EXCISE

ALSO BY DANIELLE GIRARD

DR. SCHWARTZMAN SERIES

Exhume

OTHER WORKS

Savage Art

Ruthless Game

Chasing Darkness

Cold Silence

Dead Center

One Clean Shot

Dark Passage

Interference

Everything to Lose

EXCISE

DANIELLE GIRARD

This is a work of fiction. Names, characters, organizations, places, events, and incidents are either products of the author's imagination or are used fictitiously. Any resemblance to actual persons, living or dead, or actual events is purely coincidental.

Published by Thomas & Mercer, Seattle

www.apub.com

Amazon, the Amazon logo, and Thomas & Mercer are trademarks of Amazon.com, Inc., or its affiliates.

ISBN-13: 9781503943216
ISBN-10: 1503943216

Cover design by Damonza

Printed in the United States of America

For Chris, who always believes

1

The victim was a white male, late thirties.

That was all she knew so far. It was enough.

Dr. Annabelle Schwartzman arrived at the crime scene and parked in the farthest corner of the lot. Hal would be waiting. He'd called her almost an hour earlier to give her the address of the crime scene and the basic vitals. She preferred to draw her own conclusions, so he'd avoided any insight that might prevent her from processing the scene on her own.

Nausea and lethargy from chemo meant it had taken her longer than normal to get to the scene. She opened the driver's side door even before she had turned the engine off. The car air felt stagnant and too warm.

Her fingers found the release on her seat belt, and she slid off the driver's seat. She hadn't gotten used to the new car. It was higher off the ground than her last one. What the ads called a small SUV, as if there were such a thing. She'd gotten it so she could see around all the other massive cars and because the hatchback offered a spacious rear to carry her equipment and easily load and unload her kit.

But it felt . . . massive.

She stopped at the edge of the asphalt. Somewhere nearby was a construction project echoing with the ramming of pillars and the clang of metal on metal. The shriek of heavy machinery and a smell like burning electrical wires made her feel even worse. Bent at the waist, she wrapped her arms across her stomach and drew air slowly through her nose, then blew it out her mouth.

The temperature today would get up to the seventies, but for the moment the air was cool, and she was grateful for the moisture from the morning fog.

Saliva collected in her throat, pooled in her mouth. *In, out. In, out.* The breathing wasn't working. She was going to vomit. Again.

It would be the fourth time in two hours.

She was angry and frustrated. This was a crime scene, and she was needed inside. Given how close she lived to the victim's house, she should have been able to get there in thirty minutes.

Three and a half months ago she could have done it in twenty. But that was before the mastectomy, before the start of chemo. Between the pain from the injections and the nausea, the experience was like having a nasty case of food poisoning after being run over by a truck.

These past seven weeks, everything took longer. There was no rushing the side effects of chemo. And the side effects meant there was no rushing at all.

Another wave of nausea rose into her throat. She took a slow breath. Waited.

"Be patient," her oncologist had told her. "Take a minimum of four weeks off work," the surgeon had directed.

Four weeks out of the morgue had felt like a year. She was not born for inactivity. She liked structure and work, and she thrived on the interactions of the job. Being in her condo that long had served as a daily reminder of how empty her place was, how little like a home.

She drew another breath in through her nose, but it wasn't working. Too much saliva. The next wave of nausea rolled in her stomach and rose into her throat. She ran the few feet past the pristine landscape and vomited. Pitched forward, hands planted on her knees, she was grateful for the low fog and the bit of empty parking lot that offered some privacy.

Schwartzman drew a slow breath and knew from her overproductive salivary glands that she wasn't done being sick.

"There you are." Hal's voice.

Without turning to look at him, Schwartzman raised her palm to keep him from coming closer. Hal had been the one to drive her home post-op, to get her set up for those first couple of days when she could barely make it from bed to the bathroom and back. Since then he'd been watching her like a hawk.

"I'm almost done," she said as another wave of nausea filled her throat, and she retched again. Nothing came up but a thin string of stomach acid. She shuddered.

With a couple of deep breaths, she tested the nausea. Maybe it had passed. She shifted the waist of her slacks so that it didn't press against her stomach. She was wearing her loosest pants—they were all loose now—but the sensation of anything against her skin made the nausea worse.

Maybe she could show up to a scene in her pajamas. At least she might get there quicker.

"Take this." Hal pressed a travel package of tissue into her palm.

The pressure in her stomach was gone. She pulled a tissue free of the pouch and touched it to her mouth. "Much better."

"Take your time."

She took a few slow breaths and stood upright. When she felt confident she wouldn't vomit on the homicide inspector, she turned toward him. "How'd you know I was here? Someone hear the sound of retching?"

Hal grinned, his teeth bright against his smooth, dark skin. "I think they heard your car, but it might have been the vomit that tipped them off." He wore a gray button-down and a black blazer, more formal than usual. He looked sharp.

"I can't believe you can just stand there and watch me." She returned to the car for the tin of mints and put two in her mouth. "It doesn't make you sick, watching someone throw up?"

"Nope," Hal said a little proudly.

"It does me," Schwartzman admitted. "I watched a patient throw up in the OR in med school. The anesthesia made her sick. She'd had chicken salad for lunch, and it came back up—you could see the red peppers and the asparagus." She stopped herself before the image filled her mind. Even the thought of it made her gag. "I had to leave the room. Ran across the hall, looking for a bathroom, and ended up in an empty OR. Vomited all over the floor in a sterile room."

Hal's booming laugh made her smile. "I'll bet that made you popular with the cleaning crew."

"Not very."

"You spend enough years in homicide, and you lose your gag reflex," he said. "Anytime we get a new inspector, I end up watching somebody vomit. At least the first few scenes."

"I hadn't thought about that," she said. It took time to get used to dead bodies—the sight of them, the smells. Dead bodies didn't make her gag. Even the particularly smelly ones. She was accustomed to rotting flesh and decomp. But someone else vomiting—that was gross. Better, then, that she worked with dead patients rather than the live ones.

The dead didn't vomit.

She folded the tissue inside out, used it to dab the moisture from her eyes, and handed the package back to him.

"Keep it," he said. "I borrow them from Hailey's desk."

Schwartzman smiled, and a beat passed between them.

He scanned her face, examining her. She knew he was wondering, *How bad does she feel? How much energy does she have?* He was going to tell her to go home, to rest.

She lifted her hand. "Don't say it."

"You don't have to be here," he said at the same time.

"I'm here." She opened the trunk of her car with the key fob for her crime scene kit. Hal stepped in and picked it up for her.

It was awkward to stand aside and let him take it. After her first chemo treatment, she had argued about carrying her own case. She must not have been that convincing, because Hal didn't listen. And she didn't fight him. Before, she would never have allowed someone else to carry her equipment.

But this was after.

Today, she was grateful. She had read all the warnings about how the chemo would make her feel—the exhaustion, the nausea, the sores—but she had sworn she would make it through. "I won't barf on your scene."

"You might. You haven't seen him yet."

Hal carried her case toward the entrance.

Schwartzman looked up for the first time, taking in the swanky structure. It was maybe thirty stories high, and the building had a rounded roofline and huge semicircle windows on the top level. The penthouse. Where their victim was.

The residential building was one of the new projects that ran along the Bay Bridge, condos that started at a few million for the basic model and rose quickly in amenities and faster in price. Full of Silicon Valley millionaires whose companies had migrated up to the city. She was ready to move out of the condo she was in, which held memories of the deaths that Spencer, her soon-to-be ex-husband, had brought to its doorstep.

Hal hit the "Handicap" button with his hip and nodded for her to go first. As soon as they entered the building's bright foyer, he whistled. The place was dense with foliage—as though they were entering a lush greenhouse. It smelled of wet jungle, and she imagined it would have been a peaceful place to come home to, if you weren't already nauseated.

Schwartzman swallowed, hoping that she wouldn't be sick again. "Who's the victim?"

"Todd Posner. He's—"

"The oncologist?" Schwartzman halted.

"You know him?"

How many times had Dr. Fraser assured her that Todd Posner was the best surgical oncologist in the city? Breast cancer wasn't his specialty. He was normally sought after for more involved procedures. Despite that, he had ended up taking her case. She'd met him once, for ten or fifteen minutes, before he'd performed her double mastectomy.

"Posner did my surgery." Nausea rose in her throat again. Another connection to her. Another person dead. *Spencer.* But he was in prison, awaiting trial.

That didn't mean he couldn't get to her. He could have someone else doing his bidding. Just like before.

Hal shook his head firmly. "No. You're not thinking of him."

But she was. Hal had obviously thought of him, too. How long would it be before his name wasn't the first to enter her mind when someone died?

"No way, Schwartzman," Hal went on before she could answer. "No way Spencer's got anything to do with this. The DA down there is on every conversation, every interaction. When that bastard flosses, they know about it."

"You're right," she said. Spencer was safely behind bars, and so was his accomplice. There was no way either of them could have killed Posner. "Posner's not my oncologist anyway." Spencer wouldn't want him dead. There would be no reason. "He was my surgeon, and the surgery is already done."

"Right," Hal agreed as though that was all it took. But the words weren't convincing in her own head.

They continued through the foyer and rode the elevator to the thirtieth floor. Hal hovered in the corner and watched the numbers above the doors. She knew he hated elevators. She wanted to distract him—it was the least she could do—but she couldn't shake thoughts of Spencer. She started to tell Hal but stopped herself. *Get a grip.*

The elevator doors opened with a ping, and Hal exhaled as though he'd held his breath the whole way up. They passed two patrol officers who stood guard in the hallway. She scanned their faces, nodded.

The men nodded in return. They were familiar, but she didn't know them. There had been some changes while she was gone. They included a new group of patrol cops, fresh from the academy. A new lab assistant, a new custodian. She missed the old faces.

In particular she missed seeing Patrol Officer Ken Macy at her crime scenes. Still limited to desk duty after the stabbing, Ken would not be there. She and Ken had seen each other regularly since her return from South Carolina, usually in the evening, for a dinner at whatever new ethnic restaurant Ken had discovered. Occasionally on the weekend. Despite knowing he wasn't back on patrol, Schwartzman looked for him at every scene.

She and Hal stepped from the dark entryway into a brilliant-white apartment. Floor-to-ceiling windows without shades added to the feeling that the sun shone directly in from all sides. Sleek furniture in oranges and reds was carefully placed around a room that otherwise seemed stark and bare. The furniture was strangely uninviting, as if it was meant as an artistic statement rather than something to actually sit on or use.

A modern metal sculpture—red and gold geometric pieces soldered together—moved in a quiet circle in the center of the main room. On the opposite side, a spiral staircase painted in gold led to a loft that filled one corner. She could just make out a grand piano sitting in the center of the raised space. She wondered how they'd gotten the piano up there. Or how someone would get it down.

"What do you call this style?" Hal asked, pausing to stare into the living room.

"No idea," Schwartzman said. It appeared expensive in the way of things that were designer one of a kinds. Like the bizarre dresses that came down the runway. Nothing you would ever buy. Except Dr. Posner had.

"Nouveau ugly," Hal muttered.

Hallways led off in both directions from the main room. Around the corner was an expansive kitchen in the same gleaming whites. White cabinets, white slabs on the counter surfaces—marble or maybe some new composite material. An oversize Sub-Zero refrigerator in stainless steel sat beside a floor-to-ceiling wine cooler. This was beyond a nice house. Posner was rich.

"He must have done well," she commented.

"We're doing a check on his finances, but he *was* a doctor."

Few doctors these days were rich—not in the way of corporate CEOs and those in the financial or tech sectors. And certainly not the doctors forced to negotiate with the insurance companies. As an oncologist, Posner didn't have the luxury of being paid cash. That was for boob jobs, not for mastectomies. But maybe he did other types of surgeries. If what she'd heard was true, he was certainly talented enough. "A surgeon," she clarified. "These days the rich ones are almost all surgeons. Where's the body?"

"Den." Hal led the way. "You think he had another source of income?"

"I doubt I'll get any sense of his bankbook from the autopsy," she said.

"Maybe he's got gold teeth."

"Good point. I'll let you know."

Hal stopped in a doorway and motioned inside. The decor in the den was more subdued than the other areas of Posner's house, unless you counted some truly odd wall art and a floor-to-ceiling window with a stunning view. From his desk, Posner could see out across the San Francisco Bay to the rainbow of shipping containers stacked at the Oakland Port.

Quietly watching the scene, an Australian shepherd lay in the corner of the room under an enormous three-dimensional steel-and-wire sculpture that stuck out from the wall maybe eighteen inches into the room. The sculpture was the kind of thing no parent would own for fear a kid would run into it and impale himself. But Posner didn't have children.

Schwartzman watched the dog a moment. He didn't look like a threat, but dogs were protective. She'd come close to being bitten once by a German shepherd for examining his dead owner. She would keep an eye on Posner's dog.

Posner lay about three feet from the dog. He was facedown on a rug with a Native American print in reds and blues. The rug covered the room almost in its entirety.

Most of the right side of his face was visible, but the area below his nose was obscured by his right hand. He wore dress slacks and a button-down shirt. On his feet were short athletic socks but no shoes. He looked dressed for work.

Hal set Schwartzman's kit down on the carpet.

"Has he been moved?" she asked.

"No, ma'am." An officer stepped forward. "My partner and I were first on scene. He—that is, my partner—checked for a pulse at the throat and the wrist. There was none, so we contained the scene and called you."

Hal reached out a hand. "That was excellent work."

"Thank you, sir."

"Have you seen the crime scene guys yet?" Hal asked.

"No, sir."

Hal drew out his cell phone and stepped from the room.

Schwartzman opened her kit and pulled on a fresh Tyvek suit and a face mask before replacing her boots with the navy Crocs she wore at scenes. She spent the first few minutes photographing. Roger Sampers, head of the Crime Scene Unit, normally had his people take the photographs since they usually beat her to the scene, but Schwartzman enjoyed the process of cataloguing the space. It kept her initial focus broad. Normally her inclination was to go straight to the victim. Taking photographs made her slow the process.

The victim's legs were splayed slightly, his head toward the far side of the room. There were no obvious contusions on the back of his head, which implied he might have been facing his attacker. She took a series of images of the sculpture and additional images of Posner until she was certain she had captured everything Roger's team would want from around the victim.

The camera in her hands, she spent a moment studying the distance from Posner's head to the wire sculpture. If he had been facing his killer, that person had to have been standing close to the bulky fixture. Although much of the sculpture's motion was horizontal, it also jutted out into the room—forward and sideways—in a series of wired knots and waves.

Schwartzman set down the camera and pulled her white light from the kit, approaching the sculpture and examining the sharp wire ends. She moved across the statue's sharpest points, aiming the wand's light at the metal and searching for any signs that someone else had gotten cut.

No sign of blood on the wire. It was possible someone had wiped it clean. She would mention it to the crime scene team. She put the light and goggles away and turned her focus to the body.

Gloved up, she began with the skull, palpating for contusions and finding none. There were no visible tears in his clothing, no obvious signs of struggle. Posner's left hand was palm up, and the skin was raw and inflamed, especially along his fingers. She'd seen this type of injury, most commonly in younger physicians. The constant washing of hands—especially with the antibacterial surgical soap the hospital supplied—dried the skin and sometimes caused irritation. She took several close-up images to document the finding.

The irritation tended to happen along the knuckle line, not the fingers. Finger tissue was thicker and tougher than the skin on the knuckles. She turned the hand in her own and looked at the knuckles, but they didn't have the same raw appearance. It seemed limited to the fingers. Perhaps some sort of burn. She made a note of it.

Shifting to the other side of his body, she noticed no irritation at all on his right hand. She photographed that one, as well, front and back.

As she touched his neck for signs of injury, she found only a bright-red liquid on the skin and the carpet beneath him. She took several swab samples and put on fresh gloves.

"I want to turn him over," she told patrol. "Let's watch the dog. If he reacts, we'll have to call animal control."

The officers gave the dog a cautious glance as they approached the body. She handed each man a pair of gloves. "They'll be small, but they'll do." The dog didn't even lift his head.

The officers pulled on the gloves and then positioned themselves on either side of the body, one at Posner's shoulders and one at his thighs.

"On three, we roll him toward me," Schwartzman said. "One, two, three."

Schwartzman watched the dog as they rolled Posner. No reaction. As the victim's back touched the floor, his hand dropped to his side.

The whole of his face came into view.

"Oh, God," one of the patrol officers gasped, reeling away from the body.

Like the fingers of his left hand, the side of Posner's face was an angry, mottled red. The center of the affected area was a deeper crimson, as though something had burned through the epidermis to the layers beneath.

"It looks like someone took a blowtorch to his face," the other patrol officer said, his voice a raspy whisper.

The wound stretched across his lower lip and down his chin to his neck, where it eventually disappeared under his white button-down shirt. It looked like a chemical burn. The injuries around his mouth and down his chin suggested that before he'd died, he had been drinking something highly acidic. The wound glistened with blood that hadn't dried.

His collar was stained with the same bright-red liquid.

The chemical burn wasn't enough to kill him. But it was almost certainly enough to make him want to die.

2

The sound of the officer gagging brought back the taste of vomit. She'd thrown up much too recently to listen to someone else get sick. Schwartzman lowered her head and closed her eyes. Breathing slowly, she shut out the noise.

She would not vomit on a victim.

"Go on. Get out." Hal's voice was urgent. "Don't puke in here."

He was right. She would destroy the evidence. She pushed herself back from the victim to stand as Hal ushered the patrol officer from the room.

He hadn't meant her.

Because she was not going to be sick. She took a tentative swallow and drew another slow, deep breath. Then one more.

Hal returned to the room and knelt beside her. "What the hell happened?"

"Looks like some sort of chemical burn," Schwartzman said, turning to her kit.

"That had to hurt like hell."

"Yes," Schwartzman agreed. She studied the burns. Even in the areas with the most damage, the chemical didn't appear to have penetrated the basal layer, the deepest stratum of the epidermis. Not enough damage to be fatal. "But the burns didn't kill him."

"What do you think it was, Doc?"

It was too easy to look at the human exterior and guess at how someone died. And sometimes she was right—maybe more often than not. But she didn't like guessing. Any speculation meant sending Hal's investigation in one direction. Being wrong meant a waste of time and energy for him. Time they didn't have to waste. Hal knew all this.

"Just tell me what you're seeing," he said as if reading her mind. Something he did more often since she'd returned from South Carolina.

Schwartzman pointed to the bluish tint of his lips. "Looks like he was suffering from respiratory failure. It's possible the toxin affected his lungs. But it's equally possible that something else killed him before that. I won't know—"

"Until the autopsy," he finished for her. "I hear you. What about those lines in the wound? On his cheek."

Schwartzman studied the three horizontal lines on the left side of his face. "You want to know if they're scratch marks."

"I want to know if they're defensive scratch marks."

"More likely he was scratching at the skin himself. The burns would have made the skin more fragile, easily damaged." She showed Hal the irritated skin of Posner's left hand. "The chemical burned his fingers, too."

"Makes sense if he's left-handed," Hal agreed. "I'll find out. I can't imagine he drank this stuff on his own."

Schwartzman bagged the victim's hands for transport and then examined the victim's eyes. No burns there. His pupils were enlarged black disks ringed in a thin circle of brown iris. Pupil dilation was a common response of fight or flight. She studied the burns again.

"No. If I had to guess, I'd say he was coerced." She checked his wrists. "No ligature marks."

"Maybe someone held a gun to his head," Hal suggested.

She studied his temples. No impressions in the skin. A gun wouldn't necessarily leave a mark. "It's possible."

"On second thought," Hal said, "maybe I'd risk the gunshot."

It was true. The pain of the chemical in his throat had to have been excruciating. What threat would have been strong enough to compel Dr. Posner to drink poison? Schwartzman considered what it would take to convince her. A threat to her family, perhaps? Would she have swallowed poison to save Ava? She wasn't sure.

Her father? *Probably.*

It was human nature to fight, to survive. Unless someone had convinced Posner that it wouldn't kill him? But the burning. He must have known that the liquid was a strong chemical. He was a doctor.

"I'll use alternate light sources to check for evidence of restraints in the morgue," she said. "And I'll swab the wounds. The presence and density of white blood cells will indicate how long before the death the injuries occurred." Using what looked like a long Q-tip, she took two samples from the center of the wound on Posner's chin. "You ever seen this kind of red chemical?"

"Sure," Hal said. "Transmission fluid, motor oil—they're both red."

"But darker than this."

"Generally," he agreed. "And more viscous. This is more like tropical punch."

She gave him a look.

"Well, it's not, obviously. I'm sure there are plenty of red chemicals around." He studied the stain on Posner's shirt. "But you're right. It doesn't look like automotive chemicals—at least not the ones I've seen."

"Plus, those chemicals shouldn't create these kinds of burns," Schwartzman said. "Not on their own and not so quickly." She studied the bright color on his white shirt. Hal was right. It *was* the color of fruit punch.

"Maybe he didn't realize it was a poison?"

"Like he thought he was drinking a Gatorade?" she asked.

"Is it possible?" he asked.

She leaned in and smelled the chemical. The scent was pungent. Posner would have known it was dangerous by the smell. "I don't think so." She studied the depth of the burn. Assuming the poison didn't take hours to kill him, the burn had been rapid. "It would have hurt almost immediately."

"Burned his mouth," Hal clarified.

"Absolutely."

"I think I got some of that on my hand," the patrol officer said from the corner of the room.

"Go wash it well—for two minutes at least," she told him. "Use a mild soap."

The officer hurried from the room as his partner, the gagging one, returned.

Across the room, the dog lifted his muzzle off his front paws and whined. "He's been doing that since we arrived," the officer said. The rug was dark in front of him where a puddle of drool had accumulated. The dog yawned, and his tongue uncurled. More drool dripped from his mouth.

Schwartzman changed to a fresh pair of gloves and patted her leg. "Come here, boy. Come on."

The dog lifted his head as if preparing to stand but, within seconds, sank back onto the rug.

"Anyone know his name?"

When no one answered, Schwartzman crossed to the dog and checked the collar. "Buster Posey."

"Great name," one of the officers said.

She stepped back a few feet and called the dog. "Come here, boy. Buster, come."

The dog swung his snout into the air and lifted himself onto his front legs, took two tentative steps, and collapsed.

"He must be old," the officer said.

"I don't think so," Schwartzman said, opening the dog's jaw to peer into his mouth. The gums around the front teeth looked swollen and inflamed. "I think Buster ingested whatever killed Posner." Schwartzman turned to the patrol officer. "We need to get the dog to an emergency vet."

"Call animal services," Hal said to the officer. "Tell them what we've got."

Schwartzman replaced her gloves with a new pair and shined her flashlight in Posner's mouth. His tongue was raw and red, his gums inflamed. There were several areas that were raw enough to bleed. Not unlike her own. As she worked, her tongue automatically explored one of the small red wounds in her mouth—a condition called oral mucositis. The chemotherapy damaged the fast-growing cells of the soft tissue, making it difficult for the mouth to fight off germs and heal itself. The result was sores—on the tongue, along the gums, the roof of the mouth, down the esophagus . . . another side effect of the treatment.

She pushed aside his tongue and spotted something white in the corner of his mouth. Most likely it was sputum, a mixture of saliva and the mucus in the respiratory track. Not uncommon in poisoning victims.

She reached farther into his mouth to touch it.

"Dr. Schwartzman."

She jumped at the sharp voice.

Roger entered the room, followed by one of the Crime Scene Unit's junior techs, Naomi Muir. They were winded, and Roger was frowning.

Something was wrong.

"What is it?"

Roger nodded to Hal. "Your patrol officer found this in the kitchen trash can." He lifted a plastic evidence bag. Inside was a clear medicine bottle, like the kind that might be filled with cough syrup. At the bottom were dregs of a bright-red liquid. Roger handed the bag to Hal. Schwartzman pulled her gloves off, balling them up inside out.

"What is it?" Hal asked.

Schwartzman scanned the label.

The bright-yellow label read, "Doxorubicin." Below that in a red box were the words "For Intravenous Use Only. Cytotoxic Agent."

Schwartzman was on her feet in seconds. She knew that drug. "Doxorubicin. That's another name for the drug Adriamycin."

"What is *that*?" Hal again.

"It's used for chemotherapy." She stepped away from the body, motioning the others back. "We need to clear this room until we can mitigate the spill."

"She's right," Roger said. "We'll need something alkaline."

"Baking soda?" Hal suggested.

"Not strong enough," Roger said. "Naomi, see if the victim has any ammonia; then call for a hazmat team. We'll need full protection and proper disposal equipment."

"They call that stuff Red Devil," Schwartzman added.

"Red Devil," Hal repeated, holding up the plastic bag to examine the bottle inside. "It looks like whoever killed him used all of it." He turned to Schwartzman. "How did you know what it was?"

"It's the chemotherapy treatment for breast cancer."

"You can't examine the body without full protective gear," Roger said.

Roger was right. There was clear protocol in cases of suspected toxic poisoning. She would follow it, of course. But it was ironic that she would be jumping through bureaucratic hoops to avoid exposure to the same drug that was pumped into her body every three weeks.

She looked back down at Posner. Some of the sputum in his mouth settled away from his teeth, and the white thing in his mouth took shape. It was not sputum but something small and balled.

Using a small set of surgical clamps from her kit, Schwartzman extracted the white bolus and laid it on a clean paper evidence bag. There, she used the end of the long tweezers to stretch it out.

It was blank on one side, but when she flipped it over, it read, "For Sandy, acute myeloid leukemia."

Hal squatted beside her so that their shoulders almost touched. "What's acute myeloid leukemia?"

"I'm not familiar with it, but *myeloid* relates to bone marrow or the spinal cord. And leukemia, of course, is a cancer of the blood-forming tissues."

Hal put a palm on her shoulder. "Let's get out of here. You don't need any more exposure to this Red Devil than you've already got, and I need to try to find Sandy with acute what-you-call-it."

"Myeloid leukemia," she said.

"Right."

She stood up and stepped back. As far as she knew, Red Devil was used only for breast cancer. There was no connection between Red Devil and the treatment of other types of cancer. No connection between myeloid leukemia and Red Devil.

She had cancer.

Spencer knew that.

Her cancer was being treated with Red Devil, and Posner had performed her mastectomy.

Would Spencer connect her to her surgeon? Because he'd performed the surgery to remove her breasts? It sounded absurd. But Spencer's logic was nothing if not twisted. Then why leave a note about a woman with acute myeloid leukemia, a completely different cancer from her own?

Was there some connection the killer wanted them to make? Or did the killer not know as much about cancer as he—or she—wanted them to think? That thought brought a brief breath of relief. Spencer was not careless. He would not make a mistake like this.

Spencer had nothing to do with Posner's death.

Maybe.

She followed Hal from the room, glancing back at Posner's body.

Spencer remained at the front of her mind. Her surgeon dead. On her watch. From the drug being used in her chemo treatments.

Was that really just a coincidence?

God, she hoped so.

But coincidences were for other people. Lucky people. And she wasn't lucky, not with Spencer still in her life.

3

He stopped in the red zone at the end of the block and stared at his house. A white van was parked at the curb in front. No sign of the driver, and his view of the front door was blocked by the gaudy monolith. The van's pipe rack was painted lime green. A large green-and-yellow emblem on the side was like a neon flashing sign.

Trent, he thought immediately.

This was his brother's doing. This was not staying under the radar. This was not keeping a low profile. His brother was going to blow the whole fucking thing. Months of work—of tiptoeing, of tedious planning, of running interference.

Not for the first time, his mind shifted to murder.

His gaze took in the enormous buildings that made up the street. This had been a quiet neighborhood once, small, worn-down homes in an overlooked area of San Francisco. Nothing in San Francisco was overlooked now.

Investors had swallowed up the neighboring apartment buildings in order to tear them down. People paid millions for a tiny lot and destroyed perfectly good houses to rebuild things two or three times the size of the originals. Triplexes and fourplexes had become single-family homes. But it was responsible building, they all touted. They were working hard for the planet, they said. Not that they said this to him. He didn't talk to the neighbors.

The new owners were young dot-commers with more money than God. He'd read about them in the paper—how they were so proud because their houses were solar powered, and they'd bought a thousand acres of forestland in Minnesota to offset their carbon footprint. And since they'd done that, they could justify building end to end on the lots, their greenhouses and decks looking down on his own rotting shingles.

The white van might have been there for any of those monstrosities. But it wasn't. Construction crews on these new homes came in teams like police to a raid. There was never just one van. There was a truck, an SUV, a BMW or Mercedes or Tesla or—in the case of the big asshole at the end of the block—a bright-yellow Lamborghini.

This white van with its gaudy emblem—starting to peel at the bottom-right corner, he saw—was there for their home. For their dilapidated corner of the block.

He wanted to believe that perhaps the worker had parked it there to go get food in San Francisco's Italian area, a few blocks away. During the week you had a better chance of getting struck by a car than finding a parking spot on the street—a much better chance. But he had that sinking feeling that this was Trent's doing.

Trent was in there alone. His brother knew better.

His brother. His brother. *Oh, hell.* Maybe he didn't know better. How long since Trent had stopped thinking straight? How many years ago had the pressure of their mother's disdain and their father's fury finally done him in?

Anger washed over him with the answer—since they were five years old. That's how many years it had been. And he'd been cleaning up after Trent ever since. He wrung the steering wheel in his hands as though he might relieve the pressure in his head if he squeezed tightly enough.

It was not uncommon when parents lost children. How often had he heard that?

Neither of their parents had ever recovered after their sister died. It was as though looking at the two boys made Becky's loss worse rather than better. If there couldn't be three children, there ought to be none.

As a child, he had been horrified when his father had told him why his sister died—a hole in her heart. He was only five, but he had known better than to ask. That fear lived with him beyond the age of fantasies and bogeymen, until he went through his own medical training. Becky had a congenital heart defect. It was the only logical explanation for her death. After that Trent had become fragile, always imagining some malady, every ache a cancer, every virus deadly.

From then on, nothing either boy did had ever been quite right. But it was worse for Trent. Always worse. On the rare occasions when their father had spoken to him kindly, it was often about Trent. "You're twin A," he used to say. "You must watch out for your younger brother. He is your responsibility."

Had his father recognized that the world would be too hard for Trent? That he would fall apart simply in the course of growing up?

Did his father know that the focus of his life would be taking care of Trent? Helping him get medical care and nursing him through the recoveries? Did his father wonder how the two boys could look identical and be so totally opposite?

As these thoughts ran through his head, he became convinced that the white van was there for Trent. Now the question was what to do about it. He could hardly sit there all day and wait, so he drove the boring gray sedan into the garage and parked in his reserved spot. From there he had a clear view of both the front door and the white van.

He had planned on going out this evening, taking a break from his brother. God, how he needed a release.

He smoothed the driving gloves over his knuckles, stretching his fingers and feeling the leather tighten across his knuckles. He inhaled the scent. Leather smelled like sex.

It had been way too long.

He focused on the gloves, on the stretch of the leather, the way the stitching felt against the smooth steering wheel. He'd chosen black with a bit of red piping this time. The third pair this month. He could afford more pairs. It was finding another store that carried the Fratelli Orsini brand. Couldn't keep going back for replacements. Not at $400 a pop. The clerk would certainly remember him.

Perhaps he ought to pick up a few extra pairs of less expensive ones. But they really didn't feel the same.

The door to his home opened, and out came a workman. He gripped the steering wheel, furious that he'd been right. The workman was heavyset, bearded. Twisting his hands back and forth, he silently urged the workman to leave. Instead the man turned back to talk to whoever was in the doorway.

Not whoever. *Trent.*

Trent stood in the doorway, open for all the world to see. It had to be Trent because Trent was the only one in the fucking house. Unless he'd screwed that up, too.

A hand, the brush of light hair. A flash of his face. He cringed at the sight. His own face, only grotesque. The bearded worker held a large blue tackle box in one hand. The other was waving at his side as he ran at the mouth. *Talk, talk, talk.* What on earth were the two of them talking about? And why were they doing this out on the street?

The beard stopped talking. For a moment, it seemed the beard was leaving. But then he remained in the doorway, not leaving. Now he was listening. Listening and nodding. Trent was running at the mouth.

Dear God, had Trent not learned one damn thing from the last time?

The beard set down his tackle box, talking again. They were standing in the doorway, shooting the shit.

Rage pulsed through him, along with adrenaline. Heat flushed his face as moisture collected under his arms and at his brow. Something would have to be done.

He scanned the other buildings, searching for a face in a window. Someone would see Trent. How many people would need to be silenced? But he saw no faces in the windows. Most were shaded by dull, accordion-style blinds. There was no subtle shifting of curtains like in the old days, back when Mrs. Brighton lived across the street. He could always tell when Mrs. Brighton was watching by the sway of her dingy lace drapes. Dead three years, thank God.

The beard remained in the doorway.

Anger rose in his throat like bile.

He could kill Trent. How many times had he thought about it? How easy it would be. Trent was so unsuspecting, so naive.

He clenched and unclenched his fists inside the new gloves. The smell of leather, some mixture of oak and pine and sex to his senses—filled the car. Before his mother had died, he'd owned a car that smelled like leather. Not the manufactured pleather that infused cars these days—the genuine scent of Italian leather. Along with the alloy wheels, the smooth, polished wood of the dash, the car had handled like a race car. He would know. He'd driven race cars.

When his life had been his own.

Before his mother had died and left him to manage Trent.

The beard lifted the tackle box off the porch. *Finally.* The anger simmered into an internal steam. He would need to control himself, to prepare.

The beard turned from the door and started down the steps. A sliver of Trent's face was visible as he waved. This was his brother's fault. If he would just obey directions. If he would just stay undercover for a while. But no. It was like he *wanted* to fuck things up for them.

There was no one to clean up Trent's mess except him.

He popped open the glove box and found the silver spray canister and the silk handkerchief. Put one in each pocket. Added a bottle of artificial tears and a small foil package with a wet wipe into the pocket with the handkerchief.

He locked the car and zipped his keys into the inside pocket of his windbreaker. He pulled up the hood and jogged across the street as the serviceman loaded up the back of his van.

This was not the ideal location.

He kept his face down and to the left. The yuppie neighbors might have video surveillance. Not that anyone would come checking. Not if he did it right.

He approached the van from the front. Checking that the man was still loading up the back, he took a moment to stare into the driver-side window. Cigarettes, a cell phone. Paperwork. A parking ticket.

His pulse quickened. He had an idea. He slid the gloves off his hands, tucked them into his pockets, and rounded the passenger side of the van. "Hey."

The man gave him a smile and then eyed his clothes. His expression turned into a funny double take. The name tag on his dingy uniform read "Ben."

"Ben, sorry to bother you." He pointed to the house. "It's me. I'm wondering if you could drop me off. I looked at getting an Uber, but the wait is like fifteen minutes."

Ben was staring at the closed house door. "You—"

"I know. Quick change, right?"

Ben frowned. "Actually, I've got another job I need to get to."

"It's only about six blocks from here," he went on, ignoring Ben's no. "I left my car in the parking lot across from the Exploratorium, and, of course, the damn meter is going to expire. Those tickets are outrageous."

"They are," Ben agreed. He could see the dumb lug's brain moving. "I got one this morning. A hundred bucks."

"Yeah. I'm sure mine will be at least that. And it's not my first this month." He pretended to think—good to act as slow as they were, he thought—and pulled his wallet from his back pocket, nodding and smiling. Like the idiots did. He slid a fifty from his wallet. "How about you give me a ride to my car, and I'll split the ticket with you?"

Ben eyed the bill. "Seriously?"

"That way we both win," he said with another smile. He touched his wrist even though he wasn't wearing a watch. "But only if we can go soon because if the meter runs out . . ." He reached out, the fifty-dollar bill almost touching Ben's hand.

There was no hesitation. "No problem," Ben said, pocketing the cash and moving to finish loading his gear. His shirt hiked up on one side as he lifted the tackle box into the back of the van. He closed the doors and yanked the shirt down over his doughy midsection.

Face shadowed by the windbreaker, he kept his eye on Ben as he slipped on a glove, opened the passenger-side door, and got in. With the same hand, he gathered the clipboard and paperwork, shuffling it into his lap. The speeding ticket lay on top. The fine at the bottom was sixty-five dollars. Not one hundred, but sixty-five.

So Ben was a liar, too.

He slid the pile to the middle console and slipped the glove off his hand as Ben climbed into the driver's seat.

Ben started up the engine and took the paperwork, setting it down at his feet. The idiot's gaze paused on the parking ticket, but he didn't look over.

Peering out the window, he slid on his sunglasses while Ben pulled away from the curb. Probably curious about why the hood of his windbreaker was up. He made a little internal bet. Ben wouldn't ask about the hood. He wasn't the confrontational type. The moron glanced in his direction and sped up a little. *Passive-aggressive.* He never did understand passive-aggressive personalities. He'd grown up with only aggressive ones.

As the van bounced over a pothole, Ben signaled to turn left.

"Green Street doesn't go all the way through," he said. "You'll have to go down to Broadway and cut across Sansome. Get to Green that way."

Ben glanced at his phone. Like this was taking too much time.

Sorry, Ben. You took the fifty bucks. Too late now.

"It's just a couple more blocks, Ben. I really appreciate it."

The smile was tight on his face. A dimwit like Ben who probably barely finished high school should feel damn lucky to make fifty bucks for ten minutes of work. When would he ever make that much money again? Never.

A nervous laugh caught in his throat. Ben gave him a strange look.

"Sorry. Just thought of something funny." Only the idiot wouldn't think it was funny.

He studied Ben out of the corner of his sunglasses, wondering why he was pretending to be in a hurry. Hell, from the look of it, he would have stood on the porch with Trent for another half hour.

He knew why, of course. People were drawn to Trent. It had always been like that. Women especially. As identical twins, their appearance could fool people, but give a woman five minutes with both of them, and she invariably went for Trent.

He had pretended to be Trent on more than one occasion. Slept with two of Trent's girlfriends in high school, posing as his brother. Jill might have figured it out. She was different afterward. Looked at him with those beady eyes narrowed. Creepy, really.

He remembered the smooth curve of her butt, the flawless, taut teenage ass. She was a sophomore when they were seniors. But experienced. The first girl he'd been with who knew what she was doing—how to move her hips, the noises to make, the muscles she tightened inside.

He shifted on the seat, adjusting the crotch of his slacks to give himself more space. He was going out tonight. Ginger or Stacy, maybe.

One of them would be up for some fun. Of course, Ginger wanted more, some sort of commitment. Didn't they all?

Ben stopped at a light. The street was quiet. He would have liked to finish their business right there at the light, but a car came up behind them. A stoplight was not a smart choice.

Ben swung a left on Broadway.

"Turn on Sansome. It's a little faster."

Ben shot him a frown, looking more frazzled.

"We're going to make it. You saved me a hundred bucks," he said, slapping Ben's shoulder. "Well, fifty bucks, right?"

Ben stiffened.

Maybe it was too much, the slap. As if they were buddies. How had Trent acted inside? Did Ben realize they were two different people? Or did he think they were the same person with two personalities?

Trent probably hadn't mentioned him. Didn't think of himself as a twin, didn't think of his brother much at all. Trent thought of himself with a unique focus.

"Take a right on Green and the lot is just up ahead," he said. He was pleased at his choice to come down Green. The street was quieter. Fewer stoplights, so fewer cameras. He was breathing more easily now.

Ben drove the van into the lot, taking the curb so that he bounced off his seat. He put his hands in his pockets to pull the gloves into his lap. Nodding his chin toward the end of a row, he slipped his hands into the gloves. "That's me there on the end."

"Can you get out here?"

"It'll be easier to turn around down there," he said.

Ben sighed.

"I sure appreciate it."

Ben drove to the end of the row and scanned the cars. "Which one's you?"

"That one there," he said, nodding to an older-model car on their left as he dug into his pockets. "The black one, second from the end."

His right fingers found the canister. His left bunched the silk handkerchief. "You see any ticket?"

Ben shifted in his seat to look at the car. "Can't see one."

"You sure?" He released his seat belt and let it slide off his shoulder. Hands out of his pockets.

Ben leaned forward for a better view. "You've got Colorado plates?"

He grabbed hold of the gearshift beside the wheel and jerked the car into park.

"How come—" Ben turned toward him, his lips folded in anger. "What the hell?"

"Didn't want you to roll forward."

Ben's gaze tracked to his hands, to the gloves. His eyes widened. He reached for the gearshift. As though the idiot could escape.

He sucked in a breath, covered his mouth with the handkerchief, and swung the canister into Ben's face.

Ben gasped at the spray. Like a baby does when you blow in its face. The instinctive reaction to surprise was to inhale. *Perfect.*

He held the nozzle down for a slow count of two and then cracked his door to slide from the van. Exhaled and breathed his lungs full of clean outside air. Reaching back into the van, he turned the air on high, closed the door, and watched through the window.

His belt still strapped across him, Ben writhed in his seat. His hands were pressed to his face. He touched his nose as though surprised to find it there. His mouth opened and closed like a fish out of water.

Ben's eyes looked wild as they scanned his surroundings. He clutched his neck, the steering wheel, and then his neck again.

It was arousing, watching Ben struggle to breathe. Ginger had tried to convince him to try that once. Breath play, she'd called it.

Ben stared in his direction, but the spray would have gotten in his eyes. He probably couldn't see anything.

He stood outside the car and watched Ben's last breaths. The cyanide wouldn't reach him outside, but to be safe, he kept the handkerchief to his face.

Ben lurched upright, the motion like a terrifying climax. Then, with a terrific thump, he slumped sideways against the door. Dead. His last orgasm.

Sorry, Ben.

He waited another minute before climbing back into the van to turn the air down and shut off the engine. When he pressed his gloved hand to Ben's jugular, he felt only the beating of his own heart in his fingertips.

Adrenaline galloped through his racing heart, and the erection was tight in his pants. He was slightly ashamed of his body's reaction to the murder. It had done it last time, too. Why was that? Perhaps he and Trent were more alike than he wanted to admit.

No. They were nothing alike.

He focused on Ben again. There was no detectible pulse. With Ben's head pressed backward, he squeezed drops into Ben's eyes to wash away any trace of the cyanide and used the wet wipe on Ben's face, focusing on the area around his mouth and nose where the chemical would have left a slight sheen. The bright sunlight made it difficult to see, so he wiped broadly to be safe.

Content that Ben looked as normal as a dead man could, he returned the paperwork to the passenger seat, leaving the parking ticket on top. He removed the driving gloves and put them in his pocket with the spray canister. He was ready to leave when he remembered the fifty Ben had so greedily shoved into his pants pocket.

Using the handkerchief to push open the khaki trouser pocket, he felt for the money. Through the thin layer of the pocket's lining, Ben's thigh was warm against his hand. He imagined Ginger's thighs around his waist.

His fingers found the bill, and he wrapped it in the handkerchief and shoved it in his own pocket.

He retrieved the bottle of eye drops and the used wet wipe, then looked around for the foil packaging. It wasn't under the seat or on the ground outside the van. Where had it gone? The silver caught his eye from where it had fallen between the middle console and Ben's seat. *Damn.*

He put a glove back on and tried to reach his fingers into the narrow space. Behind him, a car pulled into a spot in the lot.

He jammed his hand farther down, feeling the edge of the wrapper against the tip of his middle finger. He couldn't get hold of it. He was breathing heavily.

Two women emerged from a black Lexus SUV and walked toward the Embarcadero. The van wasn't parked in a spot. Someone would notice it soon.

The situation was no longer sexy. His erection was gone, and he was growing increasingly angry.

Time to go.

He put the glove in his pocket and double-checked that he had everything. Everything except the foil wrapper. He used the handkerchief to open the door and closed it with his hip. Then he crossed in front of the van, hugging the north edge of the lot until he reached its western edge. Head down, he walked casually until he reached Green Street and made his way home.

Backtracking a few blocks, he disposed of his various tools. By the time he finally reached the house, he had thrown the wet wipe into a trash can on a quiet corner of Vallejo and deposited the windbreaker and eye drops in a dumpster behind a popular Italian restaurant on Broadway. The gloves, the spray, and the handkerchief were rolled into his sweater, which was tucked under his arm as he walked the remainder of the way home in his shirtsleeves.

He unlocked the door, and immediately Trent was calling for him.

"I'll be up in a minute," he said, heading straight into the living room, where he started a fire. He slid the canister behind the stack of firewood and added two thick logs to the fire. Briefly he studied the strange blue flames that emerged from the pair of $400 gloves. If he dumped the gloves along his route, someone would find them. The homeless were always searching for treasures in the trash, and those gloves would certainly be a treasure.

They were too distinct, too unique to be thrown away. It would take a few fires to burn them enough to make them unrecognizable. Thankfully he was the only one who used the fireplace.

Trent hadn't screwed that up yet.

He stared at the fire, the handkerchief in his hands. He should have destroyed it, too, but it had been his father's, and, oddly, he couldn't bring himself to give it up. He slid it behind the stack of wood with the canister and found Ginger's number on his cell phone.

4

Even though the room temperature was where she always kept it, Schwartzman was sweating heavily beneath the protective face shield. The double layer of hand protection—heavy utility gloves over her examination ones—made the autopsy on Todd Posner awkward and inefficient. She had wanted to complete the autopsy this morning, but it had taken most of the day to get the body released from the hazmat team. It was no easy feat to find a place where they could safely autopsy a body that had ingested a toxin in such a large concentration.

In the end the hospital had loaned her a quarantine room for the procedure. Being in the strange room added to the bizarre sense that she was performing her first autopsy. At least the nausea had mostly passed.

Posner's body had been x-rayed, and the films were displayed on a giant screen along one wall. From them she identified a broken clavicle on his right side and a hairline fracture of his left ulna. Both showed remodeling that indicated they were several decades old. Nothing in the X-rays offered any direction for cause of death.

Schwartzman drew blood from the femoral artery to test for the presence of drugs or toxins. Would the Adriamycin have gotten into his blood system? Through his stomach maybe or through the thin tissue of his mouth? There were multiple ways to absorb a toxin.

She'd know more when she opened him up.

Recording as she went, Schwartzman did her external exam of his clothing first. She collected several hairs that might have been Posner's own and a few she would wager belonged to Buster, his Australian shepherd, as well as a variety of fibers. Some she recognized as carpet fibers. Most would likely be useless in identifying a suspect, but it took only one.

Once she collected what was visible, she turned off the overhead lamp and used her flashlight to create indirect light, hoping for some surprise in the shadows and creases of Posner's clothing. She found nothing. As a last step before undressing Posner, she removed the paper bags that covered his hands, scraped under his fingernails, and took clippings to send to the lab to test for the presence of epithelial cells other than his own. She studied the scrapings from his left hand and the scratches on his face. It was a safe bet that they would find little under those nails that didn't belong to Posner.

She then undressed him and packed his clothing into plastic bags to be submitted into evidence. With the naked victim on the table, she studied his skin, beginning with his scalp and moving downward. No injuries to his cranium or his jaw. Aside from the burns on his face, there were no markings on Posner's body to suggest a cause of death other than the poison itself.

In addition to the bolus she'd pulled from his mouth at the scene, she found something adhered to his first molar. It was half the size of a pencil eraser, and flesh-colored, but it didn't have the consistency of flesh. It was more like gum. A strange color for gum. Maybe nicotine gum.

Had Posner been a smoker?

From habit, she bent down to smell and realized it was impossible through the heavy gear. She collected the evidence carefully, trying to retain the imprint on the sample in case it had come from something they might match later. The strange substance kept her focus on the victim's mouth longer than warranted. Aside from the gum and the paper bolus, it was absolutely clean. Nothing between his teeth when she flossed them. Though the Red Devil had caused some staining along the plaque at the gum line, there was no other residue in his molars.

Posner wouldn't have ingested the Adriamycin without a fight, so there should have been some evidence of a struggle. And yet there wasn't. No signs that he'd been bound. No defensive wounds.

It was possible that he was incapacitated when the liquid was poured down his throat. But if the liquid hadn't been administered in tiny doses, he would have choked on it. Was that what had caused the burns on his face? Had he been drugged first?

Her examination of the stomach would tell her. But if he had been unconscious, why were there burn marks on his fingertips? Perhaps touching his face had been an involuntary reaction to the burning sensation.

Then, the question would be, what killed him if not ingesting the Adriamycin?

From her kit, she removed a small fluorescent light, long and thin like a wand. She examined the anterior of the body in the fluorescence, searching for things she might have missed—other fibers or, better yet, biological samples left by the killer. Maybe even a fingerprint.

There was nothing.

She repeated the exercise with a UV lamp and peered through a pair of goggles she held up to the glass of her hazmat helmet. Again she found no additional evidence on Posner's corpse.

With the exterior exam of Posner's anterior complete, she moved to the hospital phone to request two orderlies to help her flip the body. With the exception of obese victims, Schwartzman used to be able to turn the bodies herself. But since the surgery, she'd needed help. The doctor wanted her to avoid lifting heavy objects for twelve weeks. Plus the chemotherapy sapped her energy. Some days she could hardly lift her own legs to climb a flight of stairs. Still dressed in her hazmat gear, she pushed the "Speaker" button for the hospital phone and shouted awkwardly through the mask.

Then she waited. The process seemed to take forever. The hazard risk of the toxin meant the orderlies had to suit up fully in order to enter the room. Schwartzman could have used the time to get something to eat. Or—as she was parched—to drink. But that meant going through the full decontamination process only to have to suit up again.

Her hunger and thirst could wait.

As soon as the orderlies were gone, she went back to work on the posterior. Her first interesting find was two burn marks on the deceased's posterior, just above his right kidney. Each mark measured five and a half millimeters in diameter, and the two marks were six and a half centimeters apart. She'd seen these before.

Taser marks.

So that was how the killer had coerced him. She examined his posterior for additional burn marks, but it appeared the Taser was used only once. She viewed the burns under a handheld magnifying glass. Attached to one of the burns was a single pinkish fiber. She collected the fiber and was depositing it into a small paper coin envelope when the door opened.

Hal stepped in, wearing the largest hazmat suit she'd ever seen. She laughed at the sight of him. He raised his arms and looked down. "What?"

"You look great."

"Of course I do," he said, joining her at the table. "God, it's hot in here."

"The thermostat says sixty-seven."

"In all this gear, it feels like eighty."

"Turn it down."

Hal was already punching at the thermostat with a heavily gloved hand. "I figured you'd be almost done by now."

Schwartzman stared at the uncut body. Precautions slowed things down. And she was slower. For now. She would not always be slow. One more round of chemo. Another three weeks—twenty days actually—and she'd be done and on the road to being herself again.

"Don't do that," Hal said.

"Do what?"

"Think about being slow." He pointed at her face. "I can see all your worrying in those scrunched eyebrows."

That he could see anything under her shiny face mask was surprising. "I'm not worried about being slow." She tried to release the tension in the muscles of the glabellar complex between her eyes and the frontalis muscle of her forehead. It was harder than she expected. Those were her thinking muscles. Women her age used Botox to erase those lines, but Schwartzman didn't mind the proof that she was thinking.

She knew from experience—not thinking had never served her well.

Hal laughed. "Now I don't know what you're doing up there."

"I was trying to relax those muscles."

"Well, don't."

She returned to the body and checked the two burn marks with the magnifying glass. They were consistent with the injury from a Taser. She spent another moment to make sure she hadn't missed anything else. "I'm almost done with my external exam. I'd love your help flipping the body again."

"Sure. I can wait. You have anything yet?"

She handed him the envelope. "Collected a fiber off these burn marks."

Hal studied the burn marks. "He was Tasered. You find others?"

"No. Just that one place." She continued her exam. There was a small abrasion—about six centimeters wide—beneath the base of the fibula. Again she used the magnifying glass to study it. The abrasion was covered with a thin, shiny layer of serum, the fluid in blood that remained when platelets coagulated to create a scab. The presence of serum suggested the injury was either pre- or perimortem.

Either way, it had happened before Posner's heart stopped pumping.

Schwartzman documented the abrasion even though there was nothing telling in the wound. Abrasions often preserved the pattern of whatever caused the injury. She had once used an abrasion to match a specific shoe tread that led to an arrest. Maybe they'd get lucky here, too. She swabbed to test for foreign substances and noted a large mole on the inside of Posner's left heel. It was a compound nevi—a raised mole.

"That thing's huge," Hal said over her shoulder.

Schwartzman measured it. "Fifteen millimeters diameter." She was surprised it hadn't been removed. Dermatologists tended toward removal in the case of moles, especially the large ones that came with an increased risk of melanoma.

"And right there—it must have driven him crazy in shoes," Hal said over her shoulder.

Schwartzman observed a small divot in the crest of the mole. Through the magnifying glass, a puncture mark was evident. She handed the glass to Hal. "Take a look at that."

Hal leaned over. "It's like a hole in the center? What is that from?"

"I think it's a needle mark." With a scalpel, she removed the mole, taking with it a narrow edge of skin around its circumference. "We'll be able to tell under a microscope if it's a needle mark. We'll want to run a tox screen on a sample, too."

"Maybe the Taser was used to stun him so the killer could inject a longer-lasting sedative."

"If the goal was to get Posner to drink that poison, he'd have to be alert."

"So injecting him with a sedative would defeat the purpose."

"Too much sedation would make it hard to get him to drink." She thought again of the scratches on his face. "There are signs that he scratched himself—the burns on his fingertips and the skin and blood under his nails—so it's unlikely that he was unconscious." Schwartzman studied the mole in her petri dish. Definitely a puncture site. It was possible that the doctor injected himself, but there was no evidence of scarring, which she would expect if the site was used regularly. And why hide it so carefully? If it wasn't the doctor who had injected himself, was it simply luck that the killer found such a camouflaged spot? It would be an easy place to overlook in an autopsy—especially considering the burns on his face.

"How did the killer know he had that mole?" Hal asked, his thoughts running parallel to her own.

"I had the same thought," she said. "It would be covered most of the time by his shoes. Did you notice his socks this morning?"

"They were short ones, like for tennis," Hal said.

"Right. They looked odd with his dress slacks, but the mole would have been visible just above the sock." Schwartzman put a glass cover on the petri dish and set it aside. She swabbed the area around the mole and checked between Posner's toes once more. "Will you turn off the overhead light?" She drew her fluorescent wand from her kit and held it over Posner's neck and upper back.

"What the hell is that?" Hal asked as Posner's skin began to emit a pale-violet light.

"It's the fluorescence."

"The light makes him glow?"

It was hardly a glow. She recalled seeing bioluminescence for the first time, the brilliant blue beneath the water. The fluorescence gave Posner's skin a slightly purple tint. Nothing spectacular.

Hal was wide-eyed behind the mask. "Does it have to do with the poison he drank?"

"No. It's the fluorescent light. When the light strikes human skin, some of it is reflected off like regular light, but some is absorbed into the tissue. The atoms in the skin become excited, so they vibrate faster than usual. When the excitement stage ends, the excess electrical energy creates the glow."

"Damn, that's creepy."

"But sometimes it reveals things we've missed." With the magnifying glass, she went over the skin.

"Anything?"

"No." She tried to hide her disappointment and failed. She repeated the process, moving down the body while Hal continued to talk about how creepy the effect of the light was. She made it to the abrasion at his ankle and studied it carefully.

After she switched off the fluorescent wand and the body returned to the yellow-gray color of death, she used the ultraviolet light to check again. She handed Hal her extra pair of UV goggles and put on her own.

"What's that?" Hal asked immediately.

Sure enough, there was a contusion—or bruise—forming in the skin below the abrasion. It appeared to have some sort of pattern.

"Is that a shoe print?" Hal asked.

"I don't think it's big enough. Grab the camera from my bag."

Hal handed her the camera, and she took a series of close-up photographs of the markings. Standing back from the body, the two studied the images, zooming in to study the small screen. Whatever had been pressed into Posner's skin had done so with enough force to create a lasting mark. Had he lived longer, it would likely have become a bruise.

"It doesn't look like a shoe," he said.

"No," she agreed. "It's too long and thin."

"Some sort of stick."

"But it's a pressure mark, not a strike. Something held and pressed against that spot," she said, trying to make sense of the marks. "Or it's from whatever was used to hold him."

Setting down the camera, she returned to the body with the UV light and studied the other side of Posner's leg. A similar mark emerged under the UV light. "There's something here, as well." She handed Hal the UV light. "Hold this."

Again she took photos to document the pattern. Each was roughly one inch wide and around three inches long. Inside the inch-wide mark were two darker vertical lines, approximately a quarter-inch apart. Along the darker lines were a series of horizontal hash marks, and between the two lines, small half-moon shapes. She stared for some time but couldn't puzzle out what weapon would have made the pattern.

"I can't figure it out," he said.

"Me neither."

"We'll get the pictures to Roger and see if his team can match it."

She placed the light in her kit. "I'm ready to turn him over." She went to slide her hands under the victim's shoulders to help.

"I'll do it," Hal said.

"I can help you."

He watched her. "You're not supposed to lift anything heavier than a cantaloupe."

"Watermelon," she corrected.

"Whatever."

"It's a big difference," she went on. "A cantaloupe might weigh three pounds but a watermelon weighs twenty."

"Well, this guy weighs more than twenty pounds."

It was true. His head would weigh between ten and twelve pounds on its own. The restricted maximum weight for post-op patients wasn't random. Doctors granted the twenty pounds so that parents could lift their infant or young toddler postsurgery. The equivalent for her would be a dead man's head.

"Fine. Let's roll him." She was grateful not to have to call the orderlies back in even if the process with Hal took both of them. Posner probably only weighed 170 alive, but the dead effect made him feel significantly heavier.

With Posner on his back again, Schwartzman made her initial Y-incision, putting careful pressure on the scalpel to cut through the layers of skin, fat, and connective tissue but not nick any organs.

As she reached for the red-handled hedge trimmers she used as rib cutters, Hal interrupted. "As much as I love to watch you work, I'm going to head out."

"You want to take that blood and the fiber to the lab? And that, too." She pointed to the petri dish with the gum-like substance.

"What is it?"

"I don't know. I found it on one of his molars."

Hal lifted the dish and peered into it. "I'll ask Roger to run that first. Call when you're done?"

"I will," she promised. As he started for the door, she called after him. "Any luck finding Sandy?" He frowned, and she added, "Sandy with the acute myeloid leukemia."

"Not yet. We're waiting on the warrant to get access to Posner's patient files. All the patient-protection stuff makes this a real pain in the ass."

"Okay. I'll call you in a couple hours."

Hal glanced around the room. "You okay in here alone?"

"I'm not alone," she said. "Posner's here."

Hal gave her a worried look, which she returned with a smile. As soon as he left, she settled back to work. Despite what she'd told him, she was ready to get out of there as soon as possible.

5

Hal Harris headed home for a change of clothes and to check on his cat before heading to the cancer center for interviews. He'd barely slept last night, staring at the ceiling for what felt like three hours before finally giving up. For a guy in the business of catching killers, he'd always been a remarkably good sleeper, something most of his colleagues were not. He dropped off quickly, rarely woke in the middle of the night, and could usually take a call and still go back to sleep. His sister had said it was because he didn't have kids.

"There's no chance of a good night's sleep once you bring kids into this world," she'd said.

Hal didn't have any plans to find out.

It wasn't as though he slept ten hours a night. He probably averaged closer to seven. He worked late plenty of times, staying long past five at the department to puzzle together the pieces of a case. And even if he went home, he would bring everything with him and work at the kitchen table, poring over files.

The gruesome scenes didn't keep him up. He dreamed about the bodies—and their killers—but they weren't nightmares. The scenes were quiet, and he felt oddly detached from them, as though his brain were working through a complex math problem. The response didn't match the trigger. He occasionally woke with a new question that helped him get closer to the answer, but the problems seldom disturbed his sleep. The weird dreams were a fair price for a good night's rest.

But last night sleep had eluded him.

And he didn't know why.

But he had a guess that he wouldn't sleep much tonight either.

Posner's death brought back what had happened in the spring. The woman found dead in her expensive apartment. The yellow bouquet. Despite what Hollywood depicted in the movies, murders were rarely so staged, so calculated. That, in itself, had made the case stand out.

The fact that the woman looked so much like Schwartzman had made it unnerving.

Everything after that had made it terrifying.

Posner's death shouldn't have had that effect, but Schwartzman's reaction had triggered something in him. The expression on Schwartzman's face when she heard the victim was her surgeon . . . it reminded him of the days after Victoria Stein was found dead, when Schwartzman disappeared to South Carolina. Those had been some of his worst days in the department. He'd been stuck working the case in San Francisco, unable to pick up and follow her. All he could do was wait for word that she was okay, that her son of a bitch ex-husband hadn't chopped her to bits.

Husband. He wasn't even her ex. He would be soon.

Hal had kept in touch with the detective in South Carolina, and he'd talked to the DA's office, as well. Spencer MacDonald had all the traits of a psychopath—intelligent, charming, the ability to remain calm under extreme pressure, and a complete lack of empathy or remorse. And to make matters harder on the prosecution, MacDonald was both well connected and well respected in his community.

And his pockets were deep.

Hal felt protective of his colleagues, but never so strongly as with Schwartzman. There was something about her instinct to turn inward, to fight her own battle, and to cling fiercely to her independence that reminded Hal of himself. He wanted to tell her she could lean on him.

But who was he to tell her that? When had he ever leaned on anyone?

At home, Hal changed into his gray suit and went into the kitchen. Wiley jumped onto the counter and strutted under Hal's arm, rubbing against his chest.

Hal fed the cat and sat at the small bistro table to review his notes from Posner's scene while the cat ate.

His phone buzzed on his hip—a text from his partner.

Doing interviews with you. Pick me up at the station?

Coming from home. See you in fifteen, he wrote back, grateful for the company. He gathered his notes and stood from the table, his legs protesting beneath him. He stretched his arms and palmed the ceiling, feeling the tightness in his back slowly ease.

He'd played pickup ball last night for the first time in more than a month. Since college Hal had made it a point to get out to the gym off Folsom a couple of times a week. At 5:30 a.m. and 7:00 p.m., a room in back hosted pickup games.

The court wasn't regulation size, not by a long shot, but it was thirty-five bucks a month for that game. Never more than ten guys showed up. The guy who owned the gym was five two, squat, could probably bench-press Hal. Why he wanted to have a bunch of guys playing ball in his back room no one knew. But Hal was grateful. In the years since Hal had graduated college, the cost of the membership had increased five bucks. You could barely get breakfast in San Francisco for the cost of a month of games.

There was a round of applause when Hal had walked onto the court last night. Then came the ribbing.

"We thought you got shot, Harris."

"Discharge your weapon into your foot?"

"Or somewhere a little more tender—"

Roars of laughter.

Hal shook his head as he dribbled the ball slowly toward the basket, taking a shot at the free throw line. All air. Man, he was getting old.

"Don't sweat it, Harris," one of the others said, returning the ball. "It's not like you were any good to begin with."

More raucous laughter.

It was a long ninety minutes. Guys he used to run laps around were suddenly faster and taller. With only eight players, they were all on the court the whole time. By the end Hal couldn't breathe. His heart was a hammer pounding at his lungs, and his legs were half-cooked noodles, ready to buckle. He hung a towel across his head and sat on the bench until the room went quiet, after the other guys had shuffled into the showers or headed home.

His ego wasn't that easily bruised. He was out of shape, but that wasn't such a terrible thing. He was comfortable. He loved his job. He had his health, his family though he didn't see them nearly enough. Usually he even got a good night's sleep.

He stood from the bench and wiped his face, wrapped the towel across his shoulders, and started for the showers.

He hobbled like an old man.

Thirty-nine. In a few short weeks, he would be thirty-nine years old.

Thirty-nine was young. Guys his age hadn't passed their inspector exams yet, and he'd been doing the job almost a decade. And doing it well.

It wasn't the job. It wasn't even his personal life. Who knew if and when he'd have kids?

Maybe it was his dad. How much his father had accomplished by the time he was Hal's age. By thirty-nine, he had been married twenty years and had three grown kids.

Or maybe the thing that bothered Hal was that only six years later, weeks before his father's forty-fifth birthday, his father had been shot dead.

—

Hailey was standing on the curb in front of 850 Bryant when Hal pulled up. She held a Starbucks cup in each hand—one small, one huge. He could have kissed her.

Six months ago he wouldn't have been caught dead with a Starbucks cup. If he ever ended up in one of the dozen stores within a square mile of the station, he ordered drip coffee. Coffee was supposed to be black and bitter.

"You mean like you?" Hailey used to joke.

It was Schwartzman who'd changed his mind. She'd surprised him in the office after a particularly nasty domestic homicide with a Starbucks cup as big as his shoe, a size thirteen. "Mocha," she'd said.

Now it was an addiction.

Hailey got into the car and handed him the big one. Whip cream bubbled up through the hole in the lid. "Triple Venti Mocha, extra whip."

"Triple? How did you know?"

"When I woke up this morning, there were text messages on my phone sent before four a.m."

"Oh yeah. Sorry about that."

"Didn't wake me up. I slept in Ali's room."

Hailey's husband had been killed five years ago. Her daughters had been six and four years old then. How long did it take kids to get over something like that? "Is she having nightmares?"

"No. Just an impromptu slumber party."

Hal laughed. "Better than nightmares."

Hailey raised her coffee cup as if to toast. "Much, much better."

They arrived at the Bay City Cancer Center and parked in the patient lot. They would likely be here most of the day. An hour earlier, Hal had spoken to Roger, who was at the lab working through the evidence from Posner's house. Several of Roger's team would come to the cancer center to collect evidence from Posner's office and the center's pharmacy—where the Adriamycin had most likely came from.

Meanwhile, Hal and Hailey had to interview everyone who had worked with Todd Posner. Hal was grateful Hailey was able to join him. She'd been spending most of her time on a domestic violence task force, which left him working on his own. Interviewing the whole office by himself would not have been fun. These sorts of interviews were his least favorite part of the job—talking to people who barely knew the victim, each keeping his or her own secrets and clinging to some twisted perspective of the deceased, and every one of them wanting to feel important to the case.

It meant sifting through a lot of bull to find a few useful nuggets.

The Bay City Cancer Center's practice included five medical oncologists and two radiation oncologists, as well as support staff—pharmacy staff, patient coordinators, nurses, administrators, and a billing and administrative department. A total of twenty-nine people worked in the office, though only half to two-thirds were in the office at any one time.

The practice also worked closely with six surgical oncologists. Posner had been one of them. Though he didn't operate in the center, he maintained a small office in the building. For surgery, he had privileges at three hospitals in the city. According to the staff, he was in the center at most two days a week and usually only for a few hours at a time. Which meant this whole day might be a waste of time.

The breaks of homicide.

The office manager had sent them a schematic for the office along with the list of employees. From this Hal knew the center was set up with two rooms for radiation treatments and twelve stations for administering chemotherapy. There were a dozen small offices for the doctors, four exam rooms, the pharmacy with its own sealed-off room for mixing the chemotherapy agents, three administrative offices, and two conference rooms, which the office had blocked off for today's interviews.

The crime scene van was in the lot, which meant Roger's team was already there. With so many people to talk to, Hal and Hailey would split up the interviews. They each had a list of fourteen people. Whoever finished with their first fourteen would take the twenty-ninth witness. Or that was the plan.

Hailey was led into the conference room on the east side of the office, while Hal followed the receptionist to an identical room at the west end. "Dr. Fraser will be right in," she told him.

In the center of the table was a pitcher of water and four glasses. Hal poured himself one and set it beside his empty Starbucks cup. He opened to a blank page in his notebook and waited for Fraser.

Since Norman Fraser was the medical oncologist handling Schwartzman's care, Hal already knew a little about him. Posner had done her mastectomy. And now he was dead. A man she knew. Schwartzman was connecting that fact back to Spencer MacDonald. He didn't blame her. Surely she was remembering what had happened to Ken Macy when Spencer found out that they'd had dinner together. A single dinner.

Eighteen stab wounds. Macy was lucky to be alive.

But Spencer's involvement in Posner's death was impossible. Hal trusted the detective down in South Carolina. If something—if *anything*—had changed with Spencer MacDonald's incarceration, Harper Leighton would have contacted them. She regularly shared the prison reports—who came to see Spencer, who he spent time with in jail, what he did. People had attempted to visit him—some local businesspeople from Greenville as well as Schwartzman's mother. There had also been a handful of reporters who had requested access for interviews. One had come from as far north as Philadelphia. But so far Spencer had denied all visitor requests other than those from his attorney.

Hal wasn't sure of Spencer's reasoning, but for now he preferred that Schwartzman's ex have as little contact with the outside as possible.

Hal's thoughts were interrupted as a man entered the room. Breathless, his cheeks flushed, he wore a white lab coat and tan slacks. Norman Fraser.

Fraser was in his midsixties, with a full head of gray-blond hair and a strong, athletic stride. His hair was blown back slightly as if he'd been in a convertible or, more likely, the wind. Except for the circles under his eyes, he looked younger than his age.

Hal stood. "Dr. Fraser, I'm Inspector Hal Harris."

"Please call me Norman." Fraser took a seat to Hal's right, poured himself a glass of water, and drank. "Sorry," he said between sips. "I had rounds this morning. It took a bit longer than I expected, so I had to run back."

"I guess you know why I'm here."

"Of course." Fraser met his gaze. No facial tells, no wandering eyes. He didn't seem nervous. Harried and a little distracted, which was in line with what he'd told Hal about his morning.

"I'll get right to it, so you can get back to work."

"Anything I can do to help," Fraser said.

"Any ideas who would have wanted Dr. Posner dead?"

Fraser set down the water glass. "I had a feeling you'd start with something like that."

"And you have an idea?" Hal asked, pen poised.

"I have dozens of them," Fraser said.

Hal wasn't sure he'd heard the doctor correctly. "Dozens. As in dozens of people who might have wanted Posner dead?"

Fraser nodded. "I don't want to speak ill of the dead, but . . ."

"In this case, please do," Hal said.

"Posner was a real son of a bitch," Fraser said without malice. His tone held more exhaustion than anything else, as though he had dealt with a difficult situation for a long time. "Don't get me wrong," he continued. "He was brilliant, too, and the best surgeon we've worked with. And it wasn't like we didn't know that he was arrogant. Hell, when he was right out of school, he was about the most arrogant doctor I'd ever encountered, and his behavior only got worse. Posner was a golden boy—Stanford undergrad, Stanford medical school. Wealthy parents with the he-could-do-no-wrong attitude."

Hal tipped the notebook toward his lap and wrote, *Stanford x 2, golden boy, $$.* None of this was noteworthy, but he wanted to see how Fraser responded to seeing an inspector taking notes. If Fraser seemed worried about what might end up in a police report, it might mean he was hiding something.

Fraser refilled his water glass and drank again, seeming uninterested in what Hal was writing in his notebook.

Consistent. "Go on," Hal said.

"His old man was a surgeon who invented a couple of techniques that are still used today. Pretty sure Posner chose surgical oncology to get out from under his father's reach."

"So why work with him if he's such an ass?" Hal asked, matching Fraser's bluntness.

"Largely, Posner got away with bad behavior because he was such a fine surgeon. You have to understand that surgical oncology is complex. We're not talking about removing an appendix or tonsils. The tumor is a growing organism. Even though we do comprehensive scans and testing before surgery, the surgeon never really knows what he's up against until he goes in. He has to determine—in that moment—how best to remove the malignancy without damaging the surrounding tissue and organs. Not to mention the times when the tumor invades an organ. It takes incredible patience, a very steady hand, and a strategic mind."

"He must have saved a lot of lives."

"Oh, he did. Hundreds. Maybe a thousand." Fraser sighed. "But the way he behaved outside the OR . . . he was pretty awful. I can't think of a single person who considered him a friend."

So Todd Posner didn't have a lot of friends. It wasn't as if they were investigating an event on a playground. The chemotherapy agent had burned through the skin of Posner's face. Getting him to ingest that took dedication and force. Nothing about Posner's death was quick. It wasn't about killing him—it was about making him suffer and *then* killing him. They were looking for someone with sadistic inclinations—or someone who was really, really angry. "This was someone with a lot of rage toward Dr. Posner, not someone who didn't want to be friends."

"I take your point, Detective."

Inspector, Hal thought. San Francisco detectives were still called by that antiquated title. If he had a buck for every time . . . "So, when you say you have dozens of ideas about who might have killed him, can you help me understand?"

"In the last year alone, Dr. Posner was being sued by the homeowner board at his condo, by the Porsche dealership, by a pharmaceutical company . . ." Fraser raised his hands and counted on his fingers. "By two patients, and by one of the insurance companies he had negotiated fees with. Is that seven?" He looked at his hands. "No. I've missed one."

"Seven lawsuits."

"In the last year. And that doesn't include the divorce proceedings. He and his second wife, Kendra, were separated about six months ago. They're still in litigation." Hal knew about Kendra. She had been in Connecticut for a friend's wedding for almost a week. No way she'd killed Posner. And Hal couldn't see a pharmaceutical company or an insurance company torturing Posner.

"Since he and Kendra split, there have also been a number—and probably not a low number—of women Posner dated. Most of those didn't end well either."

"Can you tell me where you were yesterday evening?"

Fraser sat up straighter. "Me?"

"It's a standard question."

Fraser seemed to relax slightly. "I left the clinic around six and met my wife for dinner. We were joined by another couple—an anesthesiologist and his wife. We were home for the night by about nine."

Hal made a note of his alibi, but it sounded solid.

Fraser took a deep breath that caught Hal's attention. There was something he wanted to add.

"Dr. Fraser?" Hal prompted.

"I should tell you that we were working to fire him from the practice."

"Fire him?"

Fraser nodded. "The liability insurance premiums for malpractice have increased almost nine hundred percent with Posner over the past five years. We've tried everything else. It wasn't working."

"And when were you planning on firing him?"

Fraser hesitated. "We've been doing it very carefully. Our attorneys have been working on the paperwork and a proposed agreement for four months." He placed his hands flat on the table again. "The attorneys delivered the notification Monday. He was served at his home in the morning."

"Monday," Hal repeated. "As in the day Todd Posner was murdered?"

Fraser held his gaze. "The timing is unfortunate."

"What are you saying, Dr. Fraser? If you'd known someone was going to kill Todd Posner later that night, you wouldn't have bothered to fire him?"

Fraser had no answer to that.

6

The makeshift morgue was cooler now, less stuffy. At the same time, Schwartzman was growing accustomed to the extra layers, and the process was moving along more quickly. Plus she was finished with the external exam. She always found the internal one more interesting.

A good police officer or a crime scene analyst could interpret the contusions and abrasions on a corpse as easily as a medical examiner could. It was inside the victim's body—deep in the peritoneal cavity, beyond the ribs in the chest, or in the brain—these were the places where the medical examiner made her mark on a case.

With the chest opened up, Schwartzman removed the stomach and carefully poured the contents into a beaker. Bright red. Just like the toxin. She used a long metal probe to pick through the contents. No sign of food in the stomach, which meant Posner's last meal was at least four to five hours before his death. She measured the contents—sixty-two milligrams. Adjusting to account for normal stomach acids, she determined that Posner had ingested roughly a third of the bottle.

She poured the red liquid into a plasticized carton for tox screening, hesitating before closing the top. There were small flakes in the liquid and also some crystal-like substance. Since she was unable to use her sense of smell, she would have to wait for the lab to tell her what else might be in there.

No clear-cut cause of death yet.

She took samples of each organ to send to the lab and closed up the Y-incision. As a final step, she powered up the Stryker saw. Bone dust filled the air as she made a circular cut through the skull.

When she removed the bone piece, she noted that the brain was flat and smooth. The normal ridges and valleys of the gyri and the sulci had swollen so much that they had closed into one another. The cerebral swelling would have restricted the flow of blood to the brain, leaving the brain oxygen deprived. The resulting hypoxia would have killed him.

It would not have been a quick death.

Hungry and in need of a restroom break, Schwartzman went through the decontamination process. Rid of the bulky hazmat suit, she pulled on a sweatshirt over her scrubs top and checked her reflection in the bathroom mirror. The woman staring back looked exhausted and underfed. Both of which she was as of late.

She smoothed the hair around her forehead, testing it gently. In an effort to avoid the hair loss associated with chemotherapy, she was using something called Penguin Cold Caps. She had worn her hair long and around her face since she was a toddler and had no intention of changing that. And the caps and scarves that women in her situation usually wore would not work for her. She could not imagine dissecting a body wearing some sort of headdress.

She fingered the back of her neck. The Penguin caps, which helped preserve the hair by cooling the follicles to near freezing, didn't quite reach the lowest part of her scalp. The hair there, just above her neckline, had continued to come out, sometimes in distressing clumps at unexpected times.

Last week she'd been unlocking the door to her office and had pushed her hair off her shoulder to get it out of her way. From the corner of her eye, a long feather-like object had floated toward the floor. It had startled her, the idea that something had come out of thin air and was floating in the air beside her.

When she'd spotted the dark-brown wave and realized it was her hair, she'd stood motionless, staring.

Since beginning chemotherapy, she'd stopped brushing her hair. Instead she used her fingers after bathing it in conditioner to eliminate most of the tangles. Although she had preserved much of the dark mass, the hair she'd lost made her whole head feel more thinly covered. In turn, she felt more self-conscious about making sure the back was smooth so that it covered whatever baldness was happening underneath.

It struck her as sadly ironic that, in the face of a disease that might easily kill her, vanity still reared its head. She tucked a stray lock of hair behind her ear.

Studying her reflection, she might have been a med student, albeit an older one. Thankfully San Francisco General was a teaching hospital, so there would be other exhausted-looking doctors in scrubs milling about.

While she wasn't exactly enthusiastic about hospital cafeteria food, she dreaded the idea of going out. It was getting late in the day, and as much as she needed a break, she was anxious to be done with the autopsy. She made her way to the cafeteria and bought a bowl of chicken noodle soup and a bagel with butter.

While waiting in line, she listened to her voicemail. Two calls had come in while she was performing the autopsy. Even though she'd heard the phone ringing, the layers of hazmat protection had made it impossible to answer. Both calls were from unfamiliar local numbers. One message was from the Realtor who was working to find her a house, and the other was the bank that would be providing a mortgage should she find the right home. Nothing urgent. She saved the messages to return later.

She took a seat in a far corner and—clear of earshot—was quietly dictating her findings when her cell phone rang.

"Schwartzman."

"It's Roger. Is Hal with you?"

"Not now. He came by earlier, picked up some hairs and fibers. I thought he was going to bring them to you."

"He did."

It was unusual to hear from Roger, so she wasn't surprised that he was looking for Hal. "Is everything okay?"

"We turned up some other things at Posner's residence—might be related to his death."

"Did you leave Hal a message?"

"I texted."

"I'm sure he'll be anxious to hear what you found." When Roger remained quiet, she added, "I think he's interviewing over at the cancer center."

"He mentioned that." There was a brief pause. "Maybe you should hear it, too."

"Okay."

"Posner had a drawer of accoutrements."

"Accoutrements," she repeated and only with the word out of her own mouth did she understand what Roger meant.

"Sexual toys, some bondage equipment, media," Roger went on.

She thought of the burns on Posner's face, the injection site on the mole. In her experience, sex was often death's playmate, standing behind that rear door where lives ended. She had worked plenty of homicides in which sex was involved. But it didn't fit the murder here. "He died in the den, fully dressed. What makes you think there's a bondage connection?"

"Naomi came upon some strange fetish stuff in his online collection."

"What kind of fetish?"

"Specifically fantasies involving fire and burning. Some stuff in there about applying chemicals to the genitalia."

"To burn them, you mean?"

"Yes."

"You think the Adriamycin was a part of some fantasy?" she asked.

"The thinking part is Hal's job," Roger said. "I just report the facts."

"Me, too," she said, again struck by the fact that it was odd to have this conversation without Hal. She flipped through the mental images of the autopsy. The impression on Posner's leg. Something pressed against it. It didn't appear to be a restraint, but it might have been some sort of fetish piece. "I've got some images of an imprint on the victim's leg. It could be the result of some sex play."

A gasp and Schwartzman looked up. An elderly woman walked past, carrying a tray in shaking hands. The woman gave her a vicious frown and scurried along as though Schwartzman had made a lewd suggestion. Schwartzman was almost tempted to help her as the items slipped to one edge of the tray in her hurry to get away. "I can send them to you," she said, half whispering.

"Please do."

"I'm done with the autopsy. I just need to finish cleaning up," she said. "It took a lot longer than usual," she added, thinking about Hal's words and fighting not to explain the added layers and the awkwardness of working that way. *Don't judge yourself for being slow.*

"I'm not planning on staying too much later. My daughter has a dance performance, but I'll check the images tomorrow and see if I can locate a match among his . . . collection."

If Posner had been engaged in some sexual endeavors before his death, there may be other evidence on the body. "I'll check for burn marks on the genitalia and swab for signs of intercourse," she whispered into the receiver.

There were corpses from her internship days that still brought chills when she thought of them. But while some of the cruelest deaths she had attended were the acts of sexual predators, the killers in those cases had never used true bondage tools. They had made do with regular household items—pliers and C-clamps, duct tape and plain old nylon rope.

"Hal brought us the clothes," Roger went on. "We're checking those, too. There was one other thing."

"Sure."

"The material you found in his mouth. Any evidence of that anywhere else?"

"You mean, the paper?" she clarified.

"No, the residue in his teeth."

"Right. The gum-like stuff. No. I only found it on that one molar. Why do you ask?"

"We found a small bit of it in the carpet in the den where he died."

That made sense. If the killer had it on his or her hands, it might have ended up in Posner's mouth and on the carpet. "Can you determine what it is?"

"It's a polymer sculpting clay."

"Clay?"

"It's called FIMO."

"I've never heard of it."

"Doesn't surprise me. The only reason I know FIMO is that I've got it stuck in my own carpet."

"What?"

"It's a kid's craft dough. My girls use it to make things—ornaments and little creatures. It's like a slightly more grown-up version of Play-Doh. Soft and easy to mix the colors. Baked in the oven, it hardens."

How had they gone from talking about sexual bondage to children's craft supplies? "If it was on the carpet, it's possible that the killer tracked it in on his—or her—shoe."

"Right," Roger agreed. "But how did it get in Posner's mouth?"

She didn't have an answer for that. "Any connection between FIMO and other uses? More adult ones, I mean."

"Naomi is researching sexual fetishes. We've got a whole list of sites we can access. We're also looking for information about poisoning and acid."

"Poisoning and acid used in—" Schwartzman looked around the room. The elderly woman was well out of range, but still she whispered. "Sex play."

"Yes," Roger said matter-of-factly. "If it exists, someone has tried it."

She thought of how excruciating the acid would be. How did anyone find that kind of pain pleasurable?

But people did enjoy pain. Occasionally the ones suffering it. More often the person perpetrating the violence.

As though reading her mind, Roger said, "And if it's been done, no doubt someone's gotten off on it."

Schwartzman looked down at the chicken noodle soup and the untouched bagel and pushed the tray to the other side of the table, wishing she'd eaten before Roger called.

7

As Hal had suspected, the interviews took up the entire day. Most of what he'd learned seemed useless for the purposes of his investigation. Posner was left-handed, so Schwartzman had been correct in speculating the scratches on Posner's face may have been his own doing. They would have to wait for the results of the fingernail clippings to be certain.

Posner had inherited a big sum of money from an uncle who was part of the original Microsoft team, so that explained the palatial condominium. Hal also confirmed that Posner never wore socks. He preferred loafers without socks. But the insight did not offer any theory as to why Posner had been wearing socks when he'd died. His feet were cold? Hal himself sometimes put on socks because the floor felt dirty under his bare feet. Or once when he'd spilled a full can of Coke in his kitchen. Despite mopping it three or four times, the linoleum remained sticky for weeks. Did he imagine the murderer had dressed Posner in socks?

How was this supposed to help him find a killer?

Each interview had felt like a report of the last. The story on Posner was nothing if not consistent. "He was an impossible person to work with," two of the other doctors had said, parroting Fraser.

"He stayed with our group because he couldn't keep a staff of his own," reported Tina Munoz, the head of office administration. An attractive Latina woman—Hal guessed she was probably in her early fifties. She wore reading glasses over her hair like a headband. Even with the additional height on her head, she wasn't five feet tall. "He made everything difficult. We lost some very good employees because of him. From what I hear, the situation was the same in his personal life. And I'm not just talking about people he had to work with every day."

"Can you expand on that?" Hal asked. Others had made similar comments, but no one had offered anything concrete.

"It's just gossip," she admitted. "But I heard he had three decorators quit before he completed the remodel on his house. Supposedly he paid the last one triple her fee to stay on and finish."

Hal was confident that Posner's brutal murder was not the act of an interior designer, even a spurned one. He made a note anyway and continued the questioning. "Dr. Posner was killed with a chemotherapy agent that we believe he may have gotten from your pharmacy."

"We knew about the breach," the head admin confirmed, shifting in her chair to look over her shoulder at the door, as though worried others might hear. "The senior pharmacist alerted us at our Monday staff meeting."

This was the first Hal had heard about a breach. The head pharmacist was on Hailey's list to interview, and the other pharmacist Hal had interviewed had no idea how someone would have gotten the Adriamycin. "Do you know what was taken?"

"Yes. Just the doxorubicin—the Adriamycin," she said, adding its other name in case he didn't have them straight.

"Any idea why someone would steal this drug?"

"No," she said, shaking her head. "None. It's not used for anything other than treatment of cancer, and it's extremely toxic, which makes it risky to handle."

"I understand from one of the other pharmacists that you keep track of who enters the pharmacy."

"We do."

"It's restricted access, is it not?" Hal prompted.

"Yes. It's accessed via a keycard so we know exactly who is in and out. We went back through the records over the past two weeks, but there were no abnormalities."

"Meaning only people who were allowed in there went in?"

"Right." She paused. "Occasionally some of us from admin go in or one of the doctors—that's pretty unusual—but we have to be escorted by an authorized user."

"A pharmacist."

"Yes."

Hal confirmed the pharmacists he had on the employee list.

"That's correct. Only those people have keycards with pharmacy access."

Hal looked at the four names. He'd already spoken to two of them. "Have you had these kinds of breaches before?"

"This was our second," she said. "About two years ago, we had several bottles of cyclophosphamide stolen."

Hal started to write phonetically. "Cyclo—"

She spelled it out for him. "It's an alkylating agent."

Hal stared.

"Another drug used in fighting cancer," she explained.

"Did you discover who stole the cyclo . . . ?" He didn't bother trying to say it again.

"No. But there was also some cash in the pharmacy—about four hundred dollars. That was gone, as well. We think maybe the theft of the cyclophosphamide was a diversion, and they were after the cash. We let two employees go about two months after the theft. We had reason to believe they were involved, but without any evidence to prove it, they were let go for nonperformance issues. So no charges were filed."

"I understand there are no security cameras in the center. Is that right?"

"There hasn't been one. The laws about patient privacy are quite rigid," she said. "It's not like a bank. A recording might pick up a patient's name—on a chart or a screen." Her tone suggested the business was cumbersome. "We've always had a camera in the pharmacy's mixing lab so that someone sitting in the main area of the pharmacy can see the process. It's more a safeguard for the pharmacist who is prepping the treatment than a way to make sure nothing is taken. These chemicals are dangerous, and if something went wrong in there . . ."

"But the cameras in that room weren't recording that night?"

"No. The video is stopped and started from inside the main pharmacy. They're not like security cameras."

"Even with all the drugs in there, you didn't see a reason for a security camera?"

"We never did," she said. "These are medications for chemotherapy. They're toxic. It's not like we have narcotics on hand. There is literally nothing in there that someone *should* want to steal."

She interlaced her fingers and rested her hands on the table as she shifted forward in her chair. "That said, the doctors met with an outside consultant in response to the latest break-in. They've decided to install a single camera inside the pharmacy, above the main door. The camera will record 24-7, capturing the full view of the room, including all the drug storage areas. But from above the door, it won't capture the computer screens on the desks or pick up enough detail from files, so there should be no violations of patient privacy."

Hal considered that. "Why would someone steal a chemotherapy drug?"

She exhaled. "I don't know. I've thought a lot about that since the news on Dr. Posner. Honestly, the only people who know how to prepare those drugs are the pharmacists. No one else comes into contact with them. They're very dangerous if you don't know what you're doing."

"Any of the pharmacists had an issue with Posner?"

"No. I don't think any of them ever interacted with Posner at all. He'd have no reason to be at or near the pharmacy, and that group is not really his type—too quiet, too smart."

"Who in the office knew Posner best?"

She thought a moment before answering. "He probably spent the most time with Tamara Long. She's part of our leadership group, but she's also extremely involved in the organization that Posner worked with."

Hal wrote that down. It was the first thing he'd heard about Posner that didn't sound like a criticism. "Posner did fund-raising?"

"Actually, it was the one area of his life where he really gave back. He worked hard for that charity."

Hal made a note. "What charity?"

"It's called the Finlay Foundation, but Tamara can explain it better than I can. She handles marketing and PR for the center."

"A cancer center has a PR person?"

"Community relations," she said, wearing a smile that looked as if it was supposed to denote patience. It didn't. She glanced at her watch. "And I'm afraid I've got a meeting that started a few minutes ago."

Hal was in luck—Tamara Long was on his list. "I'll be in touch if I have other questions. Will you ask Ms. Long to come in?"

"Of course."

By the time Hal had chugged the remains of the water, he was joined by Tamara Long. In her mid to late forties, Tamara was red-haired with ruddy cheeks and almost six feet tall. She crossed from the door to the table in about three steps, stuck out her hand, and shook his firmly.

When she sat, she spread four folders in an arc on the table in front of her. To the right of those, she propped up an accordion folder that was three or four inches thick.

Without prompting, Tamara Long expressed much of the same sentiment about Posner that Norman Fraser had.

Hal didn't write down a thing she said. It was already like a loop playing in his head. Posner was an asshole. Posner was selfish, arrogant, impossible.

"I took the liberty of pulling together some records for you." She slid the first manila folder toward Hal. "This is all the information I was able to pull on the pending lawsuits he was involved with at the time of his death." Her hand lay flat on the folder as she added, "And these are only the ones we know about."

"Do you have reason to believe there were other lawsuits?" Hal asked. "Ones you don't know about?"

"A month has passed since I updated that file, so there's a good chance it doesn't include everything. Todd had a penchant for getting sued."

Todd. She was the first person to call him by his first name. That, he noted.

She watched until he was done writing and gave him the next folder. "These are the full medical records and incident reports on the two patients who have filed malpractice suits against him." She leaned in. "The insurance company would settle on these. They always do, but in my opinion, his process was exactly right. There are no grounds for malpractice in these cases."

"Todd's process, you mean?"

"Yes." She didn't bat an eye at his use of Posner's first name.

"If he did everything right, why would the insurance company settle?"

"Money," she said flatly. "It's too expensive to try the cases, and juries love their victims. Plus putting Todd on the stand would guarantee the plaintiffs would win. Jurors would hate him. Putting him in the courtroom might even guarantee a loss."

Hal wondered if there wasn't a video of Posner somewhere. He seemed too pompous to be real. There had to be more to the guy than being an excellent surgeon, a bit philanthropic, and otherwise a total douchebag. "These are helpful." He nodded to the other files. "What else have you got?"

She slid another one forward. "This file includes the work Todd did for the Finlay Foundation. He was extremely involved in their annual benefit, and he gave very generously to the charity. So much that it was a point of contention in his first marriage." She raised her hands as if to surrender. "That information is unsubstantiated, of course."

"The Finlay Foundation does cancer research?"

"More than that. They fund research, they fund treatments for people who can't otherwise afford care, and they advocate in cases in which a patient is fighting with an insurance company about coverage. It's really a remarkable organization."

"Is it based here in the city?"

"Yes. It's small. There's a board of eight or ten people, including Todd. It's really just one woman who started it—Ruth Finlay. Her husband died of leukemia—rare in a man his age. He had done quite well. The Finlays had a couple of children, but by then her children were mostly grown, so Ruth started the charity in her husband's honor. That was maybe fifteen years ago."

"But Todd Posner was involved?"

"Yes. He got involved just after medical school, I think."

"Who runs the organization now?"

"Ruth Finlay was involved until recently. There's a new executive director there, but I can't remember his name. He's not trained in medicine, which was something different, but Ruth picked him herself. The board members are mostly doctors. The board's chair is a woman named Ellen Cho, a researcher at UCSF."

"Is Mrs. Finlay deceased?"

"No. She's alive but not in great health. She's got to be in her eighties by now."

Hal slid the folder open and glanced at a newspaper clipping from the city's society page. An elegant older woman in a full-length royal-blue gown. Standing beside her, arm in arm, was Michelle Obama. "The head of office admin"—he skimmed over his list for the name—"Ms. Duarte, said you were very involved in the foundation, as well."

"I was."

"But you're not anymore."

"No. It's changed quite a bit since Mrs. Finlay was ill late last year."

"Changed how?"

"It was her energy that I loved most. The new director is good. Charming, efficient, very smart."

"But," Hal prompted.

"But he's not Ruth."

Hal tried to read Tamara's expression. The thinned lips, the slight puckering at her brow suggested her relationship with the organization had changed. Had the new director cut the ties or had she? "But Posner continued his work."

"He did. Ruth reached out to a lot of us to continue on. Todd did. I didn't. It's just the way it worked out."

He believed her. And it made sense to him. Working under the founder would have been a unique experience. "Do you know how Pos—Todd—got involved originally?"

"I believe he and Ruth Finlay met when he was at Stanford. She was a visiting speaker. Ruth could be very maternal and also very stern, matronly. I think that appealed to Todd."

Something he'd missed growing up. Hal could read between the lines.

Without additional commentary, Tamara slid forward yet another folder.

"And this one?" Hal asked.

"This file is some information on the women Posner has dated since he and Kendra separated."

Hal noticed the shift. Now that they were talking about Todd Posner dating, he was Posner, not Todd.

"Some are just names," she went on, her gaze remaining on the folder as though undecided about whether or not to share it. "Others include some estimated dates for their . . . relationships. Some of them predate the separation from Kendra."

"You keep this kind of file on all your doctors?"

"We don't keep this at all, but I didn't sleep last night, and I thought it would be helpful."

Hal was about to ask how she had gathered the information when she interjected. "There are a lot of bright women in this office, Inspector. We pay attention."

Hal flipped open the manila folder and scanned the names. Twelve or fourteen of them. Tamara's wasn't among them. "Did Dr. Posner date anyone in the office?"

"Not in a long time."

"And this was because the ladies in the office realized Dr. Posner wasn't a good prospect for a long-term relationship?"

"That might have been part of it," she said. "But also because involvement with Todd Posner was grounds for immediate termination."

"As of when?"

"About four months ago. We lost a really good employee because of an entanglement with Posner. Her name is on the list—Wendy Shapiro."

Hal put a star next to the name.

She leaned over and pointed to the mark he'd made. "Don't bother. She lives in Washington, DC, now."

He made a note next to Shapiro's name. "You and Dr. Posner never dated?"

"I'm married, Inspector Harris."

"That doesn't exactly answer the question, Ms. Long."

"I was not involved with Todd outside the foundation, and what little interaction we had was here in the office."

He made a mental note to think more about that answer. For now he let it go. "Fraser mentioned they were working to remove Posner from the practice. Was the incident with Wendy Shapiro part of that decision?"

"That I don't know." Tamara pushed her chair back and set her hands in her lap. She looked ready to leave.

But Hal wasn't done. "What's in that other folder?"

"Oh. Dr. Fraser said you wanted to see the complaints and letters sent to Todd." Todd again. He was only Posner in regard to the women. She handed him the folder. It was heavier than he had expected.

"These are all complaints?"

"There are some threats in there, as well."

Hal pulled out an unopened envelope. "This one is still sealed."

"Oh, a bunch of them are," she said. "Todd didn't care. He thought they were hilarious. He really couldn't see how angry he made people, had no idea why everyone didn't love him the way he loved himself. He'd have thrown them all away if I hadn't kept them. Last I counted, there were almost four hundred in there. I'll bet it's closer to five by now."

She had called him Todd again—in disdain now.

He thanked Tamara Long and watched her leave the conference room, mentally adding her to his list. Five hundred potential suspects in those letters—not to mention the women he'd slept with, the people in the pending lawsuits, the ex-wives.

The question was no longer about who wanted Todd Posner dead.

The question was who *didn't* want him dead.

8

With the autopsy completed and her notes dictated, Schwartzman contacted the morgue to request the attendants transport Todd Posner's remains back there. While she waited, Schwartzman did her best to sort the equipment. Everything that had come into contact with Posner's body was either discarded or double-bagged for disinfection. She sacrificed the surgical scissors used to take a sample of his stomach and liver, as well as her favorite red-handled pruning shears because the rubber handles could have absorbed the toxin. Both went into the hazmat receptacle to be destroyed.

She was a little sad to see the pruning shears go, but there was no effective way to sterilize them since the plastic would melt in the temperatures required for sterilization, and the chemicals that could be substituted for heat would destroy them.

It wasn't normal to get attached to autopsy equipment, but the red-handled pruning shears were the first thing she'd bought for herself when she'd arrived in San Francisco. They'd sat in her bedroom, ready for her first day of work, before even her bed arrived. She'd slept those first few nights on a folded blanket on the hard floor.

With the tools packed up, she used the small scrub room to change into street clothes. She pulled on her jeans first and removed the scrubs top, standing in a white tank undershirt. She pulled her button-down over her shoulders and caught motion from the corner of her eye.

The morgue attendant stared through the small window into the room.

Watching her change.

The new attendant.

She spun away from him, shoving her arms quickly into the shirt-sleeves. Buttoned the shirt and tucked it in, moving efficiently. When she turned back, he was still there, smiling. One hand in the air, he wiggled his fingers at her, the way one waved at a child.

She opened the door and stepped into the hall.

"Roy," Wally, one of the attendants who regularly helped her in the morgue, called from down the hall. "Let's get going."

"You got it," Roy said, tipping an invisible hat at Schwartzman as he went to join his colleague.

Schwartzman watched him go, anger hot in her chest. His arms swung loosely as he walked as though they were too long for his body. Slightly built with blond hair cut close to his scalp, he looked like a teenager from the back. A new addition to the morgue while she'd been away—first in Charlotte and then out for her mastectomy—Roy had moved from somewhere in Idaho.

There was something off about him.

Not to mention that it was strange that he wore long-sleeved jersey shirts beneath his scrubs. Even in the heat. And he had a habit of tugging on the sleeves, pulling them down over his wrists as though there was something there he didn't want anyone to see. At first she'd thought there might be some kind of scar—on his wrist, perhaps. But he did it on both arms, not just one.

Last week, one sleeve had gotten caught up while they were moving a corpse. Faded blue ink covered the entire front of his forearm, symbols and words in a Gothic-style print that made the tattoo impossible to read quickly.

What had bothered her most was his tendency to lurk around the morgue after his shift was done. She'd had to remind herself that he was new to town, that she, too, spent more time at work than most. But she couldn't shake the sense that he wasn't as young and innocent as he seemed at first glance.

The two men came through the door with a gurney carrying Posner's remains. "We'll be back for the rest of the equipment," Wally said. "You can leave it if you need to get going."

"Thanks," she said, feeling Roy's gaze follow her.

She carried her kit to her car and loaded it into the back. Across the lot, the morgue van sat outside a service entrance. As a rule, hospitals didn't like to send corpses through the front door.

Her phone rang as she was heading back inside for the rest of her things. *Ken.*

"Hey."

The deep notes of Ken Macy's voice made her smile. "Hi."

"Sounds like you had a long day."

"Interminable."

His low laugh. "I made you soup."

A man who could cook. She was elated. "You didn't need to do that."

"I want to bring it by, but I don't need to come up if you're too tired," he said. "I can leave it with the front desk."

"No, I want to see you," she said. The words stumbled over one another, as if they were a crowd pressed up against a door that had just opened. "I'm still at the hospital," she added more slowly. "Just loading up my equipment."

"Do you need help?"

"No." She thought of the cafeteria food, the stuffy autopsy room, the creepy morgue assistant. "I'm leaving in a few minutes."

"You tell me what works for you," he said.

She imagined the day's sweat smell, the ripe scent of death in her clothes and hair. She needed a shower and time to start a load of laundry. "Why don't you give me an hour? I'll meet you at my house?"

"An hour?"

"Make it an hour and a half. Might take a while to get the smell off."

"I used to be on animal control, remember? I've been sprayed by skunks enough times that I think the smell's in my DNA."

"Ninety minutes," she said again.

"You sure you don't need help?"

"Positive."

Schwartzman returned to the small scrub room to gather the rest of her things. On the floor was the black overnight bag she kept in the back of the car with fresh scrubs and clean street clothes. The navy Crocs she wore to crime scenes sat in a plastic bag on top. She shoved them down and reached for the plastic sack on the counter. As she grabbed hold of it, the dirty scrubs dropped to the floor. She could have sworn she'd tied it up. She looked at the edges of the bag. Wrinkled. The knot must have come loose.

When she stooped to retrieve the scrubs from the floor, there was only one piece. She shook it out—the top. No bottoms. Nothing on the floor. Nothing on the countertops.

She checked the trash.

Had they ended up in her kit? She couldn't see how.

"Doc?"

Wally stood in the hallway.

"I think we've got it all," he said. In his arms was a plastic tub filled with the bagged equipment for disinfection. No sign of her scrubs.

She scanned the hallway and noticed he was alone.

"You need anything else?" he asked.

"I'm good, thanks."

She returned the top to the bag and shoved it all into her duffel. Hurrying, she caught up with Wally down the hall. When they reached the end of the corridor, he headed straight toward the service entrance. Schwartzman turned down the main hallway toward the emergency room entrance, where her car was parked.

The pants would show up, she thought. And they were just scrubs. She had ten more pairs like them at the morgue.

It was a relief to step outside. The air was warm, Indian summer in San Francisco—a good evening to be outside. In the night air, her nausea abated. With all the focus on the new case and the autopsy, she had forgotten how miserable she normally felt the day after chemotherapy. But today her tongue, rather than constantly seeking out the sores on her gums, rested calmly in her mouth. The one thing she felt consistently with each chemo treatment was exhaustion.

It was like a weight in the center of her bones, pulling down on her. The heaviness was accompanied by a chill as though she was coming down with a cold. There was no wind, but she sensed something like a breeze on her neck. Something cooler than the outside air.

She shivered unexpectedly and glanced around. Again, the weird sensation.

Maybe fifty yards from where she stood was the morgue van. Standing at the rear was Roy. Arms crossed, back leaning against the van, he watched her. The sleeves of his jersey were pushed up to his elbows. From the distance, she couldn't make out any of the words or designs—just the faint blue of his tattoos.

He held her gaze, and she held his. What did he want? Was he trying to unnerve her, or was it simply awkwardness that shone through like malice?

Or perhaps it was her own imagination at play. After Spencer, would she always imagine a dark shadow lurking behind every interaction?

"Roy," Wally called. "Let's go."

Roy pushed off the back of the van and walked to the passenger-side door. As he walked, he pulled his sleeves back down over his tattoos.

Schwartzman got into her car and locked the doors behind her. She started the engine, turned the heat up, and punched on the seat heater. As the air grew warmer, she aimed the vent toward her. Already she could smell death in the car.

The brake lights on the morgue van were visible in the rearview mirror as it drove out of the lot. A last glance at the service entrance where the van had been parked. No one. She was tired. Maybe it was a bad idea to see Ken tonight. Maybe what she really needed was a shower and a good night's sleep.

She wasn't the least bit hungry.

Go home.

As she reached up to shift the car into reverse, she noticed a white envelope tucked under her windshield wiper. She had been so unnerved by Roy that she hadn't seen it before. She thought again about the new morgue attendant. Was it from him? Was all his strange behavior his way of trying to get her attention? She scanned the parking lot and stepped out of the car to reach for the envelope.

Back inside she relocked the doors and turned the envelope over in her hands. Her name was typed across the front. No address. No return sender. Just "Dr. A. Schwartzman."

Spencer?

She dropped the envelope into her lap as if it were on fire. She shouldn't have touched it. There might be prints. But whose? Certainly not Spencer's. Not from South Carolina. Not from jail.

She didn't want to destroy evidence, but another part of her needed to know what was inside.

Using her fingernails, she tore off one corner of the envelope, then used a pen to tear open one of the short ends. Holding it from the opposite corner, she shook the envelope until the letter fell into her lap. Using two pens like chopsticks, she opened the letter.

Immediately she recognized the design of the vital records document. A death certificate. She had signed hundreds like it in Washington and California. But this one didn't appear to be from either place. California's vital records were bordered in blue, the background pink. This page was white, rimmed in green. At first she thought it might be a problem with the ink, a failed color print, but then she read the top of the page.

Her mouth uttered an almost silent gasp. *State of South Carolina. Standard Certificate of Death.*

Her father came to mind first. Then Ava. Each had an identical document. They were both in sealed envelopes she had never opened. Both locked in a safe-deposit box at her bank. Had someone sent her a copy of her father's death certificate? Or Ava's?

But under "Name of the Deceased," this document read Joseph W. Strom. The date of death was recorded as February 17, 2003. She sifted through her memories for the name *Strom* and came up empty. Fourteen years ago.

Why would someone send her a stranger's death certificate from fourteen years ago?

Her phone buzzed on the seat beside her, sending her heartbeat into a sprint. Suddenly hot, she shut off the heat and answered the call. "Schwartzman."

"It's Hal."

She stared at the unfamiliar number. "Where are you?"

"Spent the day in Posner's office. My phone died about two hours ago. You home?"

"No. Heading there now. I was about to leave the hospital—" She stopped talking and glanced at the death certificate.

"Schwartzman?"

"Someone left a death certificate on my windshield. I just opened it. It's from South Carolina," she said before he could ask. "Deceased's name is Joseph Strom. He died fourteen years ago."

"Fourteen years," Hal repeated.

"February of 2003."

"I'm three blocks away. I'm coming."

"You don't need to," she said. "I can put it in a plastic bag and bring it in tomorrow."

"I don't want to wait until tomorrow. Where are you?"

"Parked." She took another look back at the hospital entrance, where Roy had stood against the morgue van only ten minutes earlier. "West side of the building, third row north of the emergency entrance."

"Give me ten." He hung up without saying more.

His reaction was not a comfort. He was worried there was a connection to Spencer. But what connection? And why?

She studied the document in her lap. Midway down the page was a line that read, The disease or condition directly related to death. There the coroner had typed, Hemothorax and hemoperitoneum.

Hemothorax meant blood had filled Joseph Strom's thoracic or chest cavity. The danger of hemothorax was that if blood continued to collect in the chest cavity, the pressure would eventually constrict the lungs, leading to respiratory failure. Unable to draw air into the lungs, the victim suffocated.

Hemoperitoneum was essentially the same thing—except in the abdomen.

Blood had filled Joseph Strom's chest and abdomen. Whoever Strom was, he had died of massive internal bleeding.

On the next line, under Antecedent Causes, the document read, (a) crushed chest and abdomen from (b) auto accident.

Farther down was the date of burial: February 23.

The dates meant nothing to her, but the cemetery did. Joseph Strom had been buried at Richland Cemetery. In Greenville.

She squinted to decipher the names of the officials who had signed at the bottom—the coroner, Dr. Marshall Camden, and the clerk at the office of vital records, Jeffrey Resdette or maybe Rossdale? The signature was little more than a scrawl.

Neither name was familiar, and why would it be? She'd had no interaction with the coroner's office in South Carolina. Not in the past decade since she'd started her pathology training, and certainly not before.

Using the pen in her right hand, Schwartzman flipped the certificate over, searching for some additional information. Surely if this was a message, whoever sent it wanted her to glean something from it. But what? The back of the document was blank. The imprint of the state seal showed on the bottom corner. Not a color photocopy. This was an official copy of the death certificate.

Not unusual. For ten dollars you could get an official copy from the vital statistics office.

She scanned the page again, reading every line. Strom died in a car accident. He was fifty-seven at the time of his death.

The air in the car grew stale, and she cracked a window to breathe. It had to mean something. It was too late to call her mother although she owed her a phone call. They had been talking more lately. The conversations were awkward as the two had little in common, but Schwartzman appreciated her mother's effort. She would call tomorrow, ask about Joseph Strom. Greenville had been experiencing a lot of growth over the past decade, but it had been a small town when she was growing up there. People tended to know one another—if not directly, then by minimal degrees of separation.

Which brought her to Spencer.

She did not want to think about Spencer. That was in the past.

Still manipulating the page with the two pens, she batted the death certificate onto the passenger seat as if she might be rid of it that easily. Her gaze was drawn back. She read the bottom of the page again, noting the date.

Her breath froze in her throat.

Her father had also died in 2003—May 20.

Was that the connection? But her father had died of a stroke. He hadn't been in a car accident. He'd been buried in a different cemetery.

She thought about her mother and Ava. They wouldn't lie. No. She'd seen his body. She would have known if he'd been in a car accident. And that made no sense. The deaths weren't the same night. They were almost three months apart. What connection could there possibly be?

Pressure on her arm. She reached to adjust her seat belt and felt a hand. Touched flesh. Not her own. A scream rose in her throat.

"Anna," he said.

Schwartzman shouted. Twisting in her seat, she raised her hands to fight.

9

Windows down to let in the warm fall air, Hal heard Schwartzman before he saw her. A scream. Her voice. He swerved into the first row of parking and scanned the cars. "Schwartzman!"

He listened for her response. The percussion of his pulse, the squeal of the timing belt on the department sedan. He didn't hear her. Where was her car? *What* was her car? Not the old Saab. She had something new. Big and American. Some suburban mom car.

There. One row over. The black one. He raced to the end of the parking row and came screaming into the next one. He threw it in park at an angle and had the door open before the car came to a full stop.

"Step away from her!" Hal shouted, his hand on his service weapon.

"It's me," the man said, hands raised.

Hal squinted at the form standing beside Schwartzman's car. His headlights created a shadow across the man's head, concealing his features.

"Dr. Fraser?" Schwartzman's voice.

"Yes." Norman Fraser stepped toward Hal's car, coming out of the shadows until he stood in the full beam of the headlights. He wore the same button-down shirt as earlier. A tweed blazer had replaced his doctor's coat. His hair was disheveled, his eyes frantic. His hands were raised above his hand.

In one of them was a dark object.

The pulsing energy of adrenaline pushed Hal's fingers to unfasten the lock on his holster. The urge to draw his gun seared across his chest, throbbed in his palm. This was how it happened. In these frantic seconds. Adrenaline, a possible weapon, an unknown suspect. But this was a doctor. "What's in your hand?"

"It's his phone," Schwartzman shouted. "I'm getting out of my car."

Hal stepped closer. "Don't, Schwartzman. Stay there."

But Schwartzman appeared beside Dr. Fraser, who held his hands in the air. She reached up, took the phone from his hand, and walked it to Hal.

"You should've waited," he said.

She handed him the iPhone.

Hal fastened his holster down around the gun again and drew a deep breath. Touched the moisture on the back of his neck. "What the hell are you doing out here, Dr. Fraser?"

"I was at the hospital checking on a patient who was admitted for dehydration." He turned to address Schwartzman. "It's a fairly common side effect of the chemotherapy. They're keeping her overnight to watch her fluid levels."

Doctor talk. Hal wanted to cut to the chase. It had been a long day.

Fraser's gaze returned to Hal as he motioned back to the building. "I can tell you her name, and you can confirm it. I was just in her room. Her husband is there, too. I talked to both of them."

"Fine. You were checking on a patient." He could buy that much. "Then what? You happened to see Dr. Schwartzman in the parking lot?"

"No." His attention shifted momentarily to Schwartzman and then back again. "I called the morgue, and they told me Anna was here."

Anna?

Schwartzman's brow pulled together and then released. He knew it bothered her—being called by her first name. Something to do with Spencer, he guessed, not that he'd ever asked her. But it was obvious from the way the tension mounted in her shoulders, the pull in her face.

"So you came down and looked for her?" Hal pressed.

"The gentleman at the morgue told me she drove a new black Chevy Equinox." Fraser motioned to the parking lot, hands still partially lifted.

Schwartzman's mouth tightened. Her eyebrows drew in and down. He couldn't read the reaction. What was she thinking? Hal caught her eye, but she shook her head. Hal handed the phone back to Fraser. "You can lower your hands."

Fraser exhaled. "You scared the crap out of me."

"I could say the same," Hal said.

"Me, too," Schwartzman added.

"I'm sorry," Fraser said. "I called your name twice, but you were focused on something in the car."

Hal's bet was she'd been looking at the death certificate. Had Fraser left it on her car? But he said he'd just come from a patient's room. And what connection would an oncologist in San Francisco have with South Carolina?

"What can I do for you, Dr. Fraser?" Schwartzman asked.

Fraser glanced down at his phone, back at Schwartzman, and finally at Hal. The darting gaze. He'd done something. Killed Posner? Why come forward now? The calm Hal had seen earlier had been genuine. Hal guessed it was something else.

Maybe something Fraser had just realized. Or been told. Whatever it was, it scared him.

Schwartzman eased closer. "Dr. Fraser, why did you come to talk to me? Is it about my treatment?"

"No," Fraser said quickly, standing upright again. "No, it's nothing like that."

Hal exhaled. He hadn't considered that Fraser's visit might be personal. He'd assumed it was about Posner. How had he forgotten Fraser was her doctor?

That was rare lately. It was always in his head. The cancer. Her.

Hal took another step forward, putting himself close enough to invade Fraser's personal space. A guy his size had a tendency to make people a little jumpy, a little less careful about what they said. "If you've got information on Todd Posner's death—"

"I don't." Fraser stepped backward. Then he hunched over and drew a couple of deep breaths, like someone at the end of a sprint. "Oh, hell. I came to talk to you because I didn't know what else to do, who else to go to."

"We're here now," Hal said. "Tell us what's going on, Dr. Fraser."

Fraser looked at Schwartzman, who nodded. "If anyone can help you, it's Inspector Harris," she said.

Fraser seemed resigned. He raised his phone, pointed to it as though the answers were inside. "It's my son. Patrick. He's twenty-four, in the middle of applications to Stanford medical school."

"Has something happened to him?"

"Posner," Fraser hissed. His lips drew back across his teeth, his mouth twisting in anger. The first molar on the lower left side of his jaw was gold, and it gleamed in the beams of Hal's headlights. "Posner fucking happened to him."

Schwartzman shivered beside him.

"Patrick—my son—is applying to medical school."

"You said that," Hal replied.

Fraser blinked, clearly rattled.

"How does that relate to Dr. Posner?" Hal asked. How did it relate to Schwartzman? Why seek her out?

"Patrick's had a few missteps, but he's on track. He's got a strong GPA and test scores. References. Great volunteer experience in Africa. The whole package. He could really be in the running—for Stanford, I mean."

"What does this have to do with the murder?" Hal prompted, exhaustion weighing on him.

Fraser's eyes flashed wide at *murder*. As though he hadn't considered it a murder before now. He glanced at his phone, tightening his grip on it. He looked angry. At his son? At Posner? "I'm trying to explain."

"Go on, Dr. Fraser," Schwartzman said.

"Patrick went to Berkeley undergrad. He was a little wild his first year. He'd gone to a small high school, and it wasn't easy for him. He didn't quite fit in."

A small high school. *Small* meant "private." Expensive. Hal was growing impatient. "Dr. Fraser, as interesting as this is—"

"He came out of the closet the summer before his senior year of high school," Fraser said in a quick rush.

So what? So the kid is gay. "And?" Hal asked.

Fraser dropped his head. "His mother and I didn't handle it as well as we should have. It was hard to know if it was a phase. Kids these days try this sort of thing, so we urged him not to label himself one way or the other."

"I'm still not following you, Dr. Fraser, and to be honest, it's getting late. What does your son being gay have to do with Todd Posner?"

"Pictures," he said.

Hal's gaze tracked to the phone.

"There are pictures of Patrick." Fraser's voice cracked as he spoke his son's name. "From freshman year. Horrible pictures. If Stanford got hold of these . . ."

"You're afraid he wouldn't get in to medical school," Hal said.

"It's not a sure thing, of course," Fraser said in a rush of air. "Stanford is never a sure thing. But he's a brilliant student. He has a great chance of acceptance. And it's not just Stanford. It's all the schools—"

"Dr. Fraser," Schwartzman broke in. "I'm sure medical schools don't discriminate based on an applicant's sexual orientation. Maybe twenty years ago, but certainly not now."

Fraser took his phone in both hands, shifting in the headlights. Sweat beaded on his upper lip, and a sheen glistened on his forehead.

He looked ill. "Patrick didn't want me to see these, but he had to show me. I had to know what Posner had, why Patrick was so distraught."

He turned the phone so the screen faced Hal and Schwartzman. "I know in your job you've seen things much worse than this."

Schwartzman stepped in beside Hal. "Worse than—" An image filled the screen, and Schwartzman stopped midsentence.

A white male stood, facing the camera, naked. His light hair was wavy and hung over his ears. He had a rounded, boyish face. His arms were spread wide, his head tipped back, mouth open as though he was laughing. Visible over his shoulder was his companion's head, as well as his hairy chest and one shoulder. He, too, was smiling, his focus downward. The other man's forearm was covered with hair that reminded Hal of bear fur. The furry arm was wrapped over the younger man's shoulder from behind, and it crossed his chest diagonally. Near his fingers were four red lines across the skin of Patrick's abdomen, marks, Hal suspected, from where the man had raked his fingernails across the skin.

It was hardly a shocking image. Not by a long shot. But it was made worse by the fact that there were two other men on their knees in front of Patrick. Like the first man, these two had their hands on Patrick. One man wrapped an arm across Patrick's legs and around his back. His hand was visible behind and between Patrick's legs. Both men were also hairy and larger than Fraser's kid, their faces invisible to the camera, their heads blocking his genitals. They might have been eighteen, or they might have been forty. The image was uncomfortably pedophiliac as the three men groped the boy. Patrick could only be called a boy. Hal waved the phone away. He'd seen enough. "Patrick was eighteen when this was taken?"

"Yes. That's his dorm room. He was eighteen in April of his senior year of high school, so he's definitely eighteen."

Good. That was good.

"This isn't the worst of them," Fraser said. "If anything, it might be the best." His mouth curled in distaste over the word *best*.

It was obvious why Fraser didn't want these images made public. Hal also knew stuff like this was all over the Internet. Kids were dumb about sex and drugs and drinking. And dumber about photographing and recording every stupid decision.

He didn't envy kids these days. How many crazy, stupid things had he done at that age without considering what would happen if someone found out? Not just found out. If someone had a picture of it. Or video. A hundred? More? There'd been pranks, dares from idiot friends, bad decisions driven by his own curiosity—the list was long. And today every single one would be on permanent record.

Hal felt for the kid—and his father—but he didn't understand what Fraser wanted, and more specifically why he'd come to Schwartzman.

"I can understand why you're upset, Dr. Fraser," Schwartzman said.

"What do the pictures have to do with Posner?" Hal asked again.

"Posner sent the images—five of them—to my son from an anonymous e-mail," Fraser said, drawing each word through clenched teeth.

"Just the pictures?"

"No. The pictures came along with text, which warned Patrick that the images could get out."

"An anonymous e-mail," Hal clarified. "So how do you know they're from Posner?"

"He said something about me. 'Hope your dad doesn't do anything he'll regret.'"

Hal thought about their conversation earlier in the day. "Anything you would regret, like kick Posner out of the practice?"

"I assume," Fraser said. "Who knows? Posner probably had a hundred things he wanted to use them for. It wasn't just the acceptance into Stanford. If those came out, it would be—"

"Embarrassing," Hal said before Fraser could use his own word. Hal didn't want to hear Fraser say that the images would be devastating or the end of Patrick's life. Kids like Patrick, with dads like Norman Fraser, did fine. They recovered. They succeeded. They had all the resources they needed. This was an embarrassment, nothing more.

Unless there was more.

Fraser himself looked embarrassed. "Posner knows I'd do anything for Patrick."

"And now Posner is dead," Hal said carefully, watching Fraser's reaction.

"Yes."

"So you think the pictures are somewhere in his house or on his computer."

"Yes," Fraser said again.

And Fraser wanted them back. It wasn't possible. "Everything Posner owns is evidence in his murder," Hal said.

"I know. I thought if you happened upon them . . ."

Hal shook his head. "Dr. Fraser, I don't think you understand the situation."

"I do. He's been murdered, and that is the priority. Of course."

"It's more than that. When did you find out about these pictures?"

Fraser looked confused. "Patrick called me at work today. He came by the office about an hour ago. Cindy can't know—his mother. It would break her heart." He glanced at Hal and turned to Schwartzman. "She doesn't need to know, does she?"

"Patrick still has the e-mail?" Hal asked, ignoring Fraser's question.

"Yes. I think so."

"When was it delivered?"

"Over the weekend—Friday night or early Saturday." Fraser looked back at the phone. "Patrick said he saw them on Saturday."

"And he just brought them to you today."

"Yes," Fraser agreed again, beginning to sound impatient. "But I don't understand why that matters—"

"It matters, Dr. Fraser," Hal interjected. "Because those pictures give Patrick a motive for murder."

Fraser seemed suddenly small and frail. "Oh, God."

10

He took in the spectacular view of Angel Island across the bay, his gaze sweeping across the blue water, its white crests. He'd seen sharks out there. More and more they came into the bay. One had attacked a seal fifty feet from the edge of the pier across from his building. And, once a year, two thousand idiots swam from Alcatraz to the Marina Green in the Escape from Alcatraz Triathlon. Every year he waited to hear that one of them had been picked off.

Today the bay was quiet, and the view was spectacular. That was one of the benefits of being in charge—well, being in charge and having money. These days there wasn't much else to spend money on, so the private office was a splurge. Eventually it would be different. He'd have money and freedom.

Another year maybe.

And if they made it through the next three weeks, he could get Trent out of his hair for a month. Maybe a little longer.

He rolled his shoulders in an effort to release some of the tension. This morning his brother had had the nerve to ask him if he knew anything about Posner's death, and the question still pissed him off. It was all he could do not to lash out at him. How badly he had wanted to. What did Trent think? How did he imagine this was all working? But this wouldn't be forever. It would just *feel* like forever.

First order of business was the three days of video to catch up on. A few weeks ago, he'd hardly bothered to watch these videos, happy to pass them off to his assistant. But recently it seemed important that he pay attention.

He opened the plastic container of take-out sushi. Lifted a pea-size mound of wasabi between two chopsticks and spread it on top of a piece of salmon nigiri. Dipped the whole thing into the soy sauce and put it into his mouth. The wasabi seared his nostrils and burned his eyes, and a rush of fire filled his head. He chewed slowly, savoring the heat before swallowing.

He loved sushi.

Trent hated it.

Of course. Too spicy. Too slimy.

But Trent loved raw oysters. Like they weren't slimy. Aphrodisiacs, he would say. Everything was more appealing if it related to sex. Trent was a whole box of contradictions.

With the computer booted, he logged in to the security system and opened the first video file. Clicking the space bar three times set the play mode to the fastest speed. Watched this way, he could view the entire twenty-four hours in about ten minutes. He scanned the faces as people appeared, slowed and sped up to watch what they did.

All normal activity.

Sitting next to the computer was the list of who should be there. Beside each name was a thumbnail picture. The faces were all familiar by now.

A few more days, he might pass this job back to his assistant. But so soon after Todd, it seemed smart.

He was nothing if not smart.

His brother being an idiot meant he had to be very smart.

He took another bite of salmon as the first video ended. A little extra wasabi this time. To get the same rush required increasing amounts. His nose threatened to run. He sniffed deeply, blinking back the tears.

His phone rang as he launched the third video—the one from last night. The house number. His brother.

"Hello."

"I'm bored."

Trent.

He gritted his jaw, took a breath. *Sound chipper.* "How about if I bring home pizza and a movie?"

"I want to go to the stables, visit Ribbon."

That was a terrible idea. The last time they'd been to visit Trent's horse, he'd thrown a fit over some comment one of the stable guys made. What did he expect from a bunch of redneck cowboys?

"I want to leave," Trent went on in his whiny voice. "I don't need to be here."

He clenched and unclenched his fists. His mouth was suddenly dry from the wasabi. "Just for a few more weeks."

"I can't leave the house," he went on. "I could do the same thing from Athens . . . or Barcelona."

How many times had Trent uttered those same words? And how often had he responded to his brother with the same lame encouragement? He was desperate to shout, "Go. Go and see how you manage, you fucking moron."

You cannot do that. You need Trent. For a little while longer.

Another breath.

"I know this sucks, Trent. I don't know how you're managing it," he said slowly. *Not very well,* he thought. *Like a big baby, really.* "Maybe there is another way," he added, offering his brother a little dash of hope. He'd learned at their mother's death that threatening Trent was a sure way to make him more difficult. *String him along. Once the paperwork is signed, we are home free.*

"So I can go?" Trent asked.

"Why don't you pick a few places you want to go? Then we can see how easy it would be to make it happen?"

"You're putting me off."

"I'm not," he said in a quiet voice. His patient voice. "I'm doing what is best for both of us—for the long term. We need the paperwork completed."

"Why don't we just tell the lawyer we want it now?"

"You know why, Trent."

Trent was quiet. He knew he wasn't ready. Not yet.

"I'm not staying. Not for three more weeks," Trent warned.

"Okay. We'll try to make the appointment for sooner."

"This week."

"I'll call and see—" He caught movement on the screen, stopped the video. The pharmacy was dark. In the center of the room was a familiar redhead. *Denise.* What was she doing in the pharmacy? He stopped the video. Heart pounding, he scanned the list of names of those who had access to the pharmacy. No Denise. Of course there was no Denise. She was not supposed to be in there. She did not have access to the pharmacy.

"Hello?" Trent demanded.

"Sorry. Something going on here. Can we talk about it tonight? Over pizza?" He backed the video slowly.

Why was it dark?

The time on the button of the screen read 11:49 p.m.

Midnight. She was there at midnight. He backed the video by an hour, then two hours.

His brother's voice in his ear again. "Yes, but I want it from Orgasmica," Trent demanded, referring to the pizza place way out on Filmore Street.

His phone pressed to his ear, he played it forward until she came into view. Then he slowed it, watched frame by frame. Each time it stopped, the time stamp quivered on the screen.

"Sure," he told his brother. "I can get out there."

On the screen, Denise continued to move forward in tiny, stiff motions. Through the pharmacy. Alone. At midnight. "Text me the order, and I'll pick it up." He minimized the video and double-clicked on the log folder, scanning for the file that would show which badges had been used to enter the pharmacy in the past twenty-four hours.

"How soon?" Trent asked.

"I've got a couple of hours of work left."

"Forget it. I'll get an Uber to pick it up."

On the log file, the entry at 11:48 p.m. was Sarah Washburn. He returned to the video. That wasn't her. Sarah was a ditzy blonde who lived in one of the ugly industrial apartment buildings within walking distance from the office. A good thing because she liked to go to the bar straight from work and drink until she could hardly walk.

"Good-bye," Trent said.

Trent's voice echoed in his head. Something about getting an Uber. Trent was leaving the house? He hadn't been listening. "Wait," he said, tearing his focus off the screen. "Don't hang up."

The line was silent.

"Trent!" he shouted.

"What?"

"What did you say?" His gaze was drawn back to Sarah's name on the log.

"I said I would get the pizza myself," Trent snapped.

"No." He turned his back to the computer screen. *Deal with Trent first.* He could not have his brother going out. "Don't you understand, Trent? You have to stay inside. Unless you want to move out of that house and find a job flipping burgers or drying women's hair." He was breathless, trembling.

"There's no reason to be so testy," Trent said as if he hadn't just been baiting him.

He swung back to the computer. Denise's face remained frozen in the corner of his screen. There was every reason to be testy. "I'll pick up the pizza and be home as soon as I can."

Trent said nothing. No doubt he was pouting.

"Okay?" he said softly.

"Fine," Trent replied with flat disinterest.

The line went dead. He pounded his fist into the desk. *Damn. Damn. Damn.*

He stared at the log entry, at Denise's face. Backed up the video and watched again in slow motion. Only Denise. No sign of Sarah at all.

The two were friends. He'd seen them together at one of the few office parties he'd attended. Sarah, the office alcoholic, and Denise, the office slut. He'd never talked to Sarah more than to say hello. Denise had flirted with him from time to time, in between her boyfriends. She preferred the married doctors. He recalled walking past Sarah in the parking lot. He'd noticed because it had seemed odd that she'd driven since she lived so close. In the back of her cheap Honda station wagon were four black boxes. At first they'd looked like shoe boxes. He didn't recognize the brand and figured they were something cheap. Which explained how she might have afforded four pairs.

It was only some time later that he'd remembered where he'd seen boxes like that before. In the aisle of the grocery store alongside the wines. Not shoes, boxes of wine. Four boxes of wine. No doubt her self-medication of choice.

The video rolled forward. Denise opening the refrigerator. His breath caught in his throat as she pulled out a bottle. He recognized the white-and-yellow label, the bright-red liquid. Adriamycin. She stared at the label.

Red Devil. The toxin he'd used to kill Posner.

How did she know?

She looked over her shoulder, the slightest smile on her face. In that moment, he was certain she was alone. But he had no idea what she was doing. Sarah was surely passed out somewhere, and Denise had stolen her badge to enter the pharmacy. He watched her pocket the bottle.

Was she going to confront him? Was this some sort of blackmail scheme?

Would Sarah be in on it, too?

He doubted it. Whatever she was up to, Denise would be working alone. He watched the video until she had left the pharmacy.

Then he watched it again.

Finally he deleted the video files for the past four nights, cleared them from his trash, and forced an update of the folder to the cloud. They weren't gone. Things were never gone these days, but it would slow the police. That was all he needed.

As the cloud updated, the clock icon circled on his screen. Watching it with one eye, he lifted the phone off the desk. He had to see her, find out what she knew, what she was after.

Once again he admitted that life would be easier if Trent weren't around.

If Trent had died.

If Trent disappeared . . .

How much easier everything would be.

11

Schwartzman left Hal and Dr. Fraser. They were meeting Patrick at the station for questioning, and when she had offered to join them, they'd told her she needed her rest. If she hadn't been so totally exhausted, she might have fought them on principle. But she was that tired.

She'd seen a quote once, although she couldn't remember its author. "All the women in me are tired." She felt that same, profound exhaustion, as though all the times she'd been tired before were only a preface to today. She drove home slowly, carefully, letting the air from the open sunroof blow in softly from above.

Her thoughts swirled with the air, hovering on the death certificate she'd found on the windshield. Hal had bagged it as evidence. Of what, she didn't know. South Carolina would lead them to Spencer, but he was in prison. *In. Prison.*

But that didn't mean she was safe. He had gotten a woman in San Francisco murdered without ever leaving South Carolina.

At home Schwartzman took a long, hot shower in an effort to rid her skin of the smell of death. Although the stench would remain in her nose, at least Ken wouldn't have to suffer it. She was looking forward to seeing him. She'd almost called him and begged off, but in the end she'd realized she needed the distraction. And sitting in her house, alone, would mean thinking about Spencer. Worrying about him. Spencer wouldn't come up with Ken. They would talk about work, about food, about movies and books, about his family. And not about her ex-husband.

She lingered under the water, washing her hair twice and using De-Fishing Soap before the regular one.

With Spencer in jail, a long shower had become a new luxury. Before, the shower had always felt like the most vulnerable place. Spencer had made a habit of startling her there when they were married. After leaving him, she had taken efficient showers, not long ones. If she wanted to linger in the water, she took a bath.

As Schwartzman waited for Ken to come up from the lobby, she realized it was the first time he'd been to her place since the night he was attacked. They'd been out three—no, four—times since she had returned from South Carolina, but they had never come here. Was that because he hadn't wanted to? Why had he offered to leave the soup with the front desk? She hadn't thought to ask him how he felt about it.

They barely talked about that night.

He was parked behind a desk because of that night—because of her. *No.* Not her. He was behind a desk because of Spencer. And he was okay. He was getting better. Stronger. He'd said so himself.

The elevator dinged, and the doors slid open. Ken emerged, carrying a brown sack and wearing a smile.

"You didn't have to bring anything."

"Oh, but I did. You'll love this."

He paused at the door. She hesitated, too. A moment passed between them. She smiled uneasily. "You okay?"

"Great."

She put a hand out, and Ken stepped inside. "Okay if I borrow your stove top?" he asked.

"Sure. Kitchen's right through here."

"You sit," he said. "I'm going to find what I need."

She followed him into the kitchen and took a seat at the small breakfast table. "You don't want help?"

"Nope." He set a container down on the counter and faced the cupboards. "If I was a soup pot, I'd be—"

"Bottom right beside the oven."

He snapped his fingers. "That's exactly where I'd be." He pulled out the pot, put it on the stove, and did a little three-step dance across the kitchen. "And a ladle."

"Drawer on the left."

"Seriously, I've got this," he joked, taking a wide stance as if he were going to tackle the oven.

Laughing, she raised her hands. "Okay."

"Bowls." He put a hand out. "Don't tell me." He opened the cabinet that held her glasses and closed it again. He made his way past her spices and plates before he found the bowls in the farthest cabinet from the sink.

Ken poured a yellow noodle soup from the container into the soup pot and lit the burner. She smelled ginger and something like curry.

While it warmed, he sat across from her and caught her up on his days in records. Anyone else and it might have sounded like complaining, but Ken's antics made her smile. When the soup had heated to a rolling boil, Ken shut off the burner and poured them each a bowl. The first day after chemo, most smells nauseated her, so she usually ended up surviving on toast with butter or peanut butter and an occasional yogurt.

"You don't have to eat it," he said.

She dipped her spoon and took a tentative taste. The ginger was strong without being overpowering; the chicken and noodles took the bite out of it. "It's really good."

"Thank you."

They dined in a comfortable silence, and she ate more than she'd anticipated. When they were done, Ken insisted on doing the dishes.

After a little food and an entire day on her feet, she was starting to feel sleepy. Time to curl into a ball and watch a movie.

"*Bringing Up Baby*?" Ken asked.

It was her favorite. "You remembered."

"I told you I've never seen it," he said.

Something light sounded perfect, and that movie was one of the first she remembered watching with her father. How she'd begged to own a leopard afterward.

Ken made them tea and brought steaming mugs into the living room, placing them on the coffee table before sinking into the corner of the couch. She took a sip and settled in beside him. Like an old married couple.

He put an arm around her, and she shifted closer. As she leaned into him, he moaned and sat up quickly, clutching his side. The stab wounds. She'd pressed right into them.

"I'm so sorry."

"It's okay." He rubbed his chest tenderly. "Your shoulder just hit a tender spot."

"Oh, God, Ken. I'm so sorry. Let me see." She reached for his shirt, but he caught her hand.

"I'm fine." When she didn't let go, he said, "I promise."

She wanted to see the scars. All she could recall from that night was blood—on her hands, on the sheets. It had been like a live organism, a virus, spreading across them while she fought to contain it. There had been no time to take stock of the injuries. She'd been so frantic to slow the bleeding, to take his blood and prove that they'd been drugged that night.

Eighteen stab wounds.

So often in the morgue she saw the wounds open, their rubbery edges eternally parted. The doctor in her wanted to see the scars, measure their healing. Touch the dense masses of granulation tissue that stitched the skin so it was whole again.

Ken still had hold of her hand. With his other, he pointed the remote control at the television. Then he set the remote down and tucked one of her small square throw pillows against the side of his chest. "Here," he said, patting the pillow. "Lean against this."

Schwartzman slowly lowered herself into the pillow, and Ken didn't flinch as she settled her weight in against him once more. He draped an arm across her shoulders, and she felt the comfort of his presence. Safety. Perhaps a future.

How long had it been since she had imagined that kind of freedom? And now she had it. Now she could relax.

On the screen Cary Grant stalked up the eighteenth fairway behind Katharine Hepburn, trying to explain that she was playing with his ball while she talked over and around him.

Schwartzman closed her eyes and thought of her father. Heard his laugh, the way it filled their den when they had watched this movie. How many times? Dozens at least. She felt her father's arm around her shoulder when she was a little girl, the way she had settled in against him, the way she was with Ken now.

Safe, content.

12

Spencer MacDonald spent a little extra time in front of the dull stainless steel prison mirror. His transformation was complete. Even he was shocked and, to be honest, mildly disgusted. If he weren't behind bars, he might be convinced he was addicted to something nasty. Like heroin nasty.

Of course, he would never be that weak.

In the time he'd been unjustly imprisoned, he'd managed to completely change his appearance. From handsome, polished businessman to a broken man. There was the right amount of sallowness in his cheeks. Thirty-six days of eating three bites of each meal. One bite of meat, wash that down with one bite of vegetables, and one bite of starch. Set the fork down and walk away from the table.

He was not a man who denied himself. And he wasn't accustomed to physical hunger. Not of the food variety anyway.

He caught his reflection in the glass again, and he tilted his head down to test the way the angle changed the shadows of his face beneath the industrial lighting. Down was good. It emphasized the gray-blue shade beneath his eyes.

A useful lesson from prison. How to look half-dead.

First, draw a small shape on a piece of paper with a pencil, applying heavy pressure. Fill it in deeply. Then use a fingertip to apply the gray under the eyes.

Looking half-dead was a good defense in here.

Second, add a few lesions. Use the corner of a razor, slicing from one single point until you have an almost circular wound the size of a dime. Then repeat the cutting process in uneven spaces on the neck and hands.

Third, put one on the face for good measure.

Diseased. That was the way it made him look. Even in prison, nobody wanted to touch a man who was dying of something. People gave a wide berth to the guy who had killed the bitch who'd given him AIDS. So far the story had stuck.

Now it was time to see if looking half-dead worked as well for offense. He took a last glance. He was ready.

The buzzer sawed in his ears, sounding very much like the electric chair. That was what he thought of every time the outer door opened into the visiting area.

The crowd was exactly what he'd hoped for. Mostly black men. The few white men were tattooed monoliths. She would not feel comfortable here.

The top of her head appeared over the barriers, the blonde gray of her carefully styled cut. She moved slowly. These people would terrify her. What if she left? He watched until he was sure she wouldn't stop. Then he posed, facedown, hands clasped. Like he was praying.

When he looked up, he gave her a few seconds to absorb his thin face, the blue-gray circles under his eyes. The wounds were gone. He had been careful not to create new ones before she came. She would find open sores revolting, and that would not serve his cause.

She had to want to help him.

Her mouth dropped, and she pressed her hand to her lips, as if she might cry. Thrill seared his stomach and moved downward—the first sexual excitement he'd felt since he was arrested.

He offered her a brave smile, raising his chin the way Southern men had always done in the face of adversity. She held her purse strap in two hands, the light-pink bag hanging below. The purse he had bought her for Christmas last year. He squinted his eyes in an effort to soften the focus on her face.

Imagining for a moment that she was her daughter.

The two women had the same wide-set blue eyes, but Bella was taller than her mother and considerably thinner. Where her mother was big breasted with rounded hips, Schwartzman was lithe. She also stood stronger, more confident than her mother, who was always a little timid. Especially now. And Schwartzman wore her dark hair loose and wavy where her mother's was always done. His vision was too good, better than twenty-twenty. He couldn't see his Bella, but he could imagine her.

Slipping his hand under the shallow ledge, he shifted to adjust the momentum in his pants and gave her a reassuring nod.

With a last survey of the room, Georgia Schwartzman pulled the chair back and sat, propping the pristine purse in her lap like a prize Yorkie.

He put the phone receiver to his ear. She did the same, all the while looking confused and out of sorts, like she'd never seen a movie where someone came to a prison and talked over a phone behind glass. He experienced a flash of annoyance, impatience.

This wasn't his favorite version of Georgia—her clueless damsel persona. Georgia was a chameleon. She could seem drunk on two glasses of chardonnay with a group of tittering women and an hour later recall every detail about the merger discussion happening at the next table.

And today she'd never looked so helpless. "Oh, my dear Spencer."

"Georgia, it's so good of you to come."

"I want you to know, I've been trying to come for a month, but they said you weren't taking visitors."

He leaned into the glass. "I never heard about a single visitor. They must have turned everyone away."

Georgia's eyes were narrower than her daughter's and her face slightly rounder; her nose turned up at the end. She had a tendency to keep it that way, proud of the little upturn. But propped in the air, the nose made her look like a pig. He preferred Bella's nose, a perfect forty-five-degree slope between bright-sapphire eyes.

"Isn't that illegal?" she asked.

"I'm sure it is," he went on. "But that's the whole game in here. They do whatever they want, and what can I do about it?"

Georgia sat a little straighter. "Well, something has to be done about that. What does Mr. Merckel say?"

Merckel was his lawyer.

"He's helped some, but there's not a lot he can do. The evidence against me is damning. Doesn't matter that it was obviously planted."

Georgia smiled. The power smile.

The spur of arousal came on again. He'd done too much penance. He would have to satisfy the desire soon. Today might be the day for a celebration. Because he knew that smile. Georgia was gloating.

Which meant she had it.

"I've got to find something to prove that it wasn't what it looked like that night," he said. "That someone set me up. Not Bella, of course."

"Bella would never do something like that," Georgia said quickly.

"Not in a million years. I trust Bella more than anyone," he lied. "I miss her so much." He felt a little disappointment at how quickly she'd come to Bella's defense. Served enough wine, Georgia had been known to let slip the disappointments about her life—the husband she'd chosen for his potential who had never wanted the same things she did. The daughter who took after her father rather than Georgia. How lonely it all was for poor Georgia.

But don't underestimate poor Georgia.

"I think I might have just the thing," she said.

He blinked wide eyes. "What do you mean?"

"You know that investigator you told me about? Well, I called him."

"You did?" He feigned surprise. "Why? Is everything all right?"

"I'm fine, of course. I called him to look into your case."

"You called him to help me?" He tried to appear happy. It was a stretch behind six inches of bulletproof glass, especially when he knew that wasn't how it had happened. Before his formal arrest, he had told his guy when to approach Georgia and how to get her to bite. *Check and see if she can use any help. Maybe mention the situation, how worried you are.*

"You're my son. Of course I did."

He swallowed bile. He didn't want a parent.

"He found a picture that I think you'll find very interesting." She unbuckled the purse and pulled out a small manila envelope. She took her time, enjoying his perceived anticipation.

After she drew the picture out, she pressed it against the glass awkwardly, trying to hold the phone in her other hand. As he expected, it was the photo of three girls. High school age. They stood in front of a high net, their volleyball shorts tight around their meaty teenage thighs.

"Who are they?" he asked innocently.

She set down the picture, brought out a second one, and pressed the new one to the glass. Again, he knew all about it. A close-up of the girl on the right. The top of her jersey filled the center of the image.

"I don't understand," he said to please her. As though he couldn't see it perfectly well himself.

And she was pleased, so filled with glee at her work. She tucked the phone to her shoulder so that she could tap the white-tipped nail of her other hand on the face of the girl on the right side of the picture. "This one here. She's the ticket to getting you out of here."

There it was, the scene as he'd dreamed it.

This would be like writing a master play. Setting it all up from behind the scenes and putting the actors in the right roles to make the whole thing come alive.

And come alive it would.

13

Schwartzman struggled against the bindings. Coarse. The scent of plastic. A searing pain around her wrists. She struggled to breathe. Rubbed her hands together. The binding slid across itself. Synthetic. Twine would have caught. There would have been the smell of hay. Either way it was rope, thick rope, tied tightly. Too tightly. Her skin was worn raw. It split with a series of sharp stings like splinters piercing the skin.

"Open your eyes," he said, taking hold of her chin. The smooth ends of his fingertips. The smell of aftershave and Gucci cologne.

She jerked away from him.

His fingers tightened.

"You will watch this," he said. "You will see what happens when you try to keep away from me."

She opened her mouth to scream, felt dry cloth against the roof of her mouth. She coughed, choking, fighting to draw air through the fabric. Her eyes opened instinctively as she fought for breath. Tears filled them and streamed down her face.

Spencer raised a narrow blade, pushing it close to her face. A single cutting edge, faced inward. Right-handed. She flinched, expecting the knife to come toward her.

Instead Spencer swung from the hips and drove the knife into a tan shirt. A man's scream. Schwartzman couldn't see his face, but she knew that shirt. The tan button-down.

She screamed through the gag, fought against the restraints, seeing beyond the skin, where the knife penetrated the clavicle above the second rib. Watched as it stabbed into the spongy tissue of the lung.

The tan shirt grew dark as blood soaked the fabric. The handle of the knife stuck from the chest. She knew that knife. Its bone-colored handle. It was hers—the paring knife from her kitchen set.

Spencer grabbed hold of the knife again, pressed his palm against the chest, and wrenched the knife free. Blood ran in a steady flow from the wound. Her gaze inside again, blood filled the chest cavity. She shifted to press her shoulder to the wound. Stop the bleeding.

"No one should get between a man and his wife," Spencer said as he brought the knife down again.

Before the knife struck, there was a loud pounding. Someone knocking on a door. "Dr. Schwartzman!"

She gasped, brought a hand to her face. The bindings were gone. She opened her eyes, and the living room appeared before her. Spencer was gone. She was in her living room, inside her apartment. She'd fallen asleep on the couch.

"Dr. Schwartzman, are you all right?" someone called through the door.

She sat up quickly, the room tilting sideways as the blood rushed from her head.

Voices in the hallway. Urgent. The sound of a key in the door.

She looked down at her yoga pants, the tank top she'd been wearing when Ken had come over. *Ken.* She glanced toward the bedroom as the apartment door flew open. She stood quickly as two men rushed into the room. Alan came in first, his lean frame not filling the shoulders of his blazer. His hair flopped to one side as he halted just inside the door.

When she'd received the bouquet from Spencer last spring, she had specifically asked for Alan from the front desk to come to collect the flowers, handing him a pair of gloves to help preserve the evidence to be taken to the lab. She couldn't handle doing it on her own, and his was the only name she knew. He was the only one who greeted her by name every time.

"Dr. Schwartzman." Alan held a hand at his side as though he had a gun to draw. "The neighbors heard screaming."

Schwartzman crossed to the bedroom before speaking. She pushed the door open with one hand and looked into the room, cast in the cool morning light. She saw exactly what she expected to see. The bed was made from yesterday morning, the gray-blue sheets pulled taut to the pillows and folded down over a paler gray comforter. The pillows were plumped at the head of the bed. Four of them, their open ends faced out. Two throws in the center—one circular and one oblong in a plaid and a floral. A custom mattress—Tempur-Pedic, all brand-new.

She'd replaced it all after she'd found Ken Macy in her bed, half-dead. Even the rug beneath the bed. Ken's blood had stained it all.

Alan approached without touching her. "Are you all right, Dr. Schwartzman?"

"I fell asleep with the television on," she said, not meeting Alan's eyes.

He glanced at the blackened screen. "Of course," he said quickly.

The security officer behind him made a noise, and Alan cut him a hard stare.

For several seconds her lie dissipated across the room like a bad smell.

"I appreciate you coming in to check, Alan," she said. "I'm sorry if I woke the neighbors." *If* I *woke the neighbors. Because it wasn't the television. It was me screaming because Spencer was there, stabbing Ken again. As though I were seeing it the first time. But I didn't. And Spencer didn't stab Ken Macy. He had Carol Fletcher do it for him while I was drugged in the bed beside him.*

"You sure you don't want me to take a look around?" Alan asked.

"I'm fine. Thank you again, Alan."

She followed the men to the door and locked the bolt and the chain after them. Her back to the door, she rubbed her face. Ken had been here. He'd made her soup. They'd curled on the couch and started *Bringing Up Baby*. What then? A piece of paper on the coffee table replaced the bowls and glasses that had been there the night before.

A note from Ken.

> *Good morning. You were sound asleep by ten thirty, so I borrowed the key off your ring to lock myself out. I assume you have an extra? Let's make a date to finish the movie.*
> *Baby reminds me a little of someone I know . . .*

She smiled. Her father used to say she was like Baby. Or, more specifically, like Katharine Hepburn. As a young girl, the comparison seemed funny, but she enjoyed the actress's antics. Like Hepburn, Schwartzman preferred pants to dresses and was extremely active if not exactly athletic. Schwartzman liked to think she had some of the actress's boldness, as well. But that was a long time ago.

After her father's death, Schwartzman lost the best of Hepburn's qualities. Her independence, her outspokenness, her spirit—all of it vanished entirely and seemingly at once.

It was that woman—barren of confidence and resolve—who'd married Spencer MacDonald.

An independent, intelligent woman would never have married a man who raped her on their first date. And yet she had. She'd yielded to the inner voice that told her he was the best she could do, that she owed it to her mother to marry him and take her position in society—the position her mother had wanted for her since birth.

Had that inner voice been her mother's? Or Spencer's?

She ought to be able to stitch together the fabric of who she'd been before, during, and after Spencer. Yet the edges of the tapestry between her father's death and her marriage to Spencer and the woman she was today never lined up. Their patterns had shifted entirely—from stripes to spots.

The fact that she became a person unrecognizable to herself left behind the question of whether history might repeat itself. If she was truly the strong, intelligent woman she wanted to be, how could she have let herself become a victim so easily?

Whenever she measured her success, her marriage to Spencer canceled out whatever else she had accomplished. She wondered if that would always be true, or if someday she would understand how she'd made such a mistake. And forgive herself. Schwartzman made tea and let her mind drift to the death certificate that had been left on her car. The name Joseph Strom wasn't familiar to her. She should call her mother, but she couldn't muster the energy. Instead she sent a text message.

Mama, hope you are doing well. All good here.

Except the cancer. And nightmares about Spencer.

Ran into someone from Charleston. Do you know the name Joseph Strom?

She tried to think of something else to say but came up empty, so she signed it XOX.

Her phone rang on the coffee table, a call from the morgue's main number.

She straightened her back and adjusted the pillows on the couch. "Schwartzman."

"Hey, Doc. It's Wally Jacobs."

Hearing Wally's name reminded her of Roy, the new assistant, and his weird behavior the night before. His tattoos, the missing scrub pants.

"Good morning, Wally."

"We've got an unattended death that came in last night. Paramedics responded to a man unconscious in a van off the Embarcadero at six nineteen." His inflection made it sound as though he was reading from a script. "Pronounced dead on the scene. We got photographs inside the van, and nothing showed up in X-ray. After the day with Posner and your . . ." Wally remained quiet for a second too long.

"Chemotherapy," she finished for him. "You can say it."

"Right. After that," he said, suggesting he couldn't actually say it. "The director thought this one could wait until this morning. He's in drawer twelve."

"Thanks, Wally. I'll be there within the hour. Any updates on the toxicology on Todd Posner?"

"Posner?" he asked as if he was unable to place the name. "Oh, right. Todd Posner." A short delay. "Nope. Nothing yet. I'll follow up."

She moved quickly through her morning routine, made a single cup of coffee for the road, and arrived at the morgue within the hour.

Settling in, she went straight to work on the victim in drawer twelve. The remains were of a Caucasian male, looked to be in his late thirties, approximately five nine, 190 pounds. Discoloration of the fingertips and teeth suggested tobacco use, not that she needed those signs to identify a smoker. She could tell from the second she had entered the morgue. The whole room smelled of it.

He'd been found with his wallet and ID. No signs of foul play. ID said he was Ben Gustafson. Thirty-six, so he was a little younger than he looked. Not surprising for a smoker. Lived in Albany across the bay and worked for a satellite TV company.

The autopsy on Gustafson was noneventful. He was found in his work van a short distance from the main road. Likely he'd pulled off after feeling some pain or dizziness. The case presented like sudden cardiac death, but the autopsy showed no signs of coronary thrombus, no myocardial infarction, and no signs of ruptured plaque. There were also no signs of significant coronary artery disease. Still, his weight and the fact that he was a smoker put him at a higher risk for heart failure.

In about half the cases like this one, of "sudden death," an autopsy would identify no specific pathology. The accepted conclusion in those cases was that death was caused by primary arrhythmia.

Schwartzman didn't like the cases where she was unable to identify the pathology. She liked answers.

After double-checking her findings, she set aside her organ samples to study under the microscope and stitched up the Y-incision on Gustafson's chest. As she was collecting her tools, the lights in the morgue flickered.

She happened to be standing beside the victim's head, and the flash of light caught the sheen on Gustafson's face in a way she hadn't noticed before. When the halogen lights glared brightly again, she retrieved her alternate light sources and shut off the overheads. There was no sign of abrasions or contusions on the area around his mouth where she thought she'd seen something, but under the fluorescent wand, a series of small droplets appeared across Gustafson's cheeks and chin. Expectorate could cause that type of pattern—if he'd coughed into his hand, for instance, and some of the saliva or phlegm had bounced back at his face.

But when she studied his hands, there was no sign of trace on them. He might have coughed into his shirtsleeve.

She played with the light, checking for continuity of the droplets across his face, but there was a large void around his mouth and nose. Maybe he had wiped his face. She made a note for Roger to check for traces of fluid on his clothes and took separate samples of the droplets on his cheeks and chin and the areas of void around his mouth and nose.

She returned Gustafson to drawer twelve and checked her phone. She had one text, her mother's reply to her question about Joseph Strom.

Don't know the name.

She silenced the phone and set it aside. Maybe her father had known him. There would be a lot of people he knew through work who her mother would not have met or even heard of.

Her stomach growled, and she was trying to decide what might taste good when Hal called. "You free?"

"I was thinking about food," she said honestly.

"I found Sandy. She's over in Oakland."

"Have you talked to her?"

"No. I didn't want to call, so I'm heading out now. Can you join me?"

She scanned the morgue. There was plenty of paperwork but no cases awaiting autopsy.

"I'll feed you," he added as though she was holding out for a better offer.

"How soon?"

"How soon will we eat?" he teased.

"No. How soon will you be here?"

"Ten minutes."

"I'll be ready," she said and went to pack up a travel kit. There was no reason to think she'd need it, but the kit was comforting. It reminded her that this was a job she could do.

And right now that kind of comfort was worth clinging to.

14

Hal pulled up to the morgue entrance and stopped at the curb as Schwartzman walked out into the bright sunlight. Her hair blew in the wind, and she kept her jacket tied closed although he was hot in his shirtsleeves. Her purse hung off one shoulder, and in the opposite hand was a small blue toolbox, a mini version of the large ActionPacker she took to their scenes. She looked better than she had yesterday—better even than she had the night before. Seeing the improvement reminded him how well she handled those first days after chemo.

He knew her treatments were on Mondays, three weeks apart. Four treatments total. She never talked about it, so he kept her progress in his head. It seemed important that he know how she was going to feel.

Not that he needed to remember it. Since the first treatment, her disposition had forecasted the arrival of the next. The week before the second treatment, she'd changed. Not much of a talker to begin with, she'd grown quieter. She was less patient with the morgue assistants and with the officers on the scenes. If she weren't so pleasant about it, he'd say she got grouchy. But grouchy for Schwartzman was right below saintly in his book.

He had offered to accompany her to the treatments, but she was stern in her refusal. If she'd had her way, he suspected no one would know she had cancer. But someone had to get her home from the mastectomy.

Hailey had arranged to get the day off work to help Schwartzman, but at the last minute, her daughter Ali had come down with the flu. Even if Hailey could get away, it seemed like a bad idea for her to show up after she'd been spending time with a sick kid.

So Hailey had recruited Hal.

Schwartzman had clearly been surprised when she'd woken up from surgery to find him instead of Hailey. Not surprisingly, she'd handled it the way she always did—deflecting attention, masking the pain.

He popped the trunk, and Schwartzman loaded her small kit inside. She put her hand on the car as she came around to the passenger side as if she needed it for balance or support. It had been four days since her last chemo treatment. Week two was the reprieve. She would feel mostly better by then. Her energy would return. But by week three, she'd be starting to worry again about the upcoming treatment—about feeling sick and tired, about missing work, and likely about the cancer itself.

She took off her coat before getting in the car and set it over her lap and shivered. Something else he knew from Hailey. She was perpetually cold . . . until she was boiling hot. He adjusted the vents toward himself and turned down the AC.

As soon as she was settled in the car, relief washed over him. He'd been spinning this case in his own head alone for too long. "Ready?"

"Ready," she confirmed, fastening her seat belt.

Hal put the car in gear and started toward the street. They were heading to Sandy Coleman's address of record. Coleman's name had been found in Posner's mouth, which meant the killer was trying to tell them something. Going to see her was the obvious next step.

"I've got some news on Posner." She gripped a small stack of papers with two hands. "Checked my e-mail on the way out the door and we got tox results."

"Tell me," he said, desperate for a break in the case.

"That mole?"

Hal nodded.

"It was an injection site."

"Of?" he prompted.

"Detomidine mixed with butorphanol."

Hal forgot the drug names even as she spoke them. He'd never heard of either. "What the hell are those?"

"The detomidine is an alpha-2 drug."

He shook his head. "Alpha-2?"

"It's a drug that shuts down the release of adrenaline. It's used for sedation."

Now they were getting somewhere. "A sedative. Prescribed by a doctor, I assume?"

"A vet, usually," she said.

Hal stared at her.

"It's a sedative cocktail used in horses," she explained.

"Horses?" Hal repeated.

She seemed excited. "Does that offer any clues?"

"It might." He lifted his mobile phone, put a call into the cancer center, and requested Tamara Long. He was on a brief hold before Tamara came on the line.

They exchanged quick pleasantries before Hal got to business. "I'm calling with an odd question. I need to know if anyone at the center owns horses." He put the phone on speaker and held it so Schwartzman could hear, too.

"Not that I can think of," Tamara said. "Not many people in the Bay Area keep horses."

"How about someone who grew up with horses? Or someone with a vet in the family."

"I can check."

Hal held his sigh to himself. "Call me if you think of anyone who has a connection to horses—owning, riding, anything."

"Will do," she promised, and he could hear her talking to someone else before the call ended.

"Something might come of it," Schwartzman said.

"It might," he agreed, though not convincingly.

"Where's Hailey?"

"Wondering why you're here instead?" he asked.

"It crossed my mind."

"Hailey is out on another case." For the past month, Hailey had been part of a domestic homicide task force focused on increased support for domestic abuse victims before they became homicide victims. It was supposed to be a part-time thing, but lately he rarely saw her.

"And I'm a doctor, so you thought I might be useful."

"It crossed my mind," he returned with a smile.

She paused and lifted the page again. "I've got more. The blood results from the femoral artery also came back. They show an increased level of white blood cells."

"And that means?"

"The density tells us that Posner was alive for some time after ingesting the Adriamycin. Best guess is between one and three hours."

"So he suffered." Someone had wanted Posner to suffer. "Anything else?"

"Yes. Roger and I talked about the death being possibly related to bondage, sex play—"

"I heard. He said they found some site where people burn each other with acid for kicks."

She nodded.

"Posner doesn't feel like a sex crime to me," he said. "Did you find something?"

"No," she said. "I swabbed for fluids during the autopsy. Results show no signs of vaginal or seminal fluid."

No sex. "So it wasn't about sex. If it wasn't about sex, that leaves us power, money, and love."

"Revenge," she added.

"Right," he said. "Forgot revenge."

They passed over Angel Island and onto the new section of the Bay Bridge. Until the new bridge had been built, the eastbound direction on the bridge had always been beneath the westbound one. He enjoyed getting to see the bay from this direction—the Oakland Port, the rolling hills in the background.

"You want some good news?" she asked, her voice soft.

"I could use some."

"Buster's okay."

Hal shook his head. Who the hell was Buster?

"The dog. Posner's Australian shepherd."

Hal said nothing.

"I called the vet to check on him."

"You checked on the dog?"

"He was cute."

Hal gave her a look.

Schwartzman laughed. "Okay, I thought it was good news." She folded her hands in her lap, and her expression grew serious. "What else do we know? Did you talk to Dr. Fraser's son?"

Hal nodded. "He's clean. The kid was at an engagement party—twenty of them in Lake Tahoe for the weekend. Didn't get home until Tuesday midday." Lake Tahoe was a three-hour drive without traffic. Too far away to sneak down and kill Posner. Plus there was a constant social media presence of the group from Sunday through the early hours of Tuesday. The group had posted dozens of images on Instagram and Facebook, and Patrick's Snapchat story showed images of him at the lake throughout the weekend.

"A solid alibi."

"It is." And Hal was grateful for it. He hated to think that a kid who wanted to go to medical school was the one who had injected Posner with horse tranquilizer, then forced him to ingest a toxin so he would die a slow and painful death. Hal had also confirmed Norman Fraser's alibi. He and his wife had dined with another couple the night Posner was killed. Without an exact time of death, there was still a slim possibility that Fraser could have gone back out, but Posner's death had been slow, and it didn't seem likely that Fraser could have tortured Posner and killed him inside the window Schwartzman had estimated. Hal was running background checks on the two just in case, but nothing was back yet.

"What other leads do you have?" Schwartzman asked.

"I went through the list of Posner's latest girlfriends and the pending lawsuits against him. The legal proceedings are standard. Even the two malpractice cases are pretty minor. No one died; no one's maimed."

"Not enough to warrant torturing him."

"Right," he agreed. "I'm working through the girlfriends. So far they've all been short-lived things. No one stands out." He'd spent a little extra time investigating Tamara Long, even though she wasn't on the list. She had been easy to eliminate as a suspect. The day Posner was killed, she had spent the afternoon and night in a hospital in Berkeley, acting as doula for a friend who was delivering her first baby.

"How about all those letters Posner got?"

"Roger's got someone working through them," Hal said, thankful someone else was handling that job. "A lot of irritated folks, but so far no one with a homicidal rage."

The two sat quietly for a few minutes. He had opted for Highway 13 over 880, where traffic was lighter and the highway wound through the Oakland Hills. He'd always liked this area, and he tried to anchor himself to the sense of calm he felt driving through it. This was the waiting part, the part he hated. He reminded himself that it took only one piece. He knew this from experience, and yet every time he started a new case with the same thought—what if the piece never came? What if he couldn't solve it?

Schwartzman seemed to sense his need for distraction. "Want to hear about acute myeloid leukemia?"

"Sure," Hal said, again reminded how grateful he was to have Schwartzman with him. He thought about the way she had been with Norman Fraser, the deference she'd paid to him. He was her doctor. How strange it must have been for her to think of him as a suspect.

He let go of the thought and listened as Schwartzman described Sandy's cancer.

"Rare. Acute myeloid leukemia is almost nonexistent in people under forty-five. Average age for diagnosis is sixty-seven. How old is Sandy?"

Hal shook his head. "Don't know. It was hard enough to get her full name. Took me two days of dancing around patient privacy laws. The name and her address are all I've got."

Schwartzman glanced back down at the folder and then back at Hal. "So Sandy might be . . ."

"Dead."

She said nothing in response.

"You okay?"

"Fine." She lifted the folder again. "Acute myeloid leukemia is also more common in men than women."

Hal hadn't considered that. "Sandy could be a him."

She was quiet a moment. "AML starts in the bone marrow and typically moves quickly into the blood. Stem cell transplant is required for cure." She read over her notes. "Morbidity is greater than fifty percent."

"Stem cell transplant? Is that a surgical procedure?" He was trying to figure out how Todd Posner was connected to Sandy.

"Stem cells are infused through IV. The doctor would order the treatment, but a nurse would oversee the transplant." She looked up.

"Posner's a surgeon," he said, thinking out loud. "So Posner shouldn't have had anything to do with a stem cell transplant. The order would come from a medical oncologist. Like Fraser, right?"

"Right," she agreed.

"So why was that name in Posner's mouth? And how did it get there?"

Schwartzman paused. "My guess would be that the paper was added peri- or even postmortem. There was no evidence of tooth imprints."

"Like you would've expected if he'd tried to swallow it."

"Right. If he'd wanted to swallow it, I would have expected it to be masticated."

"Chewed."

She nodded. "The process of chewing manufactures saliva in the mouth, making things easier to swallow. Plus the paper wasn't fully saturated—it was still relatively dry."

"So it hadn't been in Posner's mouth long."

"Which means Posner probably didn't put it there," she added.

"Right." Hal pulled to the curb on a quiet residential street in Oakland. The houses were well kept—freshly painted, the lawns small green plots. Most had a tall front fence, and each window was barred. It was weird to be in this neighborhood. The house he'd grown up in was less than two miles from there.

"You okay?" she asked after a few seconds.

Hal sighed and released his seat belt without answering the question. He was okay. He was okay until he thought about his dad. Now was not the time for that. If he had his way, there would never be a time for that. "Guess we should go ask about Sandy."

Hal led the way to the front door, his black notebook in his coat pocket and his badge in hand. Schwartzman held the folder to her chest, a pen clipped to the front. He rarely showed up at a house without calling first. Even in a neighborhood with a largely black population like Oakland, a strange black man on your front porch wasn't usually welcome. Another reason it helped to have Hailey with him. Or Schwartzman.

People were less likely to shoot at a white woman indiscriminately.

"Thanks for coming."

Her brows rose, and something crossed her face—nervousness or maybe excitement; he couldn't tell. Not fear. That was one expression he recognized on her, and he was relieved not to see it now.

The lace curtain beyond the barred window shifted. A woman peered out, and Hal showed his badge.

There was the sound of locks turning and a chain sliding. The door cracked open.

"Can I help you, Officer?" The woman behind the door was his age or a little younger. She wore khaki slacks and a colorful shirt with a logo that was partially obscured by the door.

"I'm Hal Harris with the San Francisco Police Department. This is my colleague, Dr. Schwartzman. We were hoping to ask you a few questions."

The door didn't budge. "San Francisco? Why would the San Francisco police want to talk to us?"

"We're here in regard to Todd Posner."

She paused a moment.

"Dr. Todd Posner. He's an oncologist."

"Yes. I remember Dr. Posner. Is everything okay?"

"I'm afraid Dr. Posner was killed."

"Killed." Her lips thinned. "We don't know anything about that."

"We don't think you do," Hal said.

"We actually wanted to hear about Sandy's cancer," Schwartzman cut in. "How Dr. Posner was involved. We won't take much of your time."

The woman behind the door shrank. The weight of Sandy's cancer. He didn't want to ask how Sandy was. Maybe he already knew.

"You're a detective, too?" she asked Schwartzman.

"I'm a medical examiner." Schwartzman pulled out her badge and passed it through the open door.

The woman returned the badge. The door closed and then reopened, wider this time with the chain undone. She waved Hal and Schwartzman into a small living room, furnished in the same sort of inexpensive oak furniture that had filled his parents' home. And like their home, this one was tidy. It smelled of lemon and something vaguely floral that he always associated with plug-in air fresheners.

"I didn't catch your name, ma'am," Hal said.

"Susan Coleman." She motioned to the couch. "I'm Sandy's mother."

Mother. So Sandy Coleman was—or had been—young.

"AML is rare in young people," Schwartzman said, taking a seat on the chair closest to the door.

"It is. Very. And even rarer in people of African descent. Sandy didn't fit any of the normal criteria."

"How was it diagnosed?"

"In that way, we got lucky. One day Sandy was a normal eleven-year-old kid. Active, good in school, happy. She finished the sixth grade, and suddenly it was the first week of summer and she couldn't get out of bed. At first I thought she was just recovering from the end of school—all the activities. But she was so sick. Fever and ached all over. It was a weird time of year for the flu. Plus she hadn't seen anyone for over a week when the fever started, and the rest of us weren't sick. We thought it was something she ate or the water. But everyone else in the house was fine."

Susan took a moment to compose herself.

Hal always felt slightly at a loss when talking to parents. Parenthood changed people. His sister had told him having a child meant part of your heart lived outside your body. Intellectually he understood. And he loved his niece and his four nephews. But he knew that fell short of what it meant to be a parent. And, in particular, a mother.

"Then she got these sores in her mouth," Susan continued.

"The flu-like symptoms and the sores . . . they're both symptoms of low white blood cell count," Schwartzman said.

Susan nodded. "So we took her to Children's Hospital, and they did blood tests. While we were waiting for those to come back, she got one nosebleed after another and started getting these bruises on her arms and thighs." Susan crossed her arms. "Now this is a kid who played soccer, a kid who had two older brothers."

Hal noticed she said *had*. She *had* two older brothers. He regretted that she had to go through this again.

"She never bruised like that," Susan said. "Children's Hospital admitted her—tests, tests, and more tests. No one would tell us what was going on. But by then Jimmy—that's my husband—he'd started reading on the Internet. He thought it was leukemia. Jimmy's sister is an oncology nurse over at San Francisco General. So we took her there."

Hal glanced at Schwartzman. Was she thinking about her own diagnosis? She'd told him her doctor had called her one morning—directly—to give her the news. Had even made her an appointment with the oncologist. How much easier it had been for her with no hoops to jump through. No endless tests. It was why she'd gotten the surgery so soon, so quickly. She'd been ushered through the process.

Because she was the medical examiner. And Sandy Coleman was a black kid from Oakland.

Hal pulled out his notebook. "Did you see Dr. Posner?"

Susan Coleman gripped her hands in her lap. "Yes. My sister-in-law knew him, so she arranged a meeting," she said. "A stem cell transplant was the only option. We knew that already. But she wasn't a candidate for an autologous transplant."

Hal looked up from his book. "An auto—"

"It means a transplant of her own stem cells," Schwartzman explained. "Once the patient is in remission, they can harvest and store her own stem cells in the case that another transplant is needed down the line."

"But she didn't have the healthy stem cells for that," Susan added.

"What did Dr. Posner suggest?" Hal asked.

"He tested us first. Her dad and I and her two older brothers, but none of us were compatible. Which was hard because that was really our best bet."

"And after that?"

"Dr. Posner put Sandy in the system, but he wasn't optimistic. He said that even if we found a compatible donor, Sandy would be in the hospital at least three months. The chances of rejection were really high and the costs enormous. We honestly didn't know what we were going to do." She stared down at her hands.

Hal waited a beat before prompting, "And then?"

"We got a call from the angel."

"The angel?" Hal repeated.

"That's what we called him—Dr. Fraser. He was the one who stepped in when Dr. Posner told us that there was nothing he could do."

A sound from Schwartzman. Like something caught in her throat. She covered her mouth and pretended to cough. "Excuse me."

Susan Coleman watched her.

"Would that be Norman Fraser?" Hal asked.

"Yes," Sandy answered. "Do you know him?"

Before Hal could answer, there was the sound of someone struggling to open the front door. After a series of thumps, the door sprang open, and a teenager in shorts and a jersey burst into the room like a hurricane. She dropped a gym bag, a water bottle, a backpack, and a soccer ball, which bounced into the dining room and knocked against the glass pane of the cabinet.

The girl wore a sheepish smile. "Sorry, Mom."

Susan Coleman exhaled. "This is Sandy."

Sandy had suffered from a rare cancer most common in white men over fifty with a high mortality rate. And here she was, a teenager in perfect health.

Schwartzman was smiling.

"Sandy, do you know Dr. Norman Fraser?" Hal asked.

"Dr. Norm," Susan explained.

"Sure. Dr. Norm helped connect us to the foundation."

"What foundation?"

"The one who paid for my treatment—right, Mom?"

"We owe Dr. Norm everything," Susan agreed. "He connected us to the Finlay Foundation, and they took care of us. We call Dr. Norm Sandy's angel."

Hal recalled the crime scene. Why Sandy's name? What did she have to do with Posner's death? There was no way this kid had injected him with a horse tranquilizer and forced him to drink a bottle of Red Devil. Even if Posner had been pessimistic about Sandy's cancer, she had gotten treatment. Norman Fraser had saved her life when Posner hadn't tried to help. Fraser, whose son was being blackmailed. Did Fraser know that Posner had blown Sandy off? Was Sandy Coleman another reason Fraser had to hate Posner?

More troubling was the fact that Fraser hadn't mentioned his involvement in the Finlay Foundation, yet he'd clearly been involved.

Seated on the arm of the couch beside her mother, Sandy Coleman spun the soccer ball on her finger.

"Did you interact with anyone other than Dr. Fraser during the treatments?"

Sandy looked at her mother. "There were tons of people at the hospital. I was there for more than a month."

"Right," agreed Susan. "The stem cell treatment is quite a production."

"Anyone stand out?" Hal asked.

Sandy stopped spinning the ball and shook her head slowly.

"Dr. Fraser didn't perform the stem cell transplant," Schwartzman cut in. "Did he?"

"No. It was a nurse named . . . ?" Again Sandy deferred to her mother.

"I don't remember her name," Susan said.

Hal waited until he was certain Sandy and Susan Coleman didn't have anything else to add. Then he stood and thanked them. At the door, he turned back. "Do you ride horses, Sandy?"

"No," she said, looking confused.

"She's never been on a horse. Not many horses in Oakland," Susan said.

Hal opened the door and let Schwartzman pass in front of him.

Walking out the door, he drew a deep breath. He needed to take a closer look at Norman Fraser.

15

Schwartzman and Hal were still parked on the street outside Sandy Coleman's house. Schwartzman glanced up at the windows, picturing the vibrant young woman in her soccer uniform.

Alive. Healthy.

She tried to imagine what that family had gone through, being told there was no hope for their eleven-year-old daughter. And then, seemingly out of nowhere, Fraser had stepped in.

Todd Posner had blown her off, and Fraser had saved her. Her interaction with Dr. Todd Posner made him seem exactly like everyone described him—a narcissist and a jerk.

Inside every monster, there is some glimpse of his angel.

Schwartzman's father had said that, but maybe he'd never met someone like Posner. She couldn't remember if he'd ever told her where it came from. Practicing law, he met plenty of monsters . . . and, she supposed, their angels, too.

It made her think of Spencer.

Would her father believe there was a sliver of angel in the man who had killed his unborn grandchild?

Again, she was back in that room. Her own image projected on the wall of the cell Spencer had created for her. Her voice crying, "Help me. Please help me." Chills scraped down the skin of her back like long talons, and heat and nausea settled in her stomach.

Hal hadn't started the car. She glanced over to find him staring at his phone. Thankful for the brief reprieve, she drew two slow breaths and pulled the seat belt across her chest.

Sandy's angel. The angel. She did not let her mind wander beyond that thought. She was done thinking about Spencer. At least for today.

Hal frowned at his phone. "Huh."

"What is it?"

"I've got a text from Roger. Says he wants to see us."

"Us?" She drew her phone out of her purse. She had a message from Roger, too. Some results in. Come by ASAP! Roger was hardly an ASAP kind of guy. And she didn't think she'd ever seen him use an exclamation point.

"Sounds urgent," Hal said. "Let's see what he's up to." He dialed and put the phone on speaker.

Naomi answered the lab phone.

"Hey, Naomi. It's Hal. Roger around?"

"Hi, Hal," Naomi said, her voice booming in the car as Hal lowered the volume. "He's been looking for you. Hang on." Relatively new, Naomi Muir had made herself valuable in the lab, and Roger had come to depend on her. Schwartzman had noticed the tech was at most of their scenes these days. She did good work.

In the background was Roger's voice. "Tell them to come in."

"We're all the way over in Oakland," Hal said.

Naomi relayed the message.

"At a scene?" Roger shouted back.

"No. We were interviewing a witness."

Again, Naomi repeated the news to Roger.

"Can't he pick up the phone?" Hal asked.

"I think he's enjoying this," Naomi whispered. "Hang on—I'll put you on speaker."

"Are you heading back into the city?" Roger again. "Do you have time to come to the lab?"

"Yes," Hal said, a hint of frustration in his voice. "And yes."

"Great. I'll be here," Roger shouted.

"He's got something to show you," Naomi told them.

"What? Can you tell us on the phone?"

"Just come in," Naomi said.

"He sounds very proud of himself."

"Oh, he is."

Schwartzman enjoyed Roger Sampers. Like herself, he was more nerd than cool kid, and he had a voracious appetite for knowledge. His chronic medical condition, alopecia universalis, had also made him a sensitive man. He had no hair on his entire body—no eyebrows, no eyelashes. Although she had never spoken to him about it directly, Schwartzman knew this had happened to him sometime in early middle school—the very age when kids were at their cruelest. He carried no chip on his shoulder and, remarkably, often joked about his condition. "I'm really *the* ideal crime scene analyst," he'd remarked once. "I will *never* leave a hair at a scene."

"We're on our way," Hal told Naomi. He did not sound pleased with the idea of having to wait until he got to the lab to find out what Roger had found.

"There is one thing I can tell you over the phone," Naomi said.

"Thank God," Hal muttered in reply.

"We got results on the DNA found under Posner's nails," Naomi said.

"And?"

Schwartzman felt the tension in the car.

"It's his," Naomi said.

"Damn," Hal muttered.

"Sorry."

"No worries," Hal said. "Thanks for letting us know."

"See you soon," Naomi said before ringing off.

On the drive back across the bridge, Hal and Schwartzman talked more about Norman Fraser.

"He was straightforward in the interview," Hal said. "He told me he didn't like Posner. Told me that he and his partners were working to boot him from the practice. So what reason did Fraser have to kill Posner? And to kill him that way?"

"The pictures of his son."

"He told us he didn't know about the pictures of his son before yesterday. I believe him. I met him earlier at the office," Hal continued. "He was calm, honest about his dislike of Posner. He didn't act like a man with something to hide. He was a different person in the parking lot. It fits that his son had just told him about Posner's threat."

"And the son has an alibi," Schwartzman said.

"Right. A good one. Fraser has one, too—he was out to dinner with another couple, but the timeline of Posner's death isn't exact and—"

"Wives have been known to lie," Schwartzman said.

It didn't make sense. They'd had little trouble connecting Sandy to both Posner and Fraser. If the killer hadn't listed Sandy's name—or alternately had left off the AML diagnosis—the reference may have remained a mystery. But "For Sandy, acute myeloid leukemia"—that was as almost as specific as a full name and address. Sandy had led them to Fraser. Why would he do that if he was the killer?

Hal was quiet. Brow furrowed, his wheels were turning.

"What are you thinking?" she asked.

"Whoever killed Todd Posner knew about Sandy," he said slowly.

"Which means the killer is someone who had access to Sandy's chart," she said.

"Exactly. Who would have access?" Hal asked.

"In a doctor's office, anyone with access to the patient system."

"So that brings us back to the cancer center."

"Yes," she agreed. "Plus, whatever labs they outsource to. Other doctors that Sandy might have seen, hospital personnel."

"Hospital?"

"The stem cell transplant would have been done in the hospital," she said.

Hal sighed. "Just when I thought I was narrowing the list of suspects, it's doubled again."

"Whoever put Sandy's name in Posner's mouth had to know you'd link it back to Fraser."

"I agree," Hal said. "The paper seems more like an attempt to set Fraser up. The question is who knew that Todd Posner had seen Sandy Coleman?"

"Seen her and turned her away." Schwartzman remembered the gossip from her days in residency in Seattle. A hospital bred rumors faster than it did germs. "It's someone in the medical community."

Hal went quiet again, and she left him to his thoughts. The new information might hint at where Hal should be looking for Posner's killer.

But he was right.

It didn't narrow the list of suspects.

—

When they arrived at the lab, Roger was fussing over a large machine propped on a counter in the corner. It was an off-white box about the size of an office printer with colored tubing in the front and a single power cord that led to a screen the approximate size of a large index card.

Roger adjusted a panel with a series of buttons. The screen shifted between different types of graphs and reports as Roger talked excitedly. Though they couldn't hear what he was saying, the animation in his voice carried across the room.

Hal paused in the doorway and watched. "No wonder he wanted us to come to him. He's got a new toy."

Roger waved them over. "Hal, Schwartzman, come see my new mass spec."

Hal chuckled as he crossed the room. "What does it do?"

Beaming, Roger stroked the side of the machine as if it were a prize horse. "It analyzes chemical compositions."

Schwartzman smiled, sharing his enthusiasm. When the morgue had installed a camera with a UV filter on a tripod for timed exposures to help her identify pre- and perimortem injury patterns under the skin, she'd been as excited as Roger was now.

Of course, at the time she'd been surrounded by dead people in drawers, so she'd kept the excitement to herself.

"Isn't she gorgeous?" Roger went on.

"Beauty's in the eye of the beholder, my friend," Hal said. "Is this what you called us in to see?"

"No," Roger said, rushing by them to his desk. "But she's the reason."

Roger always had good energy, but she'd never seen him so . . . giddy. She had assumed the lab had a mass spec since her samples had always come to the lab, and Roger or one of the other techs reported the results. "How did you do mass spectrometry before?"

"We sent them out," Roger said. "But ABC News just did a big story about the lab we were using—how there were some errors in their reporting." He waved his hand. "It happened with another of the company's clients. Not us, thankfully. Still . . . we got our own machine."

"Nothing like the threat of a scandal to encourage the department to shell out some cash," Hal commented.

"Exactly," Roger said. "I filed the request the day after the story hit. Never had a purchase requisition been approved so quickly." He flipped through pages on his desk, humming. He stopped abruptly, slid two sheets of paper from the pile, and laid them side by side. "Look."

On each page was a chart with a series of vertical peaks along the horizontal. At the crest of each one was a number, representing something labeled "Relative Abundance." It had been forever since she'd studied chemistry.

"Roger, I'm getting a headache," Hal said.

"They're identical," Schwartzman said, scanning the two.

"Exactly," Roger exclaimed.

"Okay. I get it. You're the one with the medical degree, Schwartzman." Hal rubbed his head. "I'm just a lowly criminology major. Could someone explain it to me, please?"

"We tested two chemicals."

"Okay . . ."

"One came from the swab of Ben Gustafson's face—"

"Who the hell is Ben Gustafson?" Hal asked.

Schwartzman studied the results. Not just similar. They were truly identical. Where could the other have come from? She shook her head, unable to make sense of it. "I had an unattended death come in last night," she explained to Hal. "I performed the autopsy this morning. There was no obvious pathology." She thought back. "Actually, there was nothing unusual at all."

"You mean nothing unusual other than you don't know what killed him?" Hal asked.

"Yes, but he had risk indicators for a cardiac event." Unknown pathology autopsies happened from time to time. Every two dozen or so. It certainly wasn't unheard of.

"So what made you swab him?" Hal asked.

She went back through her thought process. "There was some evidence of spatter on his face," she said.

When she didn't continue, Hal prompted her. "Nothing else suspicious about his death?"

"No. Just something like droplets under his eyes. I thought it might be saliva or sputum. It was on his cheeks and lower chin but not around the mouth."

"And you're saying it wasn't saliva?" Hal asked Roger.

"Right," Roger said. "It's not biological at all. It's a chemical residue—the exact same chemical residue found on Todd Posner's leg."

Schwartzman was stunned. *Todd Posner and Ben Gustafson?*

"What?" Hal said.

She recalled the autopsy on Posner. "His leg?"

"You swabbed it. It came in with the evidence." Roger started to page back through a file on his desk.

"Yes," she said quickly. "The mole on his leg. I swabbed it to test for a drug. I noticed a needle mark."

Hal pointed to the graphs on Roger's desk. "Was the chemical residue a drug? Like some sort of sedative?"

"In both samples, the mass spec identified benzalkonium chloride and alcohol, as well as some aloe leaf extract."

"Like a cleaning product," Schwartzman said. She thought about the area on Gustafson's face. "A wipe of some sort."

"Yes," Roger said. "Probably meant to be both antibacterial and healing."

"Right," she agreed. "The aloe." But still, there might be no connection between the two men. One had been the victim of a gruesome homicide. One was a man who'd died of an apparent heart attack. Roger would have been working with the new machine. He would have been excited, perhaps a little careless. She put her hand on his shoulder. "Is there any chance the swabs got switched, that you tested the same one twice?"

"No chance," he answered in a firm voice.

Schwartzman glanced at Hal, who watched Roger.

"There's no chance," Roger repeated. He didn't look at their expressions but put a hand up. "There's more."

"We're listening."

"Naomi," he called across the lab. "Tell them about the van."

Naomi joined them. "When Roger got the results on the cable guy—"

"Cable guy?" Hal interrupted.

"Ben Gustafson worked as a cable installer," Naomi said. "And there's no record that he's done any work at Posner's house."

"Was he a patient?" Schwartzman asked.

"Nope," Naomi said.

Hal caught Schwartzman's eye, and she shrugged. She had no idea what connection there was between the cable installer and the surgeon.

"I went to the company to take a look at the van," Naomi continued. "Gustafson was in the driver's seat when he died. There was no antibacterial aloe wipe in the car. I found the packet it came from but not the wipe itself." She took a breath and went on. "And the company said no one's touched the van since the paramedics took Gustafson. The battery was dead, so it had to be towed back to the company lot, and it was just sitting there."

Hal shook his head. "So maybe the wipe was on him when the paramedics pulled him from the van. It might have dropped on the ground or ended up in the back of the ambulance. There are a thousand reasons it wasn't there."

"Maybe," Roger said. "But Naomi dusted the packet and guess what?"

"What?" Schwartzman asked.

"There were no fingerprints on the packet," Naomi interjected.

"And Gustafson wasn't wearing gloves," Roger said.

Hal exhaled, and Schwartzman felt the humming of her pulse. So perhaps he'd opened it with his teeth or using something else. But he would have touched it at some point. Could the two men really be connected?

"What's more," Roger continued, "it appears Gustafson was prone to heavy perspiration. He left clear prints all over that van."

"You mean all over the van except on that packet," Hal added.

"Bingo." Roger exhaled.

Hal sighed. "So Gustafson is now a suspicious death. Has it been assigned to a homicide inspector yet?"

"I don't know," Roger admitted. "But whoever catches the case, you're going to want to talk to them."

Schwartzman couldn't believe it. Again her mind drifted to Spencer. Spencer was in jail. And what would Spencer gain from killing a cable installer?

Hal nudged her. "Don't."

"I'm not doing anything."

But he held her gaze, reading her thoughts as always.

"Could we be talking about a coincidence?" he asked. "I mean, wipes aren't that uncommon. Seems like everyone carries those little containers of antibacterial stuff these days. Two different killers? Both carrying wipes? Or maybe Gustafson really died of a heart attack. The wipe packet may have been there since the winter when he'd been wearing gloves . . ." His voice trailed off, and she could see he didn't believe his own reasoning. Hal did not believe in coincidences.

She was starting to feel the same way.

"In general wipes are common, like you say," Roger explained. "But the ingredients in each vary somewhat. Perfumes, content of ethyl alcohol, it's not identical."

"Not unless the product is identical," Schwartzman added, following Roger's train of thought.

"Right," Roger agreed. He turned to Naomi. "Tell him about the fiber."

"I found a pink thread caught in the passenger door mechanism of Gustafson's van," Naomi said.

"The door mechanism?" Hal crossed his arms.

"Like someone used something to cover his—or her—hand when opening the door," Naomi explained.

"Opening the door from the outside," Roger said. "On the passenger side."

"And this thread? It links to Posner?" Hal asked.

"Yes. It's identical to the thread found in the Taser mark on Todd Posner."

The four of them were silent for a moment.

Schwartzman broke the silence. "So whoever killed Ben Gustafson also killed Todd Posner."

"Yes," Roger confirmed. "It looks that way."

"So maybe this Gustafson guy installed Posner's cable—maybe he saw something he wasn't supposed to."

"No," Naomi said. "Posner uses a different company."

Hal started to speak, but Naomi raised her hand to stop him. "I talked to Gustafson's manager when I was out there. Gustafson hasn't installed any cable systems in Posner's building or at or near the cancer center. Not since he joined the company—which was over a year ago."

"Jesus," Hal muttered.

Roger motioned to the mass spectrometer in the corner of the room. "Now aren't you glad you came in to meet Rita?" Without waiting for a response, Roger smiled and returned to the mass spec.

"Rita?" Hal repeated.

"He named the mass spec," Naomi said.

Hal rubbed his head without a word.

16

Schwartzman followed Hal out of the lab and into the hallway. She could tell he was anxious to be away from there. Roger's cool new toy meant Hal would add another homicide to his already overloaded plate and, with it, more unanswered questions. Schwartzman thought about the stack of paperwork on her own desk. She checked her phone. At least no more victims. She mentally knocked on wood, as there was none available in the cold, linoleum-tiled hallway.

Her phone rang. *Like clockwork.* As soon as it occurred to her that the morgue had been a little quiet for a few hours, a victim showed up.

The phone still in her hand, she looked down at the screen. Halted. A silent gasp caught in her throat. Her chest tightened at the unfamiliar number.

It was area code 843.

"What is it?" Hal asked, stopping beside her.

"Charleston, South Carolina."

"Maybe it's Harper," Hal said. Harper was the Charleston detective who'd helped Schwartzman after Spencer had killed her aunt. And another woman. When he'd drugged Schwartzman and bound her in her aunt's garage.

She was frozen at the sight of that number. Why would Harper Leighton be calling?

Just to catch up? Or something more.

Something bad.

She wouldn't know unless she answered. She lifted the phone to her ear. "Schwartzman."

"Anna, it's Harper Leighton."

Schwartzman nodded. "Hi, Harper."

"I sent a photograph to Hal. Have you seen him?" The breathless quality in her voice made Schwartzman's heart race again.

Something *was* wrong.

"He's right here. Harper?"

"Can you ask him if he got the photograph? Please."

"Hang on." She pressed the "Speaker" button. "Harper said she sent you a photograph."

"Let me look, Harper. You okay?" Hal navigated through his phone.

Harper didn't answer, and the lines between Hal's eyes deepened. "I've got it, Harper. Picture of three girls."

"The one on the right is Lucy. My daughter."

Hal and Schwartzman exchanged a look.

Schwartzman's throat went dry.

"Is she okay?" Hal asked.

"She's fine," Harper said, her tone not the least bit convincing.

"What am I looking at?" Hal asked.

"I just got this picture from the assistant district attorney in Greenville, the one working Spencer's case."

Schwartzman felt a wall against her shoulder, as though it had come to her rather than her to it. She leaned in, allowed the dingy off-white surface to take some of her weight.

Spencer. Even when she succeeded in pushing him out of her thoughts briefly, he always reappeared.

"A picture of your daughter?" Hal said. "What does your daughter have to do with Spencer MacDonald?"

"Zoom in on her neck." Harper's voice ended in a crack.

Necklace. She'd almost said *necklace*.

Hal's large fingers fumbled on the small screen. Finally the image grew in the frame.

"She's on the right," Harper said again, as though watching over their shoulders.

The girls on the left disappeared as he zoomed in on Lucy. Her dark hair must have been her dad's, but the rounded nose, the eyes—they were Harper's. Then Lucy's head and torso were gone until the screen was filled with a section of Lucy's chin, under which hung a thin silver chain.

Hal shifted the image upward, and the pendant came into view.

Schwartzman wanted to vomit. She leaned harder into the wall, pressing her free hand into her stomach as though holding herself together from that center point.

The pendant was a small silver sea turtle.

Identical to the one that Schwartzman had as a child.

Identical to the one they'd found under the bedside table in Spencer's home, the evidence that had helped put Spencer in prison.

"Shit," Hal said.

"When did she get this necklace?" Schwartzman asked.

"I've never seen it," Harper said. The breathless quality was still there.

"Did you ask her about it?" Hal asked.

"I'm at her school now. I pulled her out of class to ask about it."

Schwartzman felt the old fear, like her body plunging into ice-cold water. It burned her scalp, dug its talons into her spine.

"Jed's with me," she added.

Hal's head dropped. "What did she say, Harper?"

"She said she found it one day in her locker at school. In a little white box with a yellow bow."

Yellow. As though prodded by an electric shock, Schwartzman started to walk. She strode a few feet down the hall until she realized she still held the phone. Walked back. She needed air.

Hal caught her eye and nodded, motioning for the stairs. They started toward the exit.

"When?" Hal asked.

"She doesn't remember. Not exactly."

Schwartzman found her voice. "When was the picture taken?"

"At a tournament in Columbia. Jed took her. I was working that weekend."

"That weekend," Hal repeated. "When?"

"It was the weekend Ava was killed."

"So Lucy got it before Ava was killed. It would've been in her locker before the tournament. Is that right?" Hal asked. He was speaking quickly, emphatically.

Scared.

"Yes," Harper confirmed. "It was after Frances Pinckney was killed but before Ava."

Frances and Ava—the two women Spencer had killed. To lure Schwartzman to Charleston. Her aunt's best friend. Her aunt. Schwartzman stopped walking, pressed her eyes closed. Spencer had involved the detective's child even before Aunt Ava died. How had he known?

Because Harper was already working Frances Pinckney's case.

"Where is the necklace now?" Hal asked.

"She doesn't know," Harper said. "She thought she'd lost it that weekend."

Spencer had gotten to a teenage girl, to Harper's daughter. But why? What had he hoped to achieve?

Hal punched open the metal door, and it slammed into the concrete building's front. Schwartzman shivered against the warm outside air.

"Harper?" Hal asked.

"Yes." Her voice broke.

"Are you okay?"

Silence. "Truth be told, I'm rattled."

"Yes," Hal agreed.

How far would Spencer take it? How far would he go to get her back? He'd already killed two people. He hadn't stopped yet. Would he kill a teenage girl? It wouldn't be about hurting the girl. Not for Spencer. It would be about hurting Schwartzman.

About getting out of jail.

"I'll be okay," Harper said, her voice sounding more like her own again.

Schwartzman was unable to speak. Her heart seemed lodged at the base of her throat.

"What else did the assistant district attorney say?" Hal asked.

A voice in the background. "Tell them." Harper's husband.

Tell them what? Schwartzman was too scared to ask.

Hal's mouth was drawn in a straight line. He felt it, too. The icy fear.

"She wasn't specific," Harper said. "There's some noise from the defense."

"What kind of noise?" Hal pressed.

"They're saying there's no evidence."

"Of?" There was a bite to Hal's tone.

"No evidence that Spencer killed them. They're claiming that Spencer was set up—that someone planted the necklace to frame him."

Schwartzman swayed on her feet, locking her knees to keep herself upright.

If the necklace found at Spencer's house was the same one Harper's daughter wore in the picture, then Spencer's attorneys could argue that it was planted. By Harper maybe. Or they might imply that Schwartzman was behind the whole scheme—that Schwartzman had deceived Harper about Spencer's guilt and convinced her to plant the evidence to help get a conviction.

After all, she *had* planted evidence.

If the defense suggested the necklace was a plant, surely that would call into question the other evidence. The evidence that she had—in an act of desperation—planted: the knee pads, the gloves, Ava's hair, the fur from Frances Pinckney's dog . . .

She couldn't breathe. Spencer would go free.

She pressed her phone into Hal's hand and walked away. No, half ran.

Awkward in her slacks and boots, she was desperate to sprint. To pull off her shoes and run in stockinged feet the way she had as a child in the big green yard behind the house.

To hell with the asphalt and the glass and the debris.

She wanted to fill her lungs, to run until she couldn't think, until she couldn't breathe.

She had done this to herself.

This is what happens when you try to push me away. When you try to get away from me. You can't, Bella. So don't even try.

But she *had* tried. Now what would he do?

17

Hal ended the call and ran after Schwartzman. She wanted to be alone, but spending too much time in her own head was a bad idea.

Hal's dress shoes were loud on the pavement as he caught up with her. Schwartzman stopped and turned back, fear on her face. When she saw him, she stopped. Shrank.

She didn't fight him when he put his arms around her.

He pulled her close. She felt tiny. She was taller than Hailey, taller than his ex-wife, but she seemed smaller than either of them now.

"He's going to get out," she whispered, her voice like a ghost's.

"Come on. We're leaving."

"Where?"

"I need a drink."

She didn't argue.

He led her to his department car and put her in the passenger's side. As he started the engine, he had to remind her to put on her seat belt.

She looked down. "I don't have my purse."

"It's there." Hal pointed to the floor where she had dropped it.

"My phone."

"Here." He put it in her hands.

She leaned back into the seat and closed her eyes as he drove toward his neighborhood. He thought of taking her to the Tempest, his newest dive bar of choice, but decided instead on Watson, which was a little quieter, more upscale.

He parked half in a loading zone, threw his department pass on the dash, and jogged around the car to help her out. Schwartzman was dazed as he led her past the neon-pink sign of the bar next door, Ruby Eyes. Two Asian women passed and eyed him suspiciously. He held his tongue and opened the door for Schwartzman, holding her arm as they entered. It was dark inside and relatively quiet as they climbed the stairs to the bar.

Hal chose the small corner table, taking a seat with a good view of the bar. Facing the room was always his preference. Today it felt like necessity.

A minute later a waitress set down two bar napkins.

Schwartzman didn't look up from the menu. "Do you have Evan Williams?"

The waitress glanced back over at the bar. "Think so. How do you like it?"

"Neat." A beat passed. "Make it a double."

Hal nodded. "For me, too."

Schwartzman pushed the food menu aside. He'd make sure she ate something before they left. He wondered what the rules were for drinking during chemo. Probably a bad idea, but this didn't seem like the time to worry about it.

Schwartzman said nothing when the drinks arrived, giving the waitress a nod as she lifted her drink and took a long pull. With a slight grimace, she swallowed, eyes closed, and set the glass down.

Hal tried the bourbon, which smelled like caramel corn and pepper. He'd never had a palate for what his dad called brown liquor. It didn't matter how expensive the bottle, brown liquor was brown liquor. And liquor—brown, clear, or anything in between—had only one purpose as far as Hal's father was concerned, getting drunk, which was why there was never any liquor in his parents' home. Beer, some wine, but never hard liquor.

Schwartzman emptied the glass and caught the eye of the bartender. Her gaze tracked to Hal's glass, but she didn't comment. He asked for a Guinness on the second round, and Schwartzman propped her elbow on the table and rested her head on her hand.

He could think of nothing but Spencer. What he'd done, what she knew. He waited for her to start talking. They had to talk about it. There was so much he didn't understand. "I never pictured you as a bourbon drinker."

She touched the glass, ran her finger across the design cut into it. "I grew up with Evan Williams." Before he could ask what she meant, she shook her head. "Not *the* Evan Williams. Just the bourbon. It was always around." Her voice dropped as she whispered, "The single barrel was my daddy's favorite."

Daddy's.

Her eyes were glassy. The word *daddy* sounded strange from a woman as accomplished as she was. It opened something up in him, maybe the hole he had from his own loss.

"You were close to your dad."

She nodded.

"Is that why you never took the name MacDonald?"

Her eyes flashed wide. She hadn't been expecting him to go straight to Spencer. She sank a little lower in the chair. "Maybe." She paused. "Or I was stubborn. It was about the only thing I never gave in on."

Hal thought of all that she had let Spencer control. Her name seemed like a strange thing to hold on to when she'd let go of so much. But maybe it was the one act of rebellion, the one way to assert the independence he had taken away.

The second round of drinks came, and Hal took a sip of Guinness.

"Spencer hated that I never changed it," she went on. "He tried a few times to change it for me. But I was never MacDonald." Schwartzman took a drink of the second bourbon. She scowled at the flavor and pushed it away. "The single barrel is so much better."

Hal watched her as he eased into the subject of Spencer. "So Annabelle Schwartzman."

She wiped her mouth and folded the napkin slowly. "I never liked Annabelle either."

"So Anna?"

"I kind of like Schwartzman. Makes me think of Dad . . . and Ava."

"Just Schwartzman?" he repeated.

She cracked a sad smile. "Too weird, huh?"

"Oprah, Bono, and Schwartzman?"

"Liberace, Banksy," she said as the waitress came to check on them.

Schwartzman watched her walk away again. Something shifted in her expression, as if she knew what was coming, as if she could read his mind. As her gaze found his, her body language started to relax, the alcohol taking effect quickly. Had she even eaten breakfast? Her shoulders drooped, her free arm draped across her legs. But her expression remained sharp, focused.

He studied her, wondered what he didn't know. About Spencer. About that necklace, the evidence that had helped put Spencer away. Schwartzman was afraid. That much he knew.

He felt the fear, too. He knew how these things went. If the defense suspected that the necklace had been planted, all the evidence that had been collected at the house would naturally be called into question. And the evidence at Spencer's house was all they had to convict. There had been no trace left at the scenes to link Spencer to the deaths of Ava Schwartzman or Frances Pinckney.

Without the evidence at his house, he would surely go free.

She took another small sip of the bourbon and grimaced again as though she'd forgotten how bad it tasted. "Go ahead." Her face was serious, but there was something about her expression that made him want to smile.

She raised her brows, waiting, and he felt the shift in her. She was all business now. But he wasn't sure what she meant. "Go ahead, what?" he asked.

"Ask."

Multiple thoughts entered his mind at once. Fleetingly the notion that she was flirting. Then questions about Sandy's cancer, the case. Spencer. Her reaction to Harper's call. The panic in her eyes when Harper had said there was noise from the defense. "What do you know about the evidence in Spencer's arrest?"

"Be more specific," she said.

It was like talking to a lawyer. "What do you know about the necklace found on Harper's daughter?"

"Nothing."

He stopped.

"Keep going," she said. "You've got more questions."

"Do you know if the necklace found at Spencer's house is the same one that was given to Harper's daughter?"

"I don't know that."

"Does Harper?"

"I'm not sure. I don't think she does."

He watched her. She had a secret. "But you know something about evidence found at Spencer's?"

She said nothing.

He thought through the items that had been found in Spencer's garage. "The gloves, the hair?"

Her gaze fell into her lap. "I should get home. We've got a big day tomorrow."

"Damn," he whispered, and she squeezed her eyes closed as if reacting to a violent murder in a horror movie.

What had she done?

18

Across the table from him, Denise wore a low-cut black top.

Her cups runneth over.

The skin was a little less taut than some of the girls he picked up in hotel bars, but she was educated. She didn't charge by the hour. She was looking for love, certainly.

But he didn't know if she was accepting the date because she wanted to go out with him, or if the date was part of some master plan that involved her being in the pharmacy two nights ago. The first order of business would be finding out why she'd been there. He'd thought of almost nothing else since he had watched the film yesterday afternoon.

He had wanted to take her out last night, but she'd had something she needed to do. That's what she'd told him. Even the words had made him uneasy. *Something she needed to do.* He'd woken in a sweat this morning. If they'd gone out last night, he would have taken care of her already. Not to mention there were fewer people out in the city on a Thursday, although fewer was a matter of magnitudes. Nothing was private in San Francisco.

He tried to tell himself there were benefits to waiting until Friday. He'd have the weekend to figure out what she was up to, to take care of things if she was a threat.

And so far she didn't seem to be any threat to him.

She was a number of years older than he was, but she didn't mention it. Neither would he. She'd been working at the cancer center for a decade. She had bad luck with men, she said, a euphemism for her attraction to married men. A grown son lived up north—Oregon or Washington. The son might be around his own age. Surely not quite but an odd thought anyway.

It almost felt like a date. His first in . . . months. It was foreign—opening doors, making a reservation for dinner rather than meeting at a hotel bar and downing a whiskey before heading to a prebooked room.

He'd forgotten that he enjoyed this part. He was not a monster. It was not just about the sex. But tonight would be neither romance nor sex. He couldn't risk it until he was sure. Tonight was about Trent, as was everything else these days. But it was a worthy cause, making sure his brother was safe.

A guilt-free date.

Even sex wasn't guilt-free these days.

He pressed his palm against the phone in his pants pocket. A phantom vibration. It seemed to happen more when he worried about Trent. Trent's ringtone was three long buzzes, so he'd know if his brother tried to reach him. He'd be pissed, but he'd know. For now all was quiet on the home front.

Denise leaned forward to talk across the table, the lace of her bra visible down the front of her blouse. He liked that she wasn't one of those anorexic types. There were so many of them these days, bony things with big breasts. Didn't they know that a man wanted some curve, something to hang on to during sex? Women got skinny and dressed up for other women.

Denise had curves. And he could tell she was enjoying the atmosphere.

She'd left work at noon today and taken the BART train in from her house, which was thirty miles away. It would have taken hours to get out there and pick her up. Plus he'd needed the extra time to get

Trent settled with his three glasses of sherry and his pint of Chunky Monkey and his Hulu watch list. Denise swore she hadn't minded. And it was clear that she'd spent the afternoon—or some of it—on her hair and makeup.

Normally he would have Ubered around the city, but tonight required extra precautions. He did not drive his own car. He did not valet park. They would not go to a hotel. He'd rented a black convertible Mercedes. There was no missing her delight as she recognized him at the curb in front of the BART station. The more appealing he made himself as a date, the better his chances of finding out what she was up to. Women like Denise didn't want to be alone.

He had booked them at the latest hot restaurant, some French-Asian fusion place where the waitstaff looked like an army of models in skintight black pants and shirts. Their waiter's name was Jacques. The nonexistent lighting and the reservation under a fake name was all part of his plan to stay invisible. The crowd was so focused on the hottest faces that his and Denise's would hardly be noticed. Not cool enough. Not flashy enough. Too conservatively dressed. Too plain, too old.

Perfect.

He encouraged her to order a cocktail. She chose a cosmopolitan, of course. For himself, he ordered a soda and bitters, whispering it in the server's ear. It looked alcoholic but wasn't. Jacques's mouth puckered in response. Nonalcoholic drinks were never a waiter's favorite. Everyone knew alcohol was what drove the big tips. Add alcohol and people drank more, ate more, ordered dessert. He wanted to tell Jacques not to be so obvious. God, it was like having Trent wait on them.

"We'll have the Grand Cru from Sauternes with dinner if you'd like to get it on ice now," he added, pointing to the $300 bottle.

The waiter perked up. Of course he did.

"We'd like it quite cold," he instructed Jacques. Ordering a good bottle meant he could be specific, particular. Chilled white went down faster than lukewarm. Truly cold white went down like water. He'd learned that from his mother.

He motioned for the server to wait and peered across the table at his date. "Do you like white wine, Denise? I've picked out a French bottle."

"It really is a lovely bottle," Jacques piped in.

"I love white wine," she said.

"Perfect," Jacques said. "I'll get that on ice for you and be back with your cocktails."

A nightcap, too, he thought.

Denise smiled across the table.

The cocktails arrived. Tiny little things, of course. Twenty bucks probably. He raised his glass to hers. "To you."

He had expected her to blush, but instead she tilted her chin upward. "To us," she said, touching her glass to his.

She brought the glass to her lips gently and swallowed the pinkish liquid as though it were something holy. A tiny drop leaked from the corner of her mouth and wound its way down her chin.

He couldn't help himself. He reached over and used his fingertip to catch it before it fell to the table. Put the finger in his mouth.

The hollow in her neck pulsed. The chemistry between them crackled.

How badly he wanted to sleep with her. How careless that would be.

Her tongue darted to the corner of her mouth.

Sitting became uncomfortable, his pants too tight.

She swallowed the rest of her drink.

He looked for Jacques and stared until the waiter sensed his gaze. He raised a single finger and pointed to Denise. *Bring her another.*

Jacques gave a curt nod.

He would not be careless.

"I was surprised you asked me out," she said, leaning across the table so that her breasts sat atop her dinner plate.

"Why?"

"I didn't think you'd ever noticed me."

"I thought you were with someone else." He knew exactly who she had been with.

Her mouth closed like the knotted tie on a balloon.

"I didn't mean to upset you."

She shook her head. "You didn't. That's over." She sat up. "It's been over for a while." She seemed different than she was at the office. Stronger. Empowered. And it suited her. Was it ending things with the married doctor? That would be odd, considering he was pretty certain she'd been dumped. But maybe it was good for her to be rid of him. He was a dullard anyway. Almost all of them were.

"I'm so glad to hear that," he said. "So what made you accept my invitation?"

"I've been watching you," she said, tilting her head sideways.

He felt himself stiffen.

Jacques set down her second cocktail, and she lifted it without pause and took a drink.

"Watching me how?"

"Just seeing how you are, who you talk to. I've been wanting to get to know you."

He scanned her eyes for some sign that she was referring to the pharmacy, to the Adriamycin. He found people were rarely as clever as they thought they were.

"Sad about Dr. Posner," he said after taking a sip of his bitters.

She blinked. "He was a jerk."

He took another sip of his drink. "Did you hear how it happened?"

She drank and leaned forward again. "They used Adriamycin, made him drink it."

Nothing in her expression suggested she was referring to him. Did she really have no idea? Was she in the pharmacy for something else?

But why would she be there at midnight? "Adria—what?" he asked innocently.

Her brow furrowed as she took the bait. "I didn't know what it was either. I had to ask."

He nodded eagerly. She did not strike him as clever enough to figure out what he had done and try to manipulate him somehow.

"It's the treatment they use for breast cancer. It's bright red." She was serious, earnest. She had no idea that he'd been in that pharmacy. If she was playing him, she would have been coy, wide-eyed and gratuitously sexual. He'd seen women in that mode plenty of times. And if she was playing a game, she would be terrified, confronting a killer.

She was neither.

Still, it seemed impossible that she'd just gone into the pharmacy of her own volition, for no reason. Maybe she had someone she wanted dead. The idea made him want to smile, but he didn't.

"Who do you think killed him?" he asked.

"Some woman he crossed, I'm sure. He was a playboy. He dated half our office, you know."

He narrowed his gaze.

She pressed her palm to her bosom and raised her glass. "But not me. I never dated him."

"So you're not the killer."

She gave him a slightly drunken smile and laughed.

Jacques arrived with their bottle of wine, and he felt himself relax. Denise was surprisingly charming. Playful and sincere, an open book.

There was more than one way to be cautious. If she cared about him, she would protect him. Then he could have her. Not for a few hours but for a whole night. Trent might be up by nine, or he might sleep until eleven. That gave him plenty of time. God, what he could do with that time.

Dinner was a swift affair. They shared food across the table, fed each other. Another bottle of wine arrived with a flick of a hand. Jacques was attentive now. The wine was frigid.

Denise was not.

He sensed their chemistry and was already making alternate plans. The reservation book full, walk-ins hovered around the bar, waiting for people to leave. He didn't want to spend any longer than necessary in a place with this many people.

He suggested a nightcap.

She suggested her house.

He motioned for the check, paid the bill in cash, and left while Jacques was far from the table. No chitchat. No pleasantries. He felt the wine as he held the door open and took her arm as she teetered in her heels. But what now? He wouldn't be driving her home. Not after all that wine. Getting pulled over with her in the car was not an option.

He left the car parked in the lot and began calculating a new plan.

She was drunk. Drunken women were normally a turnoff, but Denise was different. The alcohol didn't make her clingy or change her sultry voice into a high screech. Instead she became soft and sensual.

He knew her home address and had checked out the area and studied the traffic lights. She was on a quiet street. The neighborhood was a little run-down, built twenty-five years earlier in a surge of urban sprawl.

He would have liked to spend the night with her, go home with her and cab back later, but the voice in his mind said it was too risky. He'd erased the pharmacy recording, but how long before the police located her another way? They would surely follow up on another missing bottle of Red Devil.

The edges of the world were blurry. The plan grew fuzzy beside the desire. How long since he'd given in to desire?

Too long.

Back and forth he went.

Uber was too intimate. The trains had too many cameras and a long wait. He could not wait. The need that had grown consistently through dinner was now a persistent ache.

He hailed a cab and, before helping her into the backseat, gave the cabbie her address and passed him a hundred bucks. "Make sure she gets home okay." Then he reached through the window and took a picture of the guy's cabbie license.

He helped her into the backseat. "Good night, sweet Denise."

"Wait. Where are you going?"

He kissed her cheek. "I'll see you soon—I promise."

With that, he belted her in and shut the cab door.

He took a second cab to his house and crossed the street to the parking garage, where his boring gray sedan awaited. The trip had cost him twenty minutes. He warned himself not to drive too quickly. Not to get caught. He took the Embarcadero to the Bay Bridge and headed west. He should have planned to have his own car downtown. He could have put Denise in a cab and been two minutes behind her. Now he was twenty minutes behind. That was too much time to make up, and he couldn't risk a speeding ticket.

He maintained his speed at seven miles per hour over the limit until another car raced past him—a Porsche doing eighty-five along Highway 24. He sped up, keeping a safe three-car distance between himself and the other driver and making up some extra time.

The cabbie was at the curb when he passed Denise's address. He kept his head down, drove two blocks away, and parked in the lot for an adjacent apartment building. His car blended in with a hundred other inexpensive commuter cars.

When the cab pulled away, he hurried up the stairs, looking over his shoulder at the other units. A TV in an adjacent unit. Small windows with wood blinds. Her porch was dark, the light switched off. She was not expecting him. She might already be in bed.

He could break in. But then things would not go as he hoped.

He knocked on the door. Silence. His erection pulsed in his pants. He'd been hard since dinner. Hard when he switched cars, when he drove three cars behind the Porsche. He had planned this poorly. If only he'd known she wasn't a threat . . . if he'd known this night could have been a regular date . . .

Damn.

He shifted the erection so it was trapped under his waistband, felt the uncomfortable pull of it. He had never let sex control him, and he would not begin now. He could leave Denise and go to one of the regular places. Pay a couple hundred bucks to have one of those girls suck him off. Go home and sleep off the booze. Be safe. Keep Trent safe.

He knocked again. The sound of feet grew louder from the other side of the door.

"Hello?"

He grinned into the peephole.

The bolt unlatched, and his erection stretched taller.

"I couldn't sleep without kissing you good night," he said when she cracked the door.

The sultry smile. The door fell open. "I'm so glad you came over."

He stepped across the threshold, as happy as he'd been in months.

19

Schwartzman dreaded the weekends. Work gave the weekdays structure and purpose, while weekends became long stretches of inactivity she had to fill before she could go back to work. This weekend was no different. After the conversation with Harper on Thursday, Spencer was back in her head. In her dreams. Even in the face of a stranger whose eye she had caught from the corner of the grocery store.

And she could not stop thinking about the conversation with Hal. Had she told him too much? Too little? What would he do with the knowledge that she had planted evidence? Would he blame her? Would he understand?

What would he do now?

She thought back to the call with Harper. Her daughter had been given that sea turtle necklace, identical to the one Schwartzman had as a child. By Spencer. Of course it was him. Which meant it had to be the necklace she had found in Spencer's house.

What was Spencer planning? Something. He was not idle in prison. She would not soon forget that Spencer had found an accomplice on an online site for women who had a predilection for men behind bars. By pretending to be a man serving time at Folsom Prison for murder, he had manipulated a brokenhearted woman into killing for him. Even without access to the Internet, he would be scheming.

At the same time, she refused to live in this purgatory. While Spencer was in prison, she had to sculpt some semblance of a life for herself—something other than moving between the secured apartment building and the morgue, with stops every so often for doctors' appointments, chemo treatments, and quick runs to fill the cupboards with food. It was time she moved on.

The phone rang Sunday afternoon, startling her. *Ken.*

"I wanted to come by. You around?"

She looked down at the sweats she'd been wearing all weekend. The distraction would do her good. "When?"

"Half hour?"

"Give me forty-five minutes."

"Deal."

She stripped out of her clothes and took her robe into the bathroom. The robe slipped from her fingers as she reached to hang it from the end of the towel bar above the tub. As she picked it up, she caught sight of her naked form in the mirror.

Resisting the urge to look away, she stood in front of the mirror and examined the incisions that marked her chest. This was the body she would share with Ken. If she shared it. Lines ran parallel across each breast, as if someone had used a knife to slash through their flesh. Her nipples were gone. The flesh that gave her breasts, gone.

"Reconstruction is always available down the road," Todd Posner had told her. "But it's easier to do it now. If you wait, we have to put in expanders first and then implants."

"I'll wait," she'd told him.

"You're certain?" he'd pressed.

"I'm certain," she'd assured him. More than once.

At the time it had seemed like genuine concern, an accurate assessment of the benefits of rolling reconstruction into the initial mastectomy. That she wouldn't go through the reconstruction right away came as a surprise even to her.

The world was dominated by sex. Women's bodies were everywhere—movies, commercials, mannequins in glass storefronts—and they were supposed to look a specific way. A woman who didn't want breasts, who didn't need or want to be feminine in that traditional Playboy way, was weird. Perhaps even a freak. She had done the research herself. Most women did reconstruction—80 percent, the statistics said. The ones who went without were often concerned about other health risks or weren't prepared to undergo additional procedures. Some couldn't afford the costs, which insurance rarely paid in full. These were not Schwartzman's reasons. She felt strong and healthy. She could afford the procedures.

But it felt natural, excising that part of her—an external symbol of what she'd suffered. She had lost Ava, lost a decade of her life to a man whose sickness had become her own. And femininity in a traditional sense had only worked against her. Perhaps if she'd lost her breasts earlier, she might have been spared the past decade. Ava might be alive. Or perhaps the excision of her breasts was the final stage in excising Spencer from her life.

And still she was unnerved by the men whose gaze rested on her chest and took in the absence. Somehow those stares felt more invasive than they had when she'd *had* breasts. After a few days of feeling on constant display, she'd ordered a prosthetic bra with the smallest padding available, the equivalent of an A cup. Men didn't notice the small breasts the way they had the total absence of them. It was a relief to blend in again, but she was disappointed in herself for giving in to conformity.

Wearing nothing, she studied the angry-looking scars, ran her fingers across the place where the line ended over the rib cage that protected her heart.

She would gladly take these scars . . .

If it meant she was done with cancer.

And Spencer. Some part of her had thought that the mastectomy would keep him away, that he wouldn't want a woman without breasts. That his vanity would cause him to reject her.

Would it?

Now she wasn't so sure.

She reached into the shower and turned the hot water on full blast, waited for the steam to fill the room, erase her from the mirror. She tried to think about Ken. Gentle, kind Ken. She deserved a good man. She relaxed into the water and forced away the concerns—that there would be more wounds to come.

That Spencer wasn't done with her yet.

20

Seated at the office Monday morning, Hal stared down at the greasy film on the surface of the department coffee that filled his mug. Along with the slick oil-spill sheen, the fake creamer gave the coffee a gray tint. The combination was not appealing.

The Greenville DA's office had been his first call. Given the time difference, it was after nine there when he'd called them. He'd spoken to one of the ADAs and been told that someone would call him back.

It was almost ten thirty. No word.

He took another swig of the lukewarm coffee swill. Hard to believe he used to drink department coffee black. Now he could hardly stand the taste of it with cream and sugar. He missed the giant Starbucks mocha and hated that he'd become one of those people. He couldn't be buying coffee every day. For one, he couldn't afford it. And there was something about the coffee culture. Too yuppie, too hip. He was neither.

He checked the volume on his cell phone again. Nothing. He was starting to suspect that the DA's office wouldn't return his phone call. Hal had left a message with Harper, too, but he didn't know what more she could offer on the necklace. She'd seemed as surprised by the picture of Lucy wearing the turtle pendant as he and Schwartzman were. He thought back to the conversation he'd had with Schwartzman at the bar, wondering what it was that she had wanted him to know. Or had he imagined that?

No, he hadn't. Schwartzman knew something. She wasn't going to tell him, so he was going to have to figure it out before MacDonald used it as a way to get out of prison . . .

Spencer MacDonald.

Just the name stirred up intense rage, anger like he hadn't felt since his father's death. When the Oakland PD had announced his father was on the take. They couldn't hurt his father, so they'd hurt him and his mother, his sisters. At least his father hadn't lived through the humiliation. Wherever his dad was, he wasn't hurting.

But Schwartzman wasn't done hurting.

Spencer was always one half step off her mind. Always looming. And if he got out of prison . . . Hal wouldn't let himself consider it. There had to be a way to keep Spencer behind bars.

If only Hal knew what Spencer was planning.

He finished the dregs of his coffee and returned to the information in front of him. No surprise, he'd been officially assigned the lead on Ben Gustafson's murder, if it was a murder. The family was pressing the police to release the remains—especially since they could find no real signs of foul play, but they had allowed Schwartzman an extra day. Friday, she'd gone back to the body to examine it for any other evidence. Then she'd swabbed the droplets that remained on his face and got Roger to promise to run the material through his new toy today.

The cable company had faxed over Gustafson's schedule for the day he'd died. He was last seen at the home of a Doug and Christine Smith, where he'd installed two new devices. Hal had already spoken to Mrs. Smith. According to her, Gustafson was gone before noon. She'd worked in her daughter's kindergarten class from twelve thirty until school let out at three twenty. Thirty five-year-olds could vouch for her. Her husband had been at work the entire day. Hal put a call into Doug's workplace, but he knew the husband's alibi would hold, too.

Neither Doug nor Christine had any connection to the cancer center, Todd Posner, or Norman Fraser. Hal had checked Fraser's alibi and learned that he had been in the clinic seeing patients without so much as a break for lunch during the afternoon that Gustafson was killed. Which gave him an airtight alibi. Unless he had an accomplice, Fraser was not their guy.

Hal had gone back to the afternoon Gustafson died to look for additional clues. He'd had three more appointments in his calendar. He was due to arrive to those locations between one and five, but he'd never shown up. No GPS tracking on the van. Cell phone records would take weeks and, even then, learning which towers he'd been close to wouldn't offer enough insight, not in a place as dense as San Francisco.

Which meant Hal was at a dead end on Gustafson.

He called the cancer center to get a list of who was involved with Sandy's treatment at the hospital during her stem cell transplant and left a message. Next he called the Finlay Foundation to arrange a time to meet with the director. Left another voicemail.

Tense and frustrated, he carried the coffee mug to the tiny room that housed both the copier equipment and the coffeemaker, rinsed the mug, and returned to his desk. But he couldn't sit. He remained standing and leaned over, sorting piles of paperwork, half to organize the papers he'd been ignoring the past few days and half to have something to do with his hands. Movement, motion. He wanted to *do* something.

Caught under a catalog for high-end bulletproof vests and tactical gear was the envelope Schwartzman had found on her windshield. He caught his breath. He should have had the letter and the envelope checked for prints already.

In the chaos of dealing with Norman Fraser in the parking lot and then Sandy Coleman and the link between Posner and Gustafson, the death certificate had slipped his mind. He took the envelope by its corner and shook the folded page out onto his desk. Then he put the envelope inside an empty manila folder and, touching the page by only its corner, took the letter and made a photocopy. He added the original page to the folder and sat back at his desk.

Using the criminal database, he searched for Joseph Strom, date of birth August 9, 1947. No record found. He tried the national driver registry, but Strom wasn't there either, which meant Strom had never had his license suspended or revoked.

Impatient, Hal logged out of the system and walked out of the department with the manila folder and the photocopy of the letter. His first stop was to Records, where he requested a full search on Strom. Last address, next of kin, business—he wanted anything they could find on him. It would take a few days, they told him. If he had a chance to talk to Harper, he would ask her to look into it, too. Maybe she'd have a way to access the information more quickly.

He thought of her voice on the phone. Rattled. The sharp tone of her husband's voice in the background. "Tell them," he'd said. The defense was making noise about the evidence. God, what a nightmare.

He reminded himself Harper would contact them if she heard anything else. He would have liked to call her right then and there, but she was shaken. Scared. He needed to give her time to take care of herself and her family.

Since the mention of the evidence against Spencer—or, more accurately, the questions about the evidence against Spencer—every request, every call felt more urgent. He needed answers now.

He took the manila folder down to the lab, hoping to find Roger in the corner playing with his new toy. What had he named the machine? But Roger wasn't there.

"He's at a scene," Naomi said, spotting Hal from where she stood next to what looked like a large terrarium. She was fingerprinting. On one end of the terrarium was water, a compact heater, and the small metal container the lab used to heat the superglue to fume for fingerprints. On the other side, a long, thin blade—the kind of knife a hunter might use—was held by a C-clamp.

"What case?" Hal asked. He didn't recognize the blade.

"New evidence in last month's stabbing off Cesar Chavez."

He shook his head. "I don't remember that one."

"Vic didn't die."

Hal's phone rang. It was the department's prefix but not a number he recognized.

"Harris," he answered, walking away from Naomi.

"We got a hit on Norman Fraser."

Hal froze. "What kind of hit?"

"An assault and battery charge, back in 2010," the clerk said. "Never went anywhere, but Fraser was arrested for beating up a seventeen-year-old kid from his son's school."

"What happened?"

"Fraser allegedly attacked the kid as he was coming home after a party. Caught him outside his house and pummeled him. Broke his nose, fractured his jaw. There was some internal bleeding."

"What happened to the charges?" Hal asked.

"The kid was too drunk to make an ironclad identification, but he swore it was Fraser. Kid said Fraser was angry because he was teasing Fraser's son about being a 'fag.' Kid's word, not mine," the clerk added. "No witnesses, no surveillance cameras. Kid was drunk—and underage—so he wasn't going to make a great witness. DA ended up dropping the charges. Fraser being an upstanding citizen in the community, a doctor, no priors . . ."

"Anything else?" Hal asked.

"That's all I could find."

"Thanks." Hal ended the call. If Fraser beat up a high school kid for calling his son a fag, what would he do to someone who had threatened to release photographs that might keep him out of medical school?

Fraser had acted genuinely surprised by the photos. He was a different man than he'd been in the office when Hal had interviewed him. Was that really an act? And he had an airtight alibi for Gustafson's murder. Was there an accomplice? His son? But if one of them had been in Posner's house, why not take the computer? Posner was tortured. He would have given up the photographs long before he died. Wouldn't he?

"Everything okay?" Naomi asked, pulling him from his thoughts.

He handed her the manila envelope. "I've got something I need printed, too."

Naomi glanced at it. "For Posner?"

"Not exactly. It's not for a case. Well, not yet," he added.

Naomi nodded. "I can run it after this. Should be about twenty minutes."

Hal didn't move. He thought over the pieces of the puzzle that were still outstanding. Tamara Long had confirmed that she was unable to locate anyone at the cancer center who owned horses. No one with a vet spouse or boyfriend. Hal figured the office was small enough that if there was a horse enthusiast in the office, someone would have known about it. There were plenty of subjects that people avoided talking about in an office, but a love of horses wasn't one. And he recalled how personal the spaces in the cancer center had been. The staff's desks were decorated with family pictures, little inspirational signs on small wood boxes or ceramic plates. People tended to share interests and hobbies in a workplace like that.

He'd been disappointed when Tamara gave him the news. Bordering on desperate, Hal had asked Tamara Long if anyone had any horse pictures or figurines—even a mouse pad or a screen saver.

He might have pushed too far then. Not to mention the question placed a bias toward the women in the office. Men did not generally keep figurines and trinkets on their desks—horse or otherwise.

"I haven't seen a single horse anywhere in the office," Long had told him.

That had been his last lead. Everything else was an absolute dead end—the note with Sandy's name, the clay found in Posner's mouth, the wipes, and the wipe residue found at both Gustafson's death and Posner's. Even the sex toys and bondage equipment Roger had found.

The lawsuits were another dead end, and Hal had completed his background check on the list of girlfriends that Tamara Long had supplied. None of the women raised any red flags. Posner's recent relationships had been almost entirely one-night encounters—from his perspective as well as theirs. Most of the women Hal talked with told him that one night with Todd Posner was plenty. The others were either noncommittal themselves or had gone with it, knowing Posner was not the marrying type, at least not again and so soon. There wasn't a single spurned woman among them.

That left him with the impression Schwartzman had found on Posner's calf and yet another dead end. Roger's team had searched every corner of Posner's house for something to match the narrow imprint on his leg. There was nothing.

Nothing. His thoughts returned to Norman Fraser. He would have to talk to the good doctor again.

He glanced at his phone. Two minutes had passed.

How was he going to waste the next eighteen minutes? A walk. Clear his head. He pictured one of those damn Starbucks mochas. "I could use a coffee," he said to Naomi, who had returned her attention to her work. "You want one?"

"I can't leave now, I'm afraid," she said, pushing the hair off her face with the back of her hand.

"Oh, no. Sorry. I meant I could get us some," Hal said, cutting her off before she said anything she'd regret. He hadn't meant it as an invitation. Naomi was attractive, beautiful even. But she was in her midtwenties, and he was a decade older. He'd been through a divorce and more than ten years of this work. She felt too young . . . his mind was already making up excuses for why he didn't want to go out with her. What was wrong with him?

"Sure, I'll take a coffee," she said, appearing not to pick up on his awkwardness. "Where you going?"

"Starbucks," he admitted sheepishly.

With Naomi's order in hand, Hal walked the two blocks to the nearest Starbucks. On the way, he called the number he had in his notebook for Patrick Fraser, Norman Fraser's son. The call went to voicemail, and Hal left a message, requesting Patrick return his call. Entering the coffee shop, Hal found the line stretched all the way to the door. He considered turning around, but then he'd be in the lab waiting. Naomi said it would take twenty minutes to run the prints. He could be through this line twice in twenty minutes.

He settled into line and resisted the urge to pull out his phone, which was what everyone else had done. Instead he let his mind drift. Of its own volition, his brain steered him right back to the case. Unless the prints on the envelope or the death certificate led him somewhere, he'd have to return to his desk and consider next steps.

The Finlay Foundation was the only rock he had yet to turn over. Well, the only rock he knew about. There had to be others, but damn if he could find them.

As he waited in line, the pressure built in his lungs, and the muscles in his legs tensed. They were on day seven. Tomorrow would be a full week since Posner was discovered dead in his home, a chemical burn scarring his face. That was not a random crime. That was a crime of passion. That was rage.

Hal clenched and unclenched his fists and took a deep breath as someone nudged him from behind. He whipped around, ready to bark. Behind him was an older Asian lady, maybe half his size. Without a word, she pointed to the register, where a barista was waving for the next customer. Him.

He gave the lady an apologetic smile and ordered a Venti Mocha for himself and an almond milk latte for Naomi. He felt oddly self-conscious saying the words *almond milk* aloud. Who drank almond milk? What was wrong with cow's milk? Strong teeth and bones. When had all that changed? He forked over twelve bucks, refusing to let his brain figure out what it cost a year to come in here daily or even once a week, and stood against the far wall, waiting for them to call his name.

Since this Starbucks attracted a lot of the department employees, he recognized some of the officers and a few of the faces from the DA's office. Through the window, a dark head on the street caught his attention. She faced the other direction, but he got a glimpse of her wavy, shoulder-length hair and the way she bent into her gait, as though she were moving through heavy wind. Black slacks, a gray sweater. *Schwartzman.*

"Hal."

The barista called his name, and he picked up the two coffees.

"You need a carrier?" she asked, sticking small green plastic plugs into the spouts. All the fuss always made him slightly embarrassed.

"No, thanks."

He headed for the door as Schwartzman was coming in.

She halted inches from running into him, startled. "You scared me."

"You almost ran me down."

Her eyes wide, she seemed to need a moment to calm herself. Then she smiled. "I hardly think I could've accomplished that."

The coffee cups were burning his fingers, so he shifted them, stacking both on the palm of one hand. "I'll wait with you."

"That's okay."

"I don't mind. I'm waiting for some prints, so I've got some time to kill."

"Posner?" she asked, stepping into the line.

"Nah. Something else," he said. As soon as the words were out, he wondered why he hadn't told her. It was her business. He wanted answers. That was why. He didn't want her to think about it until he could offer her something concrete. He hoped to hell there were some prints on that thing.

She shivered and glanced over her shoulder as the door opened again. Two patrol officers entered, followed by a single man.

Hal had to step into Schwartzman's space to let the man pass. When they reached the cashier, Hal went again to the end of the counter to wait while she ordered. Shifting the coffees in his hands again, he thought the twenty minutes had probably almost passed, and the realization made him slightly anxious. He'd feel a hell of a lot better if they got a lead on something.

As he scanned the room, he noticed the man at a table in the corner. He was blond and thin, holding a newspaper spread in his hands, the pages draped across the table. No coffee. And his attention was not on the page. Hal followed his gaze. He was looking at Schwartzman. Hal tried to read his expression. Did they know each other?

He seemed to sense Hal staring. When their eyes met, Hal raised his eyebrows and the man returned to his paper. Hal had seen him come in behind the two patrol officers, but he hadn't gotten in line.

Meeting someone maybe?

Schwartzman joined him to wait for her order, and they made small talk about the case—the disappointing news that there were no obvious horse lovers or vet connections at the office, the unanswered questions about the FIMO clay found on Posner's tooth. Hal shared the news that they'd made no progress on the board of directors or the people who had cared for Sandy Coleman during her stay in the hospital.

"What about his computer?" Schwartzman asked.

"No incriminating pictures other than the ones of Patrick Fraser." Hal told her about Norman Fraser's assault charge.

Schwartzman looked stunned. "Dr. Fraser beat up a kid?"

"He was accused of beating up a kid." Hal knew what someone was charged with and what actually happened were often not the same.

"Do you think he killed Posner?"

Hal considered Norman Fraser. If Fraser had killed him over the pictures of his son, then certainly he would have taken Posner's laptop from the house. But it had been sitting there, right on Posner's desk, a few feet from his body. He was missing something. "I don't know."

"What's next?" she asked.

He had to follow up on Fraser. That much was obvious. "We're cross-referencing Posner's e-mail correspondence with Sandy Coleman's name and seeing if anything comes up."

"Something will."

He tried to absorb her confidence as they walked back down the block, then parted at the department. He promised to call her later to touch base. As soon as he'd left her side, her gait accelerated, the forward tilt of her body purposeful, efficient.

He reached the department doors and noticed the blond man from Starbucks walking past. The newspaper was gone. His hands were in his pockets. No coffee. Hal watched as he rounded the building toward the morgue.

Toward Schwartzman.

He reminded himself that the path also led to the parking lot.

His phone buzzed in his pocket. *The lab.* "Harris," he answered.

When he looked up again, the man was gone.

"It's Naomi. Got a hit."

"I'm coming down the stairs."

"Good. I was wondering about that coffee."

Naomi waited with a piece of paper in her hand, a printout of a record. Hal handed her the coffee and took the page. The print from the death certificate belonged to someone named Jake Charles. Hal scanned the report and found no priors.

"Who is he?"

"Used to be a cop, patrol out of Ingleside." The Ingleside District included the area south of the Mission and west of Bayview. Not a bad beat.

"And now?" Hal asked.

"Private investigator."

Private investigator. That meant someone had hired this Charles guy to deliver the death certificate to Schwartzman.

Spencer?

While it was the obvious guess, this didn't feel like Spencer's work. Every move Spencer had made so far was calculated to be deeply sinister. Unless Hal didn't yet understand the significance of Joseph Strom, a death certificate for a man who'd died in a car accident at the age of fifty-seven lacked the necessary scare factor. "You have a number for Charles?"

She flipped the page and pointed to a handwritten address and phone number. "Found it on Google."

She raised her coffee cup and turned back to her work.

Hal folded the page into his back pocket and carried his coffee out of the lab. He tossed the green plug from the coffee lid into a nearby trash can and took a long drink. Chocolate coated his tongue. It was no longer hot, but even lukewarm it was still pretty damn good.

He took another swig before pulling his phone out of his pocket. If he was going to go visit this Jake Charles PI, Schwartzman deserved to come along. He wished he'd told her about the prints when they were together.

He stared down at the coffee cup, then took one last pull. It wasn't even coffee. It was hot chocolate. He could save himself some real cash by buying the stuff in big canisters like his mother had done when they were kids. Still, the damn drink made him happy. And happiness—even for the moment—was something there was less of these days.

His phone buzzed in his hand. *Hailey.* Something else that made him happy. "Hey, partner. Long time."

"Where are you?" she asked.

"About to head out. Why?"

"I answered your phone," she said. Which meant she was working at her own desk. She hadn't done that in weeks.

"Who was it?"

"A Jay Schenck. He's the executive director of the Finlay Foundation. Whatever that is."

"What did he say?" Hal asked without explaining.

"That he's at the office today until three," Hailey said.

"Good, I'll go see him."

"You want company?" she asked.

"I'd love it," he said, surprised by the offer. "Are you available?"

"I am." She sounded pleased. "I'll meet you in the back lot."

"Headed there now." He palmed his phone, glad for the opportunity to catch up with his partner for the first time in weeks.

He always thought better as part of a pair. This would give him a chance to share the evidence on Posner and the strange connection with the cable installation guy. Not to mention he would be able to get her reaction to the PI's fingerprints on the death certificate Schwartzman had found on her windshield. It would be good if that was clear in his head when he approached Schwartzman with the information about Jake Charles. She had enough to worry about without him adding to it.

More than enough.

21

Coffee in hand, Schwartzman returned to the morgue, dreading the next case, her third of the day. Two victims of a vehicular accident had arrived within a few minutes of finishing her second look at Gustafson.

Thinking a cup of coffee might do her good, she had walked to Starbucks and run into Hal. But there had been something distinctly awkward about the interaction, as if he was keeping something from her.

They were both keeping secrets.

She trusted him. Whatever it was, he would tell her in time. Wouldn't he?

She hadn't told him everything. Not about what she'd done at Spencer's. She couldn't tell him. That information could only hurt him. Hurt them both.

Sitting at her desk, she drank the coffee and checked her voicemail before moving on to her next autopsy—a three-month-old baby boy. These were the worst cases.

One voicemail was from the Realtor, who called almost daily. Like most days, she announced that she had located a few potential properties that met Schwartzman's requirements and was sending links via e-mail. Schwartzman would look at them tonight, with a glass of wine. A reward for getting through this next autopsy.

At least Roy wasn't in the morgue. His day off. She was grateful not to be checking over her shoulder for him all day. Was it Spencer who had made her this way? Was she making Roy more nefarious than he was? Creating something in her mind because of what she'd been through?

She was jumpy. *Calm down and control yourself. You're in charge.*

She stared at drawer ten, the baby drawer. She had procrastinated long enough. Just as she got out a fresh kit and set up the tools on the table, the phone rang. She'd been waiting for a call from the lead inspector, so she answered it without looking at the number. "Hi."

"We've got a problem," came a female voice.

Adrenaline mixed with nausea in her gut.

"I'm sorry. Who is this?"

"It's Laura Patchett. I assumed you recognized the number."

She glanced at the screen. The 864 area code. *Greenville.*

"Laura Patchett," the voice on the phone repeated. "I'm the assistant district attorney for Greenville and Pickens Counties. We spoke a few months ago."

She recalled their first conversation, just after her return from South Carolina. Patchett had asked if Schwartzman would testify against Spencer. She had agreed. Then she'd gotten a call that they didn't need her, not in the arraignment anyway. Official charges had been made, and the judge denied bail. Across the country, Schwartzman had been weeks away from a double mastectomy, and going back to South Carolina would have delayed the surgery.

"Dr. Schwartzman."

"Yes," she said, clearing her throat. "I remember. How can I help you?" Fear pounded a furious drumbeat against her ribs. Was this about testifying? Could she do it? Go back there and face him again?

"I've sent you an e-mail," Patchett said. "The defense has come up with new evidence that is not good for our case. I need you to look at the attachment and call me back. My team and I need to create a strategy about how to approach this, so time is at a premium."

Time is at a premium.

"I'll do it now."

"You've got my number," Patchett said. Not a question. "Call me directly. No one else."

Hers was no longer the soothing, professional voice Schwartzman remembered. Patchett sounded unnerved, and the call left Schwartzman with a pit in her stomach. She locked up the morgue and hurried down the hall to her office, where her computer was. Her fingers fumbled with the lock, and then she mistyped her password as she attempted to log on.

During that first call, Patchett had told Schwartzman that she would be the ticket to putting Spencer away, that juries needed to see the victims. If you could get women jurors to identify with the witness, if you could make the male ones recognize some piece of their own mothers, wives, and daughters, Spencer would be sentenced.

They would win.

Her in-box was slow to load the twenty-three new messages. She ignored several departmental e-mails whose subject lines read, "Urgent" and "Please Respond." There it was. The subject read, "Traffic Camera Video."

Oh, God. A traffic camera.

She double-clicked on the video link.

In the center of the computer screen was Schwartzman herself. The film was grainy, heavily pixelated, as if the video had been taken from footage of a broader view, a camera a block or two away. Or more? How sophisticated were traffic cameras these days?

She recognized the house across from Spencer's, the cluster of dogwood bush she'd hidden behind. She studied her own profile. In her memory the street had been dark, much darker than it appeared on film. She hadn't noticed the porch light at the house close to her hiding place.

Standing in front of the house where she had once lived, where she had lost her unborn daughter, she had been solely focused on what she could do to finally be rid of Spencer MacDonald. But the porch light she'd overlooked then was visible in the footage. Dual-bulb and industrial looking, it illuminated a full 180 degrees, which meant it caught Schwartzman as she stood, watching the house. It caught her as she ducked behind the bushes when Spencer's Lexus backed out of the driveway.

It caught her as she started across the street.

Her dark, shoulder-length hair was unmistakable with its wave. Her gait, her posture as she moved like a woman walking to her death. She felt her own fear again, remembered the terror of that voice, of that woman's face on the wall.

The crushing realization that the woman was her.

She watched the footage until she disappeared around the side of Spencer's house and watched until the clip ended. Forty-six seconds. Not even a minute. At the conclusion, a white circular arrow filled the center of the darkened screen. To watch it again.

There was no question that it was her. Which was fine. She had been there. That was where she and Spencer had their confrontation. No one was disputing that fact. So why did the DA consider this footage so damning?

She started the video again. The footage was clearer than she would have expected for a traffic camera, and she could clearly read the make of Spencer's car as it backed out of the driveway and drove away from the camera. She was grateful not to see his face. At the same time, she wondered if seeing it might have given her some clue.

Did he know she was coming, even as he pulled away? Or had her entrance into the house triggered some sort of silent alarm that drew him back? She had never found out how he had ended up back there so soon after she'd watched him drive away. Now, with four months' hindsight, she was certain he'd had a plan.

Had he known about this camera? *He can't know everything.* And yet he seemed to.

It was only in the third viewing that she realized why Laura Patchett had called. Schwartzman slammed the laptop closed. Let out a primal shout. What had she done? Why hadn't she trusted that the police would find something to keep Spencer in jail? Why had she gotten involved? Why had she gone to South Carolina at all?

They had her on film, walking across the street in front of Spencer's house, the plastic sack she held in her right hand in full view beside her. The bag that she had taken into Spencer's house but not brought back out.

Because she had planted it in his trash can.

She put her face in her hands. Hal had told her to stay. He had told her not to go there. That it wasn't safe. But Ava was dead. Spencer had known she would come for Ava. And she had. She had fallen right into his trap.

Would they be able to enhance the footage enough to see the words *Home Depot* printed in orange across the plastic? Surely they would link the bag in her hand to the identical one in Spencer's trash—the one that held the evidence she had collected. If they checked carefully enough, if the film could be enhanced to make it all clearer, would they see that she had, in fact, been wearing gloves?

Because if so, then they would know.

That she had planned it.

That she had gathered what she needed.

Gone to his house.

And planted evidence that he was the killer.

22

The drive to the Finlay Foundation's headquarters with Hailey was filled with the easy banter that Hal had always associated with their partnership. Hailey didn't keep thoughts to herself, and she didn't mince words. In twenty minutes, she'd covered updates on her daughters, the mother-in-law who lived in the in-law apartment of their home, and the man she'd been seeing for almost a year. She'd also managed to grill Hal with two dozen questions about his own far less interesting life.

What she didn't mention was work, which was unusual. Their relationship had been built on the backs of their shared cases. It was how they'd come to trust and rely on each other. Until recently. More and more, her focus was shifted to the task force. He waited for her to bring it up.

"How's Anna?" Hailey asked, again avoiding talk of the job.

"Schwartzman," he said, a knee-jerk reaction, recalling the conversation they'd had in the bar. She didn't want to be called Annabelle. Or Bella. But *Schwartzman* was an awkward mouthful. Somehow he'd gotten used to it. "She seems okay."

"Any word on the case?"

He could still hear the fear in Harper Leighton's voice from their call. That bastard had gotten to Harper's daughter, and it filled him with rage.

"Bad news?" she asked.

"It's not good," he said tightly.

"He's going to get out? The ex-husband?"

"Let's talk about something else," he said, turning down Harrison Street. "Where is this place again?"

"Should be two blocks down on the right." She let him drive a moment. "Anything I can do?"

He glanced over.

"To help with Anna?"

He shook his head, slowing to read the numbers on the buildings.

"There," Hailey said. "Fourteen twenty-eight."

The building was a converted two-story warehouse, and there was no sign for the foundation. They parked and went inside. He wasn't convinced it was the right place until he saw the directory. There, halfway down the second-floor listings, was the listing: *Finlay Foundation*.

They climbed the stairs, Hailey in the lead, and knocked on the frosted-glass door of Suite 206. Nothing on the door marked it as the Finlay Foundation. He supposed they didn't get a lot of visitors.

"Come on in," came a male voice.

Hal followed Hailey inside. The office was a single suite, maybe half the size of the Homicide department. A large conference-room table occupied the spacious main room, and off the other side were two closet-like offices. The conference-room table was covered with glossy pamphlets, envelopes, and bright-yellow stickers that read, "Cancer Sucks."

The man who emerged from the inner office was young and trim and around five nine. His hair was cut close to his head other than a bit on top that was left long and gelled to the side. He had a full beard that was carefully groomed, hazel eyes, and high cheekbones. Without the beard, he could have been in high school.

"I'm Jay Schenck." He waved to the conference table. "We're getting ready for our annual fund-raiser. It's pretty much 24-7 these last few weeks."

"Thanks for seeing us," Hal said, nodding to a chair at the conference table.

"Of course." Jay pushed aside a stack of envelopes and sat across from Hal. Hailey took the chair beside her partner.

"Are you usually alone in the office, Mr. Schenck?"

"Jay, please," he said. "We have a part-time assistant who mostly works from home and a boatload of volunteers. Thankfully."

Hailey settled in but said nothing as Hal pulled out his notebook. "How long have you been the executive director?"

"I took over in February," Schenck said, crossing one leg over the other and folding his hands in his lap. He might have stepped out of an ad in a men's magazine. "Mrs. Finlay was very ill late last year and had to step back. Before that she was very involved. More than that—she basically ran the organization. Single-handedly. Truly, her energy was inspiring." He pointed to a picture on the wall of an attractive older woman standing next to Oprah Winfrey. Beside it was another of the same woman with Bill Gates.

"She's eighty-two now. It's quite impressive."

"And when, exactly, did she step back?" Hal asked.

"Late December or January," he said. "It was before I came." He leaned forward as though to whisper. "There was a lot of fuss over my appointment."

"Why is that?" Hailey asked.

"There was a woman here before me—Helen Tribble. She was Ruth's right-hand woman—that's Mrs. Finlay. Helen had worked alongside Ruth since the foundation was started, fifteen years ago. Helen was almost sixty-five, and the board didn't feel she could manage being executive director."

"So she quit?" Hal asked.

"I believe they let her go."

"Before you came," Hal clarified.

"Yes. This was all before me. When I arrived, the foundation was in a sort of holding pattern. They wanted someone to run it entirely on his"—he gave Hailey a glance—"or her own."

"And what is your background?" Hal asked.

"I graduated from Wharton in May."

"So you didn't have any foundation experience," Hailey said.

"Actually, before business school I worked three years for the American Cancer Society, chief analyst to the CFO."

He didn't seem old enough to have worked three years and been through business school. It made Hal feel old. The American Cancer Society also seemed like a strange place for a kid like Jay Schenck to cut his teeth. Young, polished, he looked more like someone who might work in PR or men's fashion. But, then again, what did Hal know about cancer or fashion? "So you were hired by Mrs. Finlay?"

"I was hired by the board of directors," he said. "But I've met Mrs. Finlay, and we correspond about the foundation. Mostly by e-mail. She's lovely," he added quickly.

If the whole organization had transitioned in the past eight months since Finlay stepped down, it seemed likely that Posner's killer was someone still involved in the organization. If the killer had been pushed out of the organization, why wait eight months? Why not take Posner out back then? Maybe he would finally be able to shorten his list of suspects. "Do you know the name Sandy Coleman?"

Schenck frowned. "I don't think so. Did she work for the foundation?"

"She was an eleven-year-old with a rare cancer. The foundation helped her get treatment."

Schenck froze momentarily, waiting for Hal to continue.

"She's in remission."

"Wow," Schenck said, relieved. "That is amazing. I love hearing those stories—that's part of why I took this job."

"But you've never heard of her? Sandy Coleman?"

"I haven't," he admitted. "We have stories that we use as promotional material—Sandy's would have been a great one . . . hang on." He retrieved a binder from one of the back offices and brought it back to the table. "Coleman, you said?"

"Yes."

Schenck scanned a list of names on a page at the front of the binder. "No Sandy Coleman."

"Is that a list of all the people who have received money from the foundation?" Hal asked, leaning across the table.

"Oh, God no. These are just the people who agreed to let us share their stories. We do a write-up about the person, their cancer, what they went through, and their remission. Because of the strict privacy laws, we can only share stories with written approval from the patient." He flipped to the middle of the binder to show Hal a glossy page of a man around Hal's age holding an infant in his arms. At the top it read, "Frank Delarosa, Prostate Cancer."

Hal knew there would be no way of getting a list of the patients the foundation had helped. He'd had a hell of a time just getting Sandy Coleman's name. "How many of these stories do you have written up?" he asked.

"One hundred and sixty-something at last count."

"And no Sandy Coleman?"

Schenck double-checked the list. "No."

"Mind if I take a look?" Hailey asked.

"Of course." Schenck passed the binder to her.

"How about Norman Fraser?" Hal asked.

"Was he a patient, too?"

"No. A doctor who helped Coleman."

"We've got a lot of physician volunteers," Schenck admitted. "I haven't met them all."

Hal rubbed his head. He'd hoped Schenck would be able to offer some insight into Fraser—something to put some context to the assault charge back in 2010. Fraser still hadn't called him back about that. He pulled together his thoughts before continuing. "What about the board? Have any of the members changed since Mrs. Finlay stepped away from leading the organization?"

"No," Schenck said without hesitation. "We have the same board of directors. It hasn't changed in a few years."

Hal scanned the list again. "Posner's the only one who worked for the cancer center. Do any of the other oncologists on the board live here in San Francisco?"

Schenck shook his head. "No. The other two board members who live in the Bay Area are researchers at UCSF."

The drug that had killed Posner had come from the cancer center, his own workplace, but Hal had been unable to zero in on any suspects among Posner's colleagues. Was it possible that the drug that was stolen from the pharmacy wasn't the same Adriamycin that killed him? The odds didn't make sense. So maybe Posner had stolen it himself? Only to have it used against him? But why would he have taken it? To kill someone? The same someone who'd ended up killing him?

And who the hell was that?

Hailey touched his arm, and he pushed the thoughts from his head, untwisting the questions until he could think about where he was and what he needed to know right now.

"Are there any conflicts among the board members?" Hailey asked. "Personality issues?"

Schenck paused a beat before asking, "You mean, like someone who didn't like Todd Posner?"

"As an example," Hailey said.

"Posner had a big personality, for sure," Schenck admitted. "Not everyone loved him, a couple of the retired doctors in particular. But the interactions among them were pretty limited. We meet quarterly, and the meetings are telephonic, so they're not really together."

"When was the last board meeting?" Hal asked.

"June 1. We're due to have another the week after the fund-raiser."

So it had been almost three months since the board had met. If someone on the board had it in for Posner after that last meeting, why wait so long? It didn't feel right.

"All the board members will attend the fund-raiser," Schenck offered.

One of the board members had tortured and killed Todd Posner so that they didn't have to attend a fund-raising dinner with him? *No.* He couldn't make that fit. Hal glanced at the list of questions he'd made. "Would you happen to have contact information for Helen Tribble? It might be useful to talk to her."

"Sure." Jay turned in a slow circle, scanning the room. "I don't know where it is right now, but I can get it to you."

Hal took a card from his badge sleeve and handed it over. "Just give me a call when you can locate it."

"Sure. I'll look for it today."

"Thanks," Hal said. "What did you think of Todd Posner?"

Schenck shrugged. "He loved this organization, so I thought he was pretty great. I learned this morning that Todd left his entire estate to the Finlay Foundation."

"Really?" Hailey asked. "Not to his wife?"

Schenck's face grew flushed. "Oh, they were separated, I believe. In the process of a divorce."

"And there was no other family?" Hailey went on.

"I don't know that for certain, but I have heard that he didn't have any children."

Hal thought about the penthouse apartment. Posner's estate would be worth a lot. Hal knew that Posner's soon-to-be-ex wife was not contesting their prenuptial agreement. Now a charity had inherited Posner's entire estate. That eliminated financial gain as a motive for any of Posner's love interests, but it did provide a different incentive for those people with the foundation. The foundation—and, by extension, those who worked with it—made a lot of money from Posner's death. Hal studied Jay Schenck. "Are you compensated on the money the foundation brings in, Mr. Schenck?"

"No. I'm salaried. And our assistant is paid hourly."

So Schenck didn't benefit from Posner's estate either. The only ones who did were people like Sandy Coleman. Was Posner killed as some twisted way of helping those like Sandy? A philanthropist so intent on saving lives that he was willing to murder? It seemed extreme to say the least.

His phone vibrated in his pocket. Hal recognized the number—it was their captain in Homicide, Marshall. This would not be good news. Hailey met his eye, and he nodded to the hallway.

Hailey was asking about Ruth Finlay's family as he stepped outside the office.

"Harris."

A man in a suit was coming up the stairs. He gave Hal a half wave as they met in the small space. Hal was about to step aside when the man shook his head. He turned the opposite way down the hall to the restroom.

"We got a call from a woman in Sea Cliff," Marshall announced. "Her husband's in the TV room with his head bashed in. Been dead awhile. She had been visiting her parents—since Thursday. Came home today and found him. Son saw him first—came and told his mom that Daddy was dressed for Halloween but that he smelled funny. Kid's two and a half."

Christ. "Who's the victim?"

"Name's David Kemp."

"Hang on," Hal said, patting his pockets for his notebook. "I'm writing this down. David Kemp. Spelled K-E-M-P?"

"Yep," Marshall confirmed. "He's a doctor."

"Oh, shit. A doctor?"

"Yep. At General."

Hal didn't recognize the name. "Not oncology."

"No. He's an orthopedic surgeon."

Hal hated to ask. "And I'm catching it?"

"Yep. The same red drug—the Adria-whatever—was found at the scene. Looks like someone tried to make him drink it and maybe inject him with it. When that didn't work, they bashed his head in."

"The same MO as Posner?" Hal lowered his voice. "Any leads?"

"Nothing yet. You need to get over there. We've got the crime scene team and the medical examiner en route."

"I'm on my way," Hal said.

"We need some answers, Harris. I'm about to get some very upsetting calls."

"Yes, sir," Hal said. "I'll report in as soon as I've got anything."

Hal ended the call and walked back into the Finlay Foundation office. "We've got to go I'm afraid," he announced.

Jay Schenck nodded quickly. "Of course."

"Thank you for your time," Hailey told him.

"Yes, thanks," Hal added.

The two hurried down the stairs. Above them a door opened, and Hal glanced up, hoping it would be Schenck remembering something that would break the case open. But when Hal looked, there was only the empty banister of the second-floor offices.

"I've got to go back to the station," Hailey said, reading her phone. "We've got a domestic call, too."

"I can drop you at the station on my way." Although it wasn't on his way. Not even close to it.

She stopped on the curb. "I'll grab an Uber. You go."

He turned back, wishing she could come with him. He liked it when they had two brains on a scene. Thank God he'd have Schwartzman.

"Hey," Hailey called after him. "No Sandy Coleman in that book. I went through the whole thing."

"Thanks," he said.

"Sorry."

He had his hand on the car door handle and looked up at her. Since when did Hailey apologize for the way a case was going? She avoided his gaze, too. "Thanks for coming with me."

"Like old times," she said. Her smile was a little sad, nostalgic.

"Right." He sat in the car and wondered if she was heading for a permanent change. Was she ready to leave Homicide? Was that her way of telling him? Or had she hoped to break it to him during the ride back to the station?

A part of him had known it could happen. Being a homicide inspector with two small children was no easy feat. If she worked the task force full time, she'd have a better schedule, more time with the girls.

Just because it would be good for her didn't mean he had to like it.

Which was good.

Because he didn't.

23

Schwartzman used her phone's GPS to locate David Kemp's home in Sea Cliff, arguably the wealthiest part of San Francisco. Unlike most neighborhoods in the city, Sea Cliff felt distinctly suburban. Few cars were parked on the streets, and the houses were separated from the road by a wide, grassy boulevard. Narrow strips of land ran between the homes, rare in a city where most residents shared exterior walls with their neighbors.

The style in Sea Cliff was overwhelmingly Mediterranean. Most of the homes were painted light colors—white or pale yellow—and their roofs were tiled with curved terra-cotta. Large palm trees decorated the streets at irregular intervals, making it seem almost like a Hollywood set. From Sea Cliff's high elevation, residents looked down on the Golden Gate Bridge below.

Schwartzman parked on the street between two patrol cars and retrieved what she needed from the back of the car. A week after chemo, she no longer struggled with the weight of the kit. Her appetite had returned and, with it, some of her energy. Though she was not yet her normal self, the improvement was profound, and it brought both mental and physical relief.

As Schwartzman climbed the driveway to the house, she scanned the brilliant green lawn, the flower bed with its yellow-and-red perennials.

The whole state was in a massive drought, but somehow the wealthy neighborhoods managed to keep their landscaping perfectly green.

A little sign in the corner of the perfect lawn read, "Watered with Well Water."

A bright-red tricycle lay on its side in the driveway. A baby jogger was parked with its front tire in the flower bed next to a trowel, gardening gloves, and a thin foam mat for kneeling in the dirt. It was all laid out like the owners had stepped inside for a drink of water—or fresh lemonade—and would be right back.

According to Hal, Mrs. Alison Kemp had taken her two young children down to Carmel to see her parents since her husband had the weekend on call. She'd left Thursday afternoon and returned today, about an hour before Hal called Schwartzman.

If they accepted that Ben Gustafson's death was somehow related to Posner's, and therefore Kemp's, as well, this was death number three. Three deaths made a serial killer. No two words were more terrifying to the police. The pressure, the media—it would be a storm when this hit the press.

An unfamiliar patrol officer stood at the door. She showed her credentials, and the officer wrote her name on a log and let her pass. Inside, she switched out her black boots for the navy Crocs and stepped into a spacious living room. A female patrol officer sat with a blonde woman wearing black leggings and a bright-blue jog top with a sweater pulled over it. The woman held a box of tissues in her lap, cradling it like a small dog. When she looked up, her soft amber eyes were as wide as a doe's. The wife.

The patrol officer nodded to Schwartzman and pointed down the hall to the left. The wife's gaze followed the gesture down the hallway. She seemed to focus on something there, holding it several seconds before looking away. Dropping her head, she began to cry.

Schwartzman left the inspector with the victim's wife and followed the dark-wood floors toward the back of the house, passing a bathroom and a bedroom decorated in floral wallpaper. In the center was a queen-size bed pristinely made with white linens. Pillows lined the headboard, each one balanced up on its tip like ballerinas on pointe. *The guest room,* she guessed. As she moved farther down the hall, she heard voices. *Roger. Hal.*

She had not told Hal what the Greenville ADA had sent her. They had a case to work first, and she was grateful to have time to figure out how to tell him. What to tell him. As little as possible. Nothing, if she could.

She had watched the short video a half dozen times. How could everything she'd worked for, all the freedom she'd struggled to obtain, come down to forty-six seconds of a pixelated recording?

But she knew how. The same way that political elections came down to e-mails exposed on WikiLeaks or meetings behind bathroom stalls, recordings of crass conversations on tour buses. Like Patrick Fraser's freshman escapades, everything was captured.

No. She could not compare what she had done in South Carolina to the sexual experimentation of a college freshman. She was smarter than that. She was not a woman who planted evidence.

But she had. The thought made it hard to breathe.

And now what?

Months later, what could she possibly do about it? What action could she take that wouldn't set a murderer free? She knew she was guilty of planting evidence, but she knew with equal certainty that Spencer was guilty of murder. She had no doubt about that.

She reached the end of the hallway and paused at the threshold, hearing a third voice. *Naomi.* The room was easily ten or fifteen degrees colder than the hallway. She scanned the room and saw the den's window was open. Posner, too, had been found in a den. Did it mean something? She glanced at Hal, knowing he'd already considered it.

Kemp's den was a very different space from Posner's. Here, whites and a palette of blues made the room feel as if it belonged in a beachside cottage. Two chenille-covered couches sat at ninety degrees to each other, and on the wall opposite hung a screen larger than her new car. On the far side of the couch that faced the door, the victim sat in a navy leather armchair. Schwartzman entered the room, and the group stopped talking.

She used to arrive to their scenes while the inspectors and the crime scene team were still sorting out the crime. Their silence was a sign that she was late today. She had gotten Hal's call while reviewing the traffic-camera footage.

"You okay?"

Schwartzman was startled to find Hal standing beside her. He was staring. Was she okay? *Yes.*

She nodded. "Fine."

She set her case beside the door and went straight to the body, glad for her jacket in the frigid room. Like Posner, there was red staining on the collar and the front of the victim's shirt. Red Devil perhaps but not necessarily. There was some redness around his mouth and a thin strip of irritated skin down his chin. Nothing like the injuries to Posner. If this was, in fact, Adriamycin, then this victim had been dead—or almost dead—when the toxin came into contact with his skin.

She circled the chair and took note of the matted bloody patch of hair and the clear indentation in the skull. He'd been hit with something hard enough to crack his cranium. There was blood down the back of the leather chair and around his neck and the headrest, enough blood to make her think this would likely be the cause of death. Not that she would share that supposition just yet.

As she finished her circle around the navy recliner, she noticed that the victim's left arm was dangling beside the chair. Sticking out of the medial cubital vein—the most common site for injections—was an intravenous needle.

The syringe was filled with bright-red liquid.

With her initial impression completed, she turned to Hal and nodded.

"David Kemp," Hal said. "Forty-nine. He was an orthopedic surgeon at General." Hal went quiet several seconds before asking, his voice almost a whisper, "Did you know him?"

She shook her head. "No."

Hal's expression showed his relief. This was not about Spencer. Hal said he'd known that already, but he'd still asked. He would want to be sure.

"The victim was home alone Thursday night. Security system was shut down from the inside around eleven p.m." Hal turned to Roger.

"That was unusual," Roger explained. "Shutting down the security system didn't mean just disarming the house—which we would expect if he was leaving or having someone come in. Shutting it down entailed disabling the 24-7 camera, as well."

"So there was no footage of who was here."

"None," Naomi confirmed. "When a system is shut down, the security company calls as a matter of protocol."

"Right," Roger said. "One of their representatives spoke to Dr. Kemp, who confirmed his password and said he'd shut the system down on purpose."

"They didn't ask him why," Naomi said, her tone suggesting this was a grave error.

"But it was something he'd done before," Roger added.

"Four times before," Hal clarified. "All in the last six weeks."

A mistress. The most obvious reason for disarming the house so that no film was captured was that David Kemp was expecting someone he didn't want his wife to know about.

"You want to know if this could have been done by a woman," Schwartzman said to Hal.

He nodded. "We're working to collect the traffic-camera footage from the rest of the neighborhood. See if we can pick her—or him—up on a traffic camera in the area."

Traffic camera. Schwartzman fought to slow her pounding pulse. She needed to return the ADA's call. What would she say? *No.* She could not worry about that now.

"I'm sure there's a camera on every corner in this neighborhood," Naomi said.

"Which is good for us," Hal said.

Naomi spoke to Schwartzman. "We've got photographs of everything as it was when we arrived."

"Thanks."

"I'll get in touch with the Bureau of Transportation," Naomi said. "Get started on traffic-camera footage."

Schwartzman watched her go, her thoughts pivoting again to the film of herself on camera. Almost as upsetting as the footage itself was how she would tell Hal. He had one hand on the top of his head, the way he did sometimes when he was thinking. His focus was on the victim.

With the pictures already taken, Schwartzman brought her kit and set it beside the body. Roger, too, exited the room, leaving Schwartzman to work. Hal stood off to the side, watching, but he said nothing.

Dictating as she went, Schwartzman fell into the rhythm of the exam. She studied Kemp's hands for signs of defensive wounds. There were none. She used a flashlight to check under his nails in case he might have scratched his attacker. She began with his right hand, turning it over to get a better view. The nail beds were clean. Better than that, they were pristine. Even through the gloves, she could feel the smooth texture of his skin. Dr. Kemp was a manicure man, his nails buffed to a smooth surface, the half-moon shapes perfectly round. About a millimeter of white showed at the end of each one.

"He's had a manicure recently." While it varied, human nails grew an average of three millimeters a month. "I'd say the last week or so."

Hal said nothing, and she kept working.

The nails on Kemp's left hand were as clean as those on the right. He had not scratched his attacker. There was no blood either, which meant he had not touched the wound on the back of his head.

The blow had been unexpected and almost certainly fatal.

She bagged his hands and examined the site of the needle injected in his left arm. The needle placement was technically correct—whoever had inserted the needle had managed to hit the medial cubital vein. But they had come at the skin from a ninety-degree angle—straight down. A subcutaneous injection such as a vaccine shot given in the arm was administered at ninety degrees, but an intravenous line was always done with a low-angle approach. Whoever had killed David Kemp had actually inserted the needle straight through the vein and out the other side.

Not that it had mattered for Kemp. The area showed almost no bruising. Kemp's heart had no longer been pumping when the needle went in.

Schwartzman explained the discovery to Hal.

"So it probably wasn't done by a nurse. Or a doctor."

"Hard to say with certainty."

"Right," Hal agreed. "Might've been a nurse and she—or he—was panicked out of her mind because she'd just killed him."

"I'll get him to the morgue and do the autopsy right away, see if I can find anything else."

"Murder weapon would be useful."

Schwartzman palpated the wound on the back of Kemp's head, feeling the curve in the fracture, a shelf along the edge of the wound closest to the front of the cranium.

"You've got a guess."

She glanced up at Hal. "I can do a plaster once I get back to the morgue."

"Schwartzman, I can see it. You've got an idea of what it was."

She sighed.

"You can do the plaster, too, but if you think you know—"

"A wine bottle," she said. "It might have been a wine bottle. Or something cylindrical with a flat bottom."

Hal grinned and slapped his hands together. "Okay. It's something. We can comb through the trash."

Schwartzman opened her mouth to argue.

"I know," he interrupted, palms up in surrender. He took hold of her shoulders, squeezed gently. "Thank you. It's only a guess, but damn if I don't need something to go on."

She nodded and began to pack up her kit as the morgue attendants arrived to transport the body. She was grateful that Roy was not working today.

Hal was still smiling. She saw hope, always impressed by how little it took to make him motivated, how hard he fought.

She thought about the camera footage, about the Home Depot bag. But she couldn't tell him now.

Let him have his hope.

One of them deserved to hang on to some hope. She certainly didn't have any.

24

He called the center and confirmed that Denise had left for the day.

He might beat her home. She took the train, and he could drive.

He was furious with himself. Seeing Denise on that video, in the pharmacy with that vial of Adriamycin, he had assumed she was onto him. He had never considered that she might be there for another reason. She had been seeing David Kemp—that schmuck. He knew about that. Hell, everyone did. And on Friday night, she'd said it was over. She had been different—empowered. Strange, because he thought she'd been dumped. Assumed that maybe Kemp had ended their relationship.

But Denise had ended it more permanently.

It was only a matter of time before the police zeroed in on her.

What could she tell them? She didn't know anything about how he had killed Todd Posner. Or did she?

Surely she'd gotten the idea of using Red Devil because of him. No. Not because of him. Because of Posner.

It might all be fine. There was a chance . . .

But he couldn't play on a chance.

He grabbed his keys off the desk and headed for the door. He had slept in her bed. He stopped to think back to that night. God, the sex had been great. Of course it had. She was fresh off a kill. Her first, surely. She was heady and bold.

His fingerprints were—damn, they were everywhere—the headboard, the bedside table, the counter in the bathroom, the shower, the hallway wall. He'd touched it all. And that was before they'd gone back to bed the second time. Then there was the morning. So early it was barely morning. In the kitchen.

He'd let sex cloud his judgment.

And he was furious with her.

What if he hadn't heard about Kemp's death? The police would end up at her home. Where he had been, where he had left his fingerprints and more . . . in the course of their investigation, the police would look into her life, and that might lead to him. Even if the police didn't think he was guilty of helping her kill Kemp, they would want to question him. He would be in their radar. That was risky. Way too risky. The police would come from San Francisco, wouldn't they? Her house was thirty miles from the city. Plus they would be focused on Kemp. His wife, his family. They wouldn't get to Denise tonight. He wanted to believe that it gave him time to make a plan. To make a good plan. To be calm and calculated.

But he didn't feel calm.

He was panicked, picturing his prints all over her apartment.

He couldn't eliminate his own prints. There would be too many of them. He'd wipe things down and forget somewhere. It would be much worse for the police to find his prints in some places and wiped off in others.

He had to think.

Something would come to him. First, he needed to get to her before anyone else. Before leaving the city, he texted Trent to tell him there was an issue he had to handle at work, and it might take him a couple of hours. He wouldn't text or call again. As soon as he pulled onto the street, he shut down his cell phone.

It was dangerous to be unreachable. Trent had a tendency to take an unanswered call as permission to do whatever he wanted—inevitably something stupid. But he knew enough about technology to wager that leaving the phone off was worth the risk. Where he was going—where Denise lived—was way outside his normal route. Thirty miles outside. If the police did zero in on him, his chances of avoiding prosecution for whatever was about to happen—and he knew what that was—were better if his phone couldn't be tracked bouncing between cell towers near her home.

No GPS was another benefit of the shitty car he drove.

The traffic through the tunnel was infuriatingly slow. He listened to bad local radio and clenched and unclenched his fists, one at a time. It took more than ninety minutes to reach her house. The peak of the afternoon rush hour, the apartment parking lot was a frenzy of activity. He drove past her apartment, but the single front window shade was drawn, leaving him with no idea as to whether or not she was home.

What if she wasn't coming home?

She might have gone out for drinks with Sarah, the office lush. Or had another date. A stab of something like jealousy struck him. Would she go out with someone else after Friday? *Idiot.* He was losing his focus. Too much time with Trent. He was becoming soft, distractible.

He circled the complex—a monolith of connected townhomes with ground-floor garages spanning five or six square blocks—and came back around.

He ought to know what kind of car she drove but didn't.

He made another loop, taking different side streets, and returned a third time.

As his gaze found the square window of her apartment, his heart jumped. *There.* The front shade was open. She was home. He wondered if she would be alone. If she wasn't, he'd be forced to leave. But he had to try. He had to go there, knock on her door. He had no choice.

He made a final pass of her building and parked along a side street two blocks down. The engine off, he reached across to the glove compartment and released the lock. It fell open, and his stomach drew into a tight, hard knot.

None of it was there. Not his gloves or his spray. Only two of the small wipes packets remained.

He stared at the empty glove box. *Damn. Damn. Damn.* He'd taken the spray with him Friday night, in the Mercedes, and then brought it into the house when he'd switched cars. It and the new pair of Fratelli Orsini gloves, royal blue this time with matching stitching. They were his favorite so far, bought online and mailed to the office.

Left behind. All of it.

How he wished he hadn't dumped the Taser he'd used on Posner. Why had he been too panicked to keep it? Because it looked like a weapon? Because he'd read that there were tiny variations in the prods that meant it might be traced back to him? No. He'd gotten rid of it because of Trent. The canister, the handkerchief, the gloves—they were all household goods, things he could explain if Trent came upon them. But a Taser?

What now? He palmed the two packets of travel wipes. Then, the anger building like a hurricane, he threw them back into the glove compartment and slammed it closed.

He hung his head and pulled the breath in through his nostrils.

Unprepared. Completely unprepared.

He drew two deep breaths and let them out slowly, hearing his father's scornful voice. "You've got to be responsible enough for both of you."

So he would have to work on the fly. He could do that. She was hardly Todd Posner. The doctor had weighed north of two-twenty. Denise might have been 130 pounds soaking wet.

Regaining his calm, he gathered his briefcase and coat and was about to get out of the car when another thought came to him. *Posner. The glass.* The pint glass from Posner's. He reached under the passenger seat and pulled out the grocery bag with the glass. The residue of Red

Devil stained the bottom. It had been there, under his seat, for more than a week.

He'd forgotten to get rid of it.

Another loose end he hadn't tied up.

What else had he forgotten? His mind started to spiral away from him. *No.* He had to be the clear twin, the focused one. He had to be sharper, better. Much better.

Finish Denise. Clean up this mess. Then he could figure out if there were other loose ends.

He forced another deep breath and stepped out of the car. Briefcase and coat in hand, like any other commuter, he started for her unit. Head down, he swung his keys between his fingers, caught them, swung again. A casual gesture, a man heading home after a long day.

He passed maybe a half dozen people—a couple of joggers, two mothers pushing baby carriages, a few professionals coming home. He nodded but didn't speak. People remembered a voice. There must have been eight hundred, maybe a thousand units in the development. These people didn't know all their neighbors. They didn't recognize everyone. New faces were normal.

A couple was coming out of the unit beside Denise's, so he walked past them, keeping his head low. When they had disappeared around the corner of the building, he doubled back and hurried up the steps.

With his jacket covering his hand, he checked the door. It was locked. He rang the bell. Prayed she was alone.

The house was quiet.

He thought about all the joggers. What if she'd gone jogging? *Damn it.*

He rang the bell again and glanced over his shoulder. A man crossed the parking lot toward an adjacent unit. His tie pulled loose at his collar, a jacket slung over his shoulder, he didn't look up. Another car pulled into the lot.

Damn it.

It was like Grand Fucking Central Station.

A sound at the door. He held his breath, and a moment later, it opened.

Denise stood at the threshold in a pair of yoga pants and an oversize blouse. A glass of wine in her hand.

"Surprise," he said before she could speak.

Her eyes went wide, and he felt a flash of panic. That she wasn't alone. Or wasn't happy to see him. Had other company. Was on her way out.

"What are you doing here?"

"Not bothering you, I hope," he said, shifting toward her.

She let the door fall open. "Not at all. But you're such a long way from home."

He slid into the unit, pushing the door closed with his backside before setting his coat and briefcase on the floor. "I wanted to see you."

Her eyes narrowed slightly as she searched his face. He saw doubt.

"Do you have more of that?" he asked, motioning to the wineglass. "I could use some. What a hellish commute."

"You drove?"

He nodded. "Not the best way to get here."

"God, no."

She started for the kitchen, and he stepped out of his shoes and loosened his tie, like he, too, was home for the evening. Like this was something they'd done before, a normal night. She seemed to relax as she padded through the living area to the kitchen, brought a bottle of white wine from the fridge, and took down another glass. The bottle was already half-empty, the corkscrew still on the counter. She was starting fast. That was good.

He took the glass from her hand and made note of it. The first thing he had touched. Today anyway.

The apartment looked like it had on Friday night. She had not been cleaning. Unfortunate but not surprising.

He took a gulp of the wine and wanted to reach into his pocket, wishing the cyanide spray was there. It could all be over so quickly, so neatly. God, he loved quick and neat. But he didn't have the spray.

She moved closer to him. "You seem distracted."

"Sorry," he said, snapping himself into attention. "Still thinking about work." He took her hand and gave her a little pull. She came to rest against him, and the feel of her breasts made him slightly nauseated. He leaned down and kissed her. She tasted of wine—tart and acidic. Her tongue too soft, like a raw oyster in his mouth. He forced himself to kiss her. He tried to recapture the excitement he'd had Friday night. How hot she'd been then, how sexy.

How quickly the feelings could dissipate. Vanish.

Her perfume was cloying, too sweet. Her breasts felt too soft, limp against him as she pressed in, her breath like stale bread behind the wine. He kissed her neck and noticed she smelled vaguely of sweat from the day. He pulled away, leaned against the counter and put his hand on the surface, only to grab it back as if burned.

More fingerprints. Damn it.

He drank more of the wine.

"Are you hungry?" she asked. "We could order something. There's a good Thai place nearby."

It would not do to have someone else come to the apartment. *Pull it together. Do it.*

He refilled their glasses and had downed his glass within a few minutes. Only afterward did he realize it wasn't smart. He needed to have all his faculties working. She was watching him, taking a small sip of her wine. "Must've been a bad day."

He set the glass down and leaned in to kiss her, giving it all he had, pulling his hands through her hair and reaching down to cup her buttocks. He pictured Ginger, his go-to. He lifted her off the ground. She squealed as her wineglass tipped. Wine poured down his back. He took the glass from her hand. *More fingerprints.* Put it on the counter, carried her to the bedroom, and tossed her onto her back on the bed.

She reached down to unbutton her blouse. He stood over her, gathering his nerve. Anger. He needed anger.

He got on the bed on top of her. She was wiggling out of the blouse, her wrinkled, fleshy breasts swaying side to side, when he closed his eyes and put his hands around her neck and squeezed.

He kept his arms straight, elbows locked and his eyes shut as she thrashed beneath him. She bucked her hips, catching him off guard. He almost fell over. Her fingers reached his face. Before he was able to pull away, her nails dug into his neck.

He howled and reared his head away, tightening his grip.

She scratched and clawed at his arms, pried his fingers, but he didn't let go. He watched her wide, terrified eyes. Confusion, hurt, anger all passed through them. Then there was only fear. Terror.

It made him grip harder.

Finally she stopped fighting. Then she was limp beneath him.

Still he squeezed her thin neck in his hands.

He held her there until his fingers cramped, and pain shot through the muscles in his forearms. Until it felt as though she'd never moved beneath him.

And then he forced himself to hold on longer, to be sure. Until the tremors in his muscles made it impossible to hold the grip any longer.

25

Hal drove toward the morgue to meet Schwartzman. It was early, and the streets were relatively quiet. An hour from now, the trip would take him twice as long. He'd wanted to attend the autopsy on David Kemp, but he'd been busy with interviews. After speaking with Alison Kemp, he'd gotten in touch with some of David Kemp's friends and colleagues. Each person he spoke with had offered another name.

If Posner was an utterly unlikable jerk, Kemp was his opposite. A successful orthopedic surgeon with an easygoing attitude and a great bedside manner, Kemp was liked by everyone—patients, colleagues, and friends. The story about David Kemp was as consistently positive as Posner's had been negative.

One mother who lived down the street said Kemp met her and her son in the hospital on a Sunday a couple of months back, coming in especially to set her son's wrist after he broke it skateboarding in front of Kemp's house. His friends reported that he was a regular guy—young kids, a happy marriage—at least from what they could tell. He played basketball in an over-forty league, and one of his friends joked that Kemp was almost eligible for the over-fifty group. Kemp had married at forty-three, and Alison was fifteen years younger. According to those who knew him, he'd been a playboy in his day but had mellowed with age.

Hal hoped Schwartzman could pinpoint time of death. His neighbors hadn't noticed any strange cars on the street, but the Kemps had a three-car garage, so an extra car might easily have been hidden there. And Kemp's wife didn't hear from her husband while she was gone. They were pulling his cell phone records, but so far they were unable to narrow the time of death between Thursday evening and Friday late afternoon when the hospital tried to reach him. They called several times before giving up and calling another doctor to cover Kemp's shift.

Alison Kemp said it wasn't unusual to not speak to her husband when she was gone. The on-call weekends were intense, so he slept odd hours and she worried phoning him might wake him during one of his rare chances to sleep.

She usually texted him—with little news of the day, pictures of the kids playing in the sand or at the aquarium near her parents. This weekend she hadn't gotten any response. Also not unheard of, she'd said, breaking down at the thought of her husband, who had been dead in their house for days.

Hal wished he'd brought another cup of coffee for the road. The further they got into this case, the more coffee he needed to keep going. It was eight days after Todd Posner's murder, way past the ideal time to catch a killer, and Hal was at the same dead end. He'd followed up on every lead he had. The Frasers were no longer suspects. Patrick Fraser had been at his job at UC Berkeley's Moffitt Library for eight hours when Gustafson was killed. Even with his lunch hour, there was no way he crossed from the East Bay into the city, killed Gustafson, and gotten back inside two hours, let alone the fifty-seven minutes his time card showed him out at lunch.

Hal also had a follow-up call with Norman Fraser regarding the assault charge. Fraser's story was that the kid had been a friend of Patrick's, and Fraser had gone over there "just to talk to him." When he'd arrived at the kid's house, Patrick's friend was just getting out of his car and was extremely intoxicated.

"He'd driven himself home and I was basically holding him upright," Fraser had told Hal on the phone.

According to Fraser, the kid's father had come out of the house and blown a gasket—likely furious with his kid for driving drunk and embarrassed that Fraser had found him in that condition.

Hal found Schwartzman in the morgue. A body—Kemp's he assumed—was laid out on the table, covered in a white sheet. Across the morgue, Schwartzman sat on a stool, a travel coffee mug and her laptop open on the small table in front of her. He knocked, and she waved him in.

She spun on the chair toward him and lifted her coffee mug to her lips. He could tell from the swiftness of her movements that the nausea had abated. He was glad to see her cheeks had regained a bit of their color, though she was paler and thinner than she'd been a couple of months ago.

Hal rolled the second stool toward the table where she sat and sank down on it. "What've we got?"

"Judging from the early stages of decomposition, time of death is most likely sometime between Thursday night and Friday noon. Leaving the window open helped slow things a bit, but I've taken that into account."

Hal retrieved his notebook and wrote. "Makes sense. He was due at work Friday morning and never showed."

"Also, the lab did confirm the red liquid is Adriamycin. Red Devil," she added.

"Same as Posner," Hal said.

"Yes. But other than the presence of the chemotherapy agent, there are no obvious physical connections between Posner's death and Kemp's. There is no evidence to tie the two scenes."

"Other than the Red Devil," Hal pointed out. "And the Red Devil is a big similarity. I don't know that there's ever been a case that involved death by chemotherapy agent before."

"Yes. It certainly connects the deaths," she agreed.

"But?" He knew there was one coming.

She nodded. "There was no Adriamycin in Kemp's stomach."

"So he didn't ingest it?"

"Right," she said. "And the burns on his face were minimal. It's likely he was dead or close to dead when the toxin came into contact with the skin. There was no detectable increase in white blood cells in the surrounding tissue, which we would expect to see if he were still living."

"So the injury to the head killed him."

"Yes." She rose and retrieved a metal pan with an odd-shaped piece of white plaster from the table beside Kemp's head. "This is the mold I made of the contusion."

He lifted the mold and turned it over in his hand. The straight-edged end, the rounded cylindrical side. "We didn't find any wine bottles at the scene, and not a lot of alcohol in the house in general," he said. That had struck him as odd. In his experience, affluent people usually had a lot of wine and spirits around. "Recycling was picked up Thursday morning. We found a bottle of single malt on the kitchen counter, but no evidence that it had been used as a weapon."

"The weapon was bottle shaped, but I found something interesting in the wound." She set the tray down and lifted a small plastic baggie. Inside it was a tiny fleck of blue.

"What is that?" he asked.

"It looks like some sort of paint."

Hal was thinking. "He was hit by a painted bottle?"

"A painted something that was bottle-shaped," she clarified.

"Well, what the hell would that be?" Hal asked.

"Naomi is on her way to the house to check for something we might have missed. I'm going to take this sample to the lab so they can test it. I was waiting to talk to you."

Why did the killer use Red Devil if not to kill Kemp? He could understand using the bottle as a bludgeon if the Adriamycin wasn't working, but to inject Kemp with the chemo drug after he was already dead didn't make sense. "So Kemp didn't drink the Adriamycin, but what about the needle? Did the killer try to inject it? You said last night that the needle went through the vein."

"It did," she confirmed. "I found a minimal amount of the toxin in the tissue of his arm behind the needle mark. It was only evident because of the color. Like with the tissue on his face, there were no signs of the body reacting to the toxin. No increased white blood cells, no bruising at the injection site."

"Which means he was dead when the needle went in."

"Yes," she said. "He was hit on the head before the Adriamycin was either poured into his mouth or injected into his arm. Based on the skin response, I would theorize that the Adriamycin was poured first and then injected. But he was already dead."

With Posner, Red Devil was the main event. Everything else—the horse sedative, the restraint on his leg—had been a way to get Posner to ingest it. Red Devil was related to cancer, which was Todd Posner's field. David Kemp had no connection to cancer or the cancer center. At least not that Hal could figure out.

But somehow the murders were connected.

They had to be.

"So cause of death was?" he asked after a moment.

"Severe brain injury due to blunt force trauma."

Hal couldn't motivate himself to get up. Posner had died after as long as three hours of torture, his brain so swollen that it was like a smooth lump of clay. Then there was David Kemp. Dead—or nearly dead—in a matter of minutes. And finally Gustafson. How the hell did the cable guy fit into any of this?

"You okay?" Schwartzman asked.

He nodded and rose to his feet. "You heading to the lab? I'll walk you."

"Sure. Let me grab my coat." Schwartzman slid the drawer containing David Kemp back into the wall and pulled on her coat.

They walked together to the main building. He was trying to decide what steps to take next. He'd go see Ruth Finlay, ask about any conflicts among the board members and see if anyone hated Posner enough to kill him. Then he'd hope that something came up on Kemp—the traffic cameras or some fingerprints. Something.

He would have loved to ask Schwartzman to come with him to meet Ruth Finlay, but he could see she was still not feeling 100 percent. She needed her rest. No word from Hailey today, so he was on his own again.

She stopped short of the stairs. "Have you heard anything more from Harper Leighton?"

He hadn't thought about the detective in Charleston, not since the night he and Schwartzman had talked about Spencer. He should have reached out, made sure she was okay. "Not since you and I talked to her." Hal watched her face, read fear in her expression. "Why? What's going on?"

She hesitated, her lips parting as though she was about to tell him. Then her gaze shifted over his shoulder. Her mouth snapped closed, and her eyes narrowed.

Hal turned and saw a blond man walking toward the morgue. His thin frame, his crew cut—it was the same kid he'd seen watching Schwartzman in Starbucks. "Who is that?"

"Who?"

"The blond, the one you just glared at."

Her eyes flashed wide. "I did not."

Hal held her gaze.

"He's a new assistant at the morgue," she said. "Roy."

"You don't like him."

"No," she admitted. "But I don't know why. He's practically a kid."

There was something creepy about him. A quiet anger, unusual in a kid who looked like him—young and blond. Not a bad-boy anger. Real fury.

Schwartzman stood stiffly beside him.

"Has he done anything?" Hal said, tracking the kid. "Threatening, I mean?"

She shook her head as the kid disappeared into the morgue building.

"I should go," Schwartzman said.

He thought of the questions she'd been asking. "Is there something going on?"

"No. He's just . . ."

"What is it? Something to do with the case?" Hal pressed. "With Spencer?"

"No," she answered quickly. Too quickly. "I'll see you later." And with that, she was gone.

—

Hal drove to the address Jay Schenck had given him for Ruth Finlay. He had called in advance, though the nurse couldn't guarantee that Mrs. Finlay would be well enough to talk.

Hal pulled to the curb in front of the Finlay home. The house was in an area zoned for both commercial and residential buildings. Finlay's home was two stories, and much of the exterior facade looked original, a light-yellow stucco with an ornate design along the top of the building. The house was probably built right after the 1906 earthquake. Again he had the thought that the afternoon would go better if Hailey or Schwartzman were there. He parked and stepped from the car.

If anyone had insight into who would have known about Sandy Coleman and hated Todd Posner, it was the foundation's founder.

If she wasn't senile.

Or too ill.

He was almost desperate enough to cross his fingers. Instead he jabbed the doorbell and waited.

Behind the enormous door, the doorbell echoed like a church organ. A moment later, the door opened. "Alice Williams," the woman said. "You must be Inspector Harris."

Williams was dressed in pale-yellow nurse's scrubs with a long gray cardigan. On her feet she wore black clogs. Her skin tone and features looked to be of Hispanic descent, but she spoke without an accent.

Hal shook her hand. "Thank you again for letting me come by."

Williams waved him in. "Of course."

Hal stepped into a grand marble entryway and glanced up at the chandelier hanging fifteen feet over his head. It had to weigh as much as a baby grand piano.

"I'm afraid Mrs. Finlay isn't well enough to come down," Williams explained. "She doesn't use the stairs much these days."

"I understand," Hal said. "You mentioned I might be able to go up for a few minutes."

"Certainly, she seemed up for company earlier, so I'll double-check with her. If you would wait here." Williams turned toward the stairs.

"Perhaps I could ask you a few questions first." Hal pointed into the front room. "May we?"

Williams nodded tentatively. "I don't know how I can help."

"It's pretty standard stuff."

Williams entered the sitting room. She looked around as though the room were unfamiliar before perching on the edge of an armchair.

Hal sat on the couch and opened his notebook. "How long have you worked with Mrs. Finlay?"

"This is my second week."

Hal paused. "Did you replace someone else?"

"I don't believe so—at least not recently."

Hal glanced around. The news surprised him, though maybe it shouldn't have. Schenck did say that Ruth Finlay had always been very independent. Still cooking, cleaning. A place like this took a lot to run, and from the looks of it, she could certainly afford help.

"I believe they had someone doing some cleaning once a week," Williams added. "And I know Mr. Finlay was bringing meals in."

"Mr. Finlay? That's Mrs. Finlay's son?"

Just then the sound of footsteps came from farther inside the house, and a gentleman stepped through the foyer. "That's me," he said, dropping his keys on the front table. "I'm sorry I'm late. I'm Justin Finlay."

Hal stood as the man entered the room. He looked familiar, but before he could say from where, Finlay said, "I recognize you from the foundation offices yesterday." The two men shook hands.

A six-four black man was probably pretty memorable to a guy like Justin Finlay. "Right, you were on the stairs."

"Running for the bathroom," Justin admitted. "I'd been stuck in the car for almost two hours. You and your partner were already gone by the time I got to the office."

"Yeah," Hal said, remembering the call on David Kemp's death. "We got another call."

Justin nodded. "I didn't stay long, just picking up some paperwork for Mother. Was Jay able to help you?"

"Yes. We're trying to get some information on your board of directors."

"I don't know much about the foundation, to be honest." Justin shrugged out of his coat and laid it across the back of the couch. "Please. Come sit."

"I was hoping to speak to your mother," Hal told him.

"Of course. Alice, will you tell Mother she has a guest? She'll probably want a few minutes to get ready."

"Yes," Williams said and retreated.

Justin took a seat in the armchair Williams had perched on, leaning back and crossing one leg over the other. "Are there any questions I can answer while we're waiting?"

"I was just asking Alice how long she's been here," Hal said, sitting again on the couch.

Justin smiled. "You've got her on her second week." He turned to the stairs where Alice Williams had disappeared.

"Did you have help before Alice?"

Justin shook his head. "Mother's quite proud, I'm afraid. Thinks she can do it on her own."

"A house this size requires a lot of upkeep."

"That fell mostly to me," Justin said. "I moved back in a few months ago. Mother's had a rather nasty infection that's been lingering for a few months. The doctor recommended that she remain isolated until she's stronger, so I've been having someone come in to clean the downstairs and bring meals, that sort of thing. But I've tried to keep people away from Mother. Other than her nurse and her doctors, of course."

Hal tried to envision taking care of his mother. *No.* That would fall to his sisters, thankfully. It would be impossible with his job. "You work full time?"

"I do."

"But not for the foundation?"

"No." He smiled, shaking his head. "I love my mother, but I don't want to work for her."

"What do you do?"

"I'm an efficiency expert, so I help businesses make decisions that will cut costs and improve productivity."

"You're self-employed?"

"Yes. I couldn't have managed otherwise. I have to be able to leave at the drop of a hat. Thankfully my clients are extremely understanding."

Williams came back down the stairs. "She said she's ready to see you."

"Really?" Justin said. "That was quick."

"She's on the oxygen," Williams explained. "So she'll be a bit hard to hear."

"That's all right," Hal said. "We won't keep her long."

"Thank you," Justin said, rising from his chair. "She does get tired quickly." He started for the stairs, and Hal followed. The staircase wound up to the second floor, the chandelier another ten or twelve feet above them when they reached the landing. The doors along the hallway were closed other than one at the far end.

Ruth Finlay's bedroom was twice the size of Hal's apartment. A white desk near the door was carved as ornately as the baroque design on the front of the house. A cushioned chair sat in front of it. He could see a bathroom off to one side. Light linen drapes covered the windows and were pulled open to let the light in. Hal had been expecting a hospital bed. Instead Mrs. Finlay was positioned almost in the center of a huge antique four-poster, tiny among a sea of pillows. She had a round face and deep wrinkles that ran from her eyes to her chin, giving her the appearance of a peach dried out in the sun.

From her place, she waved the men into the room with one hand as the other lifted an oxygen mask to her face.

Justin set a chair a few feet away from the edge of the bed and motioned for Hal to sit. "You should be able to hear her okay, and this way we don't need to worry that she'll get sick."

"This is fine," Hal said, taking a seat.

Justin brought another chair and set it down beside Hal's. He was about to sit when he stopped and went over to his mother. He helped straighten her in the bed, propping her back with a pillow and tucking the covers up around her neck. "Are you cold?"

"No, dear," she said.

"I'm afraid she's had tonsillitis in addition to everything else," Justin said. "So she's very raspy sounding. Can you hear her all right?"

"Fine," Hal said although the oxygen was louder than he'd expected.

Justin took the chair beside Hal.

"Thank you for seeing me, Mrs. Finlay."

She lowered the oxygen. "Of course, Detective. You've met my son."

"Yes," Hal said.

"Justin's a godsend," she said.

"He's a good son, I'm sure." Hal wanted to get right to his questions, but he sensed Mrs. Finlay was lonely.

"Do you have other children, Mrs. Finlay?"

"Oh, yes," she said, smiling behind the oxygen mask. "I have a beautiful daughter. Don't I, Justin?"

"You do, Mother."

"Does she live nearby, as well?" Hal asked.

"No, no. She's traveling. She's in Nepal now; right, Justin? We heard from her last week, didn't we?"

Justin called to Williams, who reappeared almost immediately. "Alice, would you please help Mother with a little water? It sounds like it's painful to talk."

When Williams crossed to Ruth Finlay, Justin turned to Hal. "My sister isn't in contact very regularly. Mother finds it upsetting . . ."

"I understand," Hal said. He would get right on to his questions.

"Justin," Mrs. Finlay asked from across the room as Williams backed away. Her voice was as raspy as it had been before the water. "What are you saying about your sister?"

"That she's a very talented artist," Justin told his mother.

Mrs. Finlay seemed to frown at her son, though it was hard to tell behind the oxygen mask. "Both of my children are very talented," she said.

"I was hoping to ask a few questions about Todd Posner," Hal said, ready to get to the purpose of his visit. "I assume you've heard about his death."

"I did," Mrs. Finlay said. "Awful. Absolutely awful."

"And you'd known Dr. Posner for a long time—is that right?" Hal went on.

"Oh, yes," she said. One of her feet made a slow circle under the covers, as if she was making sure it still worked. Being around old people always made Hal hope that death was swift and unexpected. His job made him hope it didn't come too soon.

"I've known Tom since he was in his twenties," Mrs. Finlay went on.

"Todd," Justin said.

She lowered the oxygen mask so that Hal saw the thin line of her lips. Deep lines ran vertically above and below them. The area around her mouth was pinker than the rest of her face, and patches of her skin were slightly raised. Like some kind of rash. Psoriasis maybe. His cousin had that. Did people get it on their faces? "What?" she asked.

"Todd Posner," Justin said again. "His first name is Todd."

"Well, that is exactly what I said," she snapped.

Justin nodded. "I must've misheard you."

Mrs. Finlay fingered the oxygen mask. "He was an advocate for our organization from the beginning. I considered Todd a dear friend." She emphasized the word *Todd* with a glance in her son's direction.

"So you didn't experience any difficulty with him?" Hal asked.

"Oh no," she went on, her voice gaining volume though it still had the deep, raspy sound he associated with a sore throat. "He was a pleasure and very passionate about our work. His death is a profound loss for the organization."

"Mother and Dr. Posner were quite close," Justin agreed, moving to the bedside again. He lifted the oxygen mask back to her mouth. She looked up at him, and Hal thought she seemed frustrated. He felt a little pity for Justin. It would be an impossible job. Certainly he couldn't imagine taking care of his own mother.

"What about Sandy Coleman?" Hal asked.

Mrs. Finlay stiffened in the bed. "Why? Has something happened to Sandy?"

"No," Hal said. "Can you tell me about her?"

"She's a young thing. A survivor," Finlay said, looking over at her son.

"I think Mother is concerned that her cancer has come back, Inspector. Is that right, Mother?"

Mrs. Finlay seemed suddenly confused.

"You were worried about Sandy Coleman, Mother. She was one of the foundation's recipients."

"I know that," Mrs. Finlay said. "Yes. Yes, I was worried."

"Sandy seems to be doing well," Hal said. "I met her last week, and she looks like a healthy teenager."

"Oh, good. That's very good." Mrs. Finlay struggled with the sheets, reaching for the corner to pull them free while holding the oxygen mask. Her shirtsleeve rode up her arm, revealing a mark on her arm like an oddly shaped bruise. The skin was pale, but she was not as frail as he'd expected.

He knew the mind could fail while the body stayed strong. Maybe that was why Justin babied her. Her mind was going—the confusion. Calling Todd by the name Tom.

His grandmother had suffered from dementia. Strong as an ox, she started forgetting things. Then she couldn't remember her children, her own house. It had killed Hal's mother to watch her like that. When she'd suffered a massive heart attack, they were lucky she'd gone as fast as she had.

Justin was up again, pulling his mother's sleeve back down, adjusting the covers. "Are you warm, Mother? Do you need water?"

Hal watched as Justin poured her more water and handed her the glass. "Hold that steady now, Mother."

Mrs. Finlay's hand shook slightly as she brought the glass to her lips.

Justin came back as Hal was pocketing his phone again. He wished again that Hailey had joined him. Or Schwartzman. Maybe she could have guessed what was killing Ruth Finlay.

With his mother settled, Justin turned to Hal. "I'm afraid she's probably getting tired."

"Sure," Hal agreed, ready to be gone himself. "One more question, Mrs. Finlay. Were there members of the foundation—board members or staff—who had issues with Dr. Posner? Any arguments you can think of? Any personality clashes?"

Justin remained at his mother's side.

When she didn't answer right away, he urged her. "Mother, there weren't issues with the board, were there? Did Dr. Posner ever fight with the others?" He looked up. "I never heard about anything."

Mrs. Finlay shook her head. The hand on her oxygen trembled slightly, and Justin took the mask. "You should rest, Mother." Justin perched over her bed and fastened the oxygen back over her mouth, looping the strap over short gray hair. He flattened the pillows behind her head so that she lay flat in the bed and pulled the blanket up over her.

Hal closed his notebook and stood. He and Hailey had once debated whether they'd rather have their minds fail and their bodies stay strong or maintain their wits while their bodies stopped working. Ruth Finlay seemed to be suffering from both a failing mind and a failing body—but maybe neither would kill her anytime soon. Or maybe death was easiest if all the faculties—mental and physical—went at once. He looked back at the small woman in the middle of the huge bed. It didn't look easy for Mrs. Finlay.

Hal made his way downstairs. As he passed Williams in the front hall, Justin called down to her. "Alice, could you get Mother some warm water? Maybe with a little honey and lemon."

"Of course, Mr. Finlay."

Hal thanked her and left.

Standing in the cool shade, he considered the irony of the murder that had been committed inside the community of Finlay Foundation, an organization whose purpose was to save lives. But the notion that the board members were all a bunch of angels was bullshit. With that much money floating around, there was bound to be ulterior motives. He just had to figure whose motives were strong enough for murder.

He glanced back at the house, his thoughts drifting to Williams, in her second week of work. Was it a coincidence that she had started work with Ruth Finlay the same week Todd Posner was killed?

But he knew the answer to that already. He didn't believe in coincidence.

26

Mrs. Finlay's hand trembled as she painted the lacquer across the nail of her ring finger. It took more concentration than it used to. She was older, of course. Justin liked to remind her that the infection had been hard on her body, and she was lucky it hadn't been worse. Staph. Not even related to the surgery. She'd caught it from being in the hospital.

It was like people said: going to the hospital was as likely to kill you as whatever you had going in. She didn't remember much of the time in the hospital. She was quite sick. But what she did remember was peaceful. As a child she had been terrified of death, terrified that it would rip her off the earth without a chance to make her mark.

But she'd made it. She could go.

Not that she could tell Justin that. He wouldn't understand, of course. She didn't know if she could articulate the sense of peace she'd felt. Resolution. As though her life had been part of a long-standing mathematical equation, and she had finally worked out the solution. It was nothing especially noteworthy—her struggles were mundane compared with most. But the puzzle of her life had been solved. And with her health as bad as it was, she often felt as if she was waiting for death.

Of course, her own death was not something she could take into her own hands. That would undo what she'd accomplished, what her life had meant.

Plus, she wanted to be able to look Saint Peter in the eye when she arrived. If he turned her away, so be it, but it wouldn't be for a lack of patience. One thing her life had taught her was patience. The second was tenacity. She had both. You didn't have to be a bear of a man to make life go your way.

She wished she'd known it would turn out this way. It was true that youth was wasted on the young. She was so much freer than she'd been in her youth, free to work in her bedroom if she desired. To hell with her mother's stupid rules. "A lady never brought work to the bedroom," her mother had said countless times. And yet there she was, seated at the same antique desk that had been in her mother's bedroom.

She'd never thought to ask her mother why she would have a desk in her bedroom if one wasn't to work there. Funny what happened with age. When her mother was close to dying, she could hardly stand to ask if her mother needed water or something to eat. And now she was full of questions for her—banal ones, important ones.

Justin had hovered during the interview with the inspector. He could be so fussy, especially recently. Which was why he went into the business he was in. *Efficiency expert. Goodness.* That would never have been a thing when she was growing up. People managed their own efficiency. Now you needed an expert.

With her nails painted, she unlocked her iPad screen and navigated to the e-mail about the fund-raiser, rereading the items that were outstanding. They didn't need her to respond. She liked to be involved if she could, although it wasn't likely that she would be able to attend the event. It wasn't worth the risk of getting worse again. Too much time on her feet. Pushing it. She was always pushing it.

These were more Justin words than hers. And she agreed with him, didn't she? Funny how she felt more like a child with each passing year.

She closed her eyes and inhaled as though simply opening her mail had been too much. Hers was merely a figurehead role, but it was her foundation. The board of directors couldn't cut her out, not when she held the purse strings.

She glanced across the room into the mirror and smoothed her hair from her face. And that would be a good long time. Aside from the recent infection, which they had assured her was minor, she was healthy as a horse.

A cupboard closed in the kitchen below. Alice was starting supper. How nice it was to hear the sounds of a household. And Justin would be home soon.

Alice had been her doing, even though Justin didn't approve of anyone in the house. On Alice's first day, he'd come straight to her bedroom. "I met Alice."

She had jumped in the bed and laughed, pressing her palm to the galloping in her chest. "Justin Theodore, you scared the bejesus out of me."

Justin had entered the room, hands to his hips. "Mother," he'd said, leaning over to kiss her cheek.

She had smiled in response. "Alice is lovely, isn't she?"

As though summoned, Alice had appeared at the door. "Can I get you anything, Mr. Finlay?"

"No, thank you, Alice."

"Dinner shall be ready in twenty minutes, Mrs. Finlay. Would you like me to set the table?"

"No need, Alice," Justin had said. "We'll eat in the drawing room."

"No," she had told her son. "I should like to eat in the dining room tonight."

Justin had frowned. Disapproving. Didn't he know he shouldn't argue with his mother?

"Please," she'd pressed. "It's not often we get to sit down to a fine meal, and Alice has done a lot of work. Haven't you, Alice?"

"It was no trouble, ma'am," Alice had said quickly, eyes to the ground.

"The dining room it is," Justin had agreed.

"I'll take care of it now," Alice had said proudly. Her clogs thumped along the hallway runner as though she were marching. It had made her smile.

Justin had sat on the edge of the bed to take her hand. "Are you happy?"

She had blinked back tears, holding his hand. "I am, darling. I really am."

"You know that it's not a good idea. Alice, I mean."

She had shaken her head, tears falling. "She's really very capable, and I do need help, Justin."

"Of course. It's just—"

"I know."

"You're not well yet. And—"

"It saves you have to go to the market and run all the errands. Really, Justin. I'll keep my distance. I'll be very careful, I promise."

"I'm going to insist that Alice not bother you. If you want her to tend to the room and such, you'll have to be in the study or the drawing room."

She had gripped Justin's hands with both of hers. Then she had taken his face between hers and kissed his cheeks—right and then left. "You are positively the most perfect son."

Justin had beamed. He really did aim to please.

"Completely perfect," she had repeated, and he'd closed his eyes.

She'd been happy he'd accepted the compliment. He didn't always. But in that moment, he had seemed to soak it in like the warmth of the sun.

And really a mother's love was like that. From it came everything.

He would let her have Alice. It was so little to ask, and she'd given him so much.

She punched the "Circle" button again, returning to the home screen, and then moved through the screens until she found the game Justin had downloaded for her. Paper dolls on her computer screen. Who would have thought? She left the desk and crossed to the bed again, careful to sit so that she didn't undo the work Alice had done on the covers and careful not to mess her fingernails, which were still tacky. She tucked her legs beneath her, pushing her stockinged feet beneath a pillow to ward off the chill in the room, and gave the game her whole focus.

First she matched a head of thick Victorian ringlets pinned up to a purple polonaise. Then she switched that out for an amber-colored one more fitting with her hair color. She created a whole line of proper Victorian ladies before switching to the 1960s and mixing Jackie O dresses—sleeveless or silk with perfectly positioned bows—with the appropriate bouffant hair or head scarf and oversize sunglasses.

It was preposterous—a grown woman playing with computerized paper dolls. Especially her, after all she'd accomplished. But it passed the time. And Justin didn't want her going out to have her nails done. He didn't want her out anywhere. Not for at least another month. And it wasn't like she had places to go.

She didn't mind being home.

Quite the opposite actually. She was as happy as she'd ever been. Happier. The pressures, the waiting, the constant proving herself—it was all over. She had arrived. How many times had she wondered if she would make it?

Until recently she'd never felt the liberty to enjoy life's tiny pleasures. Painting her nails, brushing her hair. Now it was all she did. What an odd life to be content with. For decades, there had been the struggle. To keep up with the pretenses, to please everyone around her. To be worthy.

She had thought it would be lonely, this reclusive life. But she found it suited her. The bits of correspondence, playing the role of the formidable chairperson, guiding the foundation—it gave her a sense of purpose. *Purpose is important.* How many times had her mother said that?

But at some point—soon, perhaps—nails and paper dolls would no longer be enough to fill a life.

And then she would have to decide what to do about it.

27

Schwartzman woke to the sun shining through the edges of her blinds on Monday morning. She felt off balance, out of sorts. And her thoughts kept returning to Hal. She felt hungover, except she hadn't had a drink in days. She'd spent a grueling weekend at work, taking care of one case after another—a triple homicide in the Tenderloin near Eddy Street, followed by a stabbing in Visitation Valley, followed by a hit-and-run biking death out by Golden Gate Park on Sunday morning.

Roger had worked the first two cases. She'd seen Naomi and, at one point or another, every one of the homicide inspectors in the department. Except for Hal. She hadn't heard from Hal since he'd come to the morgue Wednesday of last week, when she had shared her findings on David Kemp's murder.

Almost a week. It was the longest they'd gone without talking since she'd left for South Carolina more than four months ago. And she was sick by the fact that she had yet to tell Hal about the footage from Spencer's house.

She was pushing the covers off to get out of bed when her phone rang on the bedside table. She recognized the ADA's number in Greenville, the number that had called no fewer than twenty times since last Tuesday.

Steeling herself, she finally answered. "Ms. Patchett," she said quickly. "I'm sorry for the delay. We're dealing with a number of very intense cases here."

"We're working a pretty intense case out here, too, Dr. Schwartzman," Patchett replied. Cold, angry. "Did you watch the video?"

"I did." Schwartzman sank back onto the bed and closed her eyes.

"You were carrying a bag. When you entered Mr. MacDonald's residence. But the police have no record of you having a bag when they arrived. The defense is questioning what was in that bag. They're suggesting that you plan—"

"I can imagine," Schwartzman said, cutting her off. "When I was going to—" She did not want to say his name. "I brought tools to break into the house, in case I needed them." The lie had been building in her mind for nearly a week. They could not prove what had been in that bag, not with a video. She could not think beyond the video. Not about the trial, about what she would do if they put her on the stand. "I didn't know if he would be home."

"You were prepared to break in," Patchett repeated, a sigh in her voice.

Schwartzman stared at the blackened shades, at the stripe of sunlight at each end. She shifted so that one of the strips of sun hit her body, immediately warming her dark pajama top. "Yes."

"What did you bring? What was in the bag?"

"I believe there was a screwdriver and a small towel in case I needed to break a window," she said slowly. "And a hammer for the same reason."

"You bought these items?"

"No." Her heart pulsed in her neck. "I brought them from my aunt's house. The sack was from there, as well."

"Do you remember the brand of the hammer or the screwdriver?"

She paused, trying to recall what brands Spencer had in the house. "I don't."

"What about the towel?"

She pictured the bathroom of their home. Every bathroom. "It was a hand towel—a yellow hand towel," she answered.

Patchett asked her to explain how she'd gotten into the house. This she could do—this she'd done for the police the next day. Completely truthful, Schwartzman explained the key that she'd put under the doorjamb all those years earlier and how she'd entered through the garage.

"And the bag? The tools?"

"I believe I left them in the garage."

"You believe."

"Yes. Once I got into the house, I didn't need them."

Patchett went quiet on the line, and Schwartzman offered nothing more. Waited. Pressed her hand over her eyes. She waited for Patchett to mention the trial, to say the word *testify*.

"I'll be in touch," Patchett said.

Schwartzman did not say good-bye before ending the call. She stared at the phone, replaying Patchett's words. Did she believe that she'd brought tools to Spencer's house?

She thought of the contents of that bag. Knee pads and hair. She had tucked those items down in Spencer's garbage can, shoved the bag down in the can, as well. Would the police put that bag and the one caught on video together? Realize that she was the one who had brought the knee pads and the hair, and planted it all in Spencer's trash?

The police would figure it out. If they hadn't already.

She forced herself to move. *There is nothing you can do now. Wait. You have to wait.*

She left the phone by the bedside table and went to the kitchen for coffee.

Get through this week.

In seven days, the chemo would be over. She would be sick for the last time. Exhausted and weak, at her lowest point, but already she would be able to look forward to another good weekend. After next week they would all be good weekends.

It seemed impossible.

Her phone rang from the other room as she filled a mug with black coffee. She didn't run to answer. Her movements were slow, deliberate. It was her day off.

The phone was ringing again as she entered the bedroom with her mug of coffee.

"Hal."

"Hi," he said, slightly breathless. "Sorry to call twice, but I heard you're off today."

"I am. I was just—what's going on?"

"You have time to go see a private investigator with me?"

Schwartzman set down the mug with the sense that she might drop it. "A private investigator? Is this about Posner?"

"No. I've arranged for us to meet him at nine fifteen. Is that too soon? I'll explain on the way."

"Wait—"

"I'm here," Hal said.

"Is it Spencer?"

"Joseph Strom."

The name was vaguely familiar, but she couldn't attach it to her recent caseload. Then it hit her. *The death certificate. Greenville. Spencer.* "Oh."

"Are you okay?"

She waited to gauge her body's reaction to this news. Numb. She felt nothing. No racing heart, no cold, no dread. Or perhaps she felt everything—fear, exhaustion, shame, and a bizarre spark of elation, hope that this was some lead to overshadow what she'd done—and those feelings were too much for her.

"Schwartzman?"

"What private investigator? How—"

"Fingerprints," Hal said quickly. "On the envelope. Can I pick you up?"

"I can meet you there. Text me the address."

"It's okay. I'm close to your building. Can you be ready in fifteen minutes?"

"Yes."

"I'll be out front," Hal said and rang off.

She stood with the phone in her hand for several moments, waiting to feel something, for one emotion to rise above the rest. When none did, she hurried to dress. Fifteen minutes later, she was on the elevator down to the lobby.

She hadn't had a single sip of coffee.

28

Jake Charles was maybe five eight and built densely, like a stack of bricks. His shoulders were almost as wide as Hal's, which looked bizarre on his shorter frame, and his neck was thick, making his head seem small. Seeing him on the street, Schwartzman would have taken him for a tough guy, one who spent a lot of time in the gym.

Charles was surprisingly soft-spoken and gracious, inviting them in like a therapist would a tentative, new patient. Hal did the talking, explaining to Charles that he was connected to a document related to an open investigation. Beside Hal, Schwartzman sat as still as possible in the chair. She didn't want to field questions about why they were here. And she was keenly aware that her position as medical examiner didn't fit with Hal's assertion that this was related to a case they were working. MEs rarely worked cases. They worked corpses. But Hal referred to them as "we," looping her into the investigative team, and the PI didn't give her a second look.

Charles took a seat behind the desk and crossed one foot over the opposite knee. "I received the death certificate via express mail on Tuesday and delivered it Wednesday night of last week. At the hospital." He nodded to Schwartzman then. "I watched until you picked it up off the windshield and left."

"Can you tell us more about the sender?"

"I can do better than that," Charles said. His chair was low to the ground, making him look shorter than he was. "Normally I wouldn't share a client conversation, but this was a weird one." He looked up. "And she never requested anonymity. Here, I'll play the calls for you."

"Calls?" Hal asked.

"Yeah. I recorded her original call and the one after the job was done, which was when things got weird." He pushed a digital recorder to the edge of the desk. "That's why I wasn't surprised to hear from you this morning."

Schwartzman sat upright in the hard-backed chair, waiting for the recording to begin.

"Client's name is Margaret Buckley," Charles said.

Hal looked at Schwartzman, who shook her head. The name wasn't familiar. Her shoulders tensed, and she felt herself holding her breath, the way she did when she walked into a dark room, half expecting someone to jump out at her. Spencer. Somehow, this had to be about Spencer.

"Here's the original call."

There was a light hiss behind the PI's recorded voice. "How can I help you?"

"I need to have something delivered." The voice was soft and shaky, the accent deep. More Southern than South Carolina. Margaret Buckley had likely grown up in Mississippi or Alabama.

"Ma'am? I'm afraid I can't hear you well."

"I need to have a document delivered."

"I'm a private investigator, ma'am."

"Yes, I know," she replied sharply.

"You recognize the voice?" Hal asked.

Schwartzman scanned through voices of her childhood and shook her head. Her parents had a small group of close friends, and Margaret Buckley was not among them. Even if she hadn't seen her mother's friends in a decade, she would know their voices. And if Buckley had been in her life peripherally—through the church or the community—Schwartzman didn't remember her or recognize her voice.

The recording continued with more back-and-forth as Buckley clarified that she would pay to have him hand deliver something to Annabelle Schwartzman. The sound of her own name in the woman's deep Southern accent sent chills through her. Ever so slightly, Hal shifted closer to Schwartzman in his chair.

"I'll pay for your time," she went on. "I can send the document in the mail. I need you to put it in a plain envelope and deliver it to her."

Charles then asked more specifically if there was a message to go with it.

"Just that page."

"And she'll know what it's regarding?"

"Well, I don't know the answer to that. She's the doctor."

Charles stopped the recording, and Schwartzman continued to stare at the small black recorder as if waiting for it to offer her more. The short recording only brought up additional questions.

"Does that make sense to you?" Charles asked.

She thought about the death certificate. "He'd died from hemothorax and hemoperitoneum."

Both men looked at her blankly.

"He was in an auto accident. The impact crushed his chest and abdomen. Blood filled the cavities. Basically, he died of massive internal bleeding."

"Nothing stood out?" Charles asked.

"No. There was nothing unusual about the death certificate. And I don't know the name Joseph Strom."

The three of them sat in silence.

"If the cause of death isn't suspect, it's going to be about the victim," Hal said. "Can we contact Margaret Buckley? Maybe Schwartzman can speak to her directly."

"That's where things get weird." Charles offered no further explanation before checking a notepad and pressing several buttons on the recorder.

Hal glanced at Schwartzman, who feared something had happened to Buckley.

With his finger hovering over the "Play" button, Charles added, "This was last Friday, after I'd delivered the note to you Wednesday evening."

A phone ringing. Then a man's voice answered, "Hello." Old, Southern. It was familiar, but she couldn't quite place it.

"This is Jake Charles," the PI said across the line. "I'm trying to reach Margaret Buckley."

"Who's calling?" the man asked.

Schwartzman realized it wasn't his voice that was familiar. It was the specific hospitality of it—not rude but guarded. And the accent, of course. He was from Greenville. Amazing how she could still distinguish the differences between the Charleston accent that had stayed with her father and the Greenville one of her mother.

Charles explained that Mrs. Buckley had requested he do a job for her.

"What now?" the man grumbled.

"I'm sorry?"

"It's just—ah, hell, Margaret's got Alzheimer's. Sometimes she thinks she's out to save the world or something. Other times she's like a terrified kid." He filled the line with a long, deep sigh. "I'm her husband, Tom."

"I'm very sorry, Tom," Charles said in the awkward silence.

"Well, don't go delivering any messages from Margaret. I didn't realize she was making calls until a couple days ago. It just started."

"The calls, you mean?" Charles probed.

Schwartzman glanced at the detective across the desk. He was staring out between the blinds at the empty alley that ran beside his office. Was it simply natural curiosity that made him ask about the calls Margaret Buckley had been making? Or something else?

"Yes," Tom Buckley confirmed. "Sometime last week, she started calling folks—her old office, the wife of a colleague, the law office they used to work with, and now you." He paused. "Where the heck are you calling from anyway? Area code 415—you down in Atlanta?"

"San Francisco actually."

"San Francisco." A beat passed. "Well, who the hell was she after in San Francisco?"

There was a hesitation on Charles's end. "I really can't say," he began. "You understand, it's a matter of client—"

"Ah, for God's sake. You sound like the damned doctors. The woman is sick. I'm her husband, and most days she doesn't know me. She almost never recognizes the kids anymore. Never mind the grand-babies—" His voice rose in pitch and cut off.

His anguish seemed to transfer through the recorded voice and land in her lap, leaving her to wonder how she might help him, if there was any way she could.

Hal glanced sideways, and she met his gaze but said nothing.

"Forget it," Tom said after a pause. "I don't care. Forget it. Don't deliver any message and don't call back."

"Sir," Charles called into the line. "Please, wait."

A gruff sigh was the only sign that the man was still on the line. "What? She owe you money?"

"No, sir. It's not that," Charles said, though he didn't answer the question.

"What then?"

"Could I leave you my number? If it comes up again, I mean," Charles said.

"If what comes up? You won't even tell me why she contacted you."

Charles was quiet on the line. Across the desk, he shifted in his seat, turning back to face them, his gaze on the recorder as though he might be as surprised as Schwartzman and Hal at what they were about to hear.

"She asked me to deliver a death certificate," Charles began, the whisper of the recording slightly louder than on the earlier call.

"Whose death certificate?" Buckley asked.

Again there was a hesitation. Charles trying to decide how much he ought to tell. "Joseph Strom."

"I should've known," Buckley muttered.

"Can you explain that, Mr. Buckley?"

"All hell," he said again. "Joe's death hit her hard. Hell, it's been thirteen, fourteen years now."

"Who was Mr. Strom?"

"Her boss. He owned a big development company—mixed-used stuff—one of the first to incorporate residential and commercial in planned communities down here. Margaret was his assistant for ten, fifteen years. Before he died."

"Why would she send his death certificate—" Charles halted midsentence as if realizing he was about to give away more than he'd intended.

"Margaret was convinced he was murdered."

"He died in a car accident," Charles said.

"That's right. They ruled it an accident, said he swerved to avoid hitting a deer, but Margaret said no way. She thinks he was run off the road." A short pause. "Anyway, it's bothered her for years. Maybe I shouldn't be surprised that she was digging it all up again. Alzheimer's does all sorts of awful things—I'll tell you. I'm sure thinking about old Joe Strom again is part of this. Who knows what will be next," he added, sounding defeated and exhausted. "Listen, thanks for the call. Sorry for the bother she caused."

"Can I ask one more thing?" Charles said, speaking quickly as if he expected Tom Buckley to ring off before he finished.

"Okay," Buckley said slowly.

"Is the name Schwartzman familiar to you?"

"Schwartzman, you say?"

"Yes. Annabelle Schwartzman."

Schwartzman stiffened in her seat.

"Why do you ask?" Buckley countered.

"Margaret asked me to deliver the death certificate to her. To Dr. Schwartzman. She's a medical examiner."

Tom Buckley remained quiet another moment. "There was a Schwartzman here," he said slowly. "Not a doctor though. He was at the law firm that Margaret's company—well, Strom's company—worked with. I believe his name was Samuel Schwartzman. He was involved in the lawsuit."

Schwartzman felt the contents of her stomach turn over. *Samuel Schwartzman.* Her father. "What lawsuit?"

Both men looked up at her. Charles paused the recording.

"Sorry," she said, nodding to the recorder.

Charles started the recording again. "Can you tell me more about the lawsuit?" Charles asked Tom Buckley.

"I don't recall all the details. It's been a long time. Joe—Strom, that is—had the land under contract. He'd done a few of these developments already. Margaret said he was using a new bank, different financing or something. Anyway, the deal was set to close. In the last days, the landowner broke the contract. Turned out Joe's own banker had paid the owner to sell to him instead."

Schwartzman's fingers found the arms of her chair and clenched. *Banker. Strom's banker.*

"Guy was hardly more than a kid."

"The banker, you mean?" Charles asked Tom Buckley.

"Right. Twenties or something."

Hal's hand rested on her shoulder, and Schwartzman squeezed her eyes closed against what she knew was coming. What it had to be. Otherwise, why her? Why would she be here?

"The lawyer—Schwartzman—filed the suit, and Joe had a good case. But Joe died about a week before they were set to go to trial," Buckley continued. "Whole thing fell apart after that." The voice sounded as though it was filtered through a dense fog, coming to her in staccato bits that she had to struggle to piece together.

"I think the lawyer died a few months later. Can't remember how, but Margaret was upset about that, too."

"And this banker. Do you remember his name?" Charles's voice filled the air.

Buzzing filled Schwartzman's head, as if Charles were shouting.

There was a pause on the line. Schwartzman felt the silence like an electrical current running down the center of her bones. It couldn't be. He'd never known her father. They'd never met. Had they?

"MacDonald. Can't remember the first name."

There were more words on the recording, but Schwartzman didn't hear them. She didn't move. It was a shock to realize that her heart was beating, her hypothalamus forcing her lungs to draw breaths, her body moving forward despite the terror that was like a seizure to her every cell.

Spencer would have faced her father in court. Did that mean they'd met? And was it really possible that Spencer had something to do with Joseph Strom's death?

The man who had died three months before her father.

And if that was the case . . .

"Damn," the sound had come from Hal.

She wasn't capable of speaking.

29

Hal watched Schwartzman from the corner of his eye as he drove back to the department. She'd been completely silent since saying goodbye to Jake Charles. And he couldn't find anything comforting to say. Spencer had known her father, and her father had died not long after. Spencer had known Joseph Strom, and Margaret Buckley had suspected someone had killed him. Run off the road and his death made to look like an accident. With everything Spencer had accomplished, Hal had no doubt that Spencer had that kind of evil in him.

Fourteen years ago. Two months before Samuel Schwartzman died. Hal didn't know the circumstances of her father's death, but he bet she was thinking about it now. Her father's death had been sudden, unexpected. A stroke? A heart attack? He had imagined it was something like that.

But those things could be faked. Spencer could have made it look like a natural death. The idea that Spencer could have had something to do with the loss that defined who she had become, a loss that pushed her into Spencer MacDonald's life . . . there were no words for what that realization meant.

How many questions the possibility opened up. If Spencer was behind Samuel Schwartzman's death, did that mean he had known about Samuel's beautiful young daughter before Spencer had killed him? Or had she simply been a bonus after her father was dead?

More than fourteen years she'd been under that man's thumb, even before their first date—the night he had . . . Hal wouldn't think it. He knew what Spencer had done. And then the victim had turned against herself. Spencer made her think she was to blame, that her aggressor was her savior. As fucked-up a situation as could exist.

Hal stared at his knuckles, whitened on the steering wheel, and pried them loose, searching for something to say.

Beside him Schwartzman looked stunned, her focus on a fixed point through the windshield, unmoving. But she wasn't seeing anything. Or she was seeing everything, everything from back then. Remembering every comment Spencer might have made about her father—questions he would have asked, ways he would have pretended to sympathize.

He opened his mouth to ask, to urge her to talk, but his mobile rang in his pocket.

She glanced over, her gaze tracking his hand as he pulled out his phone, as though she suspected the call to be about her, about Spencer or her father.

"Harris."

"Inspector Hal Harris?" A man's voice. No Southern accent. How long before he'd stop associating the South with bad news? The caller was from area code 925. Out east of the city. Concord, Walnut Creek, the areas where it would be ninety degrees even as a real fall settled in the city. Too hot for him.

"Speaking."

"This is Alvin Pena. I'm with the Martinez Police Department."

Hal tried to imagine why a police department thirty miles east of the city would be calling him. "How can I help you, Officer Pena?"

"We got a call from a Sarah Washburn. She has reported a friend missing, a woman by the name of Denise Ross. Said she didn't show up for work Wednesday, Thursday, or Friday of last week. Sent a text Tuesday night that she had a family emergency."

Denise Ross. Sarah Washburn. The names were vaguely familiar. Then he remembered. They worked in Posner's office. But he hadn't talked to either of them. They'd been on Hailey's list. *What now?* "How can I help, Officer?"

"When she didn't show up to work today, Ms. Washburn contacted Denise Ross's son."

Hal tried to find a connection between Todd Posner and Denise Ross. Denise was in admin and occupied a small office with two other women—insurance and billing. Tamara Long's list of Posner's recent girlfriends did not include Denise Ross. But that didn't mean she wasn't involved with him. "And did she reach the son?" Hal asked.

"Yes, but he hasn't heard from his mother since Tuesday of last week. He's called her twice and texted, but she hasn't responded. He said they always talk over the weekend."

"You've spoken to the son?" Hal asked.

"Not yet. I've got a call in to him and am waiting to hear back. Ms. Washburn said to contact you because there was a homicide in her office—a Dr. . . ."

"Todd Posner," Hal finished when the officer's voice trailed off.

Schwartzman turned toward him, and he met her gaze.

"Yes," Officer Pena confirmed.

Was it possible Ross's disappearance had nothing to do with his case? "Have you gone to Ms. Ross's residence?"

"We're there now."

"And?"

"There are no obvious signs of a crime, but well, it's going to be hard to tell what happened."

"Why is that?"

"Denise Ross's address matches the address of a police call last week."

"What kind of call?"

"Noise complaint. Police were contacted just after two a.m. last Wednesday morning—late Tuesday night. A patrol car responded to the house. At that time there were about a dozen teenagers in Ms. Ross's apartment."

"Her son?"

"No. He is at school in San Diego. And Ms. Ross herself wasn't present. In fact, when the teenagers were questioned, none of them could recall seeing Ms. Ross that evening."

"So who were the kids?"

"A couple were from the neighborhood but most were from neighboring towns."

Hal rubbed his head. "If they weren't guests of Ross, why the hell were they in her apartment?"

"One of the boys said they were invited by a 'gentleman.' He offered the kid one hundred bucks cash and said he wanted to throw a big party for his daughter. Make it look like a big bash to get some kids from the neighborhood."

"And this guy?"

"Never showed up," Pena said. "At least, according to the kid."

"You have contact information for this kid?"

"Yeah. I talked to him already."

"And?" Hal pushed. He sensed the dead end coming.

"Not sure he's going to be real helpful," Pena said.

"Because . . ."

"His father's an attorney up in Walnut Creek. Midlevel but a big firm. Going to be hard to get the kid in for more questions."

Someone had to know something. No way this happened without someone seeing something. "What about the responding officers?"

"Yeah. I talked to one of them," Pena said. "He said the kids were pretty drunk, and the place reeked of marijuana."

So, nothing.

Hal thought about the man who had paid kids to come to "his daughter's" party. It was no coincidence. But why send a bunch of kids to her place? The kids drew attention to Ross's apartment, so bringing them there added to the risk of discovery. Or did he want it discovered that Denise Ross was missing? If so, why not contact Washburn or her son or make an anonymous call to the police?

There had to be another reason for the party. A cover-up? Why would he want a bunch of people in her place? Because he'd left something when he was there? Fingerprints, maybe. Too many to get rid of?

Then where was Denise Ross? Up until now he had killed his victims and left them. All the victims had been men. Was Denise Ross different? "Can the kid describe the man? The one who invited them to the party at Ross's house?"

"White. Older. Average height and weight."

No. That description was not going to help them find this guy.

Kidnapping didn't match with this killer's MO, but what did match it? The MO had changed with each killing. Was this another shift?

"Was he familiar from the neighborhood?"

"No."

Damn it. "They see him get into a car?"

Pena sighed. "No."

"And there's no sign of Denise Ross?"

"None," Pena said. "But we found her phone and her purse—emptied of cash—in the bedroom. Along with some blood."

"How much blood?"

"I can't say for sure. Doesn't look like enough, but this is a first for me."

"Text me the address. I'll head your way." Hal ended the call and set the phone on the seat beside him. "I've got to go to Martinez. We've got a possible scene."

"Who is it?" Schwartzman asked, her voice scratchy. She hadn't spoken in a while.

"A woman from Posner's office," Hal said. "She's missing. Hasn't been seen since last Tuesday."

"Who?" Schwartzman's torso was tense, her shoulders stiff, and her hands clasped in her lap.

"Denise Ross." He let a beat pass. Spencer slithered back into his head. "Do you know her?"

She shook her head. From her purse, she found her cell phone and worked quietly for a minute. When she looked up again, she said, "I'll come."

"You sure?"

"I'm off today."

This was not how Hal would want to spend a day off.

"If Ross died at the scene, it may be related to Posner's death," Schwartzman continued when Hal didn't respond. "I can help the county coroner if we find something."

Hal didn't need to be told twice. Unable to find the right words to help Schwartzman, he could at least provide her with a distraction. He flipped on his emergency lights and siren and crossed two lanes of traffic to make a U-turn and head for the freeway.

—

Even with the lights and siren, it still took every bit of forty minutes to reach Martinez, but it took no time at all to identify which of the identical brown block buildings housed Denise Ross's apartment. Three patrol cars were parked in front. Two officers stood on the stairs, while a group of neighbors and passersby hovered in clusters, watching and inevitably sharing theories about what was going on. One woman was rocking an infant; the woman next to her had twin toddlers encircling her legs. The two women were huddled close, talking in hushed whispers.

Pulling into a handicapped spot beside the stairs, Hal made a mental note to talk to them once he'd examined the scene. He got out of the car, and Schwartzman joined him as he walked toward the apartment.

A trim patrol officer with sideburns and a goatee approached first, his hand extended. "Inspector Harris?"

"Yes," Hal confirmed. "Officer Pena?"

The man nodded.

"This is Dr. Schwartzman. Our medical examiner."

Pena shook Schwartzman's hand and pointed to the apartment. "It's up the stairs."

"I don't have my kit," Schwartzman said, as though realizing she wasn't wearing any clothes.

"Hang on." Hal returned to the department car and popped the trunk. He grabbed a handful of gloves—size XXL—and shoved them into his pocket. He handed two to Schwartzman. Even before she put them on, they looked like clown gloves in her small hands. They would have to do for now.

Pena led them up the stairs. The main room of Denise Ross's apartment was trashed. Empty bottles littered the table tops along with half-filled glasses and bags—pretzels, tortilla chips, a half-empty container of salsa precariously tipped at the lip of the coffee table, an open box of some kind of wheat cracker. The couch cushions had been upended, throw pillows scattered on the floor. "How many people did you say were here?"

"When our guys arrived, only about a dozen, but at one point it sounded like thirty, according to the neighbors."

Which meant there would be thirty sets of prints. Was that the plan? Fill the place with teenagers to hide the evidence of the one person the police were really after?

"The blood we found was in the bedroom," Pena said.

Hal and Schwartzman followed the officer down a hallway to the bedroom. The bed was half-made. More pillows on the floor. It was impossible to know if Denise Ross had left it this way or if this was the result of a couple of horny teenagers. *Damn, what a mess.*

As Pena straightened the comforter and pointed to a bloodstain, Hal wondered what else he had touched with his bare hands. Schwartzman stepped forward, pulling on the huge gloves. She studied the bloodstain on the fabric and lifted it to check beneath. The bloodstain was visible on the other side of the comforter, but it hadn't saturated the bed. She shook her head. "This isn't enough blood loss to kill her." She scanned the bedside tables and around the bed. "No obvious sign of what cut her."

"Or him."

"Right," she agreed. "It's not necessarily Ross's blood."

"Let's take a look around the rest of the place," Hal said. "Is it just the one story?"

"She's got a small garage downstairs. Mostly storage. Doesn't look like she parked there."

"Have you located her car?" Hal asked.

"It's parked in the lot out front. Locked. Keys were in her purse."

People didn't run off without their purses and phones and cars. Wherever Denise Ross was, she wasn't there willingly. She probably wasn't alive.

"There is a small trail of blood," Schwartzman said, pointing to the floor. They followed it into the bathroom, where it disappeared at the sink. Hal moved in a circle, studying the floor and walls, looking for additional blood evidence. He found none.

They made their way back to the living room, looking for traces of blood or anything else that indicated a struggle. It was hard to tell what might have been a struggle and what was merely a bunch of kids having a party. Nothing was broken. There were no signs of blood in the living area.

"Hal."

He stopped and turned to Schwartzman, who stood in the threshold of the small galley kitchen. She pointed to a tall metal water bottle, upside down in a drying rack by the sink. He'd seen some like it. They were advertised to keep water cold for two days. This one was bright blue.

He approached Schwartzman as she lifted the bottle, putting a finger in the mouth and holding it with one gloved finger at the very edge of the base. He knew what she was thinking. The weapon that had killed David Kemp was cylindrical in shape, with a straight base. Like a wine bottle. And the bright-blue paint was chipped along the base—the same color as the chip of paint she'd found in Kemp's fatal head wound.

"We need a crime scene team," Hal told Pena. "Can you get someone out to help us?"

"Sure. I'll put a call in." Pena stepped away and got on the phone.

Schwartzman replaced the bottle, carefully returning it exactly as she'd found it. "You think the killer left it?"

He shrugged. "I've given up trying to read this guy."

"Someone will know if she used a blue water bottle. That, at least, should be pretty easy to confirm."

The only easy thing. If Denise Ross was the owner of the blue water bottle, did that mean she'd used it to kill David Kemp? Or had she been set up? And where the hell was she?

When Pena returned, he said the crime scene team would be there in thirty minutes. Hal wanted to have Roger come out, but this wasn't their jurisdiction. He and Schwartzman were here to help, which they were allowed to do as long as they had been invited. As much as he wanted to, it wasn't his place to invite the whole SFPD team. He'd have to wait and see how things played out.

"We should check downstairs," Hal said.

The stairs were narrow and poorly lit, so Hal used his phone flashlight. There were scuff marks along the white walls, which were dirty and dingy from years of wear, but it was impossible to tell which of them—if any—was recent. It didn't look like Denise Ross had ever washed the walls, and he would have bet that the paint was original to the place. So ten, fifteen years of wear and tear. Despite the mess, the rest of Ross's apartment had been decorated by someone who cared about her surroundings. The basement looked as if it belonged in a rental. An old rental.

At the base of the stairs was a small room that housed a stackable washer and dryer on one side and a set of inexpensive floor-to-ceiling melamine cabinets on the other. In between was finished sheetrock painted white. Inexpensive. Hal opened the cabinets. The shelves were filled with kitchen appliances, wrapping paper, and some random tools.

He closed the cabinets and paused to use his flashlight. Again no sign of blood or any obvious evidence of a crime. Beyond the small laundry room was a door to the garage.

He passed through first and found the light switch. As Pena had suggested, Denise Ross did not park a car here. There would have been no way. The outline of the garage was lined in boxes and large plastic bins.

"There's blood on the floor," Schwartzman said.

They all studied the concrete floor.

"Looks like it leads to the garage door," Pena said. He pulled out an industrial-size flashlight and used it to illuminate the small drops of blood on the floor. "Maybe he opened the door and took her out this way."

At the end of the blood trail was a stain roughly in the shape of a square. A few feet to the right was the garage door. Hal studied the stain again. The garbage can used to be there. It had been moved.

He approached the garbage can and used a gloved hand to flip the lid open. A large black trash bag sat on top.

Over his shoulder, Pena made a noise in the back of his throat. Hal took hold of the bag, thinking it would be heavy, but it wasn't. Not at all. Inside was a blue hand towel. Pena's flashlight caught the crusty dark stains on it. "Blood."

Hal set the towel and the garbage bag on the floor and found a white kitchen trash bag at the bottom of the can. Through the stretched plastic, he could see several boxes. Lean Cuisine meals, napkins, regular trash. Below that was another kitchen trash bag.

No body.

"Hal." Schwartzman was crouched on the garage floor.

He closed the trash can. "What is it?"

"These drops don't lead toward the garage door."

Hal sank to his haunches beside her. "What do you mean?"

"See the tails of the blood?"

He studied the drop she indicated, a roundish drop with a tiny line that came out of it, like a short-tailed tadpole. The momentum of the drop carried the blood slightly farther out on one end, an indication that the drop had come from something that was moving. Moving into the garage, not out of it.

Schwartzman was already heading back toward the laundry room. She stopped inside the door and looked left. There, against the wall, was a white chest freezer.

"Oh, God," Pena whispered.

Schwartzman aimed her phone flashlight on a box of Ziploc freezer bags that sat on the thin white wire shelving by the door. In the center of the blue cardboard was a drop of blood.

Hal gripped the corner of the freezer chest and pulled it open. There, inside, was Denise Ross.

"Oh, God," Pena said, louder and emphatically this time.

Ross was on her left side, her knees folded under her. Her torso had been wedged into the freezer, her neck at an impossible angle, probably broken after her death to get her to fit. Hal noticed her eyes had been closed. Someone the killer cared about?

"Hal."

Schwartzman pointed to Denise Ross's right hand, which was tucked up under her chin. She was missing all four fingers and her thumb.

"Why would he take her fingers?" Pena asked, his voice a whisper.

"Because she scratched him," Schwartzman said.

Hal leaned on the edge of the freezer, the cold creeping up his arms. "That would be my guess, too."

30

As Schwartzman attended Denise Ross's autopsy at the Contra Costa County Coroner's Office, one thought kept crowding into her mind: Spencer knew her father. It was barely two, and already the day had gone on longer than she'd wanted.

Exhausted, she watched the county coroner at work, although she knew what had killed Denise Ross. A cursory exam of the body revealed that her hyoid bone had been crushed. The thick red marks around her neck were further evidence of strangulation by someone stronger than herself. Likely male, though she wouldn't rule out the possibility of a female killer.

Other than the missing fingers, there were no other marks on the body. Hal confirmed that there were no signs of forced entry at Ross's apartment and no signs of a struggle.

The evidence pointed to the fact that Denise Ross knew her killer.

Which brought them back to the cancer center.

The same list of suspects.

The victim's fingers had been severed postmortem, which explained why there was so little blood at the scene. Schwartzman had noted the hesitation marks on the cuts. Even though Denise Ross had already been dead at the time, the killer had severed the fingers with difficulty.

A sign of emotion. He had closed her eyes, which were more than likely open when she'd died. Another sign of emotion.

In whatever way it was possible for a person like him, the killer had cared about Denise Ross. Killing her was not pleasurable. This meant the killer felt forced to kill her and, after that, forced to take her fingers to protect his identity.

Hal was working with the crime scene team to gather evidence at the scene, and he had convinced the attorney father to let his son look at a digital book Naomi had put together of the possible suspects from the cancer center. The kid hadn't recognized anyone.

The cancer center had been through their security footage and were able to recover deleted footage of Denise Ross entering the pharmacy after midnight two weeks earlier. Alone, she'd crossed to the refrigerator, removed a bottle of Adriamycin, and left. She'd used Sarah Washburn's access card, but there was no sign of Washburn with her.

Denise Ross had become her own dead end.

It was after three when Hal picked up Schwartzman from the county coroner's office and the two started back to the city. Traffic had slowed for the afternoon commute, and Hal didn't blare his siren or use his lights. He was obviously lost in thought and likely dreading the return to the station. Seated between them was the single piece of evidence that might answer a question—what weapon had been used to kill David Kemp. The blue water bottle was packaged in an evidence envelope, signed off by the crime scene team leader into Hal's possession. Roger was awaiting its arrival.

Schwartzman considered offering to join him at the lab, but Hal's mood discouraged talk, so she kept quiet. His captain had already called twice. Two short calls where Hal mostly listened, punctuated by several "Yes, sirs" and one "Understood."

They'd been in the car almost a half hour when Schwartzman's mobile rang. *Ken.*

"Hi," she said.

"We meeting to look at the house tonight?"

She'd forgotten all about the viewing. A half dozen text messages sat unread on her phone. Likely one of those was the Realtor, who had given up on leaving voicemails. "I think the Realtor set it up for five thirty. I'll check my messages and text you the address. Does that work for you?"

"I'm looking forward to it," he said. "I found a Cuban spot right near there—it's supposed to be great. You up for dinner after?"

"Yes." She hadn't eaten anything all day. A quiet dinner was exactly what she needed.

"I'll wait for your text. You want me to pick you up?"

"Actually, that would be great. I'll be at the station in about an hour." She felt Hal beside her, his shoulders tensing, heat from his gaze. *Anger? About what?* "I'll be in touch," she said, ending the call.

She went through her messages without acknowledging Hal. He had something to say. She sensed it. The Realtor had confirmed their showing, so she texted Ken to tell him she'd meet him in the back lot at five. She hoped they'd make it back to the station by then. Surely Hal would turn his lights on at some point.

She returned the phone to her purse.

Hal was watching her.

"What?" she asked.

"You can't seriously be thinking about buying a house." His voice was low, cautious. Anger laced with something else. *Protectiveness? Fear?* "Living alone, in a place with no security—" He clamped his mouth closed.

"Excuse me."

"Harper called me today."

Schwartzman's mouth went dry. "Is she okay? Her daughter?"

"They're running a DNA test on the necklace found at Spencer's house."

They were okay. They were processing the evidence. "Okay."

Hal's jaw popped in and out as he clenched and released.

"What is going on?"

"The video," he said in a low, angry hiss.

"Video," she repeated, the word out before she knew what he meant.

"When were you going to tell me about that?" Hal asked.

Schwartzman let her head fall back against the headrest. "I spoke to Patchett this morning—right before you called."

"But she sent the video last week."

She didn't respond.

"What was in that bag?" Hal asked.

"I told her that it had some tools, things I might have needed if I was going to break in."

"You told her."

"Yes."

"But you didn't break in," Hal went on.

"No. I found a key that I'd put outside when I lived there."

"Because he had locked you out once."

She hadn't told him that story. But Harper knew. She might have shared it with Hal. She was a victim. People always discussed victims. Her blood went hot in her veins.

"What was really in the bag?"

"What?" she asked, surprised.

"You said you told Patchett it was tools. But what was really in the bag?"

"Why would I lie to the ADA?"

Hal's gaze narrowed. "Answering a question with a question. That's how I know a suspect is lying."

"Good thing I'm not one of your suspects," she snapped.

Hal looked away. Chagrined.

She felt a flash of triumph for the sting. How dare he accuse her of lying? And yet she *was* lying. He was right. She was evading the question. She would not tell him. She could not.

"I'm on your side," Hal said, his voice raspy as if he'd been shouting. "I want to help."

She felt the tightness in her throat. At the same time she was sick to her stomach. How long had she been doing this on her own? Wasn't that why she'd kept her distance from Ava? Because she'd worried that involving her would bring down Spencer's wrath?

And it had. Despite her efforts to keep Ava safe, Spencer had killed her.

And he could kill Hal.

Hal could take care of himself. That thought was followed by the cold burn of fear. But what if he couldn't? Ken was a police officer, too, a grown man who was almost killed because of her. She couldn't risk that again. She had to find a way to defeat Spencer on her own.

Or decide to stop fighting him.

She stared at the screen on her phone. Without letting herself think about it, she texted the Realtor and told her something had come up with work. Then she texted Ken to say she needed to reschedule their dinner. She didn't want to look at a house.

Why not tonight? She was exhausted, but it wasn't just that. The urge to beg off, to postpone—was that about the house? Or Ken?

No. She wasn't changing her mind about buying a house.

She thought about her apartment in the industrial building. High up, behind security and guards. Like a modern-day Rapunzel. Without all the hair.

Ken texted that he understood. That was the thing about Ken. He always understood. For now.

One day he would give up. She would block him out one too many times.

But Hal. She turned sideways in the seat, searching for something to say to him.

Hal glanced over at her. Waiting for her to talk.

What could she say? Yes, she was grateful for his help, but no, she couldn't accept it. She would not rely on someone else. Not when it meant putting him at risk. She shifted to face front again. Closed her eyes.

The car sped up, and she jumped when the sirens blared. Beside her, Hal honked cars out of the way and pushed through the heavy traffic. She hadn't answered, and he'd obviously had enough. He probably thought she was being stubborn. Maybe she was.

But maybe being stubborn about letting him in was smart.

Or maybe it was stupid. Because it meant she was alone again.

Which was another victory for Spencer.

31

Hal's first stop Tuesday morning was Records, where he picked up the reports he'd ordered on Ruth Finlay's in-home nurse, Alice Williams, and Joseph Strom. He tucked Strom's file under his arm and read the one on Williams as he made his way to the lab. He hadn't walked more than ten feet before he had confirmed that Williams was clean. If Ruth Finlay's nurse was guilty of so much as a parking violation, she had yet to be caught.

He tucked the report under his arm with Strom's, which he would look at later, and fought not to get frustrated. At least Roger had made progress on the Kemp case.

In the lab, Roger confirmed that he had matched the paint chip, and it had definitely come from that brand and color of water bottle. Of course, there would be thousands of them. Roger was working to try to fit the shard of paint onto the bottle like a puzzle piece. If they were able to match it, they could say with absolute certainty that the water bottle found at Denise Ross's home was the weapon that had killed David Kemp. That was something, finally.

Leaving Roger to his work, Hal went to meet Sarah Washburn in Homicide's interview room. Seated at the table, Sarah Washburn wore a peach sweater so close to the color of her skin that, from the door, she looked like a giant newborn. Washburn was pale, and even through the sweater he could see she had spindly arms and a thick middle. The skin around her nose blossomed with tiny red veins. That and her bloodshot eyes told Hal she was likely a heavy drinker. Although the crying probably didn't help.

Hal introduced himself. "Thank you for coming."

"I can't believe she's gone. Who would want to hurt Denise?"

"You were aware that Denise used your access card to enter the pharmacy?"

The skin of her neck grew red and mottled. "I found out this morning. Dr. Fraser told me. I had no idea."

"Did she ever talk about getting into the pharmacy? Ever express any interest?"

"No. Never."

"Had she ever taken your access card before?"

"No. I mean, I don't think so." The mottling on her neck started to come together until the skin was simply red. "But I don't know," she confessed. "I didn't know she had it this time either."

How many interviews had he done on this case? He was already thinking this was going to be another one that added up to nothing, but he forced himself to keep going. "Was Denise dating someone?"

Washburn crossed her arms. "She'd been seeing a married man, but that was over. She ended it about a week ago." She seemed to shiver.

"Did you know who it was?"

Washburn nodded slowly. "David Kemp."

Boom. Motive for murder. "Did you speak to Denise after Dr. Kemp was killed?"

"Briefly. We went to lunch on Monday. I wasn't sure she'd heard. She didn't mention it, but when I told her, she sort of shrugged it off. Said he had it coming."

"Was that like her?"

"No," Washburn said, wide-eyed. "She was crazy about him. He was going to leave his wife for her."

"He said that?"

"Well, not to me. But to her. He said it all the time." She shook her head. "Denise said he said it all the time—"

"And did you believe that was going to happen?"

Washburn rubbed the tissue across her nose. "Denise wasn't stupid. He must've done something to make her believe it was true."

"And what about the breakup? Was she upset?"

"No. That was weird, too. She just said it was over. Said she was going out with someone new."

"Someone new?"

"Yes. She had a date with him on Friday. A nice place, too."

"Do you know who he was?"

"She said I knew him, but she wouldn't tell me. Didn't want to jinx it."

Hal shifted forward in his chair. "Did she tell you anything about him? Anything at all?"

Washburn worried the tissue between her fingers, leaving a trail of white cotton on the tabletop. "She said I'd be surprised, that he was someone she'd overlooked." She glanced up. "She said she'd always thought he was boring."

"Boring," Hal repeated, and she nodded enthusiastically, as if it was a breakthrough. As though he could identify the killer by this new evidence. He'd met half of that office. They were all boring.

Maybe he should go back to the list of employees and narrow it down by men. And then what? There were a dozen men. A dozen boring men.

"Do you know where they went for dinner?"

"She told me. It was new, flashy."

He had to resist rubbing his face. "Do you remember the name of it?"

"I know she said." She began to cry again. "But I can't think of it. It's gone from my head. I'm so sorry."

"It's okay. It might come to you," he said softly. He wouldn't have used his real name at the restaurant. Or would he?

"I have another question for you, Ms. Washburn."

She looked up expectantly.

"Do you recall if Denise used a water bottle?"

"Sure. She always had a water bottle at work. We all do. There's water in the break room, but there are never any cups."

"Was there one she normally brought to the office?"

"She kept one there, I think. Clear with a straw. It had a sticker on it from her son's school or something."

"Not a blue metal one?"

"No," Sarah said. "I have a blue one. And mine is metal. My sister gave it to me. One of those new ones. Keeps water really cold. I can fill it with cold water before bed, and it's still cold the next morning."

"You have a blue water bottle."

She nodded.

Hal found a picture on his phone. "A bottle like this one?"

"That's it. That's my water bottle." She squinted. "Is that at Denise's house? I must've left it in her car. We filled it with wine for the movi—" She stopped.

"For the movies?" he asked.

She hesitated, looking worried.

"I don't care about the wine, Ms. Washburn. When did you go the movies?"

She thought a minute. "It was a Wednesday. Not last week. Must've been the week before." Her eyes grew wide. "It was the same night."

"The same night as what?"

"The same night that she was in the pharmacy. We went to the movies, and she was going to spend the night. We made up the couch for her. Only when I woke up, she was gone."

Hal studied Sarah Washburn. A woman whose friend had gotten her drunk in order to steal her access card and break into a pharmacy for a drug that she intended to use to kill the married man who had jilted her.

She'd brought the Adriamycin with her, which meant she'd been planning to kill him. But if she had killed Todd Posner, she would have known what it took to get him to drink it. So why not use the Taser she'd used on Posner? Or the horse sedative?

He thought back. "Has Denise missed other days in the office? Besides last week?"

"No. That's why I was so surprised she didn't show up to work yesterday. A group of us were saving up vacation days to go to Mexico. A group of us were planning to go down in the early spring, you know. When it's rainy . . ." Her voice trailed off.

Ben Gustafson would have been killed while Denise Ross was at work. So were there two killers? Denise Ross and who?

He looked across the table at the weeping, red-faced woman across from him. Was she a killer? It was impossible to believe.

"Does Denise have other friends she's close to? People she might have confided in?"

Washburn shook her head. "I don't think so. She hates her ex, and she's not real close with her son."

"What about in the office?" Hal pressed. He wanted to know who the new man was. He had a gut feeling that they were on the cusp of finding this guy.

"Really only me," Washburn said. "I don't think she had a lot of friends."

His phone buzzed across the scarred tabletop. *The lab.* He'd gotten all he could from her anyway. "I appreciate you coming in," Hal told Washburn.

She was wide-eyed. "That's it?"

"That's it," he said. "We'll be in touch." Though he doubted that was true. He walked from the room, lifting the phone to his ear. "Harris."

"It's Naomi. I found something on Gustafson's phone."

"What?"

"It's an app called ProCall."

"Never heard of it."

"Pretty new, I think," Naomi said.

"What does it do?"

"Instead of calling a company to fix your appliance or install something, you can use the app to hire someone. It's cheaper and usually faster. There's a bunch of these kinds of apps popping up."

"You're saying Gustafson stopped to install cable for someone else?"

"I'm not sure yet, but he had a ProCall Service Provider account and about forty reviews on his work, so it looks like he was taking calls. Maybe evenings or weekends."

"Or maybe in between company service calls," Hal said. In the middle of the workday, which would explain the gap in his schedule. "Can you find out where he was right before he was killed?"

"Roger's got a call in to ProCall. He's hoping to bypass the warrant stage."

"Call me as soon as you get anything."

"Always do."

Hal left the building and walked down the street to Starbucks. He'd hoped to see Schwartzman. They'd left things badly the day before. Why wouldn't she tell him what was in the plastic bag she had carried into Spencer's house? Why would she have had a bag at all?

He tried to recall what he knew about the day she'd gone to Spencer's house and finally confronted him. It was all such a blur. Him trying to reach her. Harper trying to reach her. When he'd heard she was okay, he was so relieved that he'd barely bothered with why she had gone there in the first place. Maybe she'd hoped to find something to prove his guilt. Had she brought gloves so that she didn't leave prints? She could have kept those in a pocket.

From the video it looked like the plastic bag had some bulk, more than gloves could account for. She'd told him she'd brought tools, in case she needed to break in to the house. That was the story she'd given ADA Patchett, too.

What had she been planning? Was it really to break in? Or was it something worse? In which case, maybe he didn't want to know after all.

The Starbucks was quiet, a rarity, so he decided to sit awhile. He splurged on a Venti Mocha and watched the barista top him off with extra whipped cream. She gave him a nice smile. Attractive.

He took a seat in the corner, his back to the window, and opened the file on Joe Strom. Strom had graduated from the University of North Carolina at Chapel Hill in '66, gotten an MBA in '72. Strom Inc. was started in '76. All looked pretty clean. No arrests. No IRS audits. No complaints with the business bureau, no lawsuits ever filed against him. He had a few items that were settled in mediation—business stuff, likely. And then the suit that was filed in October 2002. Four months before he'd died.

The defendant was listed as Spencer Henry MacDonald.

Hal lifted the mocha and took a long drink. So there had been a lawsuit. That was a long way from linking Spencer to Joe Strom's death.

The skin on Hal's neck seemed to tighten, and he reached back to rub it. *Spencer?* The idea that he might have killed someone more than fourteen years ago? Or the fact that the odds were increasing that Schwartzman's tormentor was not going to stay behind bars?

He felt it again and looked up. A blond man stood at the end of the bar, the same man he'd seen watching Schwartzman when they were in the coffee shop last week. His hands were shoved deep into his pants pockets, his head lowered on his neck like a turtle trying to retract into its shell. The expression on his face was pure hate. Hal followed his gaze, half expecting to see Schwartzman. Instead the man was focused on the barista who had given Hal the extra whipped cream.

Hal closed the file on Strom and tucked it under his arm, taking his coffee and walking to the end of the bar. He stopped and stared at the blond man, peering down on him from five or six inches of additional height. Barely a moment passed before the narrowed, angry eyes shifted to him. They went wide, then narrowed again.

"You have a problem?" Hal asked.

The man looked around like the question was an affront. "Uh, no. I'm waiting for my coffee." He dragged the words between his teeth.

"You look angry."

"I am. That ni—" He clapped his mouth closed, shoved his hands deeper into his pockets. Fists were balled against his thighs, the shape of his knuckles visible through the fabric. "It's taking forever," he spat.

Hal crossed his arms. No way this skinny white dude was going to call her that. Before he could ask, the barista set a coffee on the counter with a thunk, sending a little toss of foam up through the lid.

She walked away, and the man stared at it and then after her.

"That's your coffee," she called back from across the bar. "Says 'Roy.' That's your name, right?"

Roy pulled a handful of napkins from the dispenser and wrapped the coffee in them before carrying it out the door. He skirted people, careful not to touch anyone as he used his foot to kick the door open and scuttle outside.

"Who is that guy?" Hal asked.

The barista shrugged. "Nut. Germaphobe or some damn thing. I've only been at this store for two weeks, but he's always like that. He's nothing," she said, waving toward the door. "You shoulda seen the guys down on Market Street near Hyde."

Market Street was home to a huge homeless population. Actually, San Francisco was home to a huge homeless population. And more coming all the time. But that guy—Roy—didn't look homeless. And he didn't look crazy—at least not mentally ill crazy.

He just looked mean.

And Hal didn't like the idea that he was watching Schwartzman.

As if he didn't have enough to worry about already.

32

Schwartzman finished work and left the morgue at three thirty on Friday. Her phone was in her pants pocket. They would be able to reach her if they needed her.

Three days until the final chemo treatment. Get through that and then decide about the house. Then she would deal with Hal.

She had not heard from him other than one e-mail to ask a follow-up question on Denise Ross's murder. An e-mail. Hal never e-mailed. He was lucky because she'd been sitting at her computer at the time. She replied within minutes.

Then nothing. No thank-you. No updates.

She had worked four homicides this week and not a single one with Hal. Walking past the department, into the morgue, she was always on the lookout for him. She considered calling. But what would she say? She couldn't tell him what she'd done at Spencer's. That would only jeopardize his job. And he wasn't going to let it go.

And she didn't know what business it was of his if she bought a house. No, she *did* know. It was none of his business. She had a right to move on, and she didn't need anyone's permission.

That morning she had arrived to two autopsies—both unattended deaths, both natural causes. She felt disjointed from the case that had been on her mind for weeks. After four related murders, there should be a flurry of action around her. But instead she'd heard nothing. Her part was done. Unless there was another body.

From the department, she drove to meet Ken at a bungalow-style house for sale in Noe Valley. It had been under contract—briefly—but the contract had fallen through on the pest report. The water damage to the tune of $65,000 probably didn't help.

She followed the directions to a tree-lined street fewer than four miles from the station. The trip took under fifteen minutes. Guerrero Street got backed up sometimes, but there were always side street options.

A good distance from work. A good neighborhood. She liked the street.

Ken was already parked in front of the house, but he pulled away when she showed up, waving her into the one-car parking spot on the curb. He returned a few minutes later from down the street where he had left his car.

He gave her a single-armed hug and a kiss on the cheek, and they stood in the street, looking at the little house.

"It's a little like a jungle," he teased.

It was true. The front of the house was a sea of overgrown fern plants and a half dozen Japanese maple trees of different sizes and ages. A camellia tree hung over the ferns on one side, and the block of bougainvillea on the other was so dense the front door was hardly visible. It reminded her of something Alice in Wonderland might enter with one of her pills. The other houses on the block had been rebuilt, expanded to the edge of their lots. This was the only one that was set back from the curb. And the only single story.

The listing advertised it as a "future four-bedroom home." A teardown. Maybe for some, but Schwartzman had no need for a four-bedroom house. The two bedrooms and den in this one, thirteen hundred square feet with two bathrooms, was already almost twice what she currently occupied.

She liked it immediately. There was a window seat with a built-in desk in the small back den, and its rustic surface reminded her of her father's desk. Was his law book still sitting on the side table in the glass case? She wondered if her mother would let her have it. Her mother had been so desperate to get rid of certain things—the rest of the Evan Williams bourbon, her father's work papers that had been stacked in the kitchen and beside his bed, the files on his desk that she knew had to go back to his office—any reason that someone from the outside might have to enter that room.

And then his clothes went—not all of them, just the casual things he wore around the house—T-shirts, pajamas, socks, and underwear. After that she wanted the older suits and more casual work clothes gone. Then, maybe a year after his death, it was the suits he'd worn around the time of his death.

Other than the active files, her mother had left his office untouched. Although it had been more than seven years ago since Schwartzman was there, it was hard to imagine the office would look different. Or that her father's tuxedo—the one her mother had so loved him in—wouldn't be at the far back of her mother's closet, still hanging behind the row of her long dresses. The tuxedo, his office—her mother cherished those items. Schwartzman herself had felt an intense desire to touch her father's tuxedo when she'd seen it hanging there. In the coat she'd found a clean white pocket square and the ticket stub from a fund-raiser at the country club.

Ken was standing at the back of the house, studying the garden through a window. There, three crossed poles had been tied like a teepee for snap peas, and boxes had been built into the ground where something still grew.

"It's garlic," Ken said, pointing to the green reeds along one row.

She'd had a garden when she was married to Spencer. Flowers mostly. It was not yet trendy to grow your own food, and Spencer would have worried what others might think, that it made her look too hippie, too alternative. Or that it made some statement on their financial security.

She tried to imagine herself out in the dirt, weeding, planting. She would have liked to be that kind of woman. She wasn't certain she was.

"Come look at the porch out back." The Realtor's voice broke through her daydream.

Schwartzman and Ken followed Sharon to the back door and down the steps into the afternoon air. It was starting to feel more like fall, and she welcomed the cool.

The plants were similar to those in the front yard, but here the concentration felt in proportion to the space—cozy rather than claustrophobic.

The entire yard was fenced, and it occurred to her that she could have a dog here. She thought of Posner's dog, an Australian shepherd–retriever mix, the vet had guessed. A dog was a huge commitment, and she was surprised at how much the idea appealed to her.

"The porch is over there," Sharon said. "The door is off the master bedroom," she added.

Schwartzman and Ken walked along a path of large flat stones and up three steps to the deck. Overhead was a lattice gazebo covered in wisteria. The vine was dormant, but a few dried flowers between the planks of the deck told her that the vine's flower was white. The vines ran along the deck and down to two similar lattices on the far side.

A rug lay across the deck's surface, a loosely woven geometrical print that made the space feel both comfortable and stylish. Along the rug's edge were a wicker love seat and two large wicker chairs. A matching coffee table sat in the center.

"Nice," Ken said.

"We're too early for it this evening, but the sunset is stunning from here." Sharon pointed to the fence that bordered the yard. "The sun sets just over there, and you get great color."

The three stared toward the place in the sky where the sun would set. Sharon excused herself.

"She's a good salesperson," Schwartzman said, trying to shake herself out of what felt like a child's dream.

"Maybe. Or you like the house."

She exhaled. "I do. I really like it."

"If you can make it work—financially, I mean—then you should buy it."

She squeezed out the thoughts that threaded into her mind like a toxic gas. When would he come? What would he do? *I am moving on. No matter what, I'm going to live my life.* If she could do it financially. And she could, especially since she didn't plan on tearing it down. She would paint and update here and there. The inheritance from her aunt Ava made financial decisions much easier. "I am."

"Are . . . ?" Ken asked.

"I'm going to buy this house."

Ken smiled and squeezed her arm. "Congratulations."

After Schwartzman went over the details of her offer with the Realtor, Ken and Schwartzman went to dinner to celebrate at the nearby Cuban place he'd been telling her about. The food was amazing, and Ken had found a rare gem on the menu to go with their meal—a Cuban single malt. She had to stop herself from having a second glass, but even one was enough to make her feel risky, adventurous. She was buying a house. No. She was buying a home.

Her home.

With heat rising in her cheeks, she invited Ken back to her apartment. They drove separately, and she beat him back by a few minutes. Quickly she changed out of her work clothes and poured them a couple of glasses of the Evan Williams reserve bourbon. As an afterthought, she splashed a little extra in her glass and swallowed it to calm her nerves.

The buzzer announced Ken's arrival. "Schwartzman."

"Dr. Schwartzman. Mr. Macy is here."

"Please send him up."

"Certainly, Doctor."

She replaced the phone in the cradle and stepped in front of the mirror that hung beside the front door. The makeup she'd put on before work this morning was gone. What was left was the gray-black shadow of mascara that had melted into a washed-out smudge below her eyes. She rubbed it away and moved the part of her hair from one side to the other, hoping it would show more of her hair's wave and less of the frizz.

Neither was better than the other.

She turned sideways and touched the hair at the back of her neck where the Penguin Cold Cap didn't reach. It had thinned from the chemo, but otherwise she still had a full head of hair.

Her heart drumming in her chest, she pinched her cheeks. After a glance at her pale lips, she dug through the purse for the lip gloss that was somewhere loose in the bottom. She painted the slick reddish tint across her lips and then promptly rubbed it off in her palm.

What was she doing? He'd agreed to come back with her. He obviously didn't care what she looked like.

Stop trying so hard.

A knock on the door.

She forced a deep breath. *Calm down.* She checked the peephole before opening the door to Ken Macy, who waited to be invited in. "I poured us some bourbon."

"Perfect."

He shrugged out of his coat and draped it across the back of the couch. He handed her a glass and raised his own. "To your new home."

There was too much air in her lungs. They clinked glasses, and she tipped hers to her lips, swallowed the liquid, and let it burn down her throat. Set the glass on the table. Ken followed suit. She took a step closer toward him, but he stopped her.

"Music," he whispered. He fiddled with her stereo until she heard the beautiful wail of Coltrane's horn.

When he returned, he took her hand and wrapped it around his waist, gripped her other hand in his, and led her across the floor.

Dancing. God, she was actually dancing. A laugh caught in her throat.

"You can't be laughing at my dancing," he said into her ear.

"I'm not. I promise."

"I was the only dance partner for five sisters. I've been slow dancing since I was five."

She laughed out loud then, and he pulled her close. Pressed against the warmth of his chest, she felt the soft cotton of his T-shirt on her cheek. He smelled of bourbon and aftershave.

The song ended. An advertisement about insurance. Ken chuckled softly, and she could feel the vibrations through his ribs. She stepped back to look at him.

The warm brown eyes. His wide smile. The tiny gap between his bottom teeth.

He caught her gaze on his mouth, leaned in, and kissed her. She caught herself off guard by kissing him back.

Seven years. She hadn't even let herself stand close to a man since her escape. Shoving the past aside, she let herself be in this moment, let him hold her, kiss her. The music purred in the background, and she recalled what it had been like to be caught up in a moment, to be swept away. Ken ran his finger along her shoulder, studying her face, as if to ask if she was sure.

And she was, and that surprised her. Until now she hadn't really accepted that this was an option, that after Spencer, there could be physical contact that was anything other than violent and cruel.

They moved across the living room, down the hall into her bedroom. She led, holding his hand. Other than the moonlight that streamed through the open blinds, the room was dark. She didn't reach for the light but let him lead her to the bed. The bed where he had . . . no.

She squeezed her eyes closed against the memory, pressed her mouth to his neck.

His fingers touched the skin of her belly, their tips grazing across her abdomen and back before he slid his hands up her back to pull her tighter to him. There was no bra to find. She'd taken the prosthetic off the second she'd come in the door. A habit. But he knew about the double mastectomy. Did he know that she'd opted not to have the reconstruction? That she no longer had breast tissue?

She started to pull away, to explain.

"You're beautiful," he whispered, meeting her gaze. His eyes assured her that she didn't need to say the words. He knew.

He tugged the shirt from her pants, lifting it gently over her arms. Cold air struck the skin on her arms. The tank top covered her scars. He moved slowly. His breath and mouth were warm and soft as he laid her back on the bed.

He yanked his own T-shirt over his head, letting it fall to the floor.

She saw the cut of his abdomen, the thick roundness of strong shoulders. Ken's chest hair formed a slightly misshapen heart. She reached out to put her fingers through it when she noticed the thick pink lines dotted throughout, like earthworms against dark pavement. Then she realized. *Scars.* A gasp escaped her lips without warning. She sat up on the bed.

Ken froze.

"I'm sorry," she whispered.

He said nothing.

Her pulse pounded.

He shook his head, not looking down at his own chest. His gaze held hers.

She had a sudden desire to leave, to turn on the lights and open the shades, to fill the space with blinding light. Instead she forced her fingers outward until they met with his chest. Felt the hair between them. Closed her eyes and fingered the ridges of keloid where the scar tissue had built up. Wondered if she could find all eighteen stab wounds by palpation.

Slowly, Ken leaned down to kiss her, his fingers on the inside of her arms, then stroking the back of her neck. She tried to focus on the kiss. How wonderful it felt to have someone so close. How much she cared about this man.

His chest was imprinted in her mind. She opened her eyes and pulled him against her, trying to push out the vision of the scars. Every time she blinked—even with her eyes closed—she saw the wounds. She had to look, had to see.

Eighteen stab wounds.

She pressed him over onto his back. Straddled above him and focused on his face. His fingers nudged the bottom of her tank top. As if to ask if she was ready.

With a quick breath for courage, she pulled the tank top off over her head. She did it slowly, to give him time before looking at the shock in his eyes. The disgust.

Even with the tank off, she kept her eyes closed, waited for the sound of his reaction, for his panic at seeing the remnants of her breasts. His fingertips trailed across her skin without hesitation. Not along the lines of her wounds. He just touched her. Touched her front as he might her back. Did he know she'd lost the sensitivity in her breasts, that the sensation he gave her was no different from a touch on her arm? No. She felt even less. The surgeries had damaged those sensitive nerve endings.

He pulled her toward him and kissed her chest. His lips pressed on the narrow scars. He didn't care.

She was both grateful and shamed. She had been so focused on how he would react to her mastectomy that she hadn't considered what it would be like to see his scars. To see what Spencer had done to him.

He doesn't blame you.

She took his chin and tilted his mouth toward her. Took it forcefully, fighting back the images in her mind. The white pallor of Ken lying beside her. The blood, her own panic. The thoughts of how narrowly he had escaped death.

Gently, she pushed him flat onto his back again.

Closing her eyes, she pressed her lips to the wounds, one by one, working her way across and down as though she were reading the history of that night by braille. Tears flowed across her face, dripped into his chest hair, across the scars.

"Anna."

He wiped them away with his thumbs. But they continued until the memories were not only of Ken dying beside her but of being in Ava's garage, tied up and alone, of being in that house, the house where she had lived as a prisoner. Then, of stumbling into the strange, dark room that Spencer had built especially for her. Of seeing herself projected onto the wall.

Her own voice crying out, "Help me. Please, God. Help me."

She brought her arms into her chest as the tears turned to sobs. Spencer was here. It didn't matter that she had new sheets or a new bed. He was still right here. He was in Ken's skin—carved there like the brand on a cow.

She could never be away from Spencer, not if she continued to live here. She had to get out. She wanted to scream, to pound her fists. She wanted out. *Let me out.* Hadn't he done enough? Hadn't he killed enough people? Ava and Frances Pinckney and now maybe Joe Strom and possibly her father and . . . God only knew who else.

Weren't they enough? Hadn't she suffered enough?

Ken's arms wrapped around her. He pulled her into his lap and held her.

"I'm sorry," she whispered. "I don't know why I'm . . ."

"You're okay. It's okay, Anna." He smoothed her hair, and she pressed against him, trying to control herself.

The sobs slowed, and she swiped at her face with the sides of one fist. She blinked hard and sat up. The tears continued to fall. She didn't know why she was such a mess.

Ken's face pressed against hers. His eyes closed. "I am here. Whatever you need, however slow."

He would wait.

She watched his face, the furrow in his brow, the emotion in the set of his mouth.

Ken would wait for her.

And then she knew. Being out of this apartment would make it easier to be away from the memories, but her problem wasn't just the house.

It was Ken.

Ken was a reminder of how easily Spencer could hurt those around her. How much there was to risk.

He forgave her for what had happened. It wasn't her fault.

How she wished that were enough. But it wasn't about his forgiveness.

It was about hers.

Because she would never forgive herself for what Spencer had done to Ken Macy. And that meant she could not love Ken Macy without simultaneously hating herself.

With that thought in mind, she wrapped her arms around him and held on.

33

Monday morning Hal made an appointment to meet with Helen Tribble, the woman who had worked with Ruth Finlay at the foundation for almost fifteen years. And though he had been avoiding Schwartzman, he left a voicemail when she was in her chemo treatment and told her he was available to come get her. He also said he looked forward to catching up. He'd meant to sound casual, friendly. They had to talk about Spencer.

After leaving her a message, he arranged his day so that he could leave at the drop of a hat to pick her up from the hospital. Hailey had more task force stuff. Surely she'd told Schwartzman that he was going to fill in for her.

But Schwartzman never called.

So she'd gotten someone else to pick her up. But she didn't have someone else. *No.* That wasn't true. She had Ken Macy. Hal considered calling down to the Northern District to check Macy's schedule, but how was that going to look? Like he was an idiot. A desperate, creepy idiot. Macy was the boyfriend. Let him pick her up.

Damn, he'd made a mess of things between them. And now it had been so long since they'd talked that things were going to be awkward. He hated this. By the end of the day, he would talk to her. He'd show up at her house if he had to.

He visited Roger in the lab and worked some phone calls on a few outstanding cases. Then he spent an hour in the DA's office in preparation for an upcoming trial where he would be a key witness in convicting a man who had stabbed and killed a tourist during a foiled robbery attempt.

After that he drove out to visit Helen Tribble in the Sunset District. Tribble had been Ruth Finlay's right hand in running the Finlay Foundation from the day it was started.

As of that moment, Helen Tribble was also the last lead Hal had on the case.

—

Tribble was a long, lean woman who appeared to be of Scandinavian descent. Her straight gray hair with a hint of blonde was cut even with her chin, accentuating a harsh, square jaw. She had two small dogs—one black and one white—that circled her feet as she stood in the doorway.

She invited Hal to enter. As he stepped into the small foyer, she pointed to his shoes. "You can leave those here."

He bent to remove his shoes, and the two dogs sniffed his fingers as he worked to loosen the laces. In his stockinged feet, he followed her into a small sitting room. He took a seat in an armchair so as not to disrupt the couches whose throw pillows appeared to have been set with a tape measure to ensure exact spacing. Tribble, however, lounged back in the center of the couch and patted twice. The two dogs hopped up and settled on either side of her.

"Thank you for seeing me," he began.

Tribble nodded, so Hal went right to it. "I understand you worked alongside Ruth Finlay."

"I did. For fifteen years."

Hal opened his notebook. "How did you meet Mrs. Finlay?"

"My niece was in the hospital at the same time as Herb—Mr. Finlay. My brother had a difficult time with his daughter's disease. Her mother was even worse off. They had two other children at home, so I took up the slack," she explained. "Ruth's kids were great with Kerry—that's my niece. They kept her entertained." She looked down at the white dog on her right, rubbed his—or her?—belly when he flipped onto his back.

Hal said nothing, waiting for her to continue.

"Cancer makes for a strange experience, especially when you're a child. Those three kids were all close in age—teenagers. My niece Kerry was almost sixteen. The three would spend hours together. Kerry was really into makeup, so they spent a lot of time doing that. She had a whole theater kit, and they'd practice. Create these fake wounds on the side of their faces. Scared the hell out of the nursing staff. Kerry made up Justin to look like Voldemort." She smiled at some memory.

She rubbed the two dogs, her hands moving naturally as she went on. "I suspect Justin had a crush on Kerry, so he was willing to sit and watch. Justin was pretty easygoing, too. His sister seemed a little crazy, but what do I know about teenage girls?"

Hal wasn't sure what he was looking for, but this wasn't it. Still, he understood Tribble's desire to remember the past. He heard this often in interviewing older people.

"It worked out well until Kerry got too sick for visitors. She died before Mr. Finlay. A few months before, as I recall. I spent some hours in the hospital, reading to some of the younger kids when I could. I never had children, so I had the time. Ruth and I kept in touch. She was in quite a spiral after her husband's death. And the kids—well, the girl in particular—they were a lot to manage."

"Sounds like your niece was lucky to have you," Hal said.

She folded her hands into her lap. The two dogs nudged at her to keep rubbing, but she ignored them.

"When did your work at the Finlay Foundation end?" Hal asked.

"January," she said. "Ruth was hospitalized. I saw her in the hospital, but when she was released, she resigned from the organization."

"And your work ended then, too?"

"Almost immediately."

"Do you keep in contact with anyone from the organization?"

"I tried to visit Ruth a few times," she said. "But they keep her very sheltered."

"Who is 'they'?"

"The children." She paused. "Well, Justin, in particular."

"You've tried to see her?"

"Oh, I've tried, all right. I've been to the house. I've called and e-mailed. I got her on the phone a couple of times, but she sounds terrible."

Hal thought about how Justin had placed his chair so far from the bed, how careful he was about the distance from the mother. "Seems like he's worried she'll get sick again."

"I know," she said, sounding resigned. "And when I've e-mailed, she's dismissive. I imagine she's worn down from the illness."

"The organization was important to her?"

"It was her life."

"That and her kids, you mean."

Tribble looked up with one brow cocked. "Ruth was almost forty when she got pregnant. She once confided that she hadn't planned to have children. She and Herb were very happy without them."

"The son is very protective of her."

"It must work for her," Tribble said, her hands returning to the dogs. "She hasn't told him to go to hell."

Despite a couple moments of frustration, Ruth Finlay had seemed to enjoy her son's fussing. He glanced at the blank page in his notebook. "Did you know Todd Posner?"

"Of course. He was one of the foundation's biggest champions. I heard he was killed."

"He was," Hal confirmed. "Can you think of someone in the foundation who would have wanted to harm him? One of the board members, maybe?"

"Oh, that guy fought with everyone. He and I had a shouting match or two, but I can't see someone killing him." The white dog rolled onto his back again, but instead of rubbing it, Tribble pushed him over as though his behavior was inappropriate for company. The dog made a small, disappointed whine and settled into the couch as she scratched behind his ears.

"He held some sway over Ruth though," Tribble went on. "I could see how that was frustrating for the board. Ruth tended to give more credence to Todd Posner than to most anyone else, including me," she added after a moment. "I don't understand why. Todd came to a charity event with his wife once, and from the way he treated her, I might have killed him."

"Do you have any idea if Dr. Posner had seen Ruth Finlay recently?"

"I don't. I haven't had any contact with Todd since I left the foundation."

"Do you know a Dr. David Kemp?"

She hesitated and then shook her head.

"What about someone by the name of Denise Ross?"

Again she shook her head. Maybe the foundation was just more dead ends. But then why was Sandy Coleman's name on that piece of paper in Posner's mouth? "Did you know Sandy Coleman?" Hal asked.

"The kid with AML? I remember her."

"Who would have known about her?" Hal asked, pen poised.

Tribble frowned at him.

"Would anyone outside the organization know what the foundation did for her? Would they know her story?"

Tribble thought about that. "I remember having a conversation about her with another oncologist—the one who took her case."

"Do you remember the name?" Hal prompted.

"Neil. No, Norman. Norman . . ."

"Fraser?" he asked when she went silent.

"Yes," she confirmed. "Norman Fraser."

"Do you recall what Dr. Fraser had to say about Sandy?"

"Well, he took over the case when Posner said he didn't think the odds made it a worthwhile gamble."

"Do you recall anything specific? Did Fraser seem angry that Posner didn't treat Coleman? Did they argue?" Hal still held his pen poised.

"I really don't know," she admitted. "I only met Dr. Fraser the one time. We were at the hospital, where several members of the foundation were meeting with Sandy Coleman and her parents."

Hal made a note. "I was under the impression that Dr. Fraser worked closely with Sandy."

"He did."

"But you only met him the one time."

"We had a number of doctors who volunteered to take a case now and again. Most of them I never met."

Hal looked down at the note he'd made. It said simply, "Fraser." Again. But he'd ruled Fraser out, hadn't he? "Anyone else stand out?" he asked.

"You mean in Sandy Coleman's case?" Tribble clarified.

"Yes. People who would have known about her condition, about the foundation's help."

"Oh," Tribble said, sitting up. "I believe there was an article in the paper about her."

Hal made a note. "Do you know which paper?"

"Pretty sure it was the *Chronicle*." She stood then. "I might have a copy. Hang on." As soon as she left the room, the two dogs ran across the room and jumped into Hal's lap. With his notepad in his left hand, he rubbed the black one on his right. The white one whined, so he set the notebook down and rubbed them both simultaneously. It made him think how hard it would be to have twins.

Tribble returned to the room. "Rice, Noodle, down!"

The two dogs hopped off Hal.

"Here it is."

Hal stood and took the article Tribble handed him. It was a human-interest piece, about four inches by six or seven. The color picture was of Ruth Finlay seated beside Sandy Coleman.

"You can keep that," Tribble told him, still standing.

"Thank you." Hal didn't sit again. "Have you had much interaction with the new executive director?"

"Schenck?" She shrugged. "He's fine. He's young but smart. I can't see him being aggressive with Posner. He's seemed more apologetic than anything."

"Apologetic for what?"

"For my getting pushed out. He offered to keep me on—said he thought it would be helpful to keep the old guard." Her lips thinned as she crossed her arms. "The old guard. That's what he called me."

Hal thanked her and left Tribble's home. Checked his phone as he reached the curb. No word from Schwartzman.

Hal got into his car and read the article about Sandy Coleman. It was a puff piece. The interview with Tribble confirmed what he already knew—Ruth Finlay was the only person who liked Todd Posner. Nothing in their conversation gave him any new persons of interest to pursue, and he had no additional reason to continue to explore Norman Fraser.

Frustrated, Hal set the article aside and thought of Schwartzman again. Why hadn't she called him? Was she okay? He dialed her number and listened to it ring. Once, twice, three . . . voicemail.

"To hell with it," he muttered, pulling away from the curb and heading toward Schwartzman's apartment building. He parked in front and went inside.

The young man at the front desk was maybe midtwenties. He was tall and lean and dressed in a maroon suit. His high cheekbones and the angle of his eyes suggested he had Asian heritage, though his green eyes suggested Caucasian heritage, as well. His name tag read "Alan." "Can I help you, sir?"

"I'm here to see Dr. Annabelle Schwartzman."

Alan eyed him. The look was less suspicious than curious. "You're the inspector," he said after a moment. "You were here the night . . ."

"Yes." Hal drew out his badge. "I'm Inspector Hal Harris."

Alan studied the badge without touching it.

"I'm not here on police business. Just as a friend," Hal said. "She had—" He was going to mention the chemotherapy. He closed his mouth.

Alan nodded. "She arrived home about two hours ago, and I helped her upstairs. She was quite sick."

Why did Alan have to help her if Macy was with her? Did it take two people? Was she that sick?

"She wasn't alone, was she?"

"She was," Alan confirmed. "She came by a car service, I believe."

"Are you sure? She wasn't with a friend?"

"I don't think so," the young man said. "The car was a black SUV, and the driver wasn't familiar. I'm pretty certain there was an Uber sign in the windshield."

So Macy didn't go to the hospital. And Schwartzman hadn't called him back so he could pick her up. Instead she'd been willing to come home from the hospital via Uber rather than take him up on his offer. The thought made him ill.

"I think she may be sleeping."

Hal wanted to go upstairs, check on her. Even if just to see that she was sleeping.

"She's usually extremely tired on the day of her treatments."

"I'd like to know that she's okay," Hal pressed.

Alan studied him. "I can ring her."

Hal exhaled. "Please."

Alan lifted a phone off the desk and dialed a series of numbers. The two men stood in silence while they waited. With every passing minute, Hal felt a heightened sense of dread. Finally Alan replaced the phone in its cradle as Hal pulled his own phone from his pocket.

I'm in the lobby, he texted Schwartzman. Want to make sure you're okay.

"I can call again a little later," Alan offered. "And I'll leave a message under her door to have her call down if she needs anything. I'm here until ten this evening."

Hal stared at the phone, willing something to happen.

The word *delivered* appeared below the message.

"Inspector?"

Hal nodded. "Yes. If you could please check in." He folded open his badge wallet and pulled a business card from the slot behind the badge. "My mobile number is here. If you would call or text me that you've reached her and she's okay."

"Certainly. I can ask Dr. Schwartzman to contact you."

"Right," Hal said. "She's got the number."

He refreshed his phone screen and saw three dots under his message. She was typing. "Wait. I think she's responding."

Alan said nothing.

Hal knew he sounded desperate. She was fine. Clearly, if she was responding, she was upstairs, breathing, probably resting.

What was wrong with him?

What did he expect? A frightening message from Spencer? The dots stopped. No message. Was she trying to ask for help?

The dots started again. His breath seemed to catch in his throat.

A small vibration and then two words popped onto the screen.

ok sleeping

Hal waited for something more. I'll call you back. Or can we talk later? Or . . . but nothing came.

"Is there anything else I can do, Inspector?" Alan asked.

It felt like a gentle brush-off. *Go on now, Inspector Harris.*

"No," Hal admitted. "Thank you."

With a last glance at his phone, he turned to leave.

She needed her rest. He knew that. Pressing her to see him, to answer his phone call, to text him more information, that was all selfish.

He would wait.

He would hate it, but he would wait.

34

Tuesday disappeared in a fugue of nausea and exhaustion. Calls piled up. The Realtor called with last-minute questions about the offer. Then Hailey and a few other women from the force called to check on her. Ken, of course. They'd had a couple of conversations since Friday night. He had wanted to see her over the weekend, but she had begged off, saying she wanted to hunker down before the final chemo. He'd been understanding, and she'd felt worse for it.

She would have to tell him. Soon.

Hal had also been in touch yesterday. Two voicemails from him and a half dozen texts. Some straight-out questions about how she was doing along with several questions about the case that she could tell were just excuses for her to call him back. She finally called him early afternoon. They spoke for less than a minute.

"You sound awful," he'd said.

"I feel worse."

"I can come," he offered. "Bring something."

"I need to sleep it off," she said. "Give me until tomorrow. If I don't surface, you can come find me."

"Are you sure?" he'd asked. "I don't mind coming by, and I can get whatever might taste good." It sounded almost like an apology.

"I'm not in danger," she promised him. "I just feel awful."

He made her promise to text or call if she needed something. His tone was so fierce, so protective, as if he felt responsible for her safety. *Absurd.* She was an adult. She could manage this alone.

Cancer, she could manage alone.

Spencer . . . she needed to figure out how to manage that on her own, too.

She woke in the evening to the ringing phone. *Ken.* She ignored the buzzing and lay back in the bed. As she stared at the ceiling, she reminded herself that the first day after chemo was the low point. She would be better soon. The worst was over. For now anyway. There would be regular tests to check for the cancer's return, but she would be optimistic. She had to be optimistic.

A double buzz indicated a voicemail. She would have to call Ken, tell him. Did he sense it? The abrupt ending to the few moments of intimacy? The fact that they didn't have sex, the awkward way they had lain together in her bed afterward before she'd rolled over and tried to sleep?

No. He was honest. He expected her to be honest.

Ken was perfect. He was kind and gentle. Funny. Strong. He respected her. He made her feel safe.

But those scars . . .

How could she see those and not remember?

But how could she punish him for getting caught in Spencer's web? She owed him.

But what did she owe him?

Did owing him mean she should date him? Be with him when the very sight of those wounds was like watching him being stabbed all over again? Like seeing Spencer? He deserved more. And despite the guilt, she knew that she deserved more, too.

Then she slept, a deep, dead sleep until the early hours of the morning. After that her rest was fitful until dawn. Moving in any fashion was painful, and the nausea grew so bad the next morning that she spent an hour vomiting into the trash can before getting out of bed. She'd sworn to tough it out without the antinausea medication, substituting home remedies like ginger rather than succumb to the drowsy side effects of the prescription medication. But this morning the nausea won. Ginger wasn't going to do the trick.

She put one of the melt-away antiemetics in her mouth, cringing as she swallowed the saliva that collected under her tongue. Her last bite of food had been before chemo yesterday, and what little water she'd had to drink wasn't sitting well. The antiemetic would also dehydrate her, but at least it would allow her to get some liquids into her system. Stuck in bed, hanging her head over a wastebasket, was the last thing she had time for.

She closed her eyes and waited for the medication to work, swallowing carefully and testing each movement for a warning that she was going to be sick again. At some point she fell asleep and woke again after nine.

Late now, she showered quickly, made herself peanut-butter toast—the only thing that she might be able to keep down—and headed for work.

—

In the morgue she went straight to the wall of metal drawer fronts. She'd been off work all weekend and yesterday, so she had no idea which drawers were occupied and which were empty. She could see their occupants on the computer, but she preferred to open the drawers and look at the deceased, as if she were meeting guests who had come to her house while she was away.

Thinking of the infant who had died of SIDS, she gripped the handle for drawer ten. Pulled it free. Inside was a black bag, a full-size adult body. She extended the drawer fully and unzipped the top of the bag. A man, somewhere between fifty-five and seventy. In the baby drawer.

She checked the computer file and confirmed that the man was an unattended death who had come in early that morning. Why would Wally have put him in that drawer? He knew better.

She pulled on a pair of gloves and opened his eyelids, one at a time. Even lifting her arms felt like exertion. She pressed the sleeve of her arm to her forehead, her body clammy, feverish. She zipped the bag back over the man, removed her gloves, and closed the drawer. Rested her forehead against the cold metal. She would need help today.

Medical examiners almost always worked with a morgue assistant, but Schwartzman had been guarded about help. She preferred being alone. But she would not be able to perform an autopsy on her own like this. She should have called in a replacement and taken the day off.

She lifted the phone off the morgue desk and dialed the front desk.

"Morgue," came a muffled voice.

"Wally?"

"No," the voice said, clear now. "It's Roy."

She pictured the strange blond man and shivered. "Is Wally there?"

"Out today on a family emergency. Afraid it's just me, Doc."

She considered working on her own but realized that was impossible. She would have to work with Roy. Schwartzman cleared the phlegm from her throat. "I'm going to need help with an autopsy. Can you come into the morgue in about ten minutes, please?"

"I'd love to," Roy said.

She thought again of the cold gaze from Roy. He worked for her. If he couldn't do the job respectfully . . . in her pocket, her phone vibrated. She was desperate to ignore it, to stay right there, but it might be a scene. She might be needed.

She pulled it out and read the words on the screen.

Everything set to make the offer today at 11:00 a.m. I'll call as soon as I have news.

The house. She was putting an offer on the house. She was going to own a home.

A flash of fear hit her, then a twinge of nausea. She drew a breath. This was good. She started to respond to the text when the phone rang. She accidentally hit the "Accept" button.

"Hello?" came a voice from the phone. A woman. A familiar voice but not the Realtor.

"Hello," Schwartzman said, lifting the phone to her ear.

"It's Laura Patchett." The ADA in South Carolina.

She swallowed back the nausea with a glance at the clock. Thirty minutes until she could take more medication. She sank onto the stool. "What can I do for you, Ms. Patchett?"

"The video that was playing in Mr. MacDonald's home? The one of you tied up?" Her tone was sharp, angry. More bad news.

"Yes," Schwartzman answered calmly.

"We have just learned that the video footage was filmed on your camera, Ms. Schwartzman."

Dr. Schwartzman. Again she imagined herself on that wall in Spencer's room. Her meek voice, calling for help. She cleared her throat, shook her head. Finally managed to say, "That's impossible."

"It's not impossible," Patchett responded, her voice tight. "The defense has pulled the data records. It's all there. The evidence suggests that *you* recorded that on your phone, and then *you* uploaded it to a Dropbox account under your e-mail."

She remembered the hours after she'd woken in Ava's garage. Trying to get untied, wanting desperately to escape before anyone saw her like that. The shame had consumed her. But there had been no way out. No way to cut the rope or pull it free. She'd had to call Harper Leighton.

She found her voice. "No," Schwartzman said through gritted teeth. "I did no such thing, Ms. Patchett. It would have been impossible since I was tied up."

"Well, that's what the defense is going to argue," Patchett said. "And we can't prove otherwise. There is no evidence that you didn't stage the whole thing yourself."

"Me? Ask Detective Leighton. She found me," Schwartzman said, hearing the tremor in her voice. "I don't have a Dropbox account. I didn't do that. He filmed it. He drugged me and tied me up!" She was shouting.

A shudder rang up her spine. *Spencer. No. Something else.* She turned.

Roy stood in the center of the morgue, staring at her. He smiled, a thin, hateful smile.

She didn't take her eyes off him. "No." She rolled the stool until her back was against the wall, lowered the receiver, and put her hand over the phone. "I need to handle this call," she told Roy. "I'll let you know when I'm ready to proceed."

Roy did not leave.

"Please go," she repeated.

"Excuse me?" Patchett said in her ear.

Roy did not budge.

"I was speaking to a colleague."

No word from Roy. His lips curled up into a smirk.

"The defense is pushing for immediate release," Patchett said. "And I've got nothing to use to hold him."

Schwartzman focused on the call. Spencer could not get out. He couldn't. "What about the necklace? The one found at his house?"

"The one seen a week earlier on Detective Leighton's daughter?" Patchett asked.

"Yes," Schwartzman said. "You need to run DNA tests on it."

"And what will that do?" Patchett snapped back. "If the DNA comes back as a match to Leighton's daughter, it looks like a plant."

"And what if it's mine?" She turned away from Roy, lowered her voice. "What if it matches my DNA?"

Patchett was quiet a moment. Schwartzman took it as encouragement. She stood and crossed to Roy, pressed the phone to her chest. "Get out of here."

"You looked scared, Doc."

She pointed. "Get out."

Roy started for the door with a little shrug.

Patchett was talking. "It would look like a plant."

"Wait," Schwartzman said. "What would look like a plant?"

"Your DNA," Patchett said. "The DA could charge *you*, Ms. Schwartzman."

Schwartzman felt a sharp pain in her chest, like an electric shock. "Charge *me*?"

"With planting evidence."

Schwartzman's voice caught in her throat.

"The Home Depot bag found in Mr. MacDonald's trash," Patchett said. "Knee pads that match the imprint on Ava Schwartzman's torso."

My aunt's torso.

"The dog hair . . . all the evidence has come under scrutiny."

Schwartzman's throat closed, and she fought to inhale. "Why? That evidence proves he did it."

"The bag found in Spencer MacDonald's garage trash can bears a strong resemblance to the sack you carried into the house, the one seen in the traffic video."

"You can't let him go," Schwartzman said, her voice losing its force.

The DA could charge her. Spencer had killed two people, motivated the death of another, and almost killed a fourth—Ken Macy—and they could charge *her*?

"It's not up to me. We have no evidence. The judge is ruling this afternoon."

Schwartzman gasped. *Today.*

"Unless there is something you can add? Something we don't know?"

The judge was ruling today on whether Spencer got out of jail. Whether he could get on a plane and show up and—

"Ms. Schwartzman?"

What did she have? What evidence could she come up with to keep him in jail? There had to be something. But she couldn't come up with a single thing. "I don't—I can't . . ."

"I'll be in touch, then," Patchett said.

The call ended, and she stared at the phone.

She had planned to testify against Spencer in court. But what if they asked her about the bag? Could she perjure herself knowing that she might be caught? That Spencer might still go free? Did she even take the risk of going back to South Carolina?

She couldn't. She wouldn't.

It wasn't just the testimony. It was the plans she'd made, plans to move forward.

How could she buy a house? How could she buy *that* house? At least in the apartment, there were guards and cameras. The front door to her condo was reinforced. Yes, Spencer might be able to sneak past the security measures, but that door? He wasn't getting through that without a battering ram or an explosive device.

The house was single level, windows all around, the wooded yard . . . moving in there would be like giving Spencer a key to the front door. The glass front door. There were a dozen easy ways inside that place. She would be a sitting duck. And now it wasn't a question of *if* Spencer would get out of jail.

It was only a matter of when.

Something touched her, and she spun around, letting out a shriek. Standing behind her, much too close, was Roy. The smile thinned, and an angry sneer took its place.

She stood from the stool, backed away from him. "What are you doing?"

"You're off the phone. I thought you'd want to work on that autopsy." There was a twang in his voice. *Southern?* Had she imagined it?

His angry smile. The hate.

"He sent you, didn't he?" she shouted. "He sent you to work here, to intimidate me. It won't work, Roy. You're done."

Roy grinned widely. He almost laughed. "I have no idea what you're talking about, Doc. Sounds like the stress is getting to you. Maybe you're not up to the job?"

"Spencer sent you. That's why you look so smug, so angry." She was shaking, her fingers trying to dial her phone. Hal.

Roy moved closer.

She put a palm out. "Stop right there."

"I don't know any Stephen," he said. He was so calm. He almost looked happy.

"Spencer," she corrected.

"You seem upset, Dr. Schwartz," Roy went on in the syrupy-sweet tone. "I wanted to make sure you're okay."

"Schwartzman," she said. "The name is Schwartzman."

"Of course, Dr. Schwartz*man*." He drew out the name with a snarl.

She fumbled to enter her passcode. *Favorites.* Why hadn't she put Hal in her favorites? *Recent calls.* She found his number. "I know what you're doing. It's not going to work."

"You don't know anything about me."

"I do," she said. "What did he tell you to do? Are you supposed to stab me? Right here, in the middle of the morgue?" The line was ringing. *Pick up, Hal. Pick up.*

"It would be fun to cut you," he admitted. "I'd enjoy it." He showed her open palms. "But enjoying cutting you has nothing to do with Stephen Whoever."

The call went to voicemail. She lowered the phone, pressed the "Call" button again. Roy was bullshitting. He knew Spencer. Of course he did.

"Why then?" she whispered, listening to Hal's phone ring again. "Why would you want to hurt me?"

"Because you're a fucking kike, and I hate kikes." Spit flew into the air.

Schwartzman froze.

Roy moved toward the door. He had the knob in his hand as though debating something. She scanned the room for weapons. Her fresh kits were in the drawer. None were within his reach.

The phone buzzed in her hand. She glanced away only long enough to see it was Hal. She answered and made some noise that he took for hello.

"Sorry I missed your call," Hal said.

"I'm in the morgue. You almost here?" Her voice was breathy, winded. Like something was sitting on her chest.

"What's wrong?" he asked.

"Yes."

"Schwartzman," Hal said. "Are you in trouble?"

"Yes. Yes, I am." She stared at Roy's back. Unmoving, he faced the door.

"Are you talking to me?" Hal asked. "What's going on?"

"Sure, Inspector Harris. I'll hold the line while you come in."

Roy faced her. The thin smile was back as he pulled the door open. "I'm glad you're okay, Dr. Schwartzman." He drew out the *man* of her name again. "I'm sure I'll see you soon."

She watched as he slithered into the hall. Only then did she allow herself to sink against the wall, fall into it, and slide downward until she was sitting on the cold linoleum floor, pressed against the hard metal of the morgue drawers.

Hal was talking in her ear. "I'm coming now. I'm almost there, Schwartzman."

"Okay," she whispered. "Okay." She held the phone to her ear, pressed it against her cheek, and sobbed until she heard Hal running down the hallway, saw him punch through the morgue door.

She was clutching the phone, listening to his breathing on the open line, when he reached her.

35

He slammed his laptop closed and spun his chair to face the view. Today, even the soothing blue of the bay couldn't calm him. The muscles in his back and neck were taut, his thighs and shoulders aching from the constant tension. It was all coming down. He could sense it. Even before the alert. He had felt close to breaking before the e-mail, as if his muscles were giant cables about to snap.

Someone had requested the history on Trent's ProCall account. If they got that, they would know that Ben Gustafson's last stop before his death was their house. The clock on his phone read 10:23 a.m. The alert had come in two hours and ten minutes ago. He'd called his tech guy immediately and then changed the phone number on the account. He changed the address, too, choosing one nearby so it would be believable if they checked Gustafson's phone records, the cell towers, which they most certainly would. But he didn't know how to wipe the history. He needed his tech guy, Nathaniel, for that.

Where the hell was Nathaniel? Probably in math class, staring out the window like a dumbass. He dialed again. Sent another text.

Things were falling apart.

If only Trent had listened. This was exactly why he didn't want Trent to see anyone.

He stood from the chair and crossed to the glass window, stared blankly at the view. White crests dotted the bay today, the sun glinting off the foamy caps like the tips of knives.

He spread his palm on the window, felt the warmth through the glass. There were views like this other places. They could leave. Pack up and leave. Without the money. Right. Without the money. He had some of his own. Eighteen, twenty thousand. That would last them awhile. Get them somewhere in Europe.

Stuck in Europe with Trent.

His brother flitting around the artist's scene while he . . . did what?

Spinning away from the window, he kicked his chair across the room. *No.* They needed it all. He called the attorney's office, barely controlling his anger as he left his name and his mobile number, tried to impress upon the dimwit on the other end of the line that it was urgent that he get a call back. And soon.

If the paperwork was done, they could go. Transfer the entire six million and go.

But if it didn't happen in time . . .

Options, he thought. What were his other options?

He froze. There was another way.

God, why hadn't he ever thought of it before?

It was Trent's ProCall account. Trent was the one with the fragile emotional state, the history of depression. There were also the attempted suicides, at least one on record. Their parents had been good at keeping those a secret. Even now Trent's mental state was questionable, at best. If the police came looking—no, *when* the police came looking, he could hand them the disturbed son, the broken one.

There would be the initial wave of shock from those who knew him. But then the idea that he was guilty would percolate, and they would remember the strange boy. It would all make sense then. "We always knew something was wrong with that one," they would say. And why not? Trent was always the crazy one.

He pictured his brother's face as he'd seen it this morning. Blushed and happy, fiddling with one of his projects in the bedroom. Like a child.

His brother would be genuinely shocked, of course. He knew nothing about what had happened. Well, he knew Posner had been murdered but not by whom. And he wouldn't have heard about Gustafson or the others.

Under heavy interrogation he might even doubt his own innocence. He might confess.

Trent would go to prison.

His stomach tightened into a fist and sank like a heavy weight. A rolling wave surged into his throat, and he doubled over to vomit in the trash can. Heaved and retched. Stomach acids and little more.

Trent in prison. *Dear God, no.* He couldn't give them Trent. Trent wouldn't survive a day in prison.

They had to leave. There was no other choice. They would take what they had and go.

He stood from his desk and scanned the surface. He didn't have time to pack up everything. He put his computer in his bag, pulled his personal files from the drawers, and searched the room. What else?

Trent. Trent wouldn't want to leave. Not suddenly, not like this. Well, he would have to. He dialed his brother's phone and listened to it ring as he glanced around the room. He loved this office. Wasn't there some way . . . ?

His call went to voicemail.

There was no way. Leaving was all they had. He stared down at his phone. God, he hoped he wasn't too late.

What if they were already at the house?

He texted his brother: Call me ASAP. He reread the words. Trent always ignored things that implied urgency. He typed again. I've got really exciting news. Really exciting. He thought of a different word. *Rad. Bomber. Awesome. Forget it.* He pushed "Send" and pocketed the phone while he took a last look around the office. Even through the panic, leaving this place cut him deeply. It was the only place that ever made him feel like a success.

He pulled the phone from his pocket as he locked up the office and dialed his brother again. “Come on, Trent.”

He hated to run, but he ran now, toward the elevators.

Hang in there, Trent.

I’m coming.

36

Hal's pulse pounded in his temple as he caught his breath. He slammed through the morgue door to find Schwartzman huddled on the floor, her cheek pressed against the cold metal drawers. An animal sound had come from his lips, and her eyes went wide when she saw him. When he reached her, she was trembling fiercely, as though she'd been out in a storm for hours, soaked to the bones. The words, when they came, were hardly discernible, but he'd gotten the most important piece of information.

The case against Spencer was falling apart, and it looked like he would get out.

"How can they let him out?"

She shook her head but said nothing. She had to know. Patchett would have told her. But she didn't want to tell him. It had something to do with the damn plastic bag she was carrying that night.

He tried to calm his panic with reason. There were other ways to ensure Spencer wasn't released. She could change her mind about testifying against him. Harper would testify. There had to be a way to keep that monster in jail. But he said nothing to reassure her. He didn't want to make a promise. How could he?

He'd seen plenty of evil men go free.

"Come on," he urged her. "Let me help you up."

She held her knees close. “I just want to stay here. Right here.”

“You can’t,” Hal said. “You’re a fighter, Schwartzman. You’ve got to fight.” He touched her shoulder. He wanted to wrap his arms around her and lift her up. He could do it, too. But it wasn’t his place. He thought of Ken Macy. Should he call Ken?

He stayed where he was and waited.

When she looked up a few minutes later, her face was tearstained, but her eyes were dry. She got slowly to her feet and pressed her arms to her stomach. Then she stared at the door. “It’s not just the call . . .” Her voice trailed off. “He said he wanted to cut me.”

Hal froze. “Wait. You talked to Spencer?”

“No. Roy.”

Anger made his limbs twitch. His hands balled into fists. *Roy.* “The blond guy?”

She nodded.

The man he’d seen watching her in Starbucks. The man who had glared at the barista. “The new guy? He said he wanted to cut you?”

“Yes. Because he hates Jews.” She shifted her weight into the wall, straightening her back. “Can you believe that? A skinhead.”

The black barista, Schwartzman. He hated them because they were black, Jewish. “Who hired that guy?”

She shook her head. “He was here when I got back from my surgery.”

“Don’t you normally weigh in on new hires?”

“Yes. Always.”

Hired while she was on medical leave. Why would they do that? “I’m getting rid of him.”

Schwartzman pushed herself off the wall, moving across the morgue. Her shoulders set back and her head up, she was starting to look like herself again. As she moved to the sink and turned on the water, Hal called over to the station. Dispatch answered.

"This is Inspector Harris. Send a couple of uniforms over to the morgue to pick up an employee by the name of Roy. He's a morgue assistant. Only been here a couple of months."

"What's the charge, Inspector?"

Hal glanced over at Schwartzman, who was running her hands through the water, staring down at it. "Assaulting an officer," he said, stretching the definition of *officer*. He didn't care. She was part of the department, damn it.

"You, sir?"

"No. The medical examiner." There was a pause on the line. "Read him his rights and hold him until I get there," Hal added.

"Will do."

Hal ended the call.

Standing at the sink, Schwartzman splashed water on her face.

"Are you okay?"

She pulled paper towels from the dispenser and wiped her hands slowly.

Of course she wasn't.

"I need some air," she said, patting her face with the towels.

"Let's go," Hal said.

She looked at him as though the idea of getting outside was his. Then she looked around the office and gave a curt nod. She took her coat off a rack on the wall and pulled it on. Her movements were slow, unsure, as if her legs were partially numb.

Hal peered down the corridor before stepping out into the hall. No sign of Roy as they left the building. Had the police already arrested him? It couldn't have happened that fast, but he saw no sign of Roy or any officers.

Surely Roy knew he was out of a job. Maybe he'd taken off.

As they reached the street, Hal's phone buzzed in his pocket. *The lab.*

"Hang on."

Schwartzman stopped walking.

"Hal," he answered.

Naomi didn't bother with hello. "I've got that info. The ProCall account that Ben Gustafson visited last is registered to a Trent Trina, and I've got an address for Mr. Trina. I'll text it now."

"You know who lives at the address?" Hal asked.

"It looks like a business. No Trent Trina in the listing. The title is registered to Anika Bouchard. I found the number for Bouchard online, but there was no answer."

"I'll head over there. Cross-reference the address with the employee list at the cancer center and call me if you get a hit."

"Will do," Naomi said. "And I'm still waiting on Gustafson's ProCall history—that should give us the address of his last call."

"Won't that be Trina's address?"

"Not necessarily," Naomi said. "Trina could've requested Gustafson at an address that isn't his record address."

"Got it," Hal said.

"I'll keep you posted."

He ended the call and turned to Schwartzman. "You want to come follow up on a lead?"

She was nodding slowly. "Posner case?"

"Yes."

"I do," she said. The anguish that had been in her expression when he'd entered the morgue had shifted to something more distanced, more measured.

Good. He had no intention of leaving her alone. Not after the news she'd gotten and the threat from Roy. They walked together to his car.

"I thought maybe Spencer sent him," she said after a while.

"Roy, you mean?"

She nodded.

Of course. Spencer could have arranged that from jail. He wouldn't have access to a computer, but he could have had someone else do it for him. Hate was an easy commodity, especially these days.

"But then he said he didn't know any Stephen."

"Stephen?" Hal repeated.

"That's what he called Spencer."

Roy had wanted to intimidate her. If Spencer put him up to it, wouldn't he want to tell her? Wouldn't Roy want to torture her with the idea that he still had access to her, even from behind bars? Certainly that seemed like Spencer's MO.

"I'm like a magnet for crazies," she whispered as they reached his car.

He studied her over the top of the car, searching for something to say.

"Come on," she said as if anticipating a pep talk she didn't want. "Let's go find the guy who killed Posner so at least one good thing can come of this day."

—

Hal parked in front of the address Naomi had texted. The address took them to a French restaurant. The proprietor, Anika Bouchard, had never heard of Trent Trina and seemed to have nothing to do with the case.

Another dead end.

Hal texted Naomi to let her know.

Dots appeared on the screen and a few seconds later, her response: Into Gustafson's records. Working on getting location for last call. Back ASAP. He was always amazed at how quickly Naomi could text. Though he was younger than most inspectors, when it came to keyboards, he was still of the hunt-and-peck generation.

To kill time Hal and Schwartzman ordered sandwiches from the deli next door. He got a meatball sub. It was an Italian delicatessen, after all. Schwartzman ordered an egg salad sandwich. His opinion of her selection must have showed in his face.

"It sounded good," she said defensively.

They took the sandwiches back to the car, and Hal cracked his window. That egg salad was going to stink up the car, but right then he couldn't smell it over the meatball sub.

Suddenly hungry, he ripped the paper off one end of the sandwich and took a bite.

"Well, that sucked," Schwartzman said, pulling a piece of bread off the corner of her sandwich.

"I should have known it wouldn't be that easy," Hal said, feeling a little better with some food heading toward his stomach.

"Seems like we're due for something to be easy," she said. She ate a piece of the crust, then took a small bite of the sandwich.

Hal thought again of Spencer. Out of jail. Walking free down the street. Any street. Spencer in San Francisco. Would he have the balls to show up here?

He'd have to.

She wouldn't have to go back to South Carolina—that was the one positive outcome from her decision not to testify. There would be no more tricks Spencer could pull. Of course, even if he were in prison—convicted and sentenced for the murders—Schwartzman would never truly be free. Even then Spencer might still be able to get to her. She would only be free when he was dead.

A dark thought crossed his mind.

Let Spencer MacDonald show up in San Francisco. This was Hal's city. All Hal needed was for the bastard to take one wrong step . . . but he already had. He'd gotten Roy hired in the morgue. No way that was a coincidence.

Had they arrested that punk? He hadn't heard from dispatch. But he hadn't told them to call him, just to put Roy in holding for him until he could get there.

Schwartzman stared at her sandwich, wrapped it up, and set it in her lap.

"You okay?"

"Lost my appetite."

He pointed to her chin, where there was a small piece of egg salad. "You have a little . . ."

Blushing, she wiped her mouth with the napkin. He realized how close he'd come to wiping it away for her, how intimate the gesture was. He thought of the way Justin had cared for his aging mother, a woman plagued by breathing problems and mysterious rashes. He wondered again what was killing her.

On his phone Hal found the picture he'd taken of Ruth Finlay, handed it to Schwartzman. "Any guess what that is, on her face?"

She zoomed in the picture. "What am I looking at?"

"See the skin around her mouth? I can't tell if it's a scar or some sort of skin disease."

"The pigmentation is different, too." She zoomed in more, tilting the phone at him. "The skin is lighter in some areas than others. But it's not like vitiligo where the skin loses pigmentation in some areas."

"Psoriasis?"

She shook her head. "Psoriasis is usually reddish and bumpy or inflamed. It doesn't look like that either." She stared at the image. "It's not like any skin condition I've ever seen." She zoomed in further. "I never saw her as a younger woman, but it looks like maybe she had some sort of cosmetic surgery. See how her chin is uneven on the left side."

Hal stared at the image. It was hard to tell. The quality wasn't good enough to make out the details clearly.

Schwartzman looked over at him. "What's the theory? You think her son's hiding her away because of a rash?"

Hal gave her a look and took his phone back. But the truth was, he had no idea. No theory. Nothing.

A text buzzed on his phone. *Naomi.*

Gustaf last call to 321 Union. No match to employees of cancer center or hospital personnel involved with Coleman.

He showed the text to Schwartzman.

"What does it mean?" she asked.

"It means we haven't got shit."

"Maybe we should drive by, take a look," Schwartzman suggested.

"Couldn't hurt," he agreed. That gave Hal an idea. "Maybe they put in a neighboring address instead of their own." He texted Naomi. Any suspects on Union? Or close by?

The response was almost immediate. No.

Hal groaned. He looked down at the remainder of his sandwich and wrapped up it up for later. He turned over the engine. "Not looking good, but what the hell. It's only a few blocks." He paused before pulling from the curb. "Unless you need to get back to the morgue."

She checked her phone. "I'm okay."

Schwartzman normally got antsy about being away from the morgue. She loved it there, but today she didn't seem anxious to go back. *Roy.* He'd deal with Roy as soon as he got to the station.

Hal drove north on Grant through the slow North Beach traffic and turned right on Union. He could have used his siren and lights, but he didn't know where he was going, so there was no rush. He passed over Varennes Street and Sonoma, small streets that he rarely had occasion to visit. Living and working on the other side of the financial district, he was seldom in this part of town. As he crossed Kearny, he realized he'd been here recently. Castle Street.

He turned right.

"Wait," Schwartzman said, pointing. "I think 321 was on the next block."

But Hal didn't slow. Instead he drove fifty feet down Castle Street and parked in the red zone across from Ruth Finlay's house.

"Who lives here?"

"The woman in the photo." Hal tossed his police pass on the dash and cracked the car door. Gustafson's last call was a hundred yards from Ruth Finlay's home. Maybe it was a coincidence. But he didn't believe in those. He wondered if Williams was in the house today. If so, he'd like to talk to her again.

Schwartzman got out, too, and they crossed the street together. As they approached, a woman came out the front door. Alice Williams.

"Ms. Williams?"

She spun around as he approached, jumping at the sight of him. "You scared me," she snapped.

"I'm Inspector Hal Harris," he said, drawing out his badge. "We met the other day."

"I remember," she said.

"I have a few more questions. It won't take long."

Her gaze shifted between his bulk and the badge he held.

"Can we go inside?" Hal asked.

Williams was staring over his shoulder at Schwartzman.

Hal looked back. Schwartzman lagged behind on the stone walk that led to the front of Finlay's house, and for a moment, Hal thought maybe she was feeling sick. The egg salad sandwich. But she hadn't eaten much of it.

"Hal," Schwartzman whispered as she stopped at the foot of the concrete stairs.

He studied Schwartzman's face, keeping Williams in his peripheral vision. "Are you okay?"

Schwartzman climbed the stairs slowly, focused on Alice Williams. "Look." She pointed to the keys in Williams's hand. He tilted his head and saw it.

Hanging from Williams's key chain was a small brown dog figurine with black ears and nose.

"May I see that?" Hal asked, reaching for the keys.

Williams's gaze tracked to her hand as though she didn't know what he was asking for. "Oh, this," she said, handing him the key chain. "It's a puppy."

Hal studied the small dog, rubbing his thumb along the smooth clay. Like Play-Doh that had hardened. Roger had said the same thing about the piece of clay found in Todd Posner's mouth. "Did you make this, Ms. Williams?"

She shook her head quickly. "No, Ms. Finlay made it." She motioned to the door. As she turned back, her expression fell as though she realized she'd said something wrong.

Hal felt the dog. "It's made of clay."

Williams nodded. "Yes. Like clay. She likes to make things with it."

"Like clay," Hal repeated.

"FIMO clay," Williams said.

A narrow collar ran around the dog's neck. It was a pinkish color. Exactly the same color as the substance found in Todd Posner's mouth.

37

Schwartzman took the clay dog from Hal, recalling the gum-like material from Posner's mouth. It had looked flesh-colored at first glance. Then it was too pink, the consistency wrong for skin, even from the mouth, which was why she'd thought it was gum. But it was a strange color for gum.

It was also the same color as the collar on the little clay dog. And the same material. FIMO clay. But what did it mean? Ruth Finlay had made it for Alice Williams. Surely an eighty-year-old woman wasn't behind the death of Todd Posner. And Gustafson. And Denise Ross.

"You're going to need to let us in," Hal told Williams.

The woman's eyes went wide. A flush reddened in her cheeks as hives trailed down her neck. Did she know something she wasn't saying? Her fingers trembled as she tried to slide the key back into the lock. She found the slot, twisted the key, and pushed the door open, leaving the key in the bolt.

Williams stepped into the hallway, glancing around quickly. Hal was right behind her.

Schwartzman paused to pull the key from the lock and followed. She tucked the key, with its clay dog, into her pocket to give to Hal. Roger would be able to compare the clay against the other sample.

Hal halted in the foyer and emitted a sound like a gasp.

Schwartzman moved in beside him, her gaze following his to the stairs.

"Schwartzman," Hal whispered. "That is Ruth Finlay."

There, coming down an elegant stairwell, was a woman with a striking resemblance to the woman in the photograph Hal had taken the day he'd interviewed Ruth Finlay. Only it couldn't have been Ruth Finlay. Finlay was in her eighties. This woman certainly was not. Mrs. Finlay's full head of gray hair had been replaced by a short, stubby ponytail. Dark brown. What had appeared as loose skin around her chin and nose, as well as the wrinkles beneath her eyes, were gone. Without them, Schwartzman saw the square jaw and the prominent Adam's apple.

The woman on the stairwell was clearly undergoing gender reassignment.

The woman's eyes opened wide, and her hand flew to her throat. Her fingers hovered over her Adam's apple the way a teenager might cover a hickey.

"You're not Ruth Finlay," Hal said. "Who the hell *are* you?"

The woman nodded slowly and turned to Williams, who stood in the corner of the foyer. "You can go, Alice. We'll see you tomorrow." The voice still had the husky edge of masculinity. To Hal, the woman said, "We weren't expecting company."

Alice Williams slipped from the room, and a moment later, the front door clicked closed.

"It's you," Hal said. "*You* were dressed up as Ruth Finlay the other day. You're Justin's brother. Or I guess sister now."

Schwartzman studied the woman. "How did you know?" she asked Hal.

"When I was here the other day, I saw that birthmark," Hal said, indicating a rich brown stain on her left arm, about the size of a half-dollar. It stood out against her pale skin. "I thought it was a bruise."

"It's called a cafe au lait stain," Schwartzman said, her gaze moving from the mark to the woman's face as she tried to put together what Hal was saying.

"You pretended to be Ruth Finlay," Hal said.

"I was Trent Finlay," the woman said. "Justin and I are identical twins." She moved slowly down the stairs. "I'm Trina. Well, I've always been Trina, but now it's official." She added a little swoosh with her arms for emphasis.

Just then a door slammed at the back of the house.

Hal put a hand on his weapon.

"That's Justin, coming home," Trina Finlay said.

"Trent?" came a voice from the other side of the house. "Are you here? We need to—" His voice broke off as he reached the entryway and saw Hal and Schwartzman.

Justin's eyes tracked his brother, now sister, as she stepped down the last stair.

"It's okay, Justin," she said calmly. "Now we don't need to hide it anymore."

Justin Finlay froze. His gaze swept across the three of them, his shoulders reared and tensed like a cornered cat. "What is going on?" He aimed his glare at Trina. "What did you tell them?"

"They just got here," Trina said.

Schwartzman watched Justin Finlay. Could he have killed Posner? One of them was involved. She tried to fit the pieces together. Posner had been on the board of the foundation. Ruth Finlay had liked him. She was the only one.

Hal's gaze was narrowed on Justin Finlay, his stance wide, stiff. Ready to move. He was suspicious, too.

"Why don't we all sit down," Trina suggested, motioning toward the living room.

Hal glanced at Schwartzman, who nodded. The answers were here.

"I'm afraid we can't talk," Justin said, the words tumbling out of his mouth. "We've got a family emergency."

"What type of emergency?" Hal asked.

"It's our mother," Justin said after a slight hesitation. "She's back in the hospital. We need to go."

Trina stared at him, her mouth dropping open. Justin looked away from his sister. His gaze flicked across Hal's face and then hers. He was lying.

"Maybe we should all go," Hal said. "We can take my car. I have some questions for your mother."

"The doctors won't let you see her, I'm afraid," Justin went on. "That's why I had Trent dress up as Mother the other day. She's too sick to see anyone."

Where was Ruth Finlay? And why prevent Ruth from seeing Hal?

"What does your mother have?" Schwartzman asked.

Justin turned to her. "Huh?"

"What is she suffering from? What's the diagnosis?" she clarified.

"Dr. Schwartzman is our medical examiner," Hal explained.

Justin's gaze went from Hal to Schwartzman. He shook his head. "We really don't have time. I'm afraid she might not make it." He looked at his sister. "Please, Trent. We have to go."

Hal pulled out his phone, his other hand resting on the holstered weapon. "Which hospital?"

"What?" Justin's voice was breathy.

"Your mother?" Hal said. "Which hospital is she in? I'll give them a call, see how she's doing."

"They—they won't tell you," Justin stammered.

"They will," Hal assured him.

Justin stared at the floor, the wheels of his mind clearly spinning.

Trina moved toward him and put a hand on his shoulder. "Let's tell them, Justin. It's not that big a deal."

Justin shrugged off his sister's touch and shook his head. "No, Trent. Don't. Don't say any—"

"Our mom died," Trina announced.

"Shut up," Justin said, speaking through gritted teeth.

Trina winced at her brother's tone but kept talking. "She died in her sleep."

"Shut the hell up!" Justin shouted.

"Justin, for God's sake, it's not worth it." Trina crossed to the living room and sank onto the couch. "Our mother died," Trina went on from the couch, leaning over to adjust a vase of peonies on the side table. "Justin was worried that the will would cut me out, that I wouldn't have the money to finish my transition."

"From male to female," Schwartzman said, heading toward the living room. She'd had a few transgender victims on her table, in various stages. Unless the transition was started before puberty—which few were because of the required parental consent—it was a lengthy process that involved many surgeries.

"Yes," Trina confirmed.

Justin seemed to shrink. He eyed Hal's gun as he moved to the living room and took a seat on the love seat next to the fireplace. Hal moved in close to sit on the edge of the chair beside him, positioning himself between Justin and the door.

Schwartzman sat down on the couch where Trina was, imagining the old woman she'd seen on Hal's phone. "You used the clay to create the wrinkles, the lowered jowl."

"Yes. Uncooked FIMO clay and rubber cement. The color is never exactly right. That's a problem."

"Aren't there other materials?" she asked. "Things that are designed for theater makeup?"

Trina's eyes widened. "Oh, there are, but the FIMO clay is so much less expensive and easier to get," she added with a dramatic wave of her arm. "An old lady and her son can't have fifty pounds of theater makeup delivered every month without raising some questions."

"You're very talented," Schwartzman said.

Trina beamed proudly.

"You have to understand," Justin said, his voice low and raspy. He sounded exhausted, raw. "Trent needed tens of thousands of dollars of treatments. And she cut him off. Her own son."

"It was harmless," Trina agreed. "Mother passed away, and we decided to use her identity for six or eight months to finish up my work. The foundation does its good. No one was harmed."

Justin stared into space.

Hal and Schwartzman exchanged a glance. Was it possible that Trina didn't know about Posner? Or Gustafson? And what about Denise?

"And what was the plan after that?" Hal asked.

"We'd bury mother in a quiet service," she said as if she were discussing rearranging the furniture. "I could be Trina. And if they took the money then, we'd be fine."

Justin rubbed his face. "It was supposed to be simple, straightforward."

"But something happened," Hal said, watching Justin.

Justin eyeballed the door as though judging whether he could make it. As he moved, the light from the front window highlighted his profile. There was a slight sheen over a patch of skin just above his shirt collar, the coloring slightly off. Schwartzman could see ridges beneath the cover of makeup.

"You've got scratch marks," Schwartzman said.

Justin's head spun toward her. "What? No."

"I can see them—under the makeup," she went on. "From where Denise Ross scratched your neck."

"It was a cat," Trina said. "I covered it up with makeup."

Schwartzman turned to the sister. "Trina, a cat did not do that."

"It was a cat," Trina said again. "Justin told me."

"It was," Justin said, covering his neck.

Schwartzman shook her head. "The scratches are too far apart, the nail marks too wide to belong to a cat. Those are human."

Justin stood quickly.

"Sit down," Hal demanded.

Justin sank but shifted in his seat, the worry clear in his expression. He was involved. Was Trina, as well?

Trina looked at Hal with narrowed, suspicious eyes. "It was a cat," she said again.

"Justin, we're going to be able to prove what you did," Hal said, perched on the edge of the chair. "You can make things easier on yourself by telling us."

"What are they talking about, Justin?" Trina said. She, too, was edging forward in her seat.

Schwartzman thought about the evidence at the scene. Without Denise Ross's fingers, they couldn't match the DNA to Justin Finlay. But what about the wipes? Surely he would have some of those around. The FIMO clay, the single fiber, a horse sedative.

If Justin was the killer, there would be evidence somewhere.

"We can do this at the station," Hal said, standing. "We're going to be able to link you to these crimes."

Justin shook his head. His gaze had shifted toward the fireplace. The stack of wood. Was he thinking about something? The past? The mistakes he'd made?

"Justin!" Trina shouted. "What is he talking about? What crimes?"

Justin shifted on the chair, staring at the fireplace.

"What happened to Todd Posner, Justin? Do you know something?" Trina's voice grew shrill.

Schwartzman saw something pink on the hearth. She leaned in, remembering the single pink fiber on Posner's body caught in the burn mark left by the Taser. Folded on the stone hearth was a pink square. A silk handkerchief. Silk like the fiber that they'd found on Posner's body, the same fiber Naomi had retrieved from Gustafson's car.

"That's Dad's handkerchief," Trina said. "Alice said she found it when she was cleaning today."

Justin lunged toward the fireplace. Schwartzman was closer. She grabbed the handkerchief before he was able to reach it and turned back to Hal. "It's the pink—"

Hal took one step toward her as Justin shot past Schwartzman and picked up a small silver spray can that had been sitting beside the handkerchief. A second later his arm was a bar across her neck, the canister in her face. "Cyanide," he said. "Touch that gun and she's dead."

Hal froze, three feet away.

Too far.

Schwartzman went rigid.

"Justin, what are you doing?" Trina asked, her voice rising in pitch.

Schwartzman glanced at the pink handkerchief, which had fallen to the floor.

"What is in that can?" Trina asked. "Alice said it was behind the stack of firewood. Why was it there, Justin?"

Justin clenched tighter on Schwartzman's neck. He didn't answer his sister.

Schwartzman knew what was in the can. The spray that had killed Ben Gustafson. Cyanide. She understood the chemistry well. The poison acted as an irreversible enzyme inhibitor, preventing electrons from being transported to oxygen in the process of aerobic cellular respiration. Cyanide poisoning would make her dizzy and weak. She wondered if, after the confusion, she would feel a sense of suffocation as her blood pressure dropped, her heart slowed, and she finally lost consciousness. Within minutes, she would experience respiratory failure.

Trina rose from the couch. "Justin, what did you do? What's going on?"

"Shut up," Justin said. "You ruined everything."

"Let's stay calm," Hal said. "No one else needs to get hurt."

"What do you mean 'no one else'?" Trina pressed.

Hal didn't respond.

"What did you do, Justin? What did you do?"

Silence.

"Nothing," he said emphatically. "I didn't do anything."

"You're lying!" Trina shouted, her voice undeniably male. "Stop lying to me."

"Trent! Shut. The. Fuck. Up."

There was a moment of quiet before Trina Finlay began shrieking.

38

Hal watched the canister in Justin's hand. Was it a foot from Schwartzman's face? Closer? How close did it have to be? How powerful was the spray?

Surely it was close enough to kill her.

If Justin's finger hit that trigger, Schwartzman would inhale cyanide. She would die. No chance he could get his gun unholstered fast enough to save her, let alone aim it and shoot. And that was if he had a clean shot, which he didn't.

Her eyes found his. Pleaded. What could he do?

Trina had stopped screaming and was huddled on the couch, sobbing.

"Let her go," Hal said. "There's no way out of this, Justin."

Schwartzman's fingers gripped the arm braced around her neck. Could she drop and free herself? Spin out of his grip? Justin might spray her. And if she ended up on the ground, he might still spray her before Hal could shoot.

Hal wanted to scream, to jump across the room and tackle Justin Finlay. Instead he raised his hands. "Trina," he whispered.

She looked up from the couch.

"Talk to your brother. Tell him to put the can down."

Trina wiped her face with large palms. "He's right, Justin. You haven't done anything. We didn't kill Mother. Don't make this worse."

"You only pretended to be your mother, right?" Hal asked.

Trina nodded quickly. "Yes. Right."

"What about seeing your mother's friends?" Hal asked like it was a casual conversation. "Didn't anyone realize that you weren't her?"

"We didn't see them," Trina explained. "Other than the surgeries, I stay here. Inside."

"What about Alice Williams?" Hal asked.

"What about her?" Trina said.

"She didn't know my mother," Justin cut in.

Schwartzman jumped slightly, and Hal leveled his palm at his waist, pressing down to try to communicate that it was going to be okay. Tried to promise her he would get them out of this.

But how? Distraction. Focus on distraction.

"Alice takes care of Trent," Justin added.

"But you were calling her 'Mother,'" Hal continued. "Surely Alice has figured out that she's not—" Hal stopped and looked at Trina. "Your mother."

"She knows. Alice thinks I've got some dementia, that I'm brain damaged," Trina said with a little smile.

It made sense. If Trina had some sort of mental illness, she might actually believe she was Justin's mother, and Williams might play along, keep her mouth shut. Trina could want to make herself up as an older woman and stay secluded in the house, and Williams wouldn't say anything as long as she got paid.

"But Todd Posner figured it out," Hal said.

"What are you talking about?" Trina asked. She turned to her brother. "What does he mean?"

"It's nothing. He's lying."

"You're lying," Trina snapped. "I can tell you're lying. Tell me what happened. Tell me what you did!" she shouted, rising from the couch.

Justin said nothing.

Trina moved toward her brother. "Stop treating me like a child, Justin. Like a moron. Tell me what is going on!"

"Stand back."

"No. This isn't only about you," Trina said.

"What a fucking joke!" Justin shouted, spit flying through the air. "It's never about me. It's only ever been about you. Every damn thing, for our entire lives, has been about you."

Trina's mouth dropped open in shock.

Hal eased forward, focused on the can. Again he wished he knew how far it would spray, how much would kill them all.

"Screw you, Justin. I don't need you."

"Like hell you don't!" Justin yelled. "You don't have a fucking clue. You never have. You live in a wonderland, worried about hair and nails while I am out there protecting you."

Her brother's words seemed to knock Trina backward.

Hal eased forward again. Surely Justin wouldn't spray the canister where it could strike Trina. Not after all he'd done for her. And the human body could survive some cyanide. But Schwartzman's chemo meant she was compromised. Would the effect be stronger on her?

"You think it, too," Trina whispered.

"Think what?" Justin spat at her.

"You think I'm a freak," Trina said, her low, masculine voice cracked high. "Just like Mom, just like Dad."

"That's bullshit. I've stood by you every step," Justin said, his voice dropping, too, slowing down. "I fought Mom to put you back in the will. I fought for them to let you do the surgery when we were in high school. I've been here, Trent. Me."

"Trina," she said fiercely. "Trent is dead. I. Am. Trina. You always call me Trent. You don't listen. You say that you're protecting me, but you're hiding me. You've never accepted me for who I am." Trina's eyes narrowed. "Todd was a better friend to me than you are."

"Bullshit." Justin jabbed his finger toward his sister.

Schwartzman started to duck, but he caught her. Yanked her against his chest.

The canister in her face again.

"Todd Posner was only in it for himself," Justin said, his jaw tight as he spoke. "He didn't give a shit about you."

Trina's mouth dropped again, her palm pressed flat to her chest. Long pink nails rested on her neck.

"It's okay," Hal said, not wanting to make Justin angry. The angrier he got, the higher the probability that he used that spray. "It doesn't have to be like this."

"What did you do, Justin?" Trina's voice cracked.

Justin shook his head. "We have to leave, Tre—Trina."

"It's over," Hal said. "You can only make things worse. You've killed three people."

"No!" Trina shouted. "Oh, my God. Todd. You killed Todd."

Justin pivoted toward his sister. Schwartzman's face was still in the V of his arm, motionless against his chest, the canister too close to her face.

Hal waited for an opportunity to pull his gun, take the shot.

Justin glanced at him, eyed the gun in his holster.

Hal raised his hands. Surrendered. He wasn't going to make a move. Not until he knew he could get her away.

Trina backed away. *Damn.* He wanted her up in her brother's face to make sure Justin wouldn't risk spraying the cyanide.

Trina had been angry, but now she was crying again. Tears streamed down her cheeks, creating a trail through her makeup. "You did it, didn't you?" she whispered.

Justin didn't answer.

"Why? Why did you kill Todd?"

"He was going to out you." Justin's voice rose. "He was going to tell people that Mother was dead, that you were an imposter."

"So what?" Trina said. "I wasn't going to be Mother forever."

"Shut up, Trent," Justin snarled, stepping backward. Schwartzman stumbled back with him, struggling to keep her feet on the ground. "You don't understand. We needed time. To get things in order."

"Todd called that night," Trina said, sinking back down. "We were out at the stables."

"No," Justin shouted. "Stop talking."

"What did Todd say to you?" Trina asked.

"Not now, Trent."

Trina's lips made a thin, angry line.

"I mean Trina," Justin said. "Posner was an asshole. You're better off." He nudged Schwartzman forward. "Now, we have to get out of here." He turned to Hal. "You're going to let us go, or I'll kill her."

Hal said nothing.

Schwartzman gave him a little nod as she worked something out of her pocket.

"You think Todd Posner was an asshole?" Trina shouted at her brother, rising again from the couch. "*You're* the asshole, Justin. You were out there protecting yourself. Your reputation. What people thought of *you*. I couldn't have cared less. I would have gone through the transition slowly, but you couldn't have a freak brother slash sister. You wanted me 'fixed,' so I could be presentable for public, so you didn't have to be ashamed of me." She reached out and grabbed her brother's arm.

Hal stepped forward.

"Stay away, Trent!" Justin shouted. "If you get sprayed, you'll die."

"What do you care?" Trina moved forward.

Justin pulled back. "I mean it, Tre—ina. Stay back."

Trina moved in again, reaching for the canister. "It would be easier if I died, wouldn't it? You wouldn't have to deal with me."

Justin's gaze flitted between Hal and his sister, trying to focus on both. He struggled to pull Schwartzman away from Trina.

Schwartzman's hand was on her thigh, the small dog key chain resting against her leg. Three fingers extended, the other two curled into her palm.

On three.

"Trent, get away."

She tapped one.

"Call me Trina!"

Two.

Schwartzman raised her right hand and, on three, drove the key into Justin's thigh.

Justin howled.

Hal drew his weapon.

Trina shrieked.

The hiss of the canister filled the room.

Schwartzman dropped to the ground.

Hal fired.

Justin fell backward, gripping his leg and screaming. Trina dropped to the floor beside him. "Justin. Justin!"

"Schwartzman!" Hal shouted.

No answer. He hurtled the table to reach her. She was on the ground, hands over her face.

"Schwartzman."

She waved her hands in her face, her mouth pinched closed. *The spray.* She'd been sprayed.

Justin tried to stand. Trina gripped his arm, helping him.

Hal scanned the room. The vase with the peonies. He yanked the flowers out and threw them on the floor. Knelt beside her and poured the water over her face.

Her eyes flew open, shocked. She coughed and choked, spit water.

He let the vase fall to the carpet, grabbed the canister from where it had fallen on the floor, and reached for her. Schwartzman wiped the water from her face.

Justin Finlay was on his feet. Hal lunged toward Justin and punched his leg. His fist struck the gunshot wound. Justin screamed and dropped like a rock.

"You move one inch, and I'll shoot you," Hal said, kneeling beside Schwartzman.

Justin's face was twisted in pain. Trina sat sobbing beside him, her arm wrapped around his shoulders.

"Are you okay?" he asked Schwartzman.

She nodded, rubbing her face and blinking a few times.

"Say something, Schwartzman!"

"I'm wet."

Relief humming through him, Hal laughed. Then he turned to look at Trina and Justin Finlay. He stood and pulled Trina off her brother.

"Justin Finlay, you are under arrest."

39

Hal wouldn't let it go, so Schwartzman agreed to go in the ambulance to General Hospital. But she was fine. She'd heard the whisper of the cyanide spray as she stabbed the key into Justin Finlay's thigh. She'd been holding her breath, and the cool spray had hit only the side of her face before she'd dropped to the floor.

It stung.

Her skin was irritated.

She was alive.

Trina Finlay had suffered a little chemical burn from the cyanide, as well. Facing Justin, Trina had likely inhaled more of the poison than Schwartzman did, but she would recover.

Justin Finlay was going to prison. For a long, long time.

Because Hal had to take Justin Finlay into custody to interview him and Trina, he arrived at the hospital almost two hours after Schwartzman. She had been asleep when the familiar sound of Hal walking woke her. He was a loud walker. Scuffed his right foot a little. Big feet.

He entered the small, curtained-off cubicle carrying her purse. "You left it in my car."

Schwartzman encouraged Hal to sit, but he would have none of it. Instead he paced a circle around the small cubicle where she was waiting to be seen. She hoped the doctor came before Hal wore through the linoleum.

"Where the hell is the doctor?" he asked.

She opened her eyes and looked over at him. It wasn't the first time he'd asked, and this time she didn't answer. She had been triaged, and she was waiting because someone else was in worse shape—a bad car accident, a gunshot wound. The doctors were working to keep some victim off her table. She was okay with waiting.

She thought again about Ken Macy, five months ago, and the eighteen fresh stab wounds peppering his body. About her waking up in a room like this with Hal asleep in the chair. About running. She wouldn't be running this time.

The doctor would get to her eventually, and the nursing staff had already treated her. There was nothing to do other than make sure the skin was thoroughly washed and apply a topical cream for the irritation. And check her lungs.

They had done a chest scan when she'd arrived and a second one after about ninety minutes to see if there was any change. Cyanide was fast acting. The damage, if there were any, would show quickly. The first scan had looked okay—no damage worth worrying about. She couldn't imagine the second test would show anything different. No doubt some particles had entered her lungs. It would have been impossible to avoid inhaling the cyanide completely.

Of course, Hal had inhaled some, too. He hadn't been holding his breath.

All of them were fine. There was cyanide in all sorts of things—almonds, of course, but also apple seeds and cherry pits. The human body could handle trace amounts.

"You can go back to the station," she said again. "I can call you."

"No."

She knew he had to go back and interview Justin Finlay again. When he arrived, he told her that he'd interrogated Finlay until he lawyered up. That was when Hal had come to the hospital. But Finlay's attorney would arrive soon, and Hal would meet with them.

"Tell me what Finlay said," she asked again. He had waved her off when she'd first asked, saying he wanted her to focus on getting better, as though the act of thinking might slow her recovery.

He opened the curtain and stared into the corridor. "I don't even see a doctor out there," he said when he came back.

"Tell me about Finlay," she repeated.

Hal hesitated.

She pointed to the plastic chair in the corner. "Sit."

He sank into the chair.

"Talk," she demanded.

"Bossy."

"Yes."

He smiled, and then his expression changed. Thoughtful. "Posner showed up at the house. Trina was dressed as Ruth Finlay, but she didn't fool Posner."

"So Posner threatened Justin, the way he threatened Patrick Fraser?" she guessed.

"Right. Posner was blackmailing Justin for more control in the organization. If he didn't get it, he would expose the fact that Trina was playing the part of their mother. Justin couldn't let that happen. Someone would start to ask questions about Ruth Finlay. They would want to see her."

"And she was dead," Schwartzman said.

"Right. And Justin knew giving Posner more control in the organization meant he and Trina would be pushed out. They would lose access to their mother's money."

"What about Fraser?" she asked. "Did he have anything to do with any of this?"

"No," Hal said. "It looks like Justin Finlay was working on his own."

Fraser had seemed so wild in the parking lot, talking about the photos of Patrick. Then they'd discovered the story of the kid Fraser had beat up. Allegedly. Even if he did it, it would be hard to blame a father for protecting his son. Was it that different from a brother protecting his sister? How many degrees of desperation had caused Justin Finlay to kill Todd Posner? Would Fraser have done something so drastic?

"It seemed like a lot of the clues pointed to him," she said.

"Fraser, you mean?" Hal said.

She nodded.

"Fraser had cut Justin Finlay's contract."

"What do you mean? What contract?"

"The cancer center was one of Justin's clients," Hal explained.

She shook her head. "I don't think I ever knew what Justin Finlay did."

"He's an efficiency expert. Was. He worked there to help trim the fat."

"That's how he got the Adriamycin," she said.

"Right," Hal agreed. "He had full access at the cancer center. And he wasn't on any of our lists because—"

"He wasn't an employee," she finished for him.

"Exactly."

"So Finlay tried to set Fraser up for the fall because he was angry about the contract?"

"Justin Finlay must have known that Posner had turned Sandy Coleman away and Fraser had cared for her."

Justin had worked alone; there was no accomplice. It was pretty clear that, aside from hiding their mother's death, Trina had nothing to do with it. Justin Finlay was going down for multiple counts of first-degree murder.

The attorney would try something to reduce the charges. They always did. Temporary insanity? She didn't see how that would work.

"Where's the mother?" she asked. "Her remains, I mean."

"In the basement. Roger's team is collecting them."

"I'll look at them tomorrow." She thought back to Posner's death. "Trina had a horse."

"Right," Hal said. "Roger confirmed that the sedative came from the stable where they boarded Trina's horse. They're sending up a sample of the sedative so Roger can confirm the compounds are identical."

"He'll get to use Rita."

"Rita?" Hal asked.

"His new mass spectrometer."

"Oh, right," Hal said. For a while he appeared lost in thought, so she gave him some time before asking, "And Gustafson was just in the wrong place at the wrong time?"

"We haven't gotten far with Gustafson yet. Best guess is Justin was worried he would talk."

A cable guy taking side calls to make a few extra bucks and cheat his company ended up at the Finlays'. Dumb luck. "You find out what made the imprint on Posner's leg?"

"Justin Finlay had a penchant for very expensive gloves—a brand called Fratelli Orsini. We're working with the company to match the imprint, but we're pretty sure that's what did it. It also sounds like Posner had a thing for wearing short socks with his dress shoes, so it's possible Finlay had noticed the mole on his leg and knew it would be harder to see a needle mark there." Hal paused. "But so far Justin's not giving us those details."

The imprint made sense to her now. Justin Finlay would have been applying a lot of pressure to hold Posner down while the horse tranquilizer took effect. "Doesn't sound like you'll need Justin to confess about the gloves in order to make your case," she said. "What about David Kemp?"

"We're not sure yet. Justin says Denise Ross killed David Kemp," Hal said. "An affair gone bad. We did find a copy of the news article about Posner's murder in her home. It looks like she might have decided to copycat Posner's death to keep the focus off herself."

That one sounded like temporary insanity.

"But we'll get Justin for Denise Ross's murder."

"She scratched him."

Hal nodded. "We're working on Justin to give us the fingers."

Justin had told Trina the scratch was from the cat, and she had applied makeup to it. Didn't Trina wonder why her brother would need to cover up a scratch from a cat? Or how he'd gotten the scratch to begin with? Or was she simply happy to be needed, to be useful?

She had trusted her brother. Since Posner died so soon after he'd discovered their secret, had she never suspected her brother was the killer? Or had she suspected him in some recess of her mind and wanted so badly to be wrong that she'd suppressed any notion that might lead her to consider his guilt?

The human brain was capable of amazing feats.

She adjusted her pillow. That very morning, she'd learned that Spencer would likely be released from jail, although if that creepy attendant was planted in her morgue by her ex-husband, then Spencer had been with her in spirit for some time. "What about Roy?"

"He's MIA," Hal said. "No one's seen him since he left the morgue."

She thought again about Spencer, about whether there really was a connection. There had to be. Otherwise she would have to accept that the morgue just happened to hire a racist morgue attendant with psychopathic tendencies while she was out on medical leave. She could not buy that Roy's appearance in her morgue was coincidence. It was Spencer.

Hal looked ready to comment when the curtain opened, and the doctor came in.

Hal shot out of the chair. "How is she?"

The doctor, a fine-boned man with warm brown eyes and silver hair, glanced up at Hal. "Hello, there. I'm Dr. Green."

"Hal Harris."

The two men shook hands.

"Dr. Schwartzman, how are you feeling?"

"Fine," she said, sitting up in the bed. "The chest scans clear?"

Green looked at Schwartzman and then back to Hal as though judging their relationship.

"It's fine to speak in front of Hal," she said.

Green pulled a thin computer tablet from under his arm and touched the screen before turning it to face her. "Here's the most recent scan." After a moment, he flicked his finger across the screen. "And the first."

He gave her the tablet and she toggled back and forth between the two scans.

Hal learned over to examine them, though she suspected he didn't know much about lung scans. If they were from a victim, she would have said there was no sign of lung damage, certainly not enough to explain a cause of death. But this wasn't an autopsy.

She wasn't dead.

She handed the tablet back to Dr. Green.

"Well?" Hal asked, shifting from foot to foot impatiently.

"They look the same," Green said. "No change, so I think she's good to go."

Hal clapped, the noise filling the small space. He didn't seem to notice.

Green peered down at Schwartzman. "If you experience any wheezing or difficulty breathing—"

"I'll come back," she said.

"Good," Green said and left the room.

Schwartzman swung her legs to the side of the bed.

Hal glanced at her bare legs. "I'll wait for you out there."

She nodded.

He hesitated before closing the curtain. "Do you want me to call someone? Ken maybe?"

She shook her head. *Ken.* She did not want to think about that now. She had to break the news to him, but not today.

"Okay."

He closed the curtain, and she rose from the bed, slowly pulling on her clothes. As she grabbed her purse, the phone inside vibrated. She pulled it out and used her fingerprint to unlock it. On her screen was a stream of messages. Harper. Laura Patchett. The word *Spencer*.

He was getting out. She hadn't read the words and already she knew. She grabbed the foot of the bed for support and drew a deep breath. Emotionally she was prepared for Spencer's release. The next step would be to prepare physically. She would not be caught off guard again.

The phone buzzed again. She glanced down as another alert slid across the screen. A calendar reminder.

Hal's birthday. Today at 5:00 p.m.

She pocketed the phone and stepped out into the corridor. "You ready to go, birthday boy?"

Hal frowned, starting to shake his head. "Wait, what day is it?"

"The nineteenth," she said.

He was staring at his phone. "So it is."

"Happy birthday."

"Thank you very much."

The two of them walked through the hospital corridors and out into the darkening sky.

40

Two weeks later

Hal had kept his thoughts to himself during the tour of the house, but she had no doubt he would speak up. A quiet agreement had emerged between them over the past few weeks. There would be no more holding back.

On the street Schwartzman noticed the crescent moon above the rise of Glen Canyon Park. San Francisco was famous for the Indian summers that happened in October. But fall was coming. The air had a crisper taste that made her think of baked apples. With it came the cold.

She was done running. *Done.* She looked back at the house. It was tiny, in need of a roof, new paint, and a lot of love.

But it was hers.

She crossed her arms and felt a chill across her shoulders, the electricity of excitement, of hope.

Hal stopped beside her, his arm brushing her shoulder. "I like the house."

"I'm glad."

"You're really going to buy it."

"I did buy it."

He winced slightly at the idea that it was done. Then he caught himself. “It’s what you want.”

“It is. It’s perfect.”

He nodded, but she saw it in his face. It was perfect . . . if not for Spencer. “Then, you’ll testify,” he said not quite a question.

“I can’t.”

“Anna.”

She smiled. “Is that like calling a child by his full name when he’s in trouble? When I’m in trouble, you call me Anna?”

“I like it.”

“Better than Schwartzman?”

His eyes narrowed. “You have to testify.”

She couldn’t. She was decided. The video was too damning. She was lucky they weren’t pressing charges as it was. Entrapment.

How preposterous to think that she might have been able to entrap Spencer. She had underestimated him. Again.

She would not think about it. She would maintain hope that some other evidence emerged. There was still the chance that the DNA on the sea turtle necklace they’d found in Spencer’s house wouldn’t match Lucy’s, that there would be some evidence of Ava on it instead. That somehow it would be enough to hold him.

It wouldn’t. Schwartzman knew the DNA would be Lucy’s.

There were other possibilities. Harper Leighton had narrowed down the day Spencer was at her daughter’s school to two possible days. There was a chance that someone in that school had noticed him when he was there. A slim chance, but a chance.

More likely he’d had a student deliver the necklace for him. But they might be able to find the student and follow the lead to Spencer. In an effort to find a witness, Spencer’s image had gone out to the entire student body, the faculty and employees, as well as the parents. Harper would be dealing with school security as a by-product, but she was determined to find some evidence of Spencer on campus. Her husband,

Jed, had created a website where kids could upload pictures taken on those days. Any pictures, anywhere on or around campus.

The way kids took pictures these days, they were betting that someone had caught something.

No matter what they found at the school, Harper would testify. She believed the necklace had been given to her daughter as a way to set her up and put all the evidence in question. She would also swear to finding Schwartzman in Ava's garage, tied up, and would assert that it would have been impossible for Schwartzman to tie herself up that way, and that there was no one else who could have helped her. Then Harper would testify about the deaths of Ava and Frances and their connection to Spencer.

Circumstantial at best. All of it.

"Schwartzman," Hal said.

Schwartzman. Not Anna. "I'm not in trouble anymore?"

"How can you joke about it?" He crossed the sidewalk to his car and leaned against the side panel. "If you don't testify . . ."

"He'll get away with it."

"Yes."

"I know." Get away with killing Ava. With killing Joe Strom and perhaps her father? Get away with tearing apart her family, isolating her? But she would not testify. She would not perjure herself. She would not risk her medical license. She would not let go of the life she'd built.

She would not start over again.

Even to keep Spencer locked away?

Even for that.

He might get away with the murders. No, he would. It felt almost certain. They'd already let him out of jail. For two weeks he'd been free. Every time the phone rang, she jumped out of her skin.

Look forward. She could not change the past, but she could direct the future. She would. She had already begun to put the pieces in place, to put the past behind her. She had told Hal about the difficult conversation she'd had with Ken Macy, how she'd broken it off. Hal knew better than to ask too many questions.

"I need your help," she told Hal now.

Hal raised his eyebrows and crossed his arms.

"I can ask someone else," she offered.

"Spit it out."

"I need to learn how to shoot a gun," she said.

His hands fell to his sides. "You don't have a gun."

"Right," she confirmed. She thought of the gun Ava had left her and wished she hadn't dumped it in the river. Would she have had the guts to shoot him? If she'd had that gun in that room, with herself projected onto the wall? She honestly didn't know.

But she knew now—for next time. Not if there was a next time. When. She would pull the trigger.

"Schwartzman?"

She took a breath and turned to Hal. "Right," she said again. "I'll need your help buying one first."

Hal's frown deepened between his brows. "You are familiar with the statistics on guns."

"I am."

"So I can't talk you out of this?" he asked.

"No."

"And I can't talk you into testifying?"

"No," she said again, going to stand beside him. She nudged him with her shoulder.

They stood there, side by side, until she could feel his warmth through her sweater.

Hal looked up at the house again. "You gonna have a guest bed in that extra room?"

She stared at the little house where she would be living in three weeks' time. "I don't get a lot of guests."

"You've got three rooms. What else would you use them for?"

"An office . . . a library." She studied the house, picturing the two smaller bedrooms as they had been when she'd first toured the house. Each had a twin bed and a small dresser, and each had a little basket of toys. Things she would never need.

"You'll still want a guest bed," Hal said. "With Spencer out of jail, you'll need an extra bed."

"Because you think he'll come live with me?" She said it as a joke, but it fell flat.

Hal pushed off the car and started down the street. With some distance between them, he turned back. She'd hurt his feelings. It wasn't only her anymore. Choices impacted him, her friends.

"Okay, I'll have a guest room," she said. Her mother might visit. Stranger things had happened. "And I'm adopting Buster."

"Buster?"

"Todd Posner's dog. I can't have him in my current place, so the vet is boarding him until I move in here."

A beat passed in silence. A dog was a good form of security. But she sensed that wasn't what Hal was thinking.

"He'll come here," Hal said, his voice barely a whisper. "You know he will."

Spencer. She couldn't argue. Spencer hadn't given up. Had it started with Joseph Strom? Were there victims before that? Would they ever know?

"So a guest room is the answer?"

"It'll be a hell of a lot more comfortable than sleeping out on the curb in my damn car," Hal barked.

Schwartzman went silent.

Hal rubbed his head and spun, heading farther down the block.

She started after him. "Hal."

He halted. "What?"

She closed the distance. "Will you help me?"

"Get a gun?" His arms were crossed again.

She nodded. "And teach me how to shoot it." She put her hand on his arm.

His stance relaxed under her touch.

"Please."

"I will," he said. "Of course I will . . ."

She sensed the hesitation. "But?"

"I wish you'd consider testifying."

"I can't."

He exhaled, and she stepped closer, leaning her forehead against his chest. "I'm sorry."

His hands fell to his sides. Then, one at a time, they reached around her and pulled her close. "Damn."

After a few moments, she pulled away gently. "We should go get a drink."

"Sure," he said, rubbing his face with both hands. "Let's celebrate."

She smiled softly. "The house or the gun?"

"The house," he said.

"Evan Williams?" she offered. She knew he wasn't a big fan of bourbon. "You haven't tried the good stuff yet."

"You're offering single barrel?" he asked.

"Single barrel."

"And you're buying?"

She laughed and threaded her arm through his. "I'm buying."

"Hell, yes, you are."

Arm in arm, Schwartzman and Hal walked back to his car.

Despite it all, she was okay. She felt healthy and content. And not terrified. That was something.

That was a lot of somethings.

But she was ready for a glass of Evan Williams. Boy was she ever.

41

Spencer faced the mirror and retied his tie. The shoulders of his jacket were slightly loose, and there was a little extra fabric at the center. His belt was tighter by two notches.

His hair was moist from the shower. He had stood under the scalding water until it went cold and stayed until his teeth threatened to chatter. He used four towels to dry himself, left them in a heap on the floor.

To be thrown away.

He tugged on the lapels of his silk suit. Everything he came into contact with for the next week would be thrown away until the prison was out of his system.

He might have put this off until tomorrow night. Taken a night to sleep in his own bed, to settle in. But they wanted to celebrate him. His partners. They thought of themselves as friends. After all, hadn't they worked together for more than a decade? They weren't his friends. He didn't need friends. It was a stupid concept, really, the giving part. The getting side he understood. That was the benefit of having people consider you a friend. They gave. He got.

And he needed Bella.

Hands flat on the countertop, he closed his eyes and clenched his jaw. *Bella. Bella. Bella.* The anger was still there. Raw and fierce. She would have to make things right before they could go back to normal.

Patience. He could not rush the process. He had waited seven years, so he could wait another one or two. With everything that had happened, he and Bella would have to end up abroad now.

He had started to research locations where women knew their place. The Middle East was appealing in that way, but he didn't want to live among a bunch of terrorists. Parts of Eastern Europe might work. He had time to find the perfect place. Build it, if he had to.

He opened his eyes and studied his reflection in the mirror. Some of the color had returned to his face. Bella had brought it back. She made his blood run hot. He turned his face left and right, studying his profile. He was thinner than he would have liked. He'd lost the weight on purpose. He'd wanted to look pathetic, but then the release had happened faster than he'd expected.

Much faster.

Not out of the woods. They could come back and arrest him, but it was unlikely without additional evidence. And there would be none of that.

He would be keeping a close eye on Harper Leighton, but she couldn't touch him. A few more weeks and the dust would settle. His case would be filed away and forgotten. And then he could reconstruct his life.

He studied his clean-shaven face. The weight loss made him look younger. Edgier. That wasn't all bad. But the circles under his eyes stole from the edge and made him look weak. That wouldn't do. Easy enough to correct.

He'd applied a little concealer under the eyes and checked it carefully. Subtle, undetectable. He took a last look and shut off the bathroom lights, headed for the garage, and got into his Lexus.

He was at the club in ten minutes. The others were already at the bar. He'd forgotten how old they all looked. Of course, all of them were older than he. Even those closest to his age looked a decade his senior.

They turned toward him, and he put on his best smile, saddling up to the bar. They handed him a Manhattan, the office favorite. A drink for geriatrics. He toasted and clinked, backed up to the bar, and set the drink down. Then he tapped the bar beside the glass with his index finger.

The bartender knew what to do.

There were jokes about everyone going to jail. Shedding a few pounds. Spencer smiled and laughed. Fake.

A few minutes later, there was a new glass on the bar. Neat. Willett single-barrel bourbon whiskey, aged twenty-two years. His own private stash was stored in a locked cabinet under the bar. Average price was fourteen hundred a bottle. He had it poured one inch at a time. Controlled, measured, refined.

Like him.

After a couple of drinks, the group moved to a table. He had just finished his first and requested a second for dinner.

It took almost no time at all to be bored by their company, but he would not leave first—a sign of weakness after what he'd been through. He needed to come across as strong, as potent as ever. Midway through the meal, his phone buzzed in the pocket of his shirt. He slid it out as one of his partners continued with yet another story about his latest golfing trip to Scotland. He saw the number on the text and breathed through his teeth.

"Everything all right there, Spencer?"

He wanted to punch the guy in the face. "Potential client. Big money," he lied. "I'll only be a moment." He rose from the table, holding his napkin in front of him until he could button his jacket. Beneath it, he was erect. Oh, how he wished he were alone at home for this.

The message he'd been waiting for. The San Francisco area code. His contact there. His access to her.

Bella.

The word filled his mouth, though he didn't speak it out loud.

He gripped the phone tightly and walked to the men's room. It was empty. He went to the last stall, closed the heavy wood door, and turned the lock. The club's bathrooms were like individual changing rooms. Each had a sitting area and a small side table. Some of the older men spent hours in these stalls, sitting on the pot, reading. All the comforts of home without the bitches, he'd heard men say.

Spencer sat on the small plush cushion across from the sink and toilet. He raised the phone and opened the text. There it was. The thumbnail loaded. He saw the dark hair, the long, lean form.

After all this time.

He double-clicked on the photo with anticipation, swallowing the saliva that collected in his mouth. Pressed his free hand on the rock-hard erection.

The image loaded. Bella on the sidewalk. Behind her was a small bungalow home with a hideous, hippie-like yard. Not where she lived now. Was she visiting someone? Moving?

Using two fingers, he moved in on the image slowly, surveying her legs, her torso, her fine shoulders . . . he zoomed in until her face filled his screen. She was pale, too thin. She was always too thin. He could help her. He would make her well again.

"Oh, Bella," he whispered, bringing the screen close. "I've missed you."

He imagined her face turning toward him, the look in her eyes as she recognized him. Terror like he'd seen in Ava's garage? Or resignation? Some relief that the time had come? Surely she knew.

He would have to wait to see, of course.

Recapturing her love was not as easy as sending someone to dispose of a cop distraction. He could not delegate Bella. And she would not come back to South Carolina. Not on her own anyway.

So he would have to go to her. And that would take very careful planning. That could not be rushed.

"Don't worry," he whispered. "I've learned to be patient."

With that, he dropped his pants and held the phone in his left hand as his right moved to relieve the pressure that had built in the few minutes of thinking of her. His eyes never strayed from her image. Even in those final seconds when it was almost impossible not to close them, he studied her, remembered her, felt her.

"Soon, sweet Bella," he whispered in that last climactic rush. "Soon."

ACKNOWLEDGMENTS

As with every book, I am incredibly grateful for the generosity of those who helped make this book possible. The good stuff is thanks to them; the errors are mine alone; and I admit fully that I sometimes bend the truth to make for a better story. Even while taking liberties with the facts, I offer my sincerest gratitude and respect to the men and women who devote their lives to pursuing justice. You have the toughest jobs and the most important ones.

For research, I am, as always, indebted to the invaluable resources at SFPD, who have been answering questions since book one. Thank you also to George Schiro, forensic scientist and crime scene investigator extraordinaire; Dr. Karen F. Ross, forensic pathologist at Ross Forensic Medicine and Pathology Consultations Inc.; Dr. Craig Nelson, associate chief medical examiner, North Carolina Office of the Chief Medical Examiner; Alison Hutchens, forensic services supervisor, crime lab unit, Durham Police Department; and Whitney Pritham NP, for her help in understanding chemotherapy and the treatment of breast cancer.

A gigantic thank-you to Meg Ruley, Rebecca Scherer, and the team at JRA for everything they do. Thank you also to the fabulous Jessica Tribble for taking such good care of this author and Schwartzman; to

Sarah Shaw and the incredible team at Thomas & Mercer; and to Leslie Lutz for her skilled guidance in the editing process.

I am endlessly appreciative of those who support the process of writing a book and especially to Randle and Shawnee and to my wonderful proofreaders: Dani, Whitney, and Tiffany. Also to Mom, Nicole, Steve, Tom, and Dad—thank you.

Most of all, my love and gratitude go to these three who put up with this insanity day and night: Chris, Claire, and Jack. For me, you guys are the moon and the sun and whatever lies beyond. I love you.

ABOUT THE AUTHOR

Photo © 2012 Janie Osborne

Danielle Girard is the author of ten previous novels, including *Chasing Darkness* and *Exhume*, the first novel featuring Dr. Annabelle Schwartzman, as well as The Rookie Club series. Her books have won the Barry Award and the RT Reviewers' Choice Award, and two of her titles have been optioned for movies.

A graduate of Cornell University, Danielle received her MFA at Queens University in Charlotte, North Carolina. She, her husband, and their two children split their time between San Francisco and the Northern Rockies.